CAN LOVE, TENDERNESS, AND HONOR SURVIVE THE FIRESTORM CREATED BY THE NEED TO DESTROY?

That is the question faced by LILA . . . whose silver tresses and black silk gowns are her trademarks, and whose title, the Black Widow, bespeaks the lust for vengeance buried deep in her wounded heart.

It is the dilemma posed to MICHAEL. . . . Equally marked by Ireland's poetic soul and Spain's passionate pride, he is determined to claim his birthright. His quest will take him around the world and plunge him into a strange culture where nothing is what it seems—and the tropical breezes whisper of mysteries that can never be solved.

It is a puzzle NORMAN refuses to acknowledge. . . . Believing himself safe at the pinnacle of the Mendoza banking empire, he is blinded by avarice and made arrogant by generations of wealth. The moment he must defend all he has taken for granted, he finds that he has no weapon stronger than Lila's rage.

Her need for an answer plunges BETH . . . lovely, young, and brave . . . into scandal. When she leaves her husband to follow her lover she finds herself on a magic island, but she is wise enough to know it can be heaven or hell—and that the choice is hers to make.

Only FERGUS believes he can solve the riddle. . . . The Irish freedom fighter has his own secrets to guard, and the power to bring down a dynasty. But can he tame the savage hatred that threatens to consume the woman he loves?

Other Bantam Books by
Beverly Byrne

A LASTING FIRE
THE MORGAN WOMEN

The Flames of Vengeance

BEVERLY BYRNE

FANFARE ™

BANTAM BOOKS
NEW YORK • TORONTO • LONDON • SYDNEY • AUCKLAND

THE FLAMES OF VENGEANCE

A Bantam Fanfare Book / December 1991

FANFARE and the portrayal of a boxed "ff" are trademarks of Bantam Books, a
division of Bantam Doubleday Dell Publishing Group, Inc.

ISBN 0-553-29375-3

Published simultaneously in the United States and Canada

Bantam Books are published by Bantam Books, a division of Bantam
Doubleday Dell Publishing Group, Inc. Its trademark, consisting of the
words "Bantam Books" and the portrayal of a rooster, is Registered in
U.S. Patent and Trademark Office and in other countries. Marca Re-
gistrada. Bantam Books, 666 Fifth Avenue, New York, New York
10103.

PRINTED IN THE UNITED STATES OF AMERICA

RAD   0 9 8 7 6 5 4 3 2 1

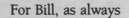

For Bill, as always

The Flames
of Vengeance

✒ Prologue ✒

CÓRDOBA, SPAIN

1869. The darkness moved and breathed as if alive. It defined everything in Lila Curran's world. She lived in perpetual night, the details of her captivity conveyed to her by all her senses except sight. Sound snaked through her black shroud, twisted around her, strangled her will to resist. The metal collar around her neck was heavy, the woven carpet she lay on rough, and the marble floor beyond the edge of the carpet was very cold. The side of the enormous carved wooden bed to which she was chained was high—the bed itself an almost unendurable torment, placed just inches too far for her to climb on.

Lila could hear her child crying. Her six-month-old son was in the room adjacent to hers. He'd been christened Miguel in the Spanish fashion, but to her—always—he was Michael. Her baby boy, the sweet tender infant, born of love and trust, or so she'd thought, had become as much an object of his father's hatred as she. A wet nurse came and fed him and attended to his needs but most the of the time Michael was alone and frightened, and he wept. And Lila tore at her chains and screamed out her fury and her pain. But no one dared admit they heard.

Around her and Michael the household in the ancient and venerable Palacio Mendoza kept to its ordinary daily routine. Lila heard through her darkness the noises of servants going about their chores, of her husband, the mighty Juan Luis Mendoza, stomping along the passage outside her door or venting his insane rages in the patio below her balcony. Occasionally she heard the voice of Juan Luis's sister Beatriz or of her husband Francisco. Her in-laws knew she was a captive. But they, too, were Juan Luis's prisoners, incapable of breaking the bonds of his tyrannical rule—in thrall to the Mendoza legacy of power and wealth.

1870. They brought her food once a day, always the same, a kind of stew of vegetables and a bit of meat in a wooden bowl. No spoon was provided and to survive she had to bury her face in the dish like an animal. Lila did it, she did whatever was necessary, because one thing she had determined in the thirteen months since Juan Luis had chained her: She would survive and she would be avenged.

Until the day when the voice of the child was silenced.

Lila listened for him, her heartbeats timed to his cries as they had been since her torment began, but there was nothing. She had thought there was no terror or fury she had not already plumbed, but the knowledge that Michael was gone—dead? murdered by his own father?—was a visitation from hell. Her pain and rage were beyond imagining. She could not scream, she hadn't the strength. All she could do was lie on the floor, her hands clasped to the metal collar around her neck.

Hours passed. And then she knew. Juan Luis had won. She was at last the victim of total despair.

"Lila, Lila, *¿puedes escuchame, mi niña?*" The voice seemed to come from far away. It repeated the guestion a second time, in labored English, an urgent whisper. "Can you hear me? It is I, your sister-in-law, Beatriz. Lila, in God's name, are you alive?"

Her name, spoken in a human voice. In all the long days and weeks and months of her agony, she had not heard her name, the acknowledgment of her existence as a separate human being. "I—I am alive." Her lips cracked and began to bleed with the effort of making words. "Beatriz, my baby, my Michael—"

"Ssh, do not talk, only listen. I am outside the door. I bribed a maid to unlock the corridor, but she would not dare to give me the key to this room. Juan Luis has terrified her, terrified all the servants." Beatriz's voice broke. "Terrified even us."

"Michael," Lila whispered. "My Michael . . ."

"That is what I have come to tell you. He is all right, *mi niña*, he is with me. Francisco and I have taken him to our apartments. I could live with it no longer, this wickedness. I prayed. I gathered courage. Then I told my crazy brother that if he did not give me the baby to look after I would make a scandal even he could not survive. To torture a helpless, it is unthinkable. All would treat him as a leper . . . Lila, do you understand? Your little Miguel, he is fine. He will be well; I will take care of him until Juan Luis comes to his senses." There was no reply. "Lila," Beatriz called again, "Lila, *¿puedes escucharme?*"

The whispered response came after some seconds. "*Sí, te oigo.* I hear you, I understand."

Her child was alive, safe and cared for. It gave her courage. Lila knew she would survive.

1882. Sometimes Michael came to the balcony of her room. It was a difficult trick, he had to be quite certain that neither his father nor any of his father's spies would see him. He had to hoist himself up to the second story using only the vines that grew on the stone walls of the palace as handholds, but he managed to do it sometimes.

Lila had been torn apart when the clandestine visits began. She longed to see her son, but she hated for him to see her. True, things were somewhat better now. The metal collar and the chains had been removed after three years of captivity—a gesture of munificence on the part of Juan Luis, some kind of relenting of his mad, unfounded jealousy. Still she was a prisoner in this single room. Her hair, once flaming red, had turned to silver, and she was as thin as a wraith, a shadow who dwelled among shadows.

"Mama! Mama, are you there?" The boy pressed his face to the glass of the balcony doors. They were locked and he had never managed to find a key that would open them, but when his mother heard his voice she usually came and parted the draperies a crack. They could peer at each other through the opening, separated, unable to touch, but with an illusion of closeness. "Mama," the boy called again. "Please answer me, it's important."

The curtains parted—only a hair; to open them wider might alert watching eyes, and was far too dangerous. "I'm here, darling. How are you?"

"I'm fine, Mama, fine."

Lila filled her being with the sight of him. He was a big child, enormous for a boy who was soon to be thirteen. He had her red hair and vivid blue eyes, darker than hers. She pressed her fingertips to the glass. If only she could touch his face. Michael . . . Michael . . . the child of her agony, of her heart, the son she had not embraced since he was three months old. "Michael," she whispered, her mouth hovering near the panes as if her breath might kiss him though her lips could not.

"Mama, listen, I have something for you. It was wonderful luck that Tía Beatriz and I saw this letter before Papa did. She said I should bring it to you."

Lila looked at the envelope; it was large and thick. She had no idea where it had come from or how she could hope to put her hands on it. It was too fat for Michael to slide between the cracks. "Michael, you cannot give it to me. It won't fit. Besides, if your father finds out—"

"I don't care," the boy said. "It's important, I know it is. I'm going to break the glass." He held up something else. A large stone.

"Michael! No, you mustn't. Your father—"

"I don't care! I'm going to break the glass and get you out. We will run away from the Palacio Mendoza. We will run so far that Papa will never find us."

There was no place on this earth beyond the grasp of the enormous wealth and power of the Mendozas, Lila knew, even if her son didn't. Besides, she had no money, no family, nothing. Where could she take him? What would they do? "No," she whispered. "No."

"Mama, the letter is important. I know it is. I feel in my bones that it is."

Lila looked at the envelope. She felt something too. Something indescribable, something she had long ago thought was dead in her. Courage, the ability to do more than merely survive, a freshening of her will to triumph. She reached out a hand as if to take the document. It drew her with a mysterious power, a sense of absolute rightness, of destiny. "Yes," she whispered. "Yes, Michael, do it. Break the glass. Only enough to get the letter in, only one pane. I can cover the break so it won't be discovered for a while."

Juan Luis came to her that night. He often came these days. He would pace up and down the room which was her prison and rave at her, tell her of her crimes, of how she had cuckolded him. She'd long ago given up remonstrating; no arguments of hers could alter his insane fixation on imagined betrayals. Her only reply was silence. Tonight she listened for long minutes, aware of the stirring of air in the room from the broken glass as yet unnoticed. The letter weighed ominously heavy in the pocket of her gown. Finally she did what she had not done in months: she spoke.

"Juan Luis, listen to me."

He froze, startled by the voice he had not heard for so long. "So you deign to answer? To what do I owe the honor?"

"To the truth, Juan Luis. To knowledge. I have knowledge, and because of it you are going to set me free. Me and my son."

"What are you talking about?"

"Power," Lila said softly. "I am talking about power. And you are going to listen."

Two days after the letter was placed in Lila Curran's hands she and her son Michael left the Palacio Mendoza. Their journey took mere weeks, but their odyssey would take many years and span two continents. They had embarked on a quest for that most elusive of all rewards—reparation for the lost years, the countless humiliations. They craved vengeance.

PART ONE

The First
Ten Days

❧ 1 ❧

MONDAY, JUNE 14, 1898
Dublin, Ten P.M.

The man walked quickly despite his severe limp, his head bent, his body hunched forward, and his left arm clutched across his chest. He looked as if he were struggling against a bitter winter storm rather than walking through a peaceful city on a mild summer evening. His clothes were as incongruous as his posture. He wore a knitted cap pulled down so it almost hid his face, a woolen jacket buttoned to the neck, and thick twill trousers from which the color had long since disappeared.

He made his way through Dirty Lane. When he drew level with Saint Catherine's Church he paused to trace a quick cross on his forehead with a grimy thumb, and used the moment to scan the street behind him. Convinced he wasn't being followed, he hurried on. The man knew the city well, but he did not take a direct route to his destination. It was almost eleven before he turned onto the quay known as Bachelors Walk and headed for the red brick public house facing the river Liffey.

A battered picture of a swan identified the pub. The sign

hung motionless on a rusty iron bracket, and the full moon highlighted peeling paint and splintered wood. The man pushed open the door with his shoulder, keeping his arm pressed to his chest.

He walked through a small narrow hall into the public bar. It was nearly closing time, but dozens of drinkers filled the large plain room. A few leaned on the oak counter that ran the length of one wall; others sat at bare wooden tables. A fireplace filled one corner, but there was no fire this warm night. Instead of the sweet smell of burning peat there was the stink of stale beer and cheap tobacco.

The man limped the length of the room, greeting no one and ignoring the vaguely hostile stares of the other customers. A tired-looking woman of about forty stood beside a pyramid of glasses and watched his progress with pale, lifeless eyes. When he took a place at the far end of the bar she moved toward him. The newcomer pulled off his hat and inclined his head in an old-fashioned bow. The gesture was jarringly formal and unexpected, and the woman lifted her eyebrows but made no comment.

The man was bald except for a fringe of jet-black hair. His eyes were almost as dark, and red rimmed with tiredness, but his greeting was cheerful. "A blessing on the house. I'll be wanting a pint of porter, if you'd be so kind."

"It's three minutes to closing time." There was no matching courtesy in the woman's tone.

"Sure, I'll drink fast. And as long as the porter's in me hand before the hour, even an English constable, may each one of them rot in hell, couldn't complain."

The woman shrugged and drew the strong black brew from a brass tap, then pushed the drink toward the man. He nodded his thanks. "That'll be four pence," she said. He gave her the coins and the woman glanced at the big clock between the windows facing the river. "Time, boys," she called. "Time."

In ten minutes most of the customers had finished their

drinks and drifted out the door. Only five remained; four men sitting at a table near the door who did not look as if they meant to leave soon, and the stranger who still stood at the bar. Despite his promise to drink quickly his glass was half full. "We're closing," the woman told him.

"Sure, I know that. But I'll be staying on a bit. I've business with the landlord."

The woman's once blond hair was drab and colorless, worn pulled back as if her only concern was to get it out of her face. Apparently life had robbed her of vanity along with joy and hope. "What business?" she asked tonelessly.

"It's private like. If you'll tell himself that Fergus Kelly wants him, I'll be much obliged."

"That's your name? Fergus Kelly?"

"Aye, so they told me when I was a bairn, and I've spent fifty years believing it."

The woman's lips twitched, as if she almost remembered how to smile, then settled into her customary grimace. She went behind a door at the far end of the bar. A few minutes later a stout man wearing a filthy apron appeared, jerked his head in acknowledgment of the four men sitting at the table, then shuffled to the end of the bar. "Fergus Kelly?"

"Aye."

"Herself said you had business with me."

"I do."

"What sort of business?"

Kelly set what remained of his porter on the bar and took his time before answering. "Seems an odd sort of question for one good Fenian to put to another," he said finally.

The landlord started. "Lower your voice, you bloody fool!"

"Why?" Kelly asked mildly. He gestured toward the men at the table, who were watching the exchange with frank curiosity. "This lot are all our brothers, are they not?"

"Brothers to some, no doubt. But that's no affair of yours. I'll thank ye to state your business and leave. It's after hours."

Kelly sighed. "Sure, when a man's been away from his country as long as I have he expects a warmer welcome when he comes home. However"—he relaxed the arm that had been across his chest all evening and loosed one button of his jacket—"you've a guest. Not the usual sort. This is for him." He withdrew a packet wrapped in brown paper, tied with string, and dotted with blobs of red sealing wax.

The landlord eyed the thing without touching it. "I don't know what you're talking about. Me only guests is them lads over there, and none of 'em knows anything about your package."

The onlookers nodded in assent.

"Don't waste my time, Patrick Shea," Kelly said. "And don't look so astonished. Sure, what would I be doing in this godforsaken place if I didn't know your name? More important, I know that the Englishman called Timothy Mendoza is to spend the night here. He's expecting this." He put the package on the bar. "See he gets it. Untampered with, mind. What's inside is important to him, but it would mean nothing whatever to you, or to the cause. And if young Mr. Timothy has aught to complain of about his visit here, the widow Curran will stop your monthly allowance. And where will all your plans be then?"

Kelly waited. The landlord only stared at the packet, then at the man who said his name was Fergus Kelly.

Kelly pulled on his hat and buttoned his jacket. He included all the men present in his broad wave of farewell. "Good night to you, boys. Long live a free Ireland. And may you all be in heaven half an hour before the devil knows you're dead."

The candles of a dozen chandeliers gleamed behind the curtains of the house on the corner of Dawson Street. The door stood open to the soft summer night, and a golden spill of gaslight tumbled down the short path leading to the tall wrought-iron gates letting onto the road. Across the way in the grassy expanse of Saint Stephen's Green, late strollers had only to look up to know that Lila Curran was giving one of her famous parties.

"Managed to inveigle God into giving her perfect weather for it," someone said. Another murmured agreement. Neither was surprised. All Dublin knew that the woman known as the Black Widow got her way in most things.

The house was called Bellereve. French sounding names had been all the fashion when it was built at the end of the previous century. Bellereve, like most Georgian houses, was perfectly symmetrical. Its stone facade was a harmony of restrained adornment and straight lines, reflecting a belief in an ordered universe. Even in the present chaotic times its appearance gave deep satisfaction. However, the happy marriage of form and function did not extend to the parts of the house the owner was presumed never to see.

Well-hidden from genteel eyes, the kitchen was below ground level, an immense cavern of a room. Tonight it seethed with frenzied activity. Billowing steam made it an inferno. The green tile walls and floor dripped moisture as if part of some primeval cave. Every pot and pan was in use, the empty hooks that normally held the vast array of copper cookware looking lethal in the flickering gaslight.

Three enormous scrubbed pine tables placed end-to-end lined the center of the room. Each was crowded with bowls and platters and tureens. A dozen scullery maids surrounded the tables, overseen by a fat cook who moved among them like a whirlwind. Sweat poured off the bodies of the servants. The sour human smells mingled with the appetizing aromas of roasting meats and simmering sauces. In the six coal-fired ovens beef, pork, and fowl pies were baking to a rich golden brown. A cauldron of potatoes bubbled on one huge hob, salmon was poaching on two others.

"More champagne!" someone shouted.

"Are you daft?" a woman's raucous voice demanded. "It's in the upstairs pantry, not down here."

A pair of feet sped back up the steps. The young footman, hired only the week before, was grateful to escape the hellish heat of the kitchen. He paused a moment in the relative freshness of the corridor leading to the pantry and drew a deep breath.

"O'Leary! There you are. When I send you for something I don't mean you to take half a lifetime to produce it." The butler slapped the boy once, a short sharp blow that glanced off his ear.

"Begging your pardon, Mr. Winston, I got confused and went downstairs—"

"Downstairs? Are you stupid as well as lazy, lad? How could there be iced champagne in that hellhole downstairs?" The butler charged off in the direction of the pantry, with the footman following.

Moments later the pair returned to the reception rooms in the front of the house, showing no sign of hurry or heat as they circulated among the throng of guests. Inexperienced though he was, O'Leary managed to carry his tray of cold sparkling wine at shoulder height, the way Mr. Winston carried his.

"Here, lad," a man said. "You've appeared at exactly the right moment." An elegant hand removed two glasses from the tray.

O'Leary was sixteen years old and until tonight he'd never seen a member of the ruling class up close . . . not a real Englishman from London. He gaped at the young gentleman who'd taken the champagne. Seemed like a god, the man did. Him with his fair curly hair and his fine black suit and his perfect manners. Bloody English, no wonder they looked as they did; ruled the world, and stole from any as they could get under their thumb.

"What are you staring at, lad? Have I egg on my face, or something equally horrible?"

"Oh, no, sir. Nothing, sir. Sure, I wasn't staring really. I only—"

"Very well, off with you. There must be other guests as thirsty as I am."

The footman dutifully went away. The Englishman turned and searched for the man to whom he'd been speaking, spotted him in the crowd and moved to his side. "Here, I managed to get us some of Mrs. Curran's excellent wine."

The other man took the proffered goblet but didn't drink. "So, Tim, as you were saying . . ."

"About what?" Timothy Mendoza asked as soon as he'd taken his first eager sip of champagne.

"About Paraguay."

"Oh, yes, Paraguay. We'll be offering shares in a new loan on the twenty-third, that's next Wednesday. Waterworks for the rural areas. The government's determined to make good on all their promises. It's a fine scheme. Sure to be a success."

"I take it you recommend I buy?"

"Definitely. Paraguay's making excellent progress since the new president took over. You're bound to do very well out of it." Timothy spoke in an almost offhand manner, as if he himself were not particularly interested in the subject of Paraguay. His gaze was raking the crowd.

"Looking for someone?" the other man asked.

"Our hostess. Haven't paid my respects yet, but I don't see the lady among us."

"No, I haven't spotted her either. Or her giant of a son."

"I'm told that Michael Curran's not expected to join us. But I did think to find Lila at her own party."

"I expect she'll make an entrance when it suits her," the other man said. "Lila Curran does everything exactly as she pleases."

"So she does. Pounces when you least expect it and eats you alive, that's the way the Black Widow does things."

The man looked startled. "Call her that too, do you?"

"Doesn't everyone?"

"Not a Mendoza, I'd have thought. One of your own, isn't she?"

"A distant cousin by marriage." Timothy flicked an imaginary piece of lint from the shoulder of his cutaway. "Besides, I meant no disrespect. I admire the lady. Black Widow's a term of affection, you might say."

The other man's eyes narrowed. "I might. Or I might not. Good evening to you, Timothy." He turned and moved away.

The Englishman stood alone for a few seconds, still surveying the crowd. Before he could decide which direction to take in search of Lila, a young lady appeared at his elbow.

"Mr. Mendoza, you remember me, don't you?"

The girl's face was vaguely familiar. Her speech had a Dublin lilt to it, but nothing that could be called a brogue. "Of course I remember you." Timothy searched his mind but couldn't recall her name.

"I saw you come in," she continued. "But of course you didn't notice me. I was so hoping I'd have an opportunity to speak with your delightful wife."

Timothy had managed to dredge up a memory while she spoke. "We met last year, didn't we? Yes, I'm sure we did. Racing at the Curragh. How nice to see you again, but I'm afraid my wife isn't here. Beth didn't come with me to Dublin this trip." He treated her to his warmest smile.

"How sad for you. You must be lonely." The girl wore a low-cut blue satin gown trimmed with black lace and carried a black lace fan with a tortoiseshell handle. She used the fan with practiced skill, letting her rapacious eyes dance an invitation above its pleated rim.

"Indeed I am. Very lonely," Timothy agreed.

They went on with the flirtation and he gave every appearance of enjoying it. The girl had no reason to suspect that three-quarters of Timothy Mendoza's mind was occupied with the problem of Lila Curran. She wouldn't have believed it if she did. There was no reason to think a woman thirty years older than she was a serious rival.

Supper was served soon after midnight. By then the entire gathering could talk of nothing but the Black Widow. The most piquant sauce of the feast was the fact that their hostess had never appeared. There were close to a hundred guests, but not one of them was offered an explanation until some time later when they collected their wraps and prepared to depart.

"Madam has asked me to convey her apologies," Winston murmured to the ladies and gentlemen as he saw them out. "She was taken ill shortly before the party began."

There was nothing anyone could say, but few believed the butler. This was simply another example of Lila Curran's outrageous behavior. She and her son, Michael, were a pair of rebels . . . and forces to be reckoned with. All Dublin knew that. Indeed, it wasn't any secret in London. As for Spain . . .

In the small hours of the morning Timothy paced the space of his mean little room above the bar of the Swan, still preoccupied with thoughts of Lila Curran. He'd planned to talk with her tonight, go over details. What in hell could have possessed her not to show her face? Damn! He should have insisted on staying at Bellereve. But her reasons for suggesting he spend the night at this public house had been convincing. That was one of the problems: the bitch was always convincing. He would never have agreed to an alliance with the Black Widow if that were not so. He knew how clever she was, but knew, too, that like her namesake she could be lethal.

He paused in his pacing and shook his head as if to clear it of thoughts of Lila. There was other urgent business. The faded curtains at the window had not been drawn, starlight illumined a bulky envelope lying on the bed. He hesitated a moment, then picked up the parcel and carried it to the table beneath the single gas jet protruding from the wall.

The key that controlled the flow of gas was sticky with grime and turned reluctantly. The first match burned down and scorched his fingers before the gas hissed forth. He cursed softly and lighted another. The jet sputtered once, then flared. The lamp had no shade. It cast a harsh yellow light on the brown envelope tied with coarse string and sealed with three blobs of red wax.

The parcel appeared intact and undisturbed. Timothy had expected as much. Patrick Shea, that grizzled sot of a landlord, had been carefully chosen. Shea's hatred of all things English would go no further than insolence. He'd never dare interfere with the affairs of a man like Timothy Mendoza. He was too dependent on Lila Curran's money for it to be otherwise.

Still Timothy did not open the packet. "I don't want it coming to my house," Lila had said. "It's too dangerous. So is any place where you might see someone you know." That was her excuse for making him stay at the Swan. It was time to find out if her caution—and his gamble—had been worthwhile. He pulled the room's single chair up to the table, sat down, and used a small pearl-handled pocket knife to break the seals and cut the string.

The wad of papers he extracted from the envelope was over an inch thick. He rifled through them quickly, then concentrated on the covering letter.

In the matter of Paraguay, I must, in strictest confidence, acquaint you with the following unpleasant facts: One, the corruption is as bad as ever, and I have reason to believe the official Mendoza agent is in the thick of it. Two, not even the finance minister believes there's a hope of completing the water project on time, if at all. Three, considering the burden of debt the Paraguayan treasury already carries, a new bond of two million pounds may prove insupportable. Four, the scheme to repay the loan by creating government-owned coffee plantations is either a fraud or a fantasy.

In the light of all this you must decide whether to offer the public this new issue. You are, naturally enough, in a most delicate position since the British investor can

know nothing of the real state of affairs so many thou-
sands of miles away, and must rely on the bank to vet
any offering . . .

There was more in the same vein, and many sheets of figures
and affadavits to back up the writer's assertions. Timothy
read through it all quickly, then twice more, paying great
attention to each word. When he was sure he'd understood
every nuance of the information, he smiled broadly and
slipped the documents back into the envelope.

This was the confirmation he'd been waiting for, proof
that what Lila had promised would indeed come to pass.
The Mendoza Bank, that venerable institution so representative of London's enormous financial power, was about to
make a catastrophic blunder. Timothy knew quite well how
catastrophic. He was a junior partner.

Even the problem of Lila Curran's whereabouts couldn't
dispel his pleasure. Timothy Mendoza slept remarkably well,
despite being away from his own luxurious room and his
adorable young wife, Beth.

Shortly before dawn a young man slipped quietly into the
lean-to behind the Swan's kitchen. The small structure was
crammed with untapped barrels of beer. There was barely
room for fat Patrick Shea to stand between them, but the
landlord was waiting. "Yer late, lad," he growled.

"Sure and how could I get away sooner?" O'Leary asked
sullenly. "There was no end of cleaning to be done after the
bloody lot of 'em left."

Shea chuckled. "Not enjoying a close look at the gentry,
eh? Nevermind, that's not what yer there for. What can you
tell me?"

"Nothing."

"What the bloody hell do you mean, nothing? I've waited
all night for your rotten little self and you've nothing to
report?"

"Mind yer tongue, Paddy Shea." O'Leary's voice shook with exhaustion and fury. "It's not from you I take orders."

"That's as may be. But I was a Fenian before you were born, and you'll show some respect." The stout man's anger ebbed as quickly as it had flared. "Ach, it's not among ourselves we should be fighting when there's so many bloody English waiting to get what we owe 'em. Tell me what happened."

"The Black Widow never showed her face at her own party. The toffs all expected her, but she never came downstairs. When they was goin' home Winston, that arse-kissing butler who's no right to call himself an Irishman, told 'em as how she'd been taken poorly just afore the party started."

Shea sucked on his fleshy lower lip. "Are you sure nobody went up to meet with her private like?"

"How could I be with nearly a hundred people in the house and bloody Winston always shouting at me to do this or get that? But if yer askin' if I seen anyone sneak upstairs, no, I didn't."

The older man sagged, then brightened. "Nevermind, ye did yer best. Come inside and have some tea afore ye go."

Shea thought hard about O'Leary's information while he fixed the tea. "Tell me one thing more," he said when he handed the younger man a steaming mug. "When did ye last see herself?"

O'Leary took a while before he answered. "Three days ago it was, early Saturday morning. I was polishing the silver in the morning room and it was perishing warm, so the door to the hall was open. She came downstairs, all dressed in black as usual, and spoke to Winston for a bit, then she went out."

"What did she say to him?" Shea demanded eagerly.

"I couldn't hear nothing. They was standing by the front door and whispering."

"Damn her soul to hell," Patrick Shea said morosely as he lifted a battered teapot and refilled both mugs. "There's something afoot, I can smell it. Could be if we knew her game we might profit by it. But she always stays one step ahead of everyone, does Lila Curran."

The young man was thinking of his return to the house on Dawson Street, and Winston's cuffs and curses. "Sure and I don't see why everyone makes so much of her. She's nothing but another bloody female, for all her airs. Women is all alike, a box and a belly and a pair of tits."

Shea shook his head. "The Black Widow's different. Do you not know her story?"

"Nothin' but what I was told, to go work there and keep me eyes open."

"You'll need 'em both wide open if yer to discover anything herself doesn't mean for you to know. A right tartar she is." Shea rolled a cigarette and lit it.

O'Leary watched enviously. "Here, have you the makings of another one of those?"

"Can't be giving smokes away, not a poor man like me. I'll tell ye a bit about Lila Curran though. Born on Moore Street she was, right here in Dublin. In some filthy cellar in the dead of winter. The man died and the da' reared her. Nothin' so unusual in that, 'cept they was Jews."

"Jews! They never were."

"Aye, tis God's own truth. Jews. There's a few of 'em in Dublin, though they hides their black and guilty faces as well they should. Not Lila Curran though, bold as brass she always was."

O'Leary frowned, as if working out a difficult problem. "You keep callin' her Curran like it was her name as a girl, but she's a widow woman . . ."

"Indeed. That's part of it. Curran she was born, though some as say it was Cohen afore her granddad changed it, and Curran she stayed. But yer getting me ahead of me story. The lass was a beauty, sure she still is after a manner of speaking, and one day when she was barely twenty, she upped and married a Spanish lord. No better than she should

be, according to some, but she took herself from Moore
Street to a palace in Spain with one toss of her red curls."

Shea took a long pull on his cigarette and exhaled through
his nose, enjoying the mixture of astonishment and envy on
his young listener's face.

"Well, go on," O'Leary urged. "Where'd she meet this
dago gent then? I wouldn't o' thought there were many of
'em in Dublin."

"No, right ye are. But this one came over from London
with one of them Mendoza Bank folks to look at a bit of
land, and happened to see our Lila and fell mad in love with
the wench. That's all anyone knew until fourteen years later
when back she comes. Only now she has a great hulk of a
son with her. Thirteen years he was, but bigger than most
grown men. And she says she's a widow woman, but she
prefers to be known by her own born name, 'cause that's
how they do things in Spain. Women don't take their husband's name, or some such folderol."

"And everybody obliged her by doin' just what she
wanted."

"Sure they did. Why not? Came home with her bustle
stuffed with money. Fierce rich she was—and is."

O'Leary was still puzzling over the details of the strange
tale. "You say she's a Jew. I ain't never seen no sign of it in
the house. Was the dago a Jew too?"

"Ach, you daft young fool, dagos is Catholics, same as
us. Sort of. Anyway, she married her Spaniard in Saint Mary's
in Liffey Street. The bishop himself conducted the ceremony.
They say there was a dispensation from the pope, allowin'
as how the Spaniard could marry his Jew girl as if she was
a proper Catholic Irishwoman." Shea hawked loudly and
spat into the ashes of the cold kitchen fire. "That's how it
goes for them what has money."

The lad drained the last cold drops of his tea. "How come
you know so much about her then?"

"Sure and don't play sly boots with me." Paddy Shea chuckled softly. "You know how I know. It's no secret she pays me a bit each month to do an errand or two for her, or that she pays dozens more as well. Has her finger in everything does the Black Widow."

❦ 2 ❦

TUESDAY, JUNE 15, 1898
London, Early Evening

It was a little past six o'clock. It would be light for hours yet, but the cold gray sky made it seem like February rather than June. Lila Curran shivered as she stood at the window of a small workman's cottage on grim Thorparch Road in the district known as Nine Elms.

A man walked along the narrow street, pausing every few steps to glance up as if he were looking for someone. Lila dropped the curtain and hastily withdrew. It was unlikely the man was hunting for her; only a few people knew she was in London and those few could be trusted absolutely, but victory was tantalizingly close and all her instincts urged caution.

She was nervous, undoubtedly because she did not want to be in this nondescript house with its pervading stench of poverty. Her hosts were Joe and Martha Clancy, an Irish couple who lived a life of too little heat, too little food, too little money. Their deprivations had an odor and it was one she knew well—and preferred to forget. She longed to be thousands of miles south in Spain, in the Palacio Mendoza in Córdoba, claiming what was hers. And Michael's. Soon, she reminded herself. Soon.

Soon was not now. Lila glanced at the ornate ormolu clock she'd put beside the bed. It looked absurd in this shabby setting. Martha Clancy was devoted to the Fenian cause and Lila had long been paying her a small monthly stipend, as she did so many others who might be useful to her. When Lila said she wished to lodge with the Clancys for a few days, Martha gave her the best room she had. Still, the room reminded Lila of the deprivations of her childhood and the risk she was taking now.

In God's name, why had she come so early? Why was she hiding here counting the minutes and worrying about Michael? It was far too soon for any word of him to reach London. At least another week was needed before Michael's efforts would bear fruit. Two, more likely. So why . . .

Lila shook her head, impatient with her own thoughts. She knew why. She simply could not remain in Dublin and play the charming hostess at a dinner dance planned before she knew that the time had come to unsheath her weapons and do battle.

A small smile turned up the corners of her generous mouth. It would have been marvelous to see her guests' faces last night when they realized she wasn't going to appear at her own party. She must have scandalized them yet again. She'd been doing so ever since she returned from Spain. The simple fact that she was a woman without a husband who openly made her own decisions and flaunted her considerable wealth was enough to scandalize them. Damn the lot of them, they should be used to it by now. Besides, they loved it. Dublin society might gossip about her but always waited avidly to see what she would do next, and invitations to Bellereve were among the most prized in the city.

All that had amused her through years of waiting. Now the waiting was almost over. She was after bigger game than the easily manipulated Irish matrons who chatted about her over their teacups, or the venal men who lusted for her in secret could imagine. She was after blood.

The four walls of the little room seemed to bear in on her. She'd chosen this temporary imprisonment, but that made it no easier to bear. Longing for some kind of physical action, she crossed to the dressing table, a small thing on spindly legs with one tiny drawer and a wavy mirror. She smoothed her already perfectly combed hair, which was silver with only the occasional strand of red to show what it had been. She knew the color of her hair became her. Her dark hazel eyes had lost none of their fire or flash; they showed up remarkably well against her pale skin and hair. Her face was unlined, the cheeks flushed a delicate pink.

She peered into the glass and was satisfied that at fifty she remained what she'd always been, a remarkably beautiful woman. "It's your dowry, me darlin'," her father used to say. "Your lovely face and your fine figure will make up for what I can't give you." He was putting a heavy burden on her looks, because the only things he could give her were a hovel in the poorest part of town and barely enough food to keep her alive.

The old Dublin cobbler had been twice cursed: first by his poverty, and second by the accident of fate that had put his Jewish grandparents on a ship bound for Dublin rather than London when they fled Belorussia in search of a better life. Ireland did not persecute them or turn them out, but it couldn't provide a host of previously arrived kinsmen to offer a lift up the ladder of prosperity. Lila's father was born poor in Dublin, and stayed poor there.

The cobbler also remained a Jew, but in his isolation he shaped the religion to his untutored understanding. It became a strange mix of superstitions and prohibitions, and mumbled prayers in a language he knew only by rote. The stories of Jewish history he told his child were a litany of unremitting misery when filtered through his limited knowledge. His aim was not to make Lila an Orthodox Jew, but to encourage her to seek freedom. Chance had made the girl beautiful, and her father believed her looks would win her the "better life" he'd never found. Instead Lila's beauty had caused her no end of grief. It was her brains that had saved her—and a letter. Those two things had won her wealth and power.

Why then was she risking all her hard-won security and social standing, her blessed financial independence? If she lost, she'd be a pauper again. Lila banished the thought. She would not lose. The will to win was too strong in her. She had laid, nurtured, and refined her plans over fifteen long years. She couldn't lose. In the end she would have a thousand times more than she had now, and Michael would have everything that was due him. That was the sweetest reward. Her son would be vindicated. It would all happen, if only she could be patient a little while longer.

She yanked open the shallow drawer of the dressing table and stared at the three things she'd put there when she unpacked. The letter of course, the much-folded often-read letter that had come from Puerto Rico in 1882, when she was a prisoner in the bedroom in Córdoba, living a life of unmitigated hell. The letter had been her salvation, and she never went anywhere without it.

There was a second piece of her life in the drawer. A gold-framed miniature of herself and Juan Luis and their infant son. Why in the name of all that was holy was she so attached to this cruel memory? Why had she taken the picture when she fled Córdoba, carried it with her ever since? Perhaps to remind herself that there had once been a happy time. In the painting she was seated with the baby in her arms. Juan stood behind her, one arm protectively enclosing his wife and child. Both parents looked proud and joyful.

The artist had captured them in the idyllic first years of their marriage, before Juan's insane, unfounded jealousy made him lock her in her room. Before he took away all her clothes and burned them. Before he chained her to the bedpost and made her eat like an animal from a dish on the floor. Before he brought his whores to the palace and carried on with them in drunken orgies that lasted for days.

Lila trembled. The memory of those days could still bathe her in cold sweat and make her stomach knot in pain. Still she never flinched from them. She'd schooled herself to remember, to nurture in secret her just hatred, her longing for retribution.

Her husband had died five years before, making her truly the widow she'd claimed to be, and displaying the extent of his malice. "I decree," Juan Luis had written in his will, "That my son Miguel Mendoza Curran is to inherit nothing of my estate. . . . I further decree that contrary to the long custom of my family, said Miguel Mendoza Curran shall not take over the Banco Mendoza on my death. He is unsuited to such responsibility, and instead I appoint my brother-in-law Francisco. . . ."

That had not, perhaps, been his final cruelty. Instead it was the way he died. His father Rafael was killed in a freak riding accident. Juan Luis's life ended when a workman on the roof of a building lost control of a huge stone and it fell, crushing his head. Lila was terrified by the legend that sudden, untimely death plagued the men of the Cordobés Mendozas. Michael was the next in that line.

Dear God, why did she torture herself with these thoughts?

Quickly she shoved the painting to the back of the drawer and pulled out a photograph of Michael taken three years before in Dublin by Eadweard Muybridge. The great photographer's reputation was based on his studies of wildlife, and he'd caught the animal vitality of her son to perfection.

Lila stared at the image for long seconds, letting her pride in Michael smother her fears, then she resolutely put it away. Her son was hers in ways that could never be severed, flesh of her flesh, the child of her agony, but not hers to command any longer. He was his own man now. Michael had joined in her present plan because he wanted his Cordobés heritage as much as she wanted it for him. In other matters he would do as he chose—which might prove to be a problem. Recently she'd discovered that her son was embroiled in a passionate affair with Beth Mendoza, Timothy's wife. Michael had not told her; she found out by chance because she'd arranged for discreet surveillance of Timothy before she approached him with her offer of an alliance.

Thinking of Michael and Beth made Lila frown. Their liaison was a rogue element in her carefully constructed strategy. It could have unexpected consequences.

She sighed, glanced once more at Michael's picture, and put it away. There was nothing she could do about her son's choice of bedmates. The affair would have to run its course, finish when one or the other of them tired of it, or some outside circumstance caused it to end. In any case, he was separated from his mistress for the moment. Michael was thousands of miles away, preparing to play his role in the unfolding drama she'd designed. Still, she feared for him. Experience had taught her that the price for fulfilling some desires could prove too high. Perhaps Michael had that lesson to learn.

Lila closed the drawer abruptly. She was growing morbid. It wouldn't do. Life was to be lived now; the past was beyond change. But the future...ah yes, the future belonged to those with the daring to seize it. Time would tell which of them had more of it, she or the Mendoza men she'd vowed to punish and defeat.

Lila's adversaries were not yet aware of her challenge. No longer based in the shabby old house in Creechurch Lane where the English branch of the great Cordobés banking family began three centuries before, they were in the Partners Room of their impressive bank on Lower Sloane Street in London's fashionable Chelsea district. James Mendoza, the present Lord Westlake, had moved them there soon after he became the senior partner. Jamie had to amuse himself somehow, he'd always been bored silly by banking.

All the partners were present at this emergency meeting. Jamie sat at the head of the table, his brothers Norman and Henry on his right, and on his left, the only male heirs the three brothers had produced: Norman's two sons Charles and Timothy.

Henry was speaking and his tone conveyed both urgency and alarm. "We must cancel the bond," he insisted. "There are rumors that the situation in Paraguay is volatile. If we put the reputation of the bank behind a new issue and we're wrong, we could ruin countless people. Worse, if we go ahead and the public chooses not to trust us . . ." Henry hesitated, cleared his throat. "If that happens we will have to support the entire bond ourselves—and, we haven't the cash. Frankly, that could ruin us."

"Nonsense," his brother Norman boomed. "You're talking rubbish, Henry." Norman was heavyset, a tall, dark, commanding figure who seemed born to be head of the bank. But he was the youngest son and his father had chosen to bow to tradition. James, the eldest, inherited not only the title and the estates, but the senior partnership. Nonetheless, Norman dominated their affairs. "Rubbish," he repeated. "Why should the public listen to rumors? Why should we?"

Henry's voice grew yet lower and more muffled, but he wasn't ready to give up. "It's too risky, Norman. For us right now, that risk is intolerable."

"So you keep saying. But banking is about taking risks. That's its nature."

"Uncle Henry does have a point, Father." It was Charles, Norman's eldest son who spoke. He was fair, as his mother had been, and he had her naturally placid temperament. There was always an element of self-effacement in anything Charles said. "I'm sure you know better than I that we're rather stretched at present. Our liquidity position—"

"The English Mendozas have always stretched themselves," Norman interrupted brusquely. "That's why we're leagues ahead of every merchant bank in Britain or on the Continent. And since Juan Luis died and Francisco took over, that includes our cousins in Córdoba."

For a moment Charles looked as if he meant to press the argument, then he simply nodded his head. "Of course, sir, no doubt you're right." He leaned back in his seat, obviously resigned to letting his father have his way.

No one else spoke. Jamie took the silence as a sign the meeting was over. "It's settled then," he said brightly, half rising. "We're going ahead with the offer, and now we can all go home."

"Sit down, Jamie." Norman waved his brother back to his chair. "We've still to hear from Timothy. At the moment he's as likely as Charles to be in charge here someday, so he'd better speak his mind."

Norman waited, watching both his sons. One of them would inherit the kingdom, there was no one else, and while theoretically the choice was Jamie's, everyone knew it would be made by Norman. The problem was that he'd yet to make up his mind between safe, steady Charles and brilliant, unpredictable Timothy.

The younger boy looked tired. There were lines of fatigue on his handsome face. That was not surprising; he'd come to the bank straight from the ship that brought him back from Dublin. Judging by his limp and creased clothing, he hadn't even gone home to change. "Well, Tim," Norman urged, "do you agree with me or with your Uncle Henry?"

Timothy's heart beat a tatoo in his chest, but he kept his face expressionless and the bitterness from his voice. He'd spent years learning to hide his hatred of his father and his contempt for Charles; by now he was expert at it. "As usual, you've been speaking it for me so well, Father, I haven't felt the need to say anything at all."

Norman leaned forward and eyed the young man. He'd been disturbed by Timothy since the lad was fifteen and his mother died. Norman had tried to spend more time with the boy then, and discovered that he never quite knew what Timothy was thinking. "Do I take it that means you believe we should go ahead?"

Timothy had thought of little besides the irrefutable arguments in the secret documents since he'd read them in Dublin the night before. The papers were actually in the small leather satchel at his feet. They made it absolutely clear that it was complete folly to go ahead. If he placed them on the table now, they would entirely validate his Uncle Henry's position. The issue would be cancelled, whatever it took to do it. The bank would face no crisis.

His father was still looking at him. Timothy met his gaze. "Definitely." His words were clear, though his mouth felt dry and his tongue thick. "The Paraguayan bond is a sound venture. In fact I've been talking to a number of clients about buying shares. I don't sense any reluctance on the part of the public."

The tension seemed to ooze out of him. He was committed now. Until this moment he hadn't been entirely sure he was going to do it. It meant putting so damned much trust in Lila Curran and her promises. Listening to his father and brother and uncles bickering tonight had decided him. They were idiots, lambs begging to be slaughtered. Lila was certain to beat them. So be it, he meant to be on the side of the victor.

His father was yet studying him. Timothy didn't flinch. "We've given our word," he said. "Of course we must go ahead."

For some seconds father and son stared at each other. It was Norman who finally looked away, turned and asked, "Well, Henry, what do you say now?"

"I suppose there really is no reason to believe . . . ," Henry murmured.

"Quite." Norman accepted the capitulation and glanced

at his elder brother. "That's it, Jamie. You can declare the meeting closed and the decision to go ahead confirmed."

"Thank goodness," his lordship said. "Consider it done." He made no effort to conceal his sigh of relief as he stood up. "If you don't mind, I'll leave you four to handle the details. My railway carriage is waiting to take me up to Westlake. The roses are at their best this week. Lovely things, wouldn't want to miss them."

By midnight Thorparch Road was shrouded in a summer fog. The gas lamps were masked by the pervasive gray mist, their glow creating only a feeble yellow circle around each pole. A man moved slowly from one illumined island to the next, straining to see the numbers painted beside the narrow front doors. At last he made out one marked by a double three and sighed with relief.

Quickly he mounted the two steps, lifted the knocker, and let it fall. The sound was muffled by the heavy atmosphere and he repeated the gesture twice more. A few seconds later the door opened a crack and a woman peered out.

"A blessing on the house," the caller said.

"And on your own head. Sure, what would you be wanting at this hour?"

"It's sorry I am to disturb your rest, Mrs. Clancy, but me business wouldn't wait."

"For the love of the Lord, tell me then. What is it?"

He understood the anxiety in her voice. He'd never met Martha Clancy, but he knew that she had three sons serving with the Fenians in Ireland. "It's not for your ears," he whispered. "It's herself I've come to see."

The woman made a quick sign of the cross with a work-gnarled finger. The man knew it was a gesture of thanksgiving because he brought her no bad news. Woman like Martha Clancy lived in terror of the midnight visitor who would tell them their menfolk were imprisoned or maimed or dead. But once her fear was assuaged her terrified expression changed to one of wariness and suspicion. "Sure and I don't know what you're on about. I'm the only herself here. It must be you've come to the wrong house."

The stranger glanced quickly up and down the street. "Would you mind very much if we argued about that on t'other side of your door? There's those we wouldn't want to know our business."

"And what business might that be?"

"Please . . ."

She waited a moment, then relented, stepping aside and swinging the door farther into the narrow entryway. "Very well, come in if you must. But don't think I'm easy prey for whatever evil thoughts you might be having. There's a blunderbuss in me kitchen and well I know how to use it."

The man smiled. "There's no need, Mrs. Clancy."

She turned her head quickly, studying him through narrowed eyes. "That's the second time you've called me that. How do you know me name?"

"Wouldn't I know it since I've a message from your youngest lad? Saw him two days past in Dublin, I did. Young Frank asked me to give his love to his mam."

She dropped any pretense of not understanding. "He's all right then? Any word of his brothers?"

"I didn't see the other two, but I'm told they're well. As for Frank, t'was he who told me how to find Thorparch Road. I wasn't sure, though herself gave me the address." The man nodded his head toward the nether regions of the little house in support of his assertion that there was another woman present.

Martha Clancy ignored his gesture. "I'm grateful for your good news of me boys. Now what else do you want?"

"Sure it's like I said, Mrs. Clancy. It's not for you I've come, though glad I am to bring a mother a bit of comfort.

It's herself I must talk to. It's very important. Now you go and get her, and I'll wait here." He spoke the final words with a ring of authority. It wasn't that his soft tones changed, only that he gave the impression of a man accustomed to being obeyed.

"You're sure she gave you the address?"

"Indeed I am. How would I have it otherwise?"

She looked at him a moment more, then seemed to make up her mind. "Very well. That's a bad leg you've got there from the look of it. There's no need to stand here in the hall. Come with me."

She led the way and the man limped after her. She wasn't wrong about his leg. Weather like this always made it worse. The ache eased, however, when he saw the homey room to which she'd led him. "Ach, 'tis a real Irish kitchen this. The night's damp as a bog and it's glad I am of the warmth of your stove." He held his hands over it, rubbing them together.

He'd completely won her over now. Her manner had changed yet again; there was a hint of deference in it as well as trust. She took a china cup from a high shelf, ignoring the tin mugs beside the stove. "Sit down and rest yourself. I'll pour you a cup of tea, then I'll fetch her."

He took the tea with murmured thanks. "Now," he urged gently, "it's getting late and—"

"Who shall I say wants her?" He told her his name and she nodded. "Wait here."

Lila was not asleep. She'd heard the muffled sounds of someone arriving a few minutes earlier. Now she was waiting to know if this midnight call had anything to do with her. When she heard Martha Clancy's step on the stair Lila sprang out of her chair and opened the door before Martha had a chance to knock. "Yes, what is it?"

"There's a man downstairs. Says he has urgent business with you. Sure and I think he's one of us, though God knows the English have spies everywhere."

"Did he give a name?"

"Aye, he told me to tell you Fergus Kelly was wanting to see you."

"Fergus! Excellent. Thank you, Mrs. Clancy. I'll come with you if I may. I think it's better if I speak with Mr. Kelly downstairs where there's no chance we can be seen from the street."

"There's no one to see you at this hour," Martha said as she led the way down the stairs. "The fog's thick as cold porridge. Besides, folks as live here work for their living. They aren't up and about at midnight."

Lila hurried after her and didn't bother to answer.

Kelly rose as soon as Lila swept into the room. Her dress was simple, pedestrian black faille with a few tucks of black satin circling the hem and the cuffs, but her elegance showed in her bearing and the faint scent of French perfume that shimmered in the air around her. She stretched out her hands in greeting. "Fergus, how are you?"

Kelly took both her hands in his. Lila was tall, but he was taller and he smiled down at her, his dark eyes alight with pleasure. "Sure, and aren't I all the better for the sight of you?" Then he turned and looked pointedly at Martha Clancy, still standing in the door behind them.

Martha seemed to understand the wordless command conveyed by his glance. "I'll be in the front room whenever you're ready to go," she said as she turned to leave.

"What news, Fergus?" Lila asked eagerly as soon as they were alone.

Kelly gazed in the direction of the door the woman had closed behind her.

"It's all right," Lila said. "I'm convinced she's trustworthy." Nonetheless, she went to the door and opened it. The hall was empty. She waited a moment so Fergus could see that for himself, then closed the door again. "What news?" she repeated.

Kelly visibly relaxed and his speech changed. The Irish lilt was still there, but now no one would call it a brogue. "A bit. Both good and bad. The good first. The arrangements are in place at the newspaper and I've seen the Russian. He'll do what we want."

Lila felt a surge of excitement, then doubt. "Will he be convincing?"

"Very. He looks as if he comes straight from the czar's court, and he knows the workings of the Imperial Treasury inside and out. Should, of course, he worked there until he was sacked for having his hand in the till."

Lila breathed easier. "Excellent. Now you'd best tell me the bad news." She steeled herself, but she wasn't really afraid. She knew that no plan this complex could run with perfect smoothness. Whatever the difficulty might be, she'd simply have to deal with it.

"It's Beth Mendoza. Brace yourself, my dear. Beth has left her husband."

"Damn!" The expletive burst from Lila. She'd expected something amiss with the intricate finances of the game, not that an empty-headed, willful girl would choose this moment to flaunt caution and convention. "Does Timothy know why?"

"I'm afraid he does. Found out a couple of hours ago, as soon as he arrived home from Dublin—after a stop at the Mendoza Bank for an urgent meeting, by the way. It seems that Beth left Timothy a note saying she was off to join his cousin Michael."

Lila pressed her hand to her heart and sank onto one of the wooden kitchen chairs. "I was afraid of something like this. But I didn't imagine she'd actually—write that she was off to join Michael. Damn the child! How did she know where to find him? How has Timothy taken it?"

"As to the first question, I can't say for sure. I expect it was Michael himself who told her. In a moment of—one of those moments when the tongue isn't guarded."

Lila felt her face warm in a blush. It wasn't the thought of Michael in Beth's bed; it was that Fergus Kelly was sharing the vision with her. "What about Timothy?" she asked again.

"He's furious, of course. My informant is his valet, a chap called Willis. I saw him half an hour before I came here. According to Willis his master had 'a right proper rage.' But apparently Timothy doesn't know where to look for the pair of them. Willis said he immediately dispatched someone to Dublin to find them."

"Well, he'll have no joy of that errand." Lila was beginning to feel a bit calmer. "Michael's not there."

"No, I realize that. But young Tim is also muttering about having his day in court."

"The fool! It's insane to go to law at this juncture."

"I agree. Look, he hasn't had time to brief his solicitor yet. I think you'd best see him. Try to get him to sit tight, at least for the moment. He could stir up more trouble than we're ready for."

Lila nodded. "Yes, I'm sure you're right. I was planning to leave here tomorrow in any case. I'll be at that new hotel, the Connaught in Carlos Place. Fergus, can you get word to Timothy? Very quietly?"

"Sure and it's no trouble at all," he said, grinning and letting the brogue grow broad again.

Lila shook her head. "The amount of pleasure you get from your play acting is absolutely indecent, Fergus."

"Why? What's indecent about pleasure?"

"I'm not sure," she admitted. "But it seems to me that it must be."

"One of my goals is to convince you otherwise."

She ignored the comment and her expression grew serious again. "Tell Tim I'll expect him at the Connaught for tea at five. Will you do that?"

"Of course I'll do it, my dear Lila. When have you asked me for anything I haven't been willing to give?"

"Never, Fergus," she said softly. "Absolutely never."

"It seems to me you're the one doing the refusing," he said with a smile.

Lila smiled back, but she said nothing.

❦ 3 ❧

WEDNESDAY, JUNE 16, 1898
London, Noon

Lila chose a dress of butter-soft peau de soie and a lace capelet that barely covered her shoulders for the journey between gritty Thorparch Road and elegant Mayfair. Her hat had three tall ostrich plumes, her gloves matched the lace of the cape, and her parasol had a handle of ivory and intricate gold filigree.

The doorman of the Connaught Hotel stepped up to the hansom cab that delivered her and knew at once that the hotel was receiving a lady of quality. "Good day, madam." He glanced at the three trunks and the six hatboxes lodged atop the carriage. "I'll have the porters deal with your luggage."

"Yes, thank you." Lila gave him her hand and he helped her descend. She had no need to pay the driver. The doorman would see to that and the item would appear on her hotel bill.

There was a pleasant flurry of activity in the elegant wood-paneled lobby. Gentlemen returned from business meetings were leaving their keys before visiting the bar for a late morning sherry. Ladies back from a strenuous round of shopping were collecting their keys so they could change for lunch. Despite all these claims on his attention, the clerk behind the desk instantly turned his attention to the new arrival. "Good afternoon, madam."

"Good afternoon, I'm Lila Curran."

"Oh, yes, we've been expecting you. Welcome to the Connaught, Mrs. Curran. I'm sure you'll be comfortable, and if there's anything you need—"

"Yes, thank you. You got my note?"

"We did, madam. It arrived the day before yesterday. We've booked the suite across from yours for the Spanish lady."

"Excellent. Has she arrived?"

"Not yet."

"Well, she's due any minute. Send someone to tell me as soon as she comes, please. And see that a table for two is reserved for lunch in the dining room. I can't say what time, it depends on the señora's arrival."

"I'll arrange everything, Mrs. Curran."

Lila smiled and swept away. She knew many pairs of eyes watched her, which was exactly what she'd meant to achieve by this so public arrival.

"It's wonderful to see you again, but you look very tired," Lila said.

Beatriz Mendoza shrugged. "It is the lot of women to be tired, is it not?" Her English was technically perfect but slightly stilted, and she tended to lisp some sounds.

"Some women," Lila agreed. She waited for the wine waiter to fill her glass with sherry before continuing. "Was the journey difficult?"

"Of course. What is this?" Beatriz waved her fork over a dish of what appeared to be flowers on ice. After a few seconds' deliberation she speared a tidbit that looked like a minia-ture rose. "But it's only a radish," she murmured when she'd taken a small bite. "Why make a vegetable look like a flower?"

"The English are fond of such conceits. How is Francisco?"

"The same. For the time being."

Lila smiled. Her sister-in-law was perhaps the most plainspoken woman she knew. Plain-looking too. The Mendoza women were unlucky. The men were often handsome, usually married gorgeous creatures, but almost always their daughters looked like Beatriz. "Does Francisco know you're in London?"

"Certainly. There was no need to lie. It would never occur to my silly husband that he should worry about my being in London or seeing you. When the storm breaks over his head he won't for a single moment connect it with my presence here."

"You're very cool about it. I hope—" Lila stopped while turtle soup was served from a huge silver tureen. She didn't continue until the three waiters who'd performed the exercise departed. "Beatriz, you're sure? No regrets?"

"None." The other woman tasted the soup. "This is delicious." Then, after two more quick spoonfuls, "Listen, it's a pity you never knew my mother. If Anna had still been alive when you married Juan Luis, you'd understand."

"Would I?"

"Of course. Anna never had any doubts about her duty, or the legacy my father left her. She made everything clear to me and to my brother. But the minute she died he chose to forget everything she'd said."

"And to marry me."

"That would have delighted my mother," Beatriz said firmly. "You had the right blood."

Lila knew she meant Jewish blood. Beatriz would not say that aloud even at this very private corner table. Nor would

Lila pursue the topic. "It's not Juan Luis we're talking about, is it? It's Francisco."

Beatriz wore her salt-and-pepper hair in the Spanish fashion, slicked back in a tight chignon, but it was wiry, obstinate hair and little strands kept escaping and curling around her face. She pushed one back with an impatient gesture and allowed herself a small ladylike snort. "My husband is not a Mendoza, that is his problem. It is not his fault. But . . ." She raised her eyebrows and shrugged.

Both women had finished their soup. A waiter removed the bowls. The wine steward brought a bottle of yellowish white Graves. Beatriz sniffed when she tasted the French wine, but she approved of the lobster in aspic that was served next. The red and white morsels shimmered in their coat of clear jelly, and Beatriz made a little noise of pleasure after her first bite. "This is wonderful. I'd never have chosen to marry Francisco, you know. Juan Luis made me do it."

"Did you never care for him?"

"It depends on what you mean by care. The way you and Juan Luis felt about each other before all the trouble started? No, it was never like that with us." Beatriz glanced up to make sure the waiters were out of earshot. "Besides, Francisco is useless between the sheets. Like a rabbit. Bim-bang and it is over."

Lila choked on her lobster. She had to cover her mouth with the damask napkin and take a sip of wine before she could speak again. "Always?"

"Always. It is no wonder I never had any children. There was never time for him to leave anything in my belly. Of course he does not see it that way. Francisco is sure it is all my fault. Lucky for you as it turns out, though, is it not?"

"Yes. For Michael's sake." There was no point in empty protests. Beatriz knew quite well what was behind Lila's passion for this venture. It was her sister-in-law's reasons that still puzzled Lila.

A man wearing a tall white chef's toque appeared at their

table and carved slices of beef from a huge joint on an elaborate silver trolley. Another waiter added roast potatoes and squares of Yorkshire pudding and asked the women if they would take gravy and horseradish cream. Lila refused the garnishes; Beatriz accepted both. The wine steward removed the Graves and filled fresh glasses with vibrant red claret.

"Will you hate it when Michael takes over?" Lila asked.

Beatriz paused, a forkful of meat halfway to her mouth. "Hate it? In heaven's name, why would I be cooperating if I were going to hate Michael taking over in Córdoba?"

"I'm not sure. But he's bound to marry eventually and his wife will be mistress of the *palacio*."

"Thank God. For me, that is one of the bonuses." Beatriz leaned against the dusky green velvet banquette. She wore a burgundy silk dress—a bad choice because the color made her skin look especially sallow—but she managed to appear a luxuriating cat as she relaxed her shoulders. "I shall travel. France I think. Deauville and Biarritz. Perhaps Austria. I've always wanted to see Vienna and Salzburg."

"Without Francisco?"

"Of course without Francisco. If he does not have a stroke or commit suicide when he is ruined I shall simply insist on a quiet separation. No more bim-bang. It will be heaven."

"Beatriz, there's one thing still worrying me. . . . What if Francisco doesn't respond the way we think he will? What if he braves the storm and finds a brilliant solution of his own?"

"Francisco?" Beatriz giggled. The laughter bubbled until she pursed her lips and choked it back. "Believe me, dear Lila, it is impossible. He will run for help like a little boy who has fallen and hurt himself. You can be sure of it." She wiped the tears from her eyes with a lacy handkerchief. "I told you, he is like a rabbit. Bim-bang, he'll run down the hole."

"You're quite incredible, you know. Will you try some of those strawberries?"

Beatriz studied the dessert cart that had been wheeled to their table. "A few perhaps. And a little piece of that cake." She smiled at the waiter and agreed that he should bathe both treats in thick heavy cream.

It was later, when they were sipping tiny cups of strong black coffee in the sitting room of Lila's suite, that Beatriz reiterated her single condition. "Michael will do what he has promised?"

"Take up the practice of Judaism, make his children Jews? Yes, he will. You have his word on it. He's already stopped eating pork," Lila added with a tinkling laugh.

Beatriz nodded approval and helped herself to a sugared almond from a silver dish. "Good. Because if he does not, I will bring him down. Much as I love him, I will do it. I do not know how, I'm not as clever at these things as you are. But I will find a way to ruin him."

The words were spoken so calmly Lila knew they were absolutly true. "There will be no need. Michael understands his obligations."

"Fine. Then everyone will be happy. And my poor dead parents can rest in peace."

"They indoctrinated you so thoroughly," Lila murmured. "How come they failed with Juan Luis?"

"Who knows? It's doubly surprising because he was nine years old when my father died. I was an infant." Beatriz sighed. "Men are all a little stupid and heartless, are they not?"

"Juan Luis was many things, but not stupid."

"Still defending him, after what he did to you?"

"I'm not defending him," Lila said. "I'm simply stating a fact."

"Very well. And we know his son is different."

"My son is wonderful."

Beatriz smiled. "I agree, so we have no problems. Only Francisco has a problem." She giggled.

"I can think of a few others who aren't going to be ecstatic about our activities," Lila said. "Jamie and Henry and Norman for a start."

"They are all traitors, pretending to be something they're not. Like their father before them." Beatriz dismissed the victims with a wave of her hand.

"Members of the Church of England you mean. But what about you?" The wine at lunch had left a pleasant little buzz in Lila's head; it made it seem possible to ask such a question. "Haven't you been pretending to be something you're not all these years?"

"It seems like that, I know. But it is not the same. No one held a gun to Joseph's head and made him become a Christian. Look, the family of my mother is from Madrid. They escaped to Italy in 1492 after the edict of banishment, but they returned about a hundred years later. Spaniards always return to Spain; it is in our blood."

"And they came back as Christians?"

"Only in public. The Caleros, my mother's people, were true marranos, secret Jews. That's why Robert and Sofía chose Anna Calero to marry their Rafael."

Lila was trying to understand how a passion this deep and everlasting could be based on an unseen God. Her own motives were so different. She thought about the various other branches of the Mendoza clan here in England. None of them had followed Joseph into Christianity; they quietly went on being Jews. After a fashion. Was that her sister-in-law's fashion as well? At lunch Beatriz had eaten her lobster with gusto. Little as she knew of Judaism, Lila did understand that the dietary laws prohibited the eating of shellfish. "Do you consider yourself a Jew?"

"Of course." Beatriz pressed a hand to her heart. "Here I am a Jew. But that will not make my mother and father's dream come true. I have no children."

Lila nodded. Michael was, as she had always known, her greatest treasure.

"Everything is ready in Córdoba," Beatriz continued. "I made all the arrangements exactly as you instructed."

"You told them the code was, minus twenty?"

"Yes. I did just what you told me to do. As soon as the cables are sent it will begin. I shall be well out of it. Jamie has invited me to visit Westlake. He does not want me, of course; I'm not decorative enough. But he has to be gracious to a visiting cousin."

"Excellent. You can keep an eye on him." Lila poured more coffee and dropped three lumps of sugar into her sister-in-law's cup. It seemed as if they'd said everything they needed to say, but she could see at least one more question in the other woman's eyes. "What is it? Why are you looking at me like that?"

"Because I have always wanted to ask you something," Beatriz said, "and never have I had the nerve."

"Ask me now."

"Will you promise to answer?"

"You know me better than that. I'd never make such an unqualified promise."

"No, I suppose you wouldn't. You have always been too clever for me," Beatriz admitted. "But to ask costs nothing, does it?"

"Nothing."

"Very well, I will ask. How did you make Juan Luis let you go, how did you force him to give you so much money? Most of all, how did you make him let Michael go?"

"I had information that he could not allow to become public."

Beatriz set down her cup with a clatter. "Lila, that is no answer at all. I know that. What information? Was it in that letter I had Michael take to you? And there's something else, how did you get Juan Luis's piece of the medallion?"

"Oh, so you know about that as well?" Lila asked softly.

"Only because I went crazy looking for it after my brother died. Francisco wanted it. He knew that the medallion was to pass to the man in charge of the bank. I didn't want him to have it because he's not a Mendoza. But I wanted it. I tore Juan Luis's rooms apart. What I found was only a little velvet pouch with a slip of paper inside. Your name was written on the paper. You took it with you when you left, didn't you?"

"Yes," Lila admitted. "I wouldn't go without it. The medallion was meant for Michael. He has it now."

"But how?" Beatriz demanded again. "How did you make Juan Luis agree to do what you wanted?"

Lila pursed her lips, thought for a moment, then smiled. "I won't tell you that, but I'll tell you a story. Or perhaps you know it. Have you heard of the man the Mendozas call Moses the Apostate?"

Beatriz waved her hand. "The Mendozas have a thousand stories. Most of them aren't true."

"This one is true."

"How do you know?"

"I won't tell you that either, but I'll tell you about Moses the Apostate." She leaned back, stretching her legs on the brocaded chaise longue, closing her eyes, speaking almost from memory.

"*Allahu akbar, Allahu akbar.* . . . That's what the muezzin says. He repeats it five times a day when he climbs up to his minaret. *La ilaha il-Allah,* there is no God but Allah. *Muhammad-un Rasulu-illah,* Mohammed is His prophet. All the while Córdoba was ruled by Islam, for nearly five hundred years, that's what the Mendozas listened to. *Allahu akbar . . .*"

"The Moors got on very well with the Jews," Beatriz said defensively. "With the Mendozas particularly."

"Yes, for a long time. But Moses the Apostate was ruler of the house in 1150, when the Christians were attacking Córdoba and a fanatical Islamic sect called Shi'ites had taken over. They decided to expel all the infidels—meaning all the Jews of course—from the city."

"And I suppose this Moses of yours wouldn't go?"

"No, he definitely wouldn't go. One Friday morning, the Moslem sabbath, Moses called everybody into that old room in the palace, the one with the mosaic freize of acanthus leaves, and pointed to the plaque. You know about that?"

"I know the story about it," Beatriz admitted grudgingly. "My mother told me the mark on the wall in that room is supposed to have been made by a plaque of the family motto."

"If I forget thee, O Jerusalem, may my right hand forget her cunning," Lila quoted. "That's what it said."

"Maybe," Beatriz said. "But nobody has seen this supposed plaque for centuries."

"No, because Moses the Apostate made it disappear. When he had his whole family in the room he told them the motto was a superstition, and they were not going to live by it any longer. He made a servant take the thing off the wall and hide it."

"Where?" Beatriz demanded.

Lila paused for a second, deep in thought. "I don't know. I've wondered about it for a long time, but she didn't tell me . . ."

"Who didn't tell you?"

"Nevermind. We're talking about Moses. Anyway, after the plaque was gone he looked at everyone in the room and told them—"

"That they were going to be Muslims?" Beatriz interrupted eagerly, caught up in the story despite her skepticism.

"Not exactly. He looked at each one of them and said, 'It is done. If there is sin in this thing be it on my head, not yours.' Then he prayed the Muslim prayer. *Allahu akbar* . . . God is Great. *La ilaha il-Allah* . . . there is no God but Allah."

The room was warm but Beatriz's fan hung forgotten from

her fingers. She stared at Lila, completely absorbed. "You sound as if you were there," she whispered.

"Sometimes I feel as if I were."

"But how do you know all this?"

Lila shook her head. "I can't tell you."

"Very well." Beatriz said scornfully. "You are a wonderful storyteller, and that is why Juan Luis let you go. Because you told him about this terrible thing the Mendozas did. I don't believe it."

Lila shrugged. "I don't know if it was so terrible. Old Moses was probably right. But anyway, that's not how it happened. Between me and Juan Luis I mean. It's the background."

"The background to what?" Frustration welled up in Beatriz and she leaned forward and beat the table with her fan, emphasizing each word. "You've explained nothing, you are only teasing me."

"No, I'm not teasing. You really do have to know about Moses the Apostate to understand the rest."

"So? What about the rest?"

"I can't tell you, not now. Instead I'll make you a promise." Lila sat up and looked directly at her sister-in-law. "I promise that when this is all over, when we've won, when Michael is in Córdoba, I will tell you."

Norman Mendoza had chosen to have his office on the ground floor of the bank. His windows looked out on Lower Sloane Street and he could see who came and left the building. Moreover, he was close to the change hall where clerks and tellers dealt with customers. At any moment he could take the pulse of the day-to-day business.

Philip Johnson, Norman's private secretary, had his desk in an alcove between the change hall and the office. Johnson was a cadaverous-looking man whose long narrow face always seemed to be disapproving of something. He'd given Norman twenty years of faithful service, and by now he felt entitled to show annoyance on his employer's behalf. He looked up and frowned when Timothy appeared. "Your father's been waiting for five minutes."

Timothy made a show of reaching for the watch tucked into the pocket of his waistcoat. "Has he, Philip? I must be running slow. It's precisely three according to my watch."

Johnson pursed his lips but said no more. He rose and shut the door to the hall, closing out the soft sounds of money changing hands and an army of clerks scratching entries into their thick ledgers. "I'll tell him you're here."

Timothy tucked his watch back in his fob pocket. He had no need to look at it a second time. It said seven minutes past three. He'd not kept the old man waiting out of spite, it was simply that he'd had to prepare himself before he came downstairs. He had to be sure that nothing in his manner or his words would reveal Beth's desertion. His father would have to know eventually, but Timothy fervently hoped that day could be delayed. His father was bound to blame him, see his wife's duplicity as somehow Timothy's failure. He couldn't face that yet. Stay calm, he told himself as he waited in the little alcove. Stay calm.

Johnson reappeared. "He'll see you." The secretary nodded his head toward the door to Norman's office, and Timothy went in without knocking.

"You're late. I told you to be here at three."

"Sorry, sir. Apparently my watch is playing up."

"Have it seen to," Norman said gruffly.

"Yes, sir. I will."

"And sit down. Don't stand there like a beggar off the streets."

Timothy took the chair across from his father's. The older man was busy signing a stack of documents. Beyond the open window people hurried up and down the street, either to the shops in Sloane Square or the private houses on Pimlico Road. A hot breeze brought the noise of the traffic and the fetid smell of the baking city past the satin curtains.

The only other sound was the ticking of the clock on the mantel. Timothy found the tension unbearable. "Turned warm for June, hasn't it?"

Norman looked at his son. "Second thoughts about the Paraguayan bond? Henry been worrying you?"

Timothy's heart was thudding again, the way it always seemed to be these days. He did his best to ignore it. "Why should I have second thoughts? We agreed the other night that Uncle Henry was being an old woman."

"Yes, so we did. Where's Beth?"

Despite Timothy's efforts to prepare himself, the question caught him off guard. It was the abruptness of the inquiry, the lack of preamble, that startled him. "She's . . . er . . . taking a holiday."

"Bollocks." Norman spoke in his normal voice, reached for a gold toothpick, and began working on a bit of roast lamb lunch had left between his teeth. "I hear she's thrown you over."

"That's nonsense," Timothy insisted. "Where did you hear it?"

"Nevermind where. I have my sources. And it's not nonsense, it's true. She's run off with Michael Curran. That's maybe the worst of it. She could have done her whoring outside the family."

Timothy's face grew very red. "Sir, I cannot permit you to speak of my wife—"

"As a whore? Why not? That's what she is. I tried to warn you. I told you years ago she was a bad choice. But you were 'madly in love' and nothing would do but that you marry her. I never should have allowed it."

Timothy fought for control, reminded himself that this was not the moment to tell the old man to go to hell. In a few weeks perhaps, but not yet. "I believe it's best if I handle my own marital affairs, Father."

"You're not managing to handle them very well, are you?

She's made a fool of you, and now she's made sure the whole world will know."

Norman watched his son's reaction, wishing that he'd followed his own base instincts a couple of years ago. He'd been quite taken with young Beth, used to invite her to go walking with him, make excuses to call when he knew Tim would be away, things like that. It never came to anything, because in the end he didn't have the stomach to cuckold his own son. Pity, considering how it had turned out. "What are you going to do about her?"

Timothy abandoned the pretense that nothing was wrong. "I haven't decided yet."

"How long's she been gone?"

"Since Sunday when I left for Dublin." The words came out muffled, strangled by Timothy's barely controlled fury.

Norman raised his eyebrows. "That long? I'll have to chivvy up my sources. I didn't hear until this morning."

"I think it's disgusting, your spying on me."

His father waved away the protest with one fleshy hand. "It's not spying. You're my son. Of course I keep an eye on you. Is Curran with her?"

"I don't know. She left a note saying she was going to join him."

"Yes, so I was told. Join him where?"

"I don't know that either."

"In Dublin perhaps?"

"No, they're not there. I've checked."

Norman nodded, glad to learn that at least the boy was doing something. "Córdoba?"

Timothy shook his head. "Not there either. He's not been seen in Córdoba since his mother took him away."

"Ah yes, Lila. You must realize that nothing ever happens without Lila knowing about it. Have you spoken to her?"

"No, she's not at Bellereve and I don't know where she is." That was true, and perhaps a more serious problem than the whereabouts of his wife and his cousin. Timothy felt sick to his stomach. Things seemed to be spinning out of control.

"Find Lila." Norman replaced the gold toothpick in its holder on his desk. "She'll be able to tell you where Michael and Beth are."

"And then?" Timothy couldn't suppress his curiosity. How would the all-powerful Norman Mendoza handle an unfaithful wife? "What do you think I should do when I find them?"

"Well, you can't thrash him, not by yourself. He's twice your size. Hire some thugs to do it for you. Quite a few thugs."

"And my wife?"

"A bit of a thrashing maybe. That you can do yourself. Nothing too violent. Then bring her home."

"I see. That's your advice, is it? Spank her bottom, then forgive and forget."

Norman had a quick mental picture of Beth's well-rounded bottom. "It shouldn't be too unpleasant a task. Besides, there's nothing else you can do."

"Yes, there is."

"What, for God's sake?" Norman demanded.

"I'm going to claim adultery and divorce her and name Michael Curran as correspondent."

Norman's response was a guffaw of laughter. "You're going to do no such thing. Are you mad, boy? Bankers don't become involved in sordid lawsuits, much less divorce. It's the kiss of death for business."

Timothy started to protest, then thought better of it. Soon he'd be so powerful he could withstand any scandal, but this was not the time to point that out. He badly needed to change the subject. "Tell me something. Have you ever heard anything of Roger?"

For a split second Norman had to think whom he meant. It was years since his father had sent Roger away. "My Uncle

Roger? What's he got to do with any of this? Whatever made you think of him?"

"He's got nothing to do with my wife. I thought of him because of a piece in today's *Times*. They say Rothschild is going to open a branch in America."

"The damned newspapers. Never trust anything they report. Liars, the lot of them. And no, I've not heard anything about Roger in years. Neither has Jamie or Henry."

"Then he's simply disappeared?"

"Looks like it. It was a daft notion anyway. My father should never have sent him to New York. Roger was no more cut out for banking than Jamie is. Putting him on his own like that in a place like New York. . . . Daft."

"Roger had a piece of the medallion, didn't he?"

Norman narrowed his eyes. At last he understood the point of this conversational diversion. "Yes, apparently he did. There's a piece unaccounted for."

"Because Grandfather Joseph split his piece between himself and his twin brothers Roger and Cecil. Eventually Joseph gave a third to each of his sons. You and Uncle James and Uncle Henry each have a piece. That's right, isn't it?"

Norman swiveled his chair so it was facing the window. The traffic was thinning as the afternoon wore on. "Yes, that's right."

"The pieces must be very small. The inscription has to be unreadable."

"There's no need to read it. We all know what it says."

" 'If I forget thee, O Jerusalem, may my right hand forget her cunning,' " Timothy quoted softly. "You'd not have thought the Mendozas would be much for the Bible."

"Some of them have been over the years. Anyway, Jerusalem in this case means the family. The business."

"When I was a boy Grandfather told me it meant Córdoba."

"I guess it did when the motto was adopted. That was long before there were any Mendozas in England."

"Does cousin Francisco have the other half of the medallion? The Cordobés half?"

Norman stood up. "Good God, lad, you're asking more questions than you did when you were six. He must have it. Robert the Turncoat, the Englishman who took over in Córdoba and married the Spanish gypsy, divided the medallion in two around 1820. He gave half to his son Rafael and half to your grandfather Joseph, who was his nephew. Rafael had two children: Juan Luis, who's dead, and Beatriz. Now that her husband, Francisco, has taken over in Spain, he must have the Cordobés half of the medallion." He stood up. "Look, it's all bloody complicated and you have other things to worry about. Besides, I have to go. I'm meeting John Baring at my club."

Timothy rose when his father did, trying not to show how interested he was in that last bit of information. Baring was head of another powerful merchant bank. It was not unusual for London's financiers to share risks, but this was the first he'd heard of Mendozas looking for a partner in the new bond. It was information that might interest Lila Curran. When he found her. "Is Barings taking a piece of the Paraguay loan?" he asked with all the innocence he could muster.

"I'm not sure. Now, about Beth and your cousin Michael. Find Lila, she'll know where they are."

"Yes, Father. I mean to find her." Timothy did not allow himself to smile at the irony.

The two men went to the office door. Timothy put his hand on the elaborately carved brass handle but did not turn it. "Father, one more question."

Norman paused. "Very well, what is it?"

"Your piece of the medallion. Who will you leave it to, me or Charles?"

"I'm not sure. I've always told you both that. The pair of you are the only male heirs; it's a serious business. I'll have to see."

"Yes, so you've said." Tim opened the door and waited for Norman to exit ahead of him. "Good afternoon, sir."

Norman waved his hand in a wordless farewell and walked through the change hall toward the street.

Bastard, Tim thought watching him. Bloody bastard. His father meant to give his piece of the medallion to Charles. He'd always intended to pass the prize to the firstborn. That's the way the Mendozas did things. That's how his father's idiotic brother James got where he was. And he'd give everything to Charles too: the title, the house. Charles was in line for all that, and the bank as well. But it wouldn't matter. By the time Norman Mendoza got around to willing his little piece of gold, it wouldn't matter a whore's tit.

Since the day was so warm Norman had no coat to leave with the porter in the lobby of Whites Club in Pall Mall. He passed the man with a brief nod and went directly to the smoking room. John Baring hadn't arrived yet, but Norman spotted someone else he knew. "Sharrick, how nice to see you."

Lord Sharrick looked up from his newspaper. "Mendoza, good to see you. It's been ages. Sit down a moment."

"Thank you. It has been a long time. You've been away?"

His lordship shrugged. "Hither and yon. You know me, eternal wanderlust."

"Indeed, the papers are always full of your exploits. Where were you this time? Plant hunting in China or looking for antiquities in Tibet?" Norman took a pipe from his pocket and filled it, tamping the tobacco down with an intricate gold tool designed for the purpose.

"China and Tibet were last year," Sharrick said. "My latest journey was to Latin America. Your bailiwick, isn't it? Financially I mean."

"Parts of it. Barings has Argentina and Uruguay and Rothschilds Venezuela, but we've picked around among what's left."

"There's quite a lot left," Sharrick said dryly. "It's a big place, Latin America. Pity it's not more stable."

Norman was fussing with a match, trying to get the pipe to light. He spoke with the stem clenched between his teeth. "It is now. Been settling down nicely. Tremendous natural resources, as no doubt you saw. Where exactly were you?"

"Paraguay mostly."

Norman looked up, ignoring the burning match in his fingers. "Really? What did you think?"

His lordship leaned back in his seat. "Mendoza, I don't think you want to know what I thought of Paraguay. I hear you're floating a huge new bond for them."

"Yes, two million. But this new president—"

"It will take more than any one politician, my friend. Look what's happened in the past ten years. One Latin American country after another has refused to pay its debts. Paraguay among them. When was the last time the country defaulted?"

"Eighteen seventy-four," Norman admitted tersely. "But that was right after their war with Argentina and Brazil. The Paraguayans made good in 1885."

His lordship raised his eyebrows. "Do you call agreeing to pay the bond holders a third of what they had coming at two percent interest making good?"

Damn the man, Norman thought. Those dark eyes always dance with pleasure when he looks at you, whatever he has to say. "You're remarkably well informed. I've never imagined that finance was one of your interests."

"The world interests me. And all the extraordinary creatures in it." Sharrick was still smiling.

"Yes, well that's admirable I'm sure. But, forgive me, you know the old expression about teaching your grandmother to suck eggs? In this case I'm the grandmother. I'm a banker, trust me, this loan is sound."

"Barings are bankers too, been at it almost as long as you have. I hear they nearly went under a few years ago."

"Nothing like as long as we have," Norman corrected. The match had long since gone out. He dropped the charred stub into an ashtray and lighted another. "For one thing, their problems were with Argentina. For another, they reorganized and came out stronger than ever."

"Then despite the fact that Paraguay's maximum total revenues are less than eighty thousand a year, you recommend I buy shares in your two-million-pound Paraguayan bond?"

"Absolutely. The government's starting a coffee-growing scheme. There's a lot of profit in coffee. Buy some shares. You'll do extremely well with them. Go on sale next Wednesday. Tell your broker today Sharrick. Don't wait or the issue may be oversubscribed."

His lordship put the folded newspaper on the table between them. "I'll think about it," he said, rising. "I'll think very seriously about your new bond. Now, if you'll excuse me . . ."

"Of course. Nice to see you again. Take care of yourself."

Norman watched the man leave the room. Amazing that the fellow managed to chase around the world despite his bad leg. Bald as a billiard ball too, but it was said that women found him extremely attractive. Filthy rich, of course, an old Anglo-Irish family. The title Sharrick of Glencree went back to Elizabethan times.

He sat there a moment longer, sucking hard on the pipe as he reflected on Sharrick's comments. Payments to Paraguay were to be by four six-month debentures of half a million each. It would take months for the matter to come to a head. A default wouldn't become obvious until such time as the bank wasn't so—what was Charles's word for it?—so stretched.

Norman thought about that. Goddamn it, he decided finally, how could they not be stretched? Making money was about risk.

Beyond the window he saw John Baring mounting the

steps of the club and he stood up, tipping the remains of
the pipe into the ashtray with a few decisive raps on the
crystal rim. He had more pressing things to think about than
the observations of Lord Sharrick. He tapped the pipe in
the ashtray one last time and the crystal shattered.

"Where have you been all week?" Timothy asked the question through clenched teeth. He held his delicate china tea-
cup in a knuckled grip.

"No place that need concern you," Lila said.

It was a little after five and they were in the residents'
sitting room in the Connaught because Lila had decided
against bringing Timothy upstairs to her suite. The public
room was pretty, comfortable, and quiet—and there was
no fear he'd push the conversation beyond the limits she
intended to impose.

Timothy's tone was shrill and he was trembling. "Under
the circumstances I think where you've been does concern
me. I have a right—"

"Lower your voice," Lila commanded. "Get hold of yourself."

"Another thing," he said more softly, but with equal
venom, "I'm not accustomed to being summoned like an
errand boy."

"Oh? Is that how it was?"

"What would you call it?"

"I haven't the vaguest idea how you were summoned."

He took a folded scrap of paper from his pocket and
handed it to her. "This appeared on my desk an hour ago.
No member of my staff will say how it got there."

The note was printed in block capitals and said simply,
THE CONNAUGHT FIVE P.M. TODAY. L.C. "It's succinct,"
she admitted.

"How did you get it onto my desk?"

"I didn't, not directly. I merely asked someone resourceful
to get word to you. Not a member of your staff, by the way.

Timothy, this is really a waste of time. What does it matter how you got the message? I'm told you've been looking for me, why?"

"Why? How in God's name can you ask me that? You must know what's happening."

"I know that a week from today Mendozas will offer the public shares in a two-million-pound bond on behalf of Paraguay. Isn't that what we've been working toward and waiting for?"

"That's a long way from all of it." He sipped his tea, then set the cup down. His hand was trembling. "Stop pretending you don't know what your vicious son is doing."

"My son is where he should be, doing what he's supposed to do."

"With my wife." He spat out the words.

Lila leaned forward and lay her hand gently over his. "Timothy, listen to me. I have heard about it and I'm very sorry. I told Michael some time ago that I considered his actions wrong as well as imprudent, but he's a grown man. I can't tell him what to do. And Beth . . . Forgive me, but I know for a fact that it was her idea to leave you. Michael had nothing to do with it. He was simply—" she hesitated, not sure how far she should go, "simply dallying," she added, rushing on before he could react with righteous indignation. "She's not worthy of you. You must see that."

"I'm going to divorce her. And I will name Michael as correspondent. Don't try to talk me out of it."

"I have no intention of doing so. You must do whatever you think best. But, dear Timothy, surely you see that this public punishment you wish to inflict must wait? You can't go to law now."

"I know that."

She relaxed a little. He wasn't an utter fool, thank God. "Good. Then I propose we discuss the really important business at hand. This other affair can wait until—"

"I want to know where they are," he interrupted.

"I can't tell you that."

"Does that mean you don't know, or only that you won't tell me?"

Lila took a sip of her tea before answering. It had grown cold and bitter. "Why is it important that you know where they are?"

"So I can gather evidence of their carryings on." He spoke the words stiffly, the picture of virtue wronged.

Lila leaned forward again. "Timothy, do you remember that when we first agreed to join forces I told you I had two secret weapons?"

"At least two, that's what you said."

"Yes. Well, it was the truth. One of my weapons is Michael. You can't interfere with that now. We need Michael to do exactly what he's doing."

"He's doing it with my wife."

She wanted to shake him, scream at him that he was a shortsighted idiot. Instead she shook her head. "He's not. I don't mean they're not together. But what Michael is doing, for you and for me as well as himself, has nothing whatever to do with Beth." She squeezed his hand. "Dear boy, I know what you're feeling. But if you'll be patient a little longer you'll have the prize you've always wanted. You will be head of the Mendoza Bank in England. Isn't that worth waiting for?"

"And your precious Michael—"

"Will be in charge in Córdoba. I've never denied that was my aim. Partnerships only work when both parties get what they want most. You should know that."

"I do know it. Until now I never begrudged him the Spanish bank or anything that goes with it. But things are different. Surely you see he's made them different."

"I do see it. I'm simply saying it doesn't matter for the moment."

He clenched his hands, the same look of murderous rage on his face. She had to go further. "Tim, I'll tell you something else. Whatever happened, Michael could never marry Beth. He has obligations to the family in Córdoba. They would never accept a divorced woman as mistress of the Palacio Mendoza. No one in Spain would accept it."

That was a new idea. Timothy's fantasies involved Michael and Beth drifting off into the sunset together, living happily ever after, himself left behind alone and forlorn. The whole point of a public divorce was to besmirch their names so thoroughly that their idyllic future would be ruined. Now Lila was saying it couldn't happen. He didn't say anything for a few moments. Then, "Do you think we could get some fresh tea?"

"Of course." She glanced toward the door of the sitting room and raised her hand. A nearby waiter saw her instantly and approached.

Lila waited until he'd gone before she spoke again. "Now tell me, is it absolutely certain Mendozas is going ahead with the Paraguayan issue?"

He was leaning forward, his hands hanging now between his splayed knees. He'd taken to clasping and unclasping them, flexing his fingers in an effort to dispel some of his nervous energy. "It looks that way. My uncle Henry was making scared noises the other night, but Father bullied him into silence as usual. It's your turn to tell me something. What weapons have you besides your bloody son and whatever he's up to?"

"Decisive weapons," she said softly. "Most decisive."

"Tell me what they are, damm it! I can't go on acting blind, putting all my trust in you."

"Yes, you can. What did you make of the report you received in Dublin?" She was probing, that report had been Fergus's idea, not hers. She wasn't quite sure what information Fergus had wanted to convey. Or why.

The waiter brought a new tea tray before Timothy could answer. Lila poured two fresh cups. Timothy didn't answer until he'd drained half of his. "The report pleased me," he admitted. "But then it would, wouldn't it? It means that my father and my uncles are about to make a horrible blunder."

It wasn't conclusive enough to tell her everything, but it confirmed some of her suspicions. Somehow Fergus had managed to bind this foolish boy closer to their alliance. "Very well, but that's not my point. Would you have had any such information without me?"

"I don't know."

"You do know. How could you have had it? You didn't for a moment suspect that the situation in Paraguay was entirely different from what you'd been led to believe. I knew and I arranged for you to find out." That wasn't exactly true, but it was true enough for her purposes. Lila waited for him to recognize the facts before pulling the leash tighter.

"Very well, I can't deny what you say," Timothy admitted. "But how far down are we going to bring them? There's not much point in grinding the bank so deep into the dust that there's nothing for me to take over." He turned to her. "Or would that suit you? It might give your precious Michael even more control in Córdoba if the bank failed here in London."

"It would do no such thing. Underneath the formal separation the house of Mendoza is a single entity. That's always been true. It's our great strength."

"Our strength? You're not a Mendoza, only a Mendoza widow."

"My son—my precious son, as you rightly call him—is as much a Mendoza as you are. Besides, I have my own reasons for wanting . . . what I want."

"So you've always said." He put down his empty cup. "According to you I'm to believe you're orchestrating everything, that you're in total control. Well, are you aware that my father is meeting with John Baring right now? Barings may take a piece of the loan. That will considerably reduce the pressure on Mendozas."

Lila smiled. "I promise you, whatever they say now, when

the time comes to put money on the table neither Barings nor any other bank will be interested in joining Mendozas in this venture."

"How in hell can you know that?" Timothy exploded. "And even if you're right, the public offering could attract a lot of subscribers. There's no telling what the small investor is likely to do. If Mendozas doesn't have a cash crisis all our plans—"

"I promise you, the issue will fail." Lila spoke with absolute certitude.

"How can you know?" he demanded again. "What are you, a witch who can foretell the future?"

Lila narrowed her hazel eyes. "Your cousin Juan Luis asked me that same question once. It was a very bad day for him. No, I'm not a witch."

"I didn't mean to offend—"

"It's all right. I realize you didn't. All the same, I'm not going to tell you how I know. But it doesn't matter. There's only a week to wait. Then you can judge for yourself if I was right or wrong."

"And if you're right and the issue fails, then what happens?"

"Then the game begins," Lila assured him.

❦ 4 ❧

Puerto Rico, Ten A.M.

As Lila and Timothy spoke in London the *Susannah Star* neared landfall half a world away.

She was a windjammer, a four-masted vessel that could spread an acre of canvas and stow eight thousand tons of cargo, riposte to the challenge of steam. The windjammers were fighting to preserve a place for sail in merchant shipping, and this one looked every inch a winner as fully rigged she made for San Juan Bay.

An enormous man stood in the forepeak watching the approaching shore. He was six feet six inches tall, with legs like tree trunks and muscles that rippled visibly beneath his fine linen shirt. He looked invincible as the freshening breeze ruffled his dark red hair and the sun flashed sparks from his blue eyes—but what he felt was fear.

For the first time in his twenty-nine years Michael Curran was not sure he had the stomach or the head for what he'd set out to do. He put his hand to his chest. Beneath the cloth he could feel the semicircle of gold that hung on a leather thong around his neck. *If I forget thee, O Jerusalem, may my right hand forget her cunning.* . . . The risks had to be taken, he reminded himself, the prize was enormous.

A lucky omen had buoyed his hopes when the venture began. The *Susannah Star* belonged to a small fleet owned by the Mendozas; she traded on their behalf. Michael had not planned to travel on a Mendoza ship. It had been an accident of chance that this one was setting sail when he was seeking a berth. The captain knew nothing of his passenger's connection with the family, but Michael found the irony heartening. He was the raider at the gate and he'd easily breached the first defenses.

The *Susannah* bore down on the shore, running before the wind with all canvas set. San Juan was distinguishable now. Michael saw a cluster of low white buildings with red roofs, dwarfed by the turrets of two lowering stone fortresses. This had been a Spanish island since the fifteenth century, and the architecture clearly showed the influence of the motherland.

He strained to see any sign of damage inflicted by the American warships that had bombarded the town a month earlier. None was evident. The incident had been merely a skirmish in the weeks-old war between Spain and the United States; nonetheless, he was convinced the Americans wanted this island. In fact, he and Lila were counting on it.

The cliffs were looming now. Michael was no seaman but suddenly he sensed danger. The windjammer appeared hellbent on a collision course. He turned to look aft and became aware of tension crackling in the air. The crew were all on deck, poised and waiting. For long seconds the only sound was the wind sighing in the sails, then the voice of Captain Judson Hughes boomed, "Ready about!" and every man jumped to his position.

There were a series of other commands, each issued by the captain and passed on by the mate's whistle. "Down helm!" and the great ship began turning into the wind. "Mainsail haul!" and men strained on winches and lines, singing to maintain their rhythm as they canted the yards to a new angle. "Let go and haul!" and the foreyards were swung round and the luffing sails once more filled with wind. Michael stood his ground in the bow, unwilling to move lest he get in the way. Once the ship lurched sickeningly, then he felt her steady beneath his feet.

The mate's whistle sounded again, and crewmen climbed some hundred and fifty feet into the tall rigging and began furling sail like demons. Seconds later the *Susannah* moved smoothly into the channel between the island of Las Cabritas and the cliffs of Puente del Morro, making for safe harbor. Michael let go a breath he'd not realized he was holding.

"There you are, Mr. Curran, I was looking for you." It was Briggs, who had acted as his steward during the two-week journey. "Will you be taking all your things ashore, sir?"

"Yes, Briggs. Everything."

The seaman was as tough and short and squat as one of the oak barrels in the hold below, but a look of almost childlike disappointment appeared on his face. Formerly the ship's cook, he'd broken his arm two days out of Liverpool and the captain, not knowing what else to do with him, had suggested that Michael take him on. It had proved a most satisfactory arrangement. As it happened, Briggs's father had been a valet. The boy had learned a lot before he ran away to sea at the age of ten.

There was a wistful note in Briggs's voice when he asked, "You'll not be leaving Puerto Rico with us, then?"

Michael shook his head. "No, I've had enough of the ocean for a while. Though thanks to you it was a most comfortable journey."

"T'was a pleasure to serve you, sir." Briggs looked ruefully at the black sling tied across his chest. "But I'd have made a better job of it with two hands." He started to leave. "I'll go below and pack both trunks."

"Hold on a moment. I've been thinking, Briggs. Would

you consider leaving the *Susannah* and coming to work for me?"

The Englishman's leathery face split into a broad grin. "I been hoping for days that you'd ask. I'd just 'bout given up."

"Done then. I'll see the captain and make the arrangements."

The Posada de San Juan Bautista was the best public lodging San Juan could offer, but that was a dubious recommendation. There were few foreign visitors to the island. The inn was used by planters who came to town on business and stayed a night or two before returning to their outlying haciendas. Apparently they did not demand luxury. Michael scowled as he surveyed the overgrown courtyard and the peeling pink wash on the stucco walls, but he led Briggs inside.

The landlord looked astonished when the big man so obviously a foreigner addressed him in perfect Spanish.

"*Dos habitaciones,* one for me and one for my man here." Michael nodded toward Briggs. "See that they're clean," he added.

"*Sí, caballero* . . . If you will wait only a little while, I will do everything necessary."

Michael turned to Briggs. "He's promised to get two rooms ready. I have to go out for a while. Can I leave you to see to everything here?"

"Yes, sir, 'course you can. But begging your pardon, Mr. Curran, I didn't know you spoke the lingo."

"Since I was a child," Michael said shortly. "I had a Spanish grandmother." That was true as far it went, and it would shut off any further questions about his background.

Michael left the inn and walked across the neglected courtyard as far as the gate to the street. He sheltered in the dappled shade of a tall oleander heavy with pink flowers. Their sickly sweet scent was almost overpowering. Glancing over his shoulder to be sure he was unobserved, he took a bit of much-folded paper from his jacket pocket.

What he held was a crude hand-drawn map that directed him from the Posada to the foothills south of San Juan. A cross in the upper right-hand corner marked his destination. Lila had given Michael the drawing in Dublin, as well as the name of the man who prepared it. The mapmaker was here on the island and eventually he'd track him down, but that wasn't his first priority.

He studied the sketchy lines and arrows, occasionally glancing up to identify a landmark. If the scale was even remotely accurate, he had some eight miles to cover. He could probably hire a carriage, but drivers talked and he wasn't ready for publicity. There might be a stable where he could get a horse—No, it would take too much time. Michael shoved the map in his pocket and strode off.

His route led him along the main thoroughfare of the town, the Calle Fortaleza, past the Banco Mendoza. It was the grandest building on the road, three stories tall with stucco walls the color of fresh cream, a red tiled roof, and intricately carved wooden balconies and doors.

Michael stood in the shadows across the street and considered this distant outpost of the Mendoza empire. It was a bastard child spawned by Robert the Turncoat when he ruled Córdoba, but founded by Ricardo de Maya, a one-time monk turned revolutionary. When de Maya died with a knife in his back it was his wife, the legendary Maria Ortega, who took over the bank. She could not read or write, but before she died in 1873 she'd made a fortune for herself and for the Mendozas, and left a thriving institution as her legacy.

It was his target, the goal of his journey to this obscure island.

Michael felt again the searing doubt that had haunted

him since he sailed from England. Once more he touched the medallion, then walked on.

In minutes he'd left the town behind and was walking along a dirt track that cut through an increasingly dense pine forest. He should have been thinking about the bank and his plans for it; instead he was oblivious to everything but his memories. He'd suppressed them until now, but glimpses of the women of Puerto Rico had destroyed the self-discipline he'd maintained in the all-male universe aboard ship.

He thought of Beth. He remembered how his two hands could span her waist, the way her small pointed breasts felt pressed to his chest, the glint of her blond hair, and the smell of lavender that she always wore. The images were achingly vivid. He felt a sudden painful longing for the woman he'd left behind in England.

"Curran, you're a horse's arse," he said aloud as he climbed a steep hill. "This is not the moment to concentrate on your crotch." But was that it? Did Beth only appeal to him because they enjoyed each other in bed? Or was it the added fillip of cuckolding his smug cousin Timothy? Hell, the basis of the attraction no longer mattered. Even if she were not already married, Beth could have no place in his future. He'd made a bargain with his mother and his aunt Beatriz; to keep it he'd have to take a Jewish wife.

There was no one else on the road; the only sounds were of birds chattering in the trees and small animals scurrying in the underbrush. He'd come to a strange place to seek his fortune. But everything about this scheme was strange and difficult and obscure. Most of Lila's plans were complex. The woman he chose to marry would be different. She'd be a sweet and docile creature like Beth, not someone he'd have to match wits with all the time.

He reached the crest of the hill and sucked in his breath, all thoughts of the future driven away by the moment's reality. A small convent was nestled into the hillside some fifty yards below. He had come full circle on a journey begun the day he scaled the wall to his mother's prison and gave her the letter that secured their freedom. He was here, and at least that mystery would be solved.

Michael scrambled down the path to a stone arch topped by a wooden cross. A small sign told him he'd arrived at the Convent of the Virgin of the Snows, Las Nieves. She was an odd patron for this tropical place, it was midafternoon and the heat was sweltering. He glanced at the cloudless sky, took a deep breath, and pulled the cord of the brass bell hanging beside the gate.

A moment went by and nothing happened. He rang again, swinging the rope hard this time. More silent seconds passed under the blazing sun. He was damned if his long quest would go unrewarded. He rang the bell a third time, tugging the rope so fiercely that the countryside echoed with the clamor.

"*Buenas tardes, señor.* I am sorry you had to wait. We were at prayers."

The small black-robed nun who unlocked the gate looked too fragile to carry the weight of her heavy veil. She was panting and her upper lip was beaded with sweat, as if she'd run all the way to answer his summons. He felt guilty about his impatience. "*Disculpa, mi hermana,* I have come to see—"

The nun held up her hand, forestalling his words. "Later, señor. You look hot and tired. Please, come in and drink some water and refresh yourself in the shade."

He stepped through the gate into an immaculately tended patio filled with crimson geraniums and a pale blue flowered shrub called plumbago that he hadn't seen since he left Córdoba. There was a well in the center. The nun drew a bucket of water and ladled some into a tin cup. "I am Sister Paloma," she told him as she handed him the drink. Michael took it with a nod of thanks, thinking that *paloma* meant dove and that the name suited her. She moved like a small bird, every now and then glancing at him shyly from under her coif.

A few seconds later, his thirst satisfied, he tried again to state his business. "I've come to see—"

"Sister Magdalena," she supplied. "I know."

He was astonished. "How did you know?"

"Because the holy sister told me." The little nun flashed him a mischievous smile. "She said to expect a giant of a man with red hair and blue eyes. It had to be you, didn't it?"

"I suppose so, but how could she—"

"Sister Magdalena can answer your questions, señor." The hint of teasing was gone. Sister Paloma was grave and properly nunlike once more. "It is best if you ask her yourself. Please wait here a moment. I will tell her that you have come. She wasn't sure if it was to be today or tomorrow."

Michael was left alone only a few minutes. When she returned, the nun said nothing but motioned him to follow. The way led along arcaded paths that edged a series of patios filled with flowers and shrubs. He heard no sound, nor saw anyone except Sister Paloma. Ahead of him she glided noiselessly across the tiles, her long black skirts swaying as she walked. Once he stumbled over an unexpectedly shallow step and cursed softly. The nun turned to him and pressed a finger to her lips. He felt bigger than he'd ever felt in his life—enormous, unweildy, and thoroughly out of place.

They came to the end of the sheltered walkways and she unlocked a gate that led to yet another patio. This one was small and bare and contained only a single gray-barked tree with dusty leaves and numerous branches that swept the cobbled ground. The rough country stones were broken in places so the gravelly earth showed through. In contrast to everything else he'd seen, this place looked desolate and forgotten.

"We are out of the convent proper here," Sister Paloma

said as if she'd read his mind. "This is not the cloister." She paused. "Do you understand?"

Michael shook his head.

"Our order is made up of nuns who take a vow of silence and enclosure, señor. Some, like me, are externs, allowed to deal with the outside world. But Sister Magdalena is neither."

Michael was impatient with her explanations. He wanted to see the old woman and talk with her; the technicalities of her life didn't interest him. But Lila had schooled him well in patience.

"We are not part of any great order, only simple Puerto Rican women who dedicate ourselves to God. The bishop himself installed us in this convent. It is he who sent us Sister Magdalena."

Michael nodded. "Very well, now can we—"

The nun held up her hand in a restraining gesture. "Wait, señor. I wish to explain what you will find." She hesitated, then went on. "The rest of us live in community; the holy sister lives alone. In there." She nodded toward what seemed a blank stucco wall. He looked at it more closely and saw a low door, half-hidden by the unruly branches of the tree.

Sister Paloma pointed to the sky. "Look up, señor. What you see is the back wall of the convent church."

Michael's glance followed her pointing finger. He saw the spire and bell tower. "I see," he murmured. He really didn't, but it was unimportant. Only the woman mattered.

"The life of an anchoress is an ancient tradition," Sister Paloma continued. "Holy women used to wall themselves up behind the altar of churches and—" She broke off, apparently reading incomprehension in his face. "Never mind. Come, I will take you in."

The wood of the old door was splintered and unpainted. It was also very low. Michael had to bend his head to follow her. A patch of sun revealed a well-worn stone threshold.

Many pairs of feet had passed through this opening. Into what?

Inside he could see almost nothing of his surroundings. The only light came from the open door, and he was blocking most of that. "*Benedicamos Domino*," Sister Paloma murmured into the dark.

"*Deo gratias*," a disembodied voice whispered.

A chill crawled up Michael's spine. There was something unnatural in this place, something that smacked of worlds unseen. Don't be a fool, he told himself. Latin incantations and obscure rituals are the way they've been controlling people for centuries. It's nothing but a blind to hide a thirst for power. These women are pawns in a game nearly two thousand years old, but you're not going to be seduced by it.

A few seconds passed. His eyes began to adjust to the half light. He could see Sister Paloma clearly, but he still couldn't make out the other woman. "Sister Magdalena?" He overcame the impulse to whisper and said firmly, "My name is Michael Curran. I need to speak with you."

Sister Paloma turned swiftly, her face full of reproach. "She knows that. But you should wait for the holy sister to speak to you. Her silence can only be violated with permission."

"It's all right, Paloma. It is his way." The faceless voice was low but musical. It didn't suit his image of a holy recluse. "Thank you for bringing my guest to me. I have been expecting him. Now, leave us please."

Paloma made a slight bow and withdrew, pulling the door shut behind her. The room was plunged into total darkness.

"Sit down, Don Miguel. There is a small stool to your right."

"My name is Michael, not Miguel. And the title isn't necessary."

"In Córdoba, in Andalusia, when you were born, they

named you Miguel," the voice said with a hint of laughter.
"But I will call you Michael if you prefer."

He let that pass. "What did you mean you were expecting
me? How could you have known I was coming?"

She laughed openly now. It was a rich, hearty laugh, but
not unkind. "I know the things Our Lord chooses to tell
me. He told me a little about you, and that you were coming
here. But you're still standing and the ceiling in this place
is too low for you. Please, won't you sit down and be a bit
more comfortable?"

"How can I be comfortable when it's as black as pitch in
here? Is there some law that says you can't have a lamp?"

"No, it is simply that I am accustomed to the dark . . ."
Her voice trailed away and he heard a match being struck,
then saw the pinpoint of flame travel in a short arc. Finally
the larger flame of a candle stabbed the darkness. "Is that
better, Michael?"

"Much," he admitted. His eyes took a moment to adjust,
then he spied the stool. He hooked it to him with his foot
and sat down, leaning forward as he tried to make out the
woman in the shadows. He saw only a huddled black shape
silhouetted against a white wall. So the old crone didn't
want to show herself. Very well, that wasn't important. "I
came because of your letter."

"Yes, I thought so. But I wrote the letter many years ago
when I was still in the world. Before I came here."

"Sixteen years ago. And you sent it to my mother in
Córdoba. Why?"

"Because Our Lord told me to do so."

"And I suppose He told you her name and address too?"
Michael did not disguise his scorn.

"No," the woman admitted. "My messages are seldom as
specific as that. I asked in the Calle Fortaleza."

"At the bank?"

"Sí, the Banco Mendoza. Doña Maria was very old, but
still alive."

"Maria Ortega knew you were writing to my mother?"

"Sí. At least I assume she did. It was Doña Maria herself who told me where I could find the woman called Lila Curran."

"I'm told the Ortega woman never gave anything away for free. How did you worm the information out of her?"

"I had certain knowledge which made Doña Maria anxious to cooperate with me."

"What information?" Michael demanded.

The reply was a few seconds coming. "I can see no harm in telling you," Sister Magdalena said finally. "Maria Ortega is long dead. She has faced her punishment or her forgiveness according to the will of the Lord." Another pause, and when she spoke again her tone was gentle and sad. "I knew the truth, you see. I knew that Doña Maria murdered her husband. It was she who put the knife in Don Ricardo's back."

Michael drew a sharp breath. "It's well known that everyone suspected as much at the time, but how did you prove it?"

"I did not have to prove it. I told her exactly what happened. When. Where. What she said and how she felt."

"By Jesus, woman!" he exploded. "Your messages from on high are pretty damned convenient, aren't they? Do you expect me to believe all this?"

"It is not up to me what you believe or do not believe, Michael. But if you do not credit my visions, why are you here?"

"How can I credit them? I can't even look into your face when you talk. As to why I'm here, if you know so damned much, why not that as well?"

"Please do not curse," the nun said quietly. "As for my visions, they tell me what I need to know. To help those whom I am to help. The rest is in God's hands and I do not trouble myself about it."

"Bloody damned convenient," Michael repeated.

She sighed. "You must believe or not, as you choose. I cannot take much more time from prayer. Tell me what I can do for you?"

"I need information."

"It is many years since I had a vision concerning the Mendozas. There were only those two, the long story I wrote to your mother, and the one about Maria Ortega that made her tell me what I needed to know. Oh, yes," she added matter-of-factly, "a few days ago Our Lord told me about you and that you were coming, but nothing more."

He stood up, needing to move, to make his mind work. "It's all too dam—too pat to be believed. I don't believe it. There's someone feeding you these stories. Someone in the bank who tells you these things. I need to know his name. For the love of Christ, woman, you have to tell me!" He took a step toward the huddled form.

"No, please—" A smooth white hand emerged from the rusty black folds of the all-encompassing habit. "You must not touch me. It will break my vows. I have told you everything I know."

He paused where he stood, leaning toward her but not making any attempt to reach her. "I don't give two hoots in hell about your vows. I mean to have the truth. You're my best hope."

"Your hope for what?"

"To save what belongs to me and to those who will come after me."

"Our true inheritance is God, Michael, and no one can take Him from us. Only we can separate ourselves from His love."

Michael's words burst from him in a strangled groan. "Don't tell me your pious stories. My family have suffered for generations from your loving God. You know. You told that story to my mother and it was true, every word of it was proved true. Because of that she was able to remove herself from a desperate situation and escape to Dublin and some peace."

"I see," Magdalena said thoughtfully. "And she took you with her?"

"Yes. I was only thirteen at the time."

"I see," she repeated. "That explains a great deal. What you meant about securing your inheritance, for example. And why you call yourself Michael Curran."

"It explains more than that, if you know the history of the Mendozas."

"But I don't. I've been telling you that. Only those two visions. Nothing more."

"Dammit! I don't believe you." He lunged toward her again.

The nun pulled back. Michael could have caught her easily, but some instinct stopped him.

"Wait," she whispered urgently. "I think . . . yes, I know what to do." Suddenly she straightened and stood. He hadn't realized she was seated until he saw the way the shadow on the wall behind her elongated. What he'd assumed to be a humped back disappeared, and her robes fell into graceful folds now that she wasn't clutching them to her.

He stared in silent fascination as Sister Magdalena reached up her arms and lifted her veil, then she leaned forward into the flickering light of the candle. "Look into my face, Michael. Then you will know that I'm not lying."

The woman who revealed herself to him was young and beautiful. He couldn't see her hair except for a dark widow's peak, but the face framed by the tight white band of her coif was a perfect oval, with a full mouth and a short straight nose and prominent cheekbones. It was a face, he realized at once, that had been marked by asceticism, but it was still lovely. The eyes were two black coals, set deep and framed by long dark lashes. The fire behind those eyes might be religious passion, but given different circumstances it could be something else entirely.

"I thought you were an old woman," he whispered incredulously.

"Many people think that. But I was twelve years old when I came to this place. Eleven when I had the vision concerning the Mendozas, the one I wrote about to your mother."

"Eleven . . . That's impossible. How could a child understand such a story, write it, send it to a place thousands of miles away—"

"That is what I'm trying to explain," Magdalena interrupted urgently. Her dark eyes never left his. "I am only a messenger, Michael. Our Lord uses me as he chooses. I understood nothing of the matter then, and not much more now."

Somewhere a bell tolled, drowning out any words he might think of to say. Instantly the nun flicked her veil forward and blew out the candle. "You must go," she said into the darkness. "The door is right behind you. There is another door in the patio. It leads directly to the road. I will hold your troubled soul in my prayers, my friend. Our Lord will take care of you; don't be afraid." He heard the sound of a metal grating open, then shut.

In seconds Michael realized he was alone in the small airless room. He turned and easily found the handle of the door. It swung open and he stepped into the brilliant sunshine of the patio. For a moment he was blinded, then he could see. The second door she'd told him to look for was there. Michael crossed and opened it and he was, exactly as she'd promised, on the road that skirted the Convent of Las Nieves and led to San Juan.

Back in the real world—with none of his questions answered.

The swift tropic dusk was falling when he reached San Juan. Michael was tired and hungry and thirsty. Still he lingered a moment in the Calle Fortaleza, staring at the bank.

The street was deserted; there were no strollers indulging

in the traditional *paseo*, the late afternoon promenade he remembered from his childhood. He suspected that the brief attack by the Americans had made the residents of San Juan aware of their vulnerability. The colossus to the north cast a long shadow, and there was the smell of fear in the sultry stillness.

Across the street a flicker of movement caught his eye. Michael stepped deeper into the shadow of a sheltering wall and watched as the door of the bank opened. Two men stood speaking. He instantly recognized Captain Judson Hughes of the *Susannah Star,* but he didn't know the second man.

The stranger was short and there was something rodentlike about him. He had to be Fernando Luz, manager of the bank. Lila's Puerto Rican informant, the man who drew the map and whom Michael knew as Rosa, had described Luz in much the same terms: ". . . a rat, but not one of real courage, one who hides down holes." Michael didn't know if the assessment was accurate, but he expected to find out.

Hughes was saying something, punching his fist into his palm to emphasize a point. Luz listened impassively. The apparent tone of the exchange was puzzling. Since the *Susannah* was owned by the Mendozas, the banker should think himself the captain's superior, higher in the pecking order. Yet it appeared that Hughes was giving orders to the Puerto Rican. Michael filed that fact away as something he might be able to use.

Minutes later the ship's captain hurried in the direction of the harbor, and the other man retreated into the ostentatious bank. It was dark now, the sky spangled with stars and a ripe full moon rising. Seconds passed, yet Michael remained where he was. Not until he saw the glow of a lamp appear on the top floor above the bank did he nod with satisfaction and stride off toward the posada.

Briggs had done well. Michael's room was spacious and airy
and had a balcony that looked toward the sea. He also found
hot water for a bath waiting, and a large glass of grog that
was more rum than water.

"I feel like a new man," Michael announced an hour later
as he fastened the studs of a freshly laundered evening shirt.
"Full marks, Briggs. You've managed superbly."

With his one good arm Briggs held Michael's cutaway
coat so his employer could slip into it. "I done me best, sir.
Mind, these foreigners are bloody difficult, what with having
no English and all."

"That hasn't seemed to stop you getting everything arranged. What's the plan for dinner? I could eat a horse. Two
if I had the chance."

"Only a chicken. But leastwise I seen to it they won't be
servin' you no pork."

The servant deftly adjusted the jacket over Curran's massive shoulders. "Them dagos downstairs kept jabbering at
me, but I didn't unnerstan' what they was saying, and I
figured they didn't unnerstan' me. Told 'em over and over
I did, no pork. I been servin' the master near three weeks,
and he never touches no part of a pig. Should o' been clear
enough, shouldn't it, sir? But I wasn't sure me message was
getting through."

"So what did you do?"

"Never made no difference about them bein' daft blokes
what don't unnerstan' English," Briggs said firmly. "I went
into the kitchen and there was a whole pig carcass hanging
there. So's I pointed at it and shook my head real strong
like, and they got the idea. T'weren't no beef I could see,
but plenty o' hens squawkin' out in the back. I made 'em
unnerstan' you'd have a chicken for your dinner."

The meal was acceptable, at least there was enough of it to
appease Michael's hunger. The only other guests in the dining room were a party of five men, locals from the sound

of their Spanish, sugar planters from the hills, no doubt. They left before Michael did, and there was no sign of them in the lobby when he went there after dinner. No one else either.

He was too full of thought to sleep. Michael went out to the street and was immediately reminded of Andalusia and his youth. In contrast to the empty inn, there were masses of people milling about. Darkness seemed to have given the natives courage. In Dublin nearly everyone would be abed by this time. Like the Spaniards, the Puerto Ricans seemed to consider midnight the shank of the evening.

He strolled idly, listening to the accents eddying around him, picking up bits and pieces of conversations, ignoring the stares attracted by his obviously foreign appearance. It wasn't any plan that took him toward the docks; he simply wandered idly, following the crowd.

Michael turned a corner into a small street and suddenly found himself in a barrio that stank of poverty and vibrated with menace. Groups of sinister-looking men stood on corners and clustered around doors that led to noisy, smoke-filled *tavernas*. It didn't occur to him to be frightened. Physical security was something his size and strength had always provided. He continued walking and observing.

Michael heard the scuffle before he saw it. He turned his head toward the sounds of fighting coming from a slit of an alley between two low buildings. There was a moment when his blood throbbed in anticipation—God but he'd love some action after all these weeks of agonized speculation!—but he pushed the notion aside. He wasn't ready to attract attention. He was about to retreat the way he'd come when he heard something that stopped him.

He stood where he was and peered intently at the melee of swinging fists and kicking feet in the alley. Something was not as it should be in that brawl. It wasn't just a covey of hoodlums settling a grievance. There was . . . yes, he was sure of it. He'd heard a woman in the center of the wolf pack. He sprang forward.

The alley was less than four feet wide. He still couldn't see the woman, but he could hear an undertone of sobs beneath the cursing and grunting of the fighters. Two men, locked in what was obviously meant to be a death grip, blocked his way. Michael planted one huge hand on the shoulder of each of the grappling men and tore the pair apart, flinging them against the opposite walls of the alley. There were sharp thuds and a crack that sounded like a breaking skull. One body crumpled to the ground and lay still. The other man didn't lose consciousness, but he cowered and stared at the avenging fury that had suddenly erupted into the fray.

Michael ignored him and hurled himself at the remaining pair of fighters. For a brief second they were transfixed, then one of them threw himself forward, grasping for Michael's throat. He flung the man off easily. The other thug stood and stared, toothless mouth agape. Michael started to lunge for him. Suddenly he felt someone climb onto his back and sink sharp teeth into his shoulder. The man he'd left conscious behind him had recovered his nerve.

Michael screamed in fury. He reached up and grabbed a handful of greasy hair, trying to pull the teeth from his flesh, but the man wouldn't let go. Michael spun around twice, gathering maximum momentum. Then he slammed his back, and the man riding on it, into the stone wall. There was the snapping sound of breaking bone and Michael felt a spurt of hot blood on his neck. The biting hold gave way and the burden fell from his shoulders.

Acting together, the two others went for him now, though a few seconds earlier they'd been mortal enemies. Michael dispatched them with one punch each. In seconds it was over. The alley was littered with bodies and there was no one left to fight. He stepped over the carcasses, searching for the woman. He couldn't see much of anything since the moon had gone behind a cloud, but gradually his eyes adjusted to the deepened dark.

A few feet ahead he saw one prostrate form that didn't look like the rest. Michael went toward it. He'd been right: it was a woman. She lay face down in the dirt of the alley, her shoulders heaving with sobs. *"No passe nada, señorita,"* he murmured. *"Ahora usted está segura."* His assurances that nothing had happened and that she was safe had an effect. The sobs died away.

"Here, let me help you." Michael extended his hand and gently took the woman's arm. She still hadn't said a word, but she allowed him to help her stand up. He was conscious of the feel of the dress she wore. It was made of cheap silk that felt sleazy to his touch. And the scent of her perfume was overpowering, mingling with the smell of fear and sweat. It was not a nice combination. A hush had fallen, and he could hear the woman's labored breathing.

At that moment a new voice shouted, *"Ay!¿Qué pasa?¿Por qué la ruida?"* It was a neighbor complaining about the noise now that it had stopped and the danger had obviously passed. A woman flung open a shutter and leaned forward holding an oil lamp, shedding a shaft of light on the scene. *"Madre de Dios!"* she gasped.

The alley looked like a slaughterhouse, full of tangled arms and legs and spattered with blood. Michael glanced up, but he wasted no time reassuring the woman hanging out the window. He was concerned only with the one he'd rescued.

Her head was bent forward. In the beam of light coming from overhead he saw that her hair was black and thick and hung down over lush breasts barely covered by her dress. "Señorita," he began.

The woman raised her face to his.

Michael stared at her, gasped, then stumbled backward, pressing himself against the wall of the alley. Her glance raked his face. Her eyes reflected back his astonishment—and his disgust.

The woman gave one cry of pain, then turned and ran into the darkness. Above Michael's head the window was shut with a decisive slam, while the neighbor still begged the Virgin to witness the carnage below.

For some seconds he stood where he was, paralyzed by disbelief. Finally he stumbled out of the alley. He was shivering by the time he reached the main road. There was a deserted bench under a palm tree. Michael dropped onto it, trying to catch his breath, to make himself accept what he'd seen.

In the moment when she raised her face to his he had recognized the woman he'd saved—the woman dressed like a tart and stinking of cheap perfume. She was Sister Magdalena, the holy recluse of the Convent of Las Nieves.

❦ 5 ❧

THURSDAY, JUNE 17, 1898
San Juan, Early Morning

For most of the night Michael stood by the french doors of his room staring at the darkened harbor. When dawn came and he watched the sun rise over the sea, he was still unsure of his next move. All his instincts drove him to return to the Convent of Las Nieves and confront the woman, but logic suggested a different direction.

Fact number one: Sister Magdalena was a fraud, a collosal and talented liar. That meant she'd lied to him about the source of her knowledge of the Mendozas. No God he'd ever heard of granted celestial messages to a whore.

Fact number two: Somebody had told her the story she'd written down years ago, somebody on this island knew incredible things about the Mendozas. He had to find out who, and the only person who could tell him was the creature pretending to be a holy recluse up in the hills.

Fact number three: It shouldn't be difficult to make her tell the truth now that he had such a hold over her. This was a Catholic island. Religion was taken seriously, so, too, was being a nun. The woman wouldn't want her guilty secret broadcast all over Puerto Rico.

The issue was whether to wait or to go back to the convent immediately. Waiting would give him a stronger position. She'd have had time to brood about their chance meeting in the alley, to recognize her position. But if he waited she might bolt. Why should she sit and wait for him to expose her? On the other hand, where could she go? They were on a small island with few opportunities to leave, and that was insurance of a sort.

There was a light tap on the door. *"Adelante,"* Michael called.

Briggs came in balancing a tray in his one arm. "What you said, sir, I figure it meant I should come in?"

"Yes, of course. I thought it might be one of the locals."

"All asleep, near as I can make out. I told 'em you always take your breakfast early, but I had to pull one of the blighters from his bed behind the stove to get this."

Briggs put the tray on the table near the balcony. "T'ain't nothin' to be had but this here coffee and crullers, sir. Not a speck of tea nor porridge in the kitchen, nor a kipper neither, far as I could tell. I'm goin' out back and see if them squawkin' hens laid any eggs, but I thought I'd bring you this first."

"It's all right, Briggs. I quite like *café con leche* and *churros* for breakfast. Don't bother about the eggs."

The Englishman looked doubtful. "Only this, sir? It's not enough for a nipper, let alone a man your size."

"It will do." Michael picked up the large bowl of coffee. "Spanish people don't eat the kind of breakfast we're accustomed to. This is a Spanish island, so we'll do as the locals do."

Briggs still looked doubtful. "I don't drink coffee, sir. Tea or grog or beer, nothin' else."

"Do as you like," Michael said sharply. He didn't want to stand here and argue about food with the Englishman.

For the first time he wondered if he'd been wise to abandon his plan to find all his servants among the Puerto Ricans. But the impetus behind his impulsive decision to hire Briggs was still valid; it could prove useful to have someone around who saw the world through British eyes and had no loyalties to anyone in Puerto Rico other than himself.

"I'll be calling on the British consul sometime soon," he added more kindly. "I'll ask him about getting some tea. Or perhaps we can buy some from the *Susannah*'s stores."

Briggs brightened. "That's a fine idea. I'll go see the quartermaster meself. Always got on fine with him. With your permission, sir, I'll do it afore the ship leaves port this afternoon."

"Permission granted. Now, go get yourself something to eat. And don't sneer at these crullers. The *churros*." Michael held out the plate of fried pastries. "They're delicious. Try one."

"Maybe later," Briggs said doubtfully. "Meanwhile, sir, I brushed all your suits when I unpacked yesterday. Which one will you be wanting today?"

"The dark blue pinstripe. I'm calling on a banker this morning."

Michael suppressed a smile at the ease and obvious pleasure with which the seaman had recalled his father's skills as a valet. And while he watched Briggs laying out the clothes it occurred to him that, for better or for worse, he'd made up his mind not to tackle the convent whore just yet.

Fernando Luz bent his head over the two letters of credit Michael had placed on his desk. "*Sí*, I see, señor. Five thousand pounds sterling with Barings, and an equal amount with Rothschilds. A considerable amount of money, señor. We will do everything in our power to make you happy with the services of the Banco Mendoza."

"I hope so, since I've no choice in the matter. Yours seems to be the only private bank on the island."

The Puerto Rican smiled. "That is true, señor."

"In Britain and on the Continent we value competition, Señor Luz. It sharpens the wits. I'm not entirely sure I feel comfortable in a situation where there is none."

Luz paused and leaned back, surveying his caller. "This is your first visit to our island, señor?"

"Yes."

"And you arrived yesterday?"

Michael knew that Luz required no confirmation of the information, but he nodded. "That's true, too."

"Then you cannot be expected to know our ways. But if you plan to remain among us for a time—"

"Perhaps permanently," Michael interrupted. "I've been looking for new opportunities. If I find them here, I'll stay." God forbid, he added mentally. He'd already decided that he liked nothing about Puerto Rico and less than nothing about San Juan.

"Very wise, Señor Curran. There are indeed opportunities on our island: A man of means such as yourself, fluent in both Spanish and English, is sure to prosper here. May I ask what you know of our political situation?"

"Not a great deal. What I've learned all points to God-knows-how-many parties and splinter factions. Spain may have granted you autonomy of a sort, but you don't seem to have a talent for self-government in Puerto Rico. What you have is chaos." Michael spoke softly, with a hint of scorn, watching to see if Luz would take offense at the words.

The banker did not rise to the bait. "True, all true. But chaos can be profitable for a man able to see the opportunities it brings. Don't you agree, señor?" Luz didn't wait for an answer. "Besides, the mother country has had difficulties of her own for over a quarter of a century."

"Longer than that," Michael said.

Luz shrugged. "We could go back perhaps to the dawn of time. It's the last quarter century that has made the difference here. When Spain abolished slavery in 1873 they made change inevitable in Puerto Rico." Luz pursed his lips in disapproval. "Now they have a queen regent who declares war on the United States of America."

"You don't approve of Maria Cristina?" Michael asked. "I thought she was universally liked."

"Liking has nothing to do with it, señor. She is a woman, and as such is easily influenced. The *norteamericanos* will eat Spain for breakfast. They have already begun. As you no doubt know, the first course was taken in Manila a few weeks ago."

Michael nodded. "I know. But what about Puerto Rico? You had a taste of the American guns as well. And San Juan seems to be preparing for war."

Luz shrugged. "A few hotheaded fools stir up the peasants and make what they call preparations. It will come to nothing. You forget, señor, it is to free Cuba from Spain's yoke that McKinley and his Congress make war. They have said so. Here in Puerto Rico we have been promised autonomy. What can the Americans want with us?"

"Do you believe all the statements made by governments, Señor Luz?"

"Almost none of them," the Puerto Rican admitted. "Politicians are all liars. And fools as well. It is because of them that today we are without the economic support of the slaves."

Michael thoroughly detested slavery, but it would be idiotic to say so now. "I take it a number of the plantations have suffered because of that?"

"Not as many as elsewhere in the Indies perhaps, but we've had our casualties. No white man can pick cane, señor, not and live a long life. I assure you this is true."

Michael studied his fingernails, as if the subject were of only passing interest. "So they tell me. But sugar prices have been unstable for years. Perhaps the answer is that no white man should plant cane, Señor Luz. But coffee, now that's another matter." He looked up, fixing his eyes on the banker's face. "Wouldn't you say so?"

"I would, señor. As a banker, I would advise anyone weighing the advantages definitely to choose coffee." His voice was very soft. The eyes Michael hadn't been able to see yesterday when the man was arguing with Judson Hughes were faded brown. They were small, tired eyes, set close together. Nature had not been kind to Fernando Luz, but he met the Irishman's piercing blue gaze without waivering. "If you are interested in a plantation, it should definitely be coffee," he repeated.

Michael stood up. "I'll bear it in mind. Now, sir, if you'll kindly open an account for me based on those . . ." He gestured to the two letters of credit still on the desk.

Luz jumped to his feet. "Of course, Señor Curran. At once." He treated his visitor to a smug smile. "Barings and Rothschilds are both fine institutions, but I think you'll find the Banco Mendoza has no equal."

None at all, Michael thought as he nodded to Luz and prepared to leave.

The banker trotted ahead of him, anxious to offer every politeness to the man who'd just deposited a fortune in his bank. "Permit me, señor." He opened the door with a flourish.

"Oh, Luz," Michael said, pausing on the threshold. "One other thing. Can you recommend a good tailor? I've nothing with me but tweeds and serge." He brushed the sleeve of his heavy woolen suitcoat. "Something lighter-weight seems in order here."

"Indeed, señor. And it's not yet truly summer." Luz smiled with satisfaction as he warned the Irishman of the heat to come. "Diego Fontes on the Calle Cristo. None better. Tell him I sent you, of course."

"Tell me, Briggs," Michael inquired that afternoon when he returned to the inn, "what do you know of horseflesh?"

"Not a thing," Briggs admitted. "Like I told you, sir. I put to sea when I was a nipper of ten."

"Yes, so you said. Very well, I'll see to it myself."

Briggs looked pained at having been found wanting. "Are you planning to buy a carriage, sir?"

"Maybe. Or perhaps only a riding stallion at first. There's a livery stable not far from here. I'll see what they have to offer. But not right now. Briggs, it's time for that admirable local custom, a siesta."

"What's that, sir?"

"A nap." Michael slipped his suspenders from his shoulders and began unbuttoning his trousers.

"Here, sir," Briggs said springing forward, "let me do that."

"No, I won't let you do it." Michael brushed the Englishman's hand away. "I told you when we were aboard ship, I take my own bath and I dress myself."

"But I wasn't really your valet then, Mr. Curran. Not like now."

"As far as this business goes, it makes no difference. Get you gone, man. Go take a nap of your own. Do you good to get into the local way of things." Michael paused with his hands still at the waistband of his trousers. "By the way, I never thought to ask, is your room satisfactory?"

"Very, sir." Briggs's morose expression vanished. "Ain't had a room to myself since I first shipped out. Nor a proper bed to sleep in neither."

"Good. Glad you're pleased with your new state. Now go and enjoy it and leave me in peace."

When Briggs had left, Michael stripped. He fingered the gold pendant a moment, but he never considered taking it off. He'd worn the thing day and night since Lila gave it to him. Sometimes, like now, it seemed to burn his flesh, but it kept him aware of the stakes in the game he was playing.

He stretched out on the bed and clasped his hands behind

his head. The ceiling had once been pale ivory, but years of neglect and the smoke of hundreds of candles had darkened it to the color of horse dung. Everything in Puerto Rico seemed dull and suffering from neglect.

He'd intended to pass the hottest time of the day deciding on his next moves, but the night spent agonizing about Sister Magdalena had taken its toll. Michael was asleep before he'd had a chance to string two thoughts together.

The High Seas

"Oh, my God." Beth Mendoza moaned. "I'm drying, Tillie."

"I don't think so, Miss Beth. The ship's doctor doesn't think so, neither. You're seasick, that's all."

The woman had been Elizabeth Turner's baby nurse before she became the girl's maid. Three years before, when nineteen-year-old Beth had married Timothy Mendoza and left her parents' home, Tillie went with her as a matter of course, an unlisted part of Beth's substantial dowry. Long familiarity had eliminated any need for deference. "Do stand up," Tillie said brusquely. "The doctor prescribed fresh air. A walk on deck will do you good."

"No, I can't possibly. Go away and let me die in peace."

The maid ignored the instruction and tugged her mistress into a sitting position, then swung the girl's legs over the side of the bed. Quite a surprise that was, a proper bed in what they called a cabin. Miss Beth even had a private bathroom. Tillie had expected to find narrow bunks and foul-smelling holes instead of proper toilets. Her only knowledge of accommodations at sea came from a brother who was a sailor on a cargo ship.

Conditions aboard the Cunard's *Persia* were not like those Tillie's brother described in his Christmas letters. The liner was enormous. When she first saw it at Southampton dock,

Tillie was convinced it must sink the moment they got underway. Instead the *Persia*'s thudding steam engines drove her in a stately, steady fashion Tillie found entirely satisfactory. And she never had a moment's seasickness. Not like poor Miss Beth.

"C'mon," she insisted, slipping Beth's small feet into leather walking shoes with squat heels and sturdy laces. "Up you get, pet. It will do you good, you'll see." Whenever her mistress was ill Tillie became yet more familiar, reverting to her role of childhood protector. "Do be a good girl," she repeated.

Beth held a crumpled linen handkerchief pressed to her mouth. She took it away long enough to say, "These shoes are awful. Where did they come from? Why did you pack them?"

"They're walking shoes. Don't you remember having them made when Mr. Norman wanted you to go walking with him in Oxford? 'Course I packed 'em, never know when you might need walking shoes in some foreign place like we're going to."

Beth frowned at the mention of her father-in-law. Then there was some subtle deviation in the ship's motion and a new wave of nausea overcame her. "Oh God..."

"That's it, we're taking you out to the fresh air right now." Tillie put one strong arm around Beth's waist and tugged her to her feet. The girl lurched as if she were drunk. Tillie marched her out of the cabin, ignoring Beth's constant moans.

In the first days of his enterprise, some fifty years earlier, the Canadian Cunard had conceived of his vessels as utilitarian ferries plying the oceans. Competition changed that. The *Persia* was one of a series of steamships that boasted every conceivable passenger comfort, as well as speed. The liner was a floating hotel that would bring her passengers to New York in ten days' time.

Beth took no pleasure in the broad teak decks or the

inviting lounge chairs, or the army of stewards and waiters ready to provide whatever any passenger might fancy. She fought back the dizziness that threatened to overcome her and the constant nausea and gritted her teeth. Her trial by sea wouldn't end in New York. She'd booked a berth on a freighter called the *Lady Jane*. At the office in Southampton they'd told her it would bring her to San Juan, Puerto Rico, in three days. She could look forward to almost a fortnight more of this agony.

Grimly she grasped the railing, ignoring fellow passengers strolling along as if they were on Brighton pier. Was Michael worth what she was enduring? The thought came and went quickly. Beth was quite convinced that he was.

San Juan, Midnight

Sister Magdalena could not stop trembling; cold sweat bathed her body despite the heat of the night. She had been kneeling in the same position for a long time, and now when she tried to rise she lurched forward and found her legs would not hold her. Slowly, painfully, she dragged herself to her feet, clinging to the stone slab that served as her bed. Eventually circulation returned and she could stand.

Her cell was dark, but the blackness in her heart was darker still. This torment had to end; she could not go on with the knowledge forced upon her. But dear sweet Lord Jesus, how could she deny it? Her lips moved as if she spoke, though she made no sound. I know, my God, I know because you tell me. But what am I to do? Who will believe me?

Suddenly she raised both arms above her head, shaking her fists in rage, and this time she cried aloud. "Leave me alone," she begged through clenched teeth. "Leave me alone!

I'm merely a woman and a terrible sinner. You cannot ask me to be Jonah. Do you hear me, Lord? Leave me alone!"

The reply was silence. The fury left her and in its place was only shame. Sister Magdalena fell upon the stone bed and wept.

❦ 6 ❧

MONDAY, JUNE 21, 1898
San Juan, Nine A.M.

The bishop of Puerto Rico was a small fastidious man who kept his robes tucked close to his person, as if afraid they'd be contaminated should they touch the world beyond his privileged comfort. While he spoke he kept twisting the heavy ring on his finger, symbol of his rank and armor against lesser mortals.

"You wished to see me, my child?"

"Yes, Your Excellency. Forgive me for troubling you. I would have come to you if it were not for my vows. I did not mean for you to make this visit so early in the morning." Sister Magdalena's eyes were lowered; she kept them fixed on her hands, which were folded in her lap. Her face was covered by her veil, and despite the lighted candle she saw only dimly the unlikely scene, the mighty bishop seated on the rough stool in the tiny room where she received callers.

"My schedule is very full. Your message said a matter of gravest urgency. This was the only hour I was free to come."

"Yes, Excellency," she murmured. "I understand, of course."

"But I do not understand. What is so urgent, Sister? Why have you sent for me?" There was an edge of fear in the bishop's voice. He did not normally jump at the request of a nun. But this one was different, as he had good reason to know. "What do you wish to tell me?" he urged.

"Our Lord sent me a vision." Her voice was barely audible.

The bishop leaned forward. "Yes? Yes? Come, my child, how can I help you if you don't tell me what you want?"

"I want nothing," Magdalena whispered. "Only to be left in peace. But Our Lord will not allow it. He said I must tell you."

"Yes? Tell me what?" It took enormous control not to shout at the woman.

"We are in great danger. Our enemies—"

"Who is *we*? Do you mean the convent here? the Church?"

She shook her head. "No, not exactly. Puerto Rico, the whole island. Terrible danger."

His Excellency sighed. When her message came he'd been terrified. Even since he had recognized that she really was a seer of sorts, the bishop had lived with the fear that some day she might discover his own secrets, accuse him to his face, perhaps even send word to Rome. But this crisis seemed to have nothing to do with him personally. "You are very removed here in your convent," he said with paternal unction. "There is a war between Spain and America. I'm sure that's what your vision meant. But there's nothing to worry about, my child. The American Navy came, but it went away and there was little damage."

"No, no, you don't understand!" Her dismay was increasing, making her voice shrill. "I know about the shelling; the nuns get news even here. My vision had nothing to do with that. Our Lord told me that all of Puerto Rico is in danger, but that the thing the people must not do is resist."

The bishop stood up. "Very well, and now you have told me. Your duty is discharged, Sister Magdalena. You may return to your prayers."

She lifted her face. He could see the faint outline of her features beneath the veil. "Excellency, you will tell them? You must explain everything to our people. That is why I was given the vision."

"I will do what I deem best," he said sharply.

She jumped to her feet, almost knocking over the candle. He grabbed it just before it fell. Hot wax burned his wrist but he ignored it, preoccupied by the sudden image dancing before his eyes—spreading fire and himself trapped in this small mean room. "Be careful! Sit down, Sister, calm yourself. There is no need for this agitation. I am your bishop, your highest authority on earth short of the Holy Father himself."

"My authority is Our Lord." She was calm now, her worst fears had been confirmed and she could only go forward. "He told me that I must tell you, but that you might not do as you should. Then the responsibility would be mine."

"Yours? That's absurd. Almighty God does not take authority from a bishop and pass it to a woman, not even you, Sister Magdalena. You will do exactly as I tell you. Remain here and pray, faithful to your vows."

"My vows are not more important than thousands of lives."

"Enough!" The bellow was startlingly loud coming from such a small man. He took a step toward the door and repeated the command. "Enough! You will not spread rumors and panic, Sister. You will do as you are told."

A number of nuns were huddled beneath the tree in the patio outside Magdalena's cell. Technically they were beyond the cloister, but this was not a time to worry about such things. The mother superior and her council, half a dozen of her most trusted advisers, waited to see what extraordinary thing must come from this urgent summons to a bishop. They heard the episcopal shouts and clung together in terror. The little door opened and the bishop came out. The nuns saw the expression on his face and knew their fear was justified.

His Excellency stood a moment, looking at them. Then he issued a series of orders, and the nuns rushed away to do as he commanded.

"These are the coffee-growing areas, are they not?" Michael's finger traced a broad curve on the map of Puerto Rico he'd spread on the desk of Fernando Luz.

"Sí, señor. The high hills of Cordillera y Central. It is good land for coffee."

"Yes, so they tell me." Michael wore the white linen suit that the tailor Diego Fontes had produced for him in only four days. On the rack near the door he'd hung a new hat of Panama straw. The big Irishman managed to look entirely at home in the tropical outfit. He was relaxed and confident as he took the seat Luz had offered him a moment earlier. "I wish to buy it."

"It? Forgive me, I do not understand. Which plantation do you wish to buy?" Luz leaned forward, studying the map. He put one finger on a spot near the village of Cayuco. "Here is the land of Don Prudencio Alvarez. It is very fine. I know for a fact that Don Prudencio would entertain a reasonable offer. Of course, there is also the neighboring hacienda of La Alboria. That is not quite so excellent perhaps, but it is owned by a widow who is growing old and she—"

"Both of them," Michael interrupted brusquely.

Luz raised his eyebrows. "That is a very large venture, Don Miguel."

"Michael. I do not care to be addressed as Miguel." Each time he heard the Spanish version of his name he remembered his father's voice. He hated the echo.

"Forgive me. Don Michael then. But as I was saying, between them La Alboria and the hacienda of Don Prudencio cover almost five thousand *cuerdas*."

Michael nodded. A *cuerda* was roughly the same as an

acre. The two plantations Luz had mentioned would come to something like seven square miles, but the calculation was irrelevant. "I'm afraid I'm not making myself clear. I wish to buy all the coffee haciendas."

The banker gazed at his client and didn't say anything. Finally he swallowed hard. Michael kept his eyes fixed on the other man's prominent Adam's apple. It went up and down two or three times. "All of them?" Luz whispered.

"That's right. At least all of them worth having. Seventeen haciendas by my count. Starting with that of Señor Morales in the west here at Lares," Michael indicated the place on the map, "and finishing with Señor Machin's land near Montaña."

Luz's eyes hadn't followed the sweep of Michael's moving finger. Instead he continued to stare at the Irishman. "Tell me, Don Michael, do you have any idea how much land that represents?"

"Naturally. Not all the holdings I want are contiguous, but together they come to approximately two hundred thousand *cuerdas*. In my terms, about three hundred square miles."

Luz leaned back in his chair, convinced now that the redheaded giant was a madman and the only thing to do was play along with him. "In your terms. Yes, I see. And in your English terms Puerto Rico is approximately one hundred miles long by thirty-five miles wide, about thirty-five hundred square miles. So permit me another question. Since what you propose to buy represents such a large proportion of our little country, how much money do you expect it to cost?"

"A great deal." Michael smiled and took a cigar from his coat pocket. "May I, Señor Luz?"

"But of course. Allow me, please." The banker struck a match and held it a hairsbreadth from the tobacco. Michael leaned forward and sucked the flame toward the cigar. It caught instantly, filling the office with a sweet smell.

Michael sat back, keeping the cigar clenched between his teeth. "A great deal of money," he repeated.

"Yes, millions of pesetas. Millions and millions."

Michael's blue eyes crinkled at the corners in a hint of silent laughter. "But maybe not so many millions as before this war."

Luz threw up his hands. "The war means nothing here. I told you—"

"Yes, you told me. The Americans are trying to free Cuba, they have no territorial ambitions. The gospel according to President McKinley. But let us not waste time, Don Fernando. The war matters because soon you will have new masters. A number of your citizens are not pleased with the thought of being ruled by the gringos from the north. Some of my seventeen targets are bound to be among them."

"Targets." Luz repeated the word as if he'd not understood it. "Targets. I presume you mean some of those whose land you wish to buy?"

"That's right."

"And you think they will sell cheap because they expect the *norteamericanos* to take us over?"

Michael exhaled cigar smoke and watched it rise toward the ceiling. "Right again."

"Even if I grant you all your premises, Don Michael, for the sake of our discussion, how cheap is cheap? Coffee is our main export crop, our chief source of foreign revenue. Ten thousand pounds will not buy two hundred thousand *cuerdas* of our best coffee land."

The cigar had developed a long gray ash. Michael flicked it carefully into the brass ashtray on Luz's desk. "You mean the deposit with which I opened my account in your bank? No, of course not. But this might." He took an envelope from his inside breast pocket and placed it beside the ashtray.

Luz picked up the envelope. It was addressed by hand to Coutts and Company in London. Coutts was one of the oldest British merchant banks, almost as old as the Mendoza Bank. The envelope was unsealed. Luz was sweating as he withdrew the single piece of paper it contained. Beads of moisture made his shirt stick to his narrow back and left his fingerprints on the document as he read it. Finally he raised his eyes to the Irishman's. The foreigner was smiling.

"That might do it, don't you think?" Michael asked.

"Señor, there must be some mistake. This is a demand for . . ." His voice trailed away. He couldn't form the words because the number was so enormous.

"For a million pounds sterling, and it's no mistake," Michael said easily. "Now, my friend, do you wish to negotiate for me? Or should I find someone else?"

"Of course I—"

Luz never had a chance to finish the sentence. The door burst open. A woman entered. The spicy scent of gardenias entered with her, mingling with the sweet smell of Michael's cigar. She headed straight for the desk, ignoring the broad back of the man in front of it. "Fernando, I told you—"

"Doña Nuria, please, not now. I am busy as you see. If you'll only wait—"

"I am not waiting a moment longer. A week ago I told you to find the girl and she's still missing. What do you think you're doing? How can you be so incompetent?"

Her frock was made of brilliant blue and white cotton, printed in the geometric manner black slaves had brought to the island in the early part of the century. Its cut, too, owed more to Africa than to Europe. The material was wrapped close around her body from her shoulders to her knees, then hung free to swirl about her ankles.

Curran and Luz had stood the moment she entered. Her height was the first thing the Irishman was aware of. He hardly had to lower his eyes to see her breasts as they rose and fell with the intensity of her agitation. He moved his gaze to take in her waist, her hips, the sweep of her long legs outlined beneath the vivid fabric. Finally he raised his eyes to her face. Michael couldn't see her hair because it was wrapped in a turban made of the same material as her dress. She was turned away from him, looking at the banker, but her profile was enough. He drew in his breath and bit back an exclamation.

She was still badgering the banker. "What do I pay you for? Don't you understand that I cannot have a girl simply snatched away from me like this? There will be no discipline left if I don't get her back. From the militia I expect nothing, they're idiots. But from you—"

"Please, calm yourself. Everything will be taken care of. It is simply a matter of time. Allow me to introduce you to a newcomer to our island. Don Michael Curran, from London. This is Doña Nuria Sanchez Palmera."

She turned. Michael stared at her, but this was not like the time in the alley. He'd had a few seconds to study her profile, and he knew who she was before he saw her dark eyes and her sharply pronounced cheekbones and the prominent widow's peak below the wrapping of the turban. "We've met," Michael said. "In different circumstances."

"You!"

"Yes, me." He inclined his head in a brief bow that was not obviously insolent. "Michael Curran, at your service. Doña Nuria, is it?"

She was nonplussed, but only for a moment. She recovered herself quickly. "I'm sorry I didn't thank you the other night. I was very upset."

"I'm sure," he said softly.

Luz was looking from one to the other, aware of undercurrents, but not of their meaning. This was his bank, his office. It was important that he maintain control. "Señor Curran has just arrived in San Juan—" he began.

"Almost a week ago now," Michael interjected. "And from Dublin by way of Liverpool, as it happens. London didn't come into it. But then, the señorita knows all about me. She told me so."

Her brown eyes had little gold flecks in them. They seemed to spark, then Nuria Sanchez turned away, dismissing him with one toss of her head. "I need to know what is happening, Fernando."

"And you shall." The banker had recovered his composure. He came out from behind the desk and took the woman's arm, moving her toward the door. "Go home and calm yourself, my dear. I will come [this afternoon] after the siesta and we will discuss everything."

Nuria Sanchez allowed him to lead her as far as the door, then she stopped and turned back to Michael. Their eyes met and held. He could not read what hers were saying. In seconds the contact was broken because Luz gently pushed her through the door.

Nuria swept through the bank, ignoring equally those who nodded to her and those who turned their heads and pretended not to see her. Her carriage was waiting outside the door. It was small and shiny black, with two matched black horses, their manes braided with gold. There was a driver and, in a custom which everyone but she had forsaken a century earlier, a footman who rode standing in the rear. Both servants were black and former slaves; both wore flashing blue and gold livery.

The footman helped his mistress into the open cab, then jumped to his stand at the back, grasping the pair of handles that kept him from falling off. The driver was ancient. The face he turned to his mistress was deeply lined, and a fringe of pure white close-cropped hair showed beneath his blue silk top hat. He spoke in the singsong pidgin Spanish that was unique to those of his race and his history. "*Verdad* where we go to go, Missy Doña?"

"Home," Nuria murmured. She'd intended to go to the Indian market and see a new pair of captured macaws she'd heard about, but the meeting in the bank had made her forget about birds, however beautiful. "Take me home," she repeated. "Right away." The smart little carriage performed a quick turnabout and clattered off down Calle Fortaleza in the direction from which it had come.

Usually Nuria enjoyed the attention her rig commanded. She'd planned it that way. Today she was too disturbed to notice that people in the street stared. It wasn't only that Carmen was still missing, she'd been worrying about the child for ten days and still managed to live her normal life. It was the man.

Michael Curran. An Irish giant. Why did he unnerve her so? Since last Tuesday night in the alley the dreams had been worse than ever before, and the black times came more frequently when she was awake. Darkness, terror, the sense of falling through space. . . . And afterward she could remember nothing. The black times were worse than the nightmares.

At first she'd blamed the intensified onslaught of her secret demons on her shame at the way she'd allowed those thugs in the *taverna* to get the better of her. It had been crazy to dress up like a whore and go looking for Carmen on the waterfront. The four bandits would have raped her in that alley if they hadn't begun fighting between themselves about who would be first. And if the Irishman hadn't appeared . . . After he saved her the black times came two or three times a day. The more she thought about it the more she was convinced it was his fault. The way he'd looked at her, as if she were a witch out of hell. A look such as that could be responsible for anything.

Her head was throbbing. Nuria reached up and yanked off her turban, letting her dark hair fall free, running her fingers through it and relishing the breeze caused by the swift movement of the carriage.

Nuria Sanchez had left as much confusion in Fernando Luz's office as she'd carried away with her.

"I apologize for the interruption." The banker closed the

door behind the woman and returned to his place at the desk. "Doña Nuria is a remarkable lady, but very excitable. There is a private matter I've been——"

"Who is she?" Michael demanded, still staring at the spot where he'd last seen her.

"She is—I mean she——" Luz broke off, apparently unable to define her in any terms he found adequate. "A business-woman," he added finally. "She is very well known in Puerto Rico."

"What kind of business?" Michael leaned forward, propped both hands on the desk, and stared at Luz. His gaze burned with the intensity of his need to know. "How often does she come into San Juan?"

"Come . . . ? I don't understand, señor. Doña Nuria lives in San Juan. But please, this is unimportant. We have still not settled the matter we were discussing."

Luz picked up the demand letter, read it again, and again broke into a cold sweat. The numbers hadn't changed. "A million English pounds," he whispered.

Michael forced himself to pay attention. It was for this he'd come to the island and to the bank. Sister Magdalena and her brazen double life and her sources of information were a secondary issue, a bonus perhaps. He would deal with them after he'd finished with Luz. "Yes, a million. You know Coutts, of course."

"Of course. A most respectable institution. I'm sure that they——"

"Will honor my request," Michael finished for him. "Yes, they will. And naturally you will check with them. Now, as I recall, you hadn't answered my question before we were interrupted. Will you negotiate on my behalf?"

The banker hesitated a moment. Finally he nodded. "If you wish it, yes."

"I wouldn't have asked if I didn't wish it. The bank will take its usual commission, of course. And you——"

Luz looked up, staring into Michael's eyes. "Yes?"

"—you will be rewarded personally for your efforts."

"That isn't necessary, señor."

It was a game and a lie. Of course it was necessary. Luz was simply unaccustomed to having the rules stated quite so plainly. "Three percent of the final purchase price for all seventeen holdings," Michael said. "And ten percent of any difference between seven hundred thousand and a million. Here are the names of the places I want." He placed a second sheet of paper on the desk.

"Don Miguel—"

"Michael," the Irishman reminded him.

"Forgive me. Don Michael. I was simply about to ask if you brought the names with you, or if you decided on these particular properties after you arrived?"

"Some of them I knew before. About five. The rest I've chosen since I came."

"You have been very busy, señor."

"Yes." Michael moved to the hat rack to reclaim his panama. As before, Luz rushed to open the door. The Irishman accepted the courtesy without acknowledgment. "I'll return Thursday morning and you can tell me how things are proceeding."

"Very well. But in case I should need to see you before then, you are still at the Posada of San Juan Bautista?"

Michael nodded. Lila's way would have been to rent or buy immediately the grandest house in the town and hire a flock of servants. He considered that a distraction. "Once I own the plantations I'll choose a house to live in." He paused. "One more thing, Luz. Doña Nuria, where does she live?"

"In the Calle Cruz, near the port. But—"

Michael left without waiting to hear what the but signified.

Luz stared after the man who had just made such an extraordinary proposal. He didn't close the door until Señor Curran had left the bank and could no longer be seen, then he slammed it and turned the key. There was a safe in the wall behind the picture of Maria Ortega that overlooked his desk. Luz removed the picture and turned the dial.

Only two people knew the combination to the safe. Himself and Don James in London. Luz had never actually seen Don James; sometimes he wasn't sure the man existed. But he was quite certain of Michael Curran's existence. Damn the man. Why had he come here and upset everything?

Luz wanted only a quiet life. He'd managed to put a fair amount of money in his accounts in New York. As soon as this last bit of business with Captain Judson Hughes was completed, he intended to retire and go live in America. Now this Curran had arrived and was stirring the waters. Still, three percent of seven hundred thousand pounds, ten percent of the difference between that and a million. *Madre de Dios,* that would translate into a great many dollars. He could live in a mansion on Fifth Avenue if he had as much money as that.

Both telegrams that had arrived two days earlier were still in the safe where he'd put them. Luz took them out and read them again. He had difficulty with spoken English, the pronunciation was impossible, but he could read and write the language well enough. The Baring and Rothschild banks had each answered his inquiry by confirming that the letters of credit were genuine and that Mr. Michael Curran was a valued customer who should be shown every courtesy. Sweet Señor Jesus, it might be that the demand on Coutts would be honored as well. He was perhaps dealing with a man who had a million pounds sterling to spend, and wished to do so in Puerto Rico.

The Calle Cruz was a short, narrow street angled off a small plaza in front of one of the ubiquitous churches of San Juan. Michael reined in his mare and hitched her to a post at the top of the road.

There were half a dozen houses on the street. He didn't

know which one belonged to the Sanchez woman, and at first glance there was no way to tell. A gardener was trimming a hibiscus hedge belonging to the house on the corner. "*Buenos días*," Curran said. "I'm looking for Señorita Sanchez."

The gardener was a mestizo, half black, half Indian. His skin was the color of red clay, and when he smiled he displayed bright pink toothless gums. "*Buenos días, señor*. It is very early for the señorita."

"I know she's awake. I saw her in town less than an hour ago."

The gardener chortled as if the stranger had made some enormously funny joke. "Awake, yes, I'm sure of it." He pointed with the hand that held his clippers. "The last house on the right, señor." He was still laughing when Michael strode off.

The house was large, built of the usual white stucco. The wrought-iron railings of the front porch were draped in purple bougainvillea. Michael climbed the steps to the door, then lifted the brass knocker and let it fall twice in rapid succession.

The door opened before the echo of the knocker faded. A very large black woman wearing a bandanna and a voluminous white apron faced him. "We don' let in no callers what is callin' before de darktime," she announced.

"I wish to see Doña Nuria. Please tell her it's Michael Curran."

"No callers until de darktime," the woman repeated. "And is *verdad*. Missy Doña ain't here."

Curran tried to see past the woman's bulk. He could make out only a dim passage. "When do you expect her?"

"Is *verdad* strangers come in de darktime." She said it louder this time, as if perhaps he were deaf, and she started to close the door.

"Wait a minute." Michael put up his huge hand.

"Now looksee, Señor Estranjero, is *verdad* I tell you nice

like. If you don' pay no heed I'll call my boys and they's gonna tell you theys own way. Not nice like. Is *verdad*."

Short of knocking her down, there was little he could do. "I'll be back," he said as he turned away.

"Sure you come back, suh. In de darktime. Is *verdad* you be big welcome after de sun is gone away."

He'd unhitched the mare and mounted her before he put together the things the woman calling herself Nuria Sanchez had said at the bank, and the remarks of the black servant. Jesus God almighty! The place was a bordello. The nun wasn't a whore when she was away from her convent; she was a madam.

He sat astride the horse for a moment, examining the wonder of it, the incredible cheek. Then he made up his mind and gave the animal a gentle prod with his spurs. The mare took his lead and headed out of town.

The journey was a lot shorter on horseback than it had been on foot. In forty-five minutes he'd almost reached the Convent of Las Nieves. The track into the hills was rutted and stony, but the mare picked her way with ease. They were cantering comfortably when Michael rounded a bend and saw a carriage coming toward him.

"Whoa girl," he called softly, tugging on the reins. The horse slowed, then stopped.

There wasn't room for him to pass the rig. Michael backed the horse off the path into a stand of pine trees. The driver of the carriage nodded a curt thanks and came on.

Michael watched while it pulled level with him. He was curious about the passenger, but the cab was entirely closed and curtained. He was so busy trying to get a peek inside that he almost missed the arms blazoned on the door, a pair of crossed keys and a shepherd's staff. He'd seen those arms before in his wanderings around San Juan; they were prominently displayed above the entrance to the bishop's residence.

He waited until the carriage had turned a corner and passed out of sight, then spurred his horse on toward Las Nieves.

Ten minutes later he arrived. The convent looked exactly as it had when he had come on his first day in Puerto Rico: silent and peaceful, all the gates shut against the outside world. Michael glanced briefly at the bell beside the main entrance, then circled the walls until he came to the door he'd used when he left Sister Magdalena. It was locked.

The walls were high, but not unscalable. Michael hoisted himself out of the saddle with the help of an overhanging tree branch. In seconds he was standing on the top of the wall, looking down into the shabby patio. When he spotted the low door that pierced the blank stucco wall he cursed softly. It had been barred from the outside with a hefty piece of timber that was padlocked into position.

Perhaps he could break through those defenses, but it wouldn't be easy. And possibly counterproductive. Michael lowered himself back into the saddle, rode around to the front of the convent, and tugged on the bell rope.

This time he didn't have to wait. It was almost as if his movements had been observed and the gatekeeper was waiting for him. The door opened instantly. "¿Si?"

It wasn't Sister Paloma. The nun who faced him now was twice the size of the little dove, and thick featured and unintelligent looking. "I wish to see Sister Magdalena, the recluse," he said.

"The holy sister is receiving no visitors." The nun started to swing the gate shut.

"Wait, she'll see me. I know she will. She's expecting me. Tell her it's Michael Curran."

"She is in deep silence, señor. Seeing no one. On the orders of the bishop. Please go away."

"Where's Sister Paloma? I'll speak with her if I can't see Sister Magdalena."

"Sister Paloma is unavailable."

He searched his mind for a way to avoid dismissal. You didn't live sixteen years in Ireland and not absorb something of the way convents were organized. "I'll speak with the mother superior," he blurted out a second before the gate shut.

"You must leave, señor. We are in retreat, on the instructions of His Excellency the bishop."

The gate closed with a thump of finality. This time the Convent of Las Nieves had not offered him even a cup of water.

It was after ten when Michael returned to the house on the Calle Cruz. The big black woman wasn't wearing her apron when she came to the door. She had on what looked to Michael like a pinafore. It was printed in red and white flowers and her enormous bosom was hung with strings of multicolored beads. She greeted him with a broad smile. "You come back like I tell you. That be very good. *Verdad*, you have good time here, long as it be de darktime."

"I want to see Doña Nuria."

The woman threw back her head and laughed. "Missy Doña be de only thing you no can have, Man Irish. But you come look and you won't mind."

Michael followed her toward a set of double doors. "How do you know I'm Irish?"

"Assunta know all de things in San Juan what *verdad* she want to know. Like who is big red hair man."

"Is that your name? Assunta?"

"*Verdad*. 'Course I got me other names. Some is real powerful. But dey is not for you to worry. Come in here, I bring you good things, take all worries from you mind."

She threw open the doors and Michael saw a salon furnished with dark wooden setees covered in fringed crimson velvet, numerous chairs with satin cushions, and little round tables draped in lace. The walls were dotted with bad paintings in elaborate gilt frames, and every horizontal surface was cluttered with porcelain knickknacks and geegaws. The room could have come straight from some house in London or Dublin. Or from someone's imagination of what such a room would be like.

"Obadiah, you bring yourself over by here," the black woman said in her slurred singsong dialect. "Carry de Man Irish some punch."

A lad as black as she was hurried toward them with a glass. Michael took it with a nod of thanks. The rum punch went down easy, and sipping it gave him something to do while he looked around. There didn't seem to be any females in this bordello. "Where are the women?"

"You is *verdad* in a big hurry. De ladies is coming once you sit yourself and be comfortable."

He took the chair she indicated. "I'm not really here to look for a companion for the evening. I have to see Doña Nuria."

The black woman cocked her head. "What for you want Missy Doña?"

"To talk to her. She knows about what."

"If she know she tell Assunta. And Missy Doña *verdad* no tell me nothing."

"Tell her I'm here. Please," Michael added, taking Assunta's hand and pressing a thick wad of pesetas into her palm.

The woman slipped the money into her pocket without any sign of surprise. "I can tell her. But is *verdad* I don't know if Missy Doña see you. She don't do nothin' but what she wants."

"Tell her," Michael repeated.

Assunta nodded, then turned to the boy who acted as barman. "Obadiah, you see dis Man Irish no be thirsty while I is gone."

Nothing happened for nearly ten minutes. Michael drank his punch, the boy watched him, the room stayed empty of either customers or whores, the street beyond the windows was silent. "How long have you worked here?" Michael asked when eventually Obadiah approached, carrying a pitcher filled with more rum punch.

"I be *verdad* borned in this house, *señor*."

"I see. How long ago was that? How old are you?"

"I have twelve years, señor."

Twelve years old and he was barman in a whorehouse. The woman who called herself Doña Nuria when she was in San Juan had a lot to answer for. "Does your mother work in this house?"

"My mother is *verdad* dead, señor." Obadiah blessed himself, making the sign of the cross with his right hand while his left poured more punch into Michael's glass. "She be in heaven with Señor Jesus. Missy Doña, she take care of me."

Michael could think of no reply. He continued to watch the double doors, waiting for Assunta to return. Instead a pair of drapes on the other side of the room was suddenly parted. Nuria Sanchez stood in the opening, holding the curtains back with her hands and studying him.

Michael put down the glass of punch and got to his feet. He looked at her as brazenly as she was looking at him. She wasn't wearing the blue-and-white native dress any longer. Instead she had on a green gown printed with white stylized ferns and made of some sheer material that fell in loose folds from her shoulders. It did not disguise her wonderful body. He let his eyes travel the length of it, stopping for a moment at her full breasts. Then his gaze met hers and they stared at each other for some seconds. "What do you want?" she asked at last.

"To speak with you. It's past time, don't you think?"

"I have nothing to say to you."

"Yes, you do. This time you're going to tell me the truth."

Before she could answer the door knocker clattered, and they heard Assunta's laughter and the sound of chattering men. "You have customers," Michael said.

"Yes." She hesitated only a moment, then jerked her head in the direction from which she'd arrived. "Come with me."

He followed her through the draperies, the gardenia scent she wore filling his nostrils. The corridor she led him down was dark and he couldn't see her clearly. She moved ahead of him like a wraith, a spirit goddess, conjured up perhaps by his imagination. They came to the end of the passage and she opened another door and led him onto a small patio.

Michael heard a noise that belonged to the night but was not natural in this place. It was of creatures stirring, preparing for something, muted crawlings and cawings and rufflings in a readiness for protest and attack.

"Be quiet, my pretties, go back to sleep. It's all right." Then, over her shoulder Nuria murmured to him, "They don't know you."

The full moon of his arrival in Puerto Rico was on the wane, but there was light enough for him to see a small fountain in the center of a floor of vividly painted tiles, and stucco walls hung with cages of every size and description. He took in flashes of color, green and pink and purple and azure and scarlet, a tumult of exotic plumage, before he saw tiny heads and curved and pointed beaks and folded wings, all captured behind intricately carved bars. "You keep birds," he murmured.

Nuria didn't answer. She hurried across the tiles, and Michael followed her through another door into what seemed a second house built behind the first. She led him into a small sitting room lighted by half a dozen candles.

This place was different from the parlor where he'd waited for her. The white stucco walls were without ornament, and the tables and chairs were made of bamboo and covered in the same brilliantly figured cotton cloth as Nuria's dresses. She started to speak, then something on one of the tables caught her eye. Nuria dashed to it and snatched up the object. Michael couldn't see it clearly, but it looked like a tiny doll of some kind.

She put whatever it was into a cupboard hanging beside the door, then turned to him. "What do you want?"

"I've already told you. The truth."

"I don't know what you're talking about."

"Look, let's stop playing games, Nuria or Magdalena or whatever you wish to be called. I know who you are and you know that I know. I saw the bishop's locked trap this afternoon. I'm not sure how you got out of it, but frankly I don't give a damn what you do or how. All I want is the name of whoever gave you the information about the Mendozas. If you don't tell me, I'll see that everyone in San Juan knows about your double life."

She frowned, staring at him with an expression composed of perplexity and wonder. "I thought I was crazy, but maybe it is you. What does the bishop have to do with me? And do you mean the Mendozas of the bank?"

"Do you know any others?"

"I know none. At the bank I know only Fernando Luz. He tells me there are Mendozas in England and in Spain, but none of them have ever come to Puerto Rico."

Michael was swiftly losing patience. "The letter—"

"What letter?"

"Goddamm it, woman! I don't intend to go on with this nonsense. Now sit down and begin at the beginning and tell me what I want to know."

"Stop shouting! This is my place, Señor Curran. I am queen here. If I ring," she gestured to a small brass bell on one table, "men will arrive instantly and you will be thrown out."

"Did you forget your bell the other night in the alley? Where were those men then? And do they know about your little masquerade as a nun?"

"A nun . . . *Madre de Dios*, now I know you are crazy."

"Do you have the barefaced cheek to stand there and

deny that when you're not here running this whorehouse you're pretending to be a nun at the Convent of Las Nieves? I don't believe it. It never occurred to me you'd try to brazen it out."

She sat down hard in one of the bamboo chairs, a rocker as it happened. Her body tilted backward and forward and she put her elbows on her splayed knees and her chin in her hands and stared at him. "You are crazy," she repeated.

"Why are you doing this?" Michael asked, suddenly weary of the charade. "Why not simply admit that I'm on to your game and tell me what I want to know? I've already told you, I don't care what you do. If you cooperate, I've no reason to expose you."

She looked at him a few seconds more. His big body was sagging and she realized he was very tired. "Sit down. Tell me why you think I am a—" she had difficulty saying it, laughter stifling the word, "a nun," she managed finally. "Yes, Don Miguel, I'd like to know why anyone should think Nuria Sanchez is a nun."

Michael didn't bother to correct her pronunciation of his name. "You're forgetting that I saw you." He took the chair she indicated. It had been a very long day and exhaustion was nearly overwhelming him. "The other day, when we talked about the letter. You threw back your veil and showed me your face."

"I don't know anything about any letter. In my whole life, Don Miguel, no one has ever sent me a letter."

"Not one you got, the one you sent," he said impatiently. "The one you mailed to my mother in Córdoba."

Nuria shook her head. "Poor man. You really believe what you're saying, don't you?"

Michael ran his fingers through his hair, which tended to curl. Since he was a boy he'd hated that. Only girls should have curly hair. In the heat and humidity of Puerto Rico his hair always seemed to be in ringlets. "Sweet Jesus," he whispered, "I've too many other things to worry about to deal with this insanity. The only thing I need to know is who gave you the information about the Mendozas. Tell me that and I'll go away and not trouble you again. Was it Maria Ortega?"

"Maria Ortega has been dead for many years, Don Miguel." She spoke as if to a demented child, softly and with exaggerated patience.

"I know that. But we're talking about something written years ago."

"By Doña Maria Ortega?"

"No, by you."

"Then you cannot be correct." She stared directly at him, her eyes peering into his. Her face reddened and her voice lowered, but she did not falter. "I can neither read nor write, Don Miguel. I was never sent to school. Anyone in San Juan can tell you that is so."

He was drenched in her honesty. It was truth made credible by shame and it washed over him like a tide.

❧ 7 ❧

TUESDAY, JUNE 22, 1898
San Juan, Daybreak

Fernando Luz went to the telegraph office himself. The nightman was still on duty when he arrived, sleeping in his chair, a broad-brimmed sombrero pulled down to cover his face. Luz knocked on the tiled top of the counter.

"*¡Despiértate!* Wake up! *Madre de Dios*, what do they pay you for?"

The clerk pushed his hat back with one hand and blinked repeatedly. When he registered the identity of the caller he sprang out of his chair. "Señor Luz, I was just on my way to the bank. This very moment I was coming to deliver your cable myself."

"Your mouth is full of shit," Luz told him without emotion. "You came out of your mother's womb lying. Give me the cable. It's from London?"

"*Sí*, señor. From London. An answer to the message you sent yesterday—"

Luz leaned forward grasping the man's thin shirt in his hand. "Listen to me you son of a whore. The messages you send and receive are private. Private. Do you hear me?"

"*Sí*, Señor Luz. Of course I hear you. Naturally whatever words come from my machine into my fingers, never do I put them in my head. I know nothing." He covered his eyes with his hands to demonstrate.

"Liar," Luz said again, releasing his grip on the man. "But any leak of information would be immediately traceable to you. And if such a thing happens I will personally see that the militia hangs you, after they cut off your balls and gouge out your eyes."

"Don Fernando, I only copy down the words. I do not even know English! I assure you—"

"I am not interested in what you say, only in what you do and don't do. Give me my cable."

The message was passed across the counter. Luz wanted to read it immediately, but he would not allow himself such a lapse of dignity in front of the telegraph clerk. He put the unopened envelope in his pocket and left the office, walking slowly the short distance to his bank like a man with all the time in the world. But he took the stairs to his apartment two at a time, gasping for breath when he reached the sitting room overlooking the street.

There was no one in the house to spy on him. He was a bachelor who lived alone. The servants came by day and would not arrive for at least an hour. Luz went to the window and parted the curtain and looked down on the Calle Fortaleza. It too was deserted. Satisfied, he took the cable from his pocket and ripped it open.

The bank in London was parsimonious with words that cost a penny each to transmit.

CONFIRM SECURITIES HELD IN NAME OF MICHAEL CURRAN STOP FACE VALUE BEYOND AMOUNT OF INQUIRY STOP REQUIRE LETTER SIGNED BY SAME TO RELEASE FUNDS SIGNED HAMMERSMITH FOR COUTTS.

Madre de Dios! The Irishman really had more than a million pounds with Coutts. The whole crazy thing was real. This Curran could afford to buy two hundred thousand *cuerdas* of coffee land. And if he did, when he did, some of that incredible amount of money would stick to Fernando Luz.

He sat down because his legs were trembling too badly to hold him. "It was a very good day that brought you to Puerto Rico, *estranjero,*" he murmured after he'd read the cable a second time. "For me, it was a very good day."

Luz was in Michael's room at the inn of San Juan Bautista by half past eight. "You will understand, Don Michael, I had to inquire of Coutts."

"Naturally. Have some coffee. Briggs!" he shouted into the corridor. "I have a visitor. Get him a coffee and some *churros.*"

"Please, señor, it is not necessary."

"It is. No one can do business on an empty stomach. Sit down, Luz. I take it you've had a satisfactory response from the bank?"

"Yes, of course. Very satisfactory."

Michael sat on the bed. Luz took the single chair in the room and looked around. Everything in this place was old and worn out. Why in the name of the Holy Virgin would a man with more than a million pounds live like this? All foreigners were a little crazy, apparently the Irish were crazier than most. "You are comfortable here?" he asked.

"No, I'm not comfortable. But it will do." Michael dipped one of the crullers into his coffee and took a large bite. "Until I choose my hacienda," he added.

"Yes, your hacienda. There is one thing, Don Michael—"

"What thing?"

"Coutts has said . . ." Luz let the sentence die away. Briggs entered without knocking. His arm had healed and he used both hands to carry a tray that held a big bowl of coffee frothy with milk and a plate of steaming *churros*.

"Thank you," Luz murmured. His stomach was so knotted with excitement he was sure he could eat nothing, but he took a sip of the coffee and found it soothing.

"You were saying?" Michael asked when Briggs had left.

"Only that naturally enough the bank in London, Coutts, will not release the funds on the basis of a cable. You must send them a letter with your signature."

"Of course. I already have." Luz looked surprised. "The letter I gave to you," Michael continued. "That's what it's for. Send it to London."

"Ah, the letter you gave to me. I see. I will do so, of course. There's no ship in just at the moment, but the *Susannah Star* is due to return any day, and there's a steam driven freighter, the *Lady Jane,* which I think will be here around the third of July."

"Excellent, either one will do. Send the letter with whichever ship docks first."

"*Sí*, Don Michael. And as soon as the money is credited to—"

"You're not suggesting you'll wait to speak with the owners until the transaction clears," Michael said in tones of astonishment. "That will take weeks. Luz, haven't you understood anything I've been telling you? There's a war on. Puerto Rico is up for grabs." Luz started to protest but Michael waved him silent. "I know. You don't agree. It doesn't matter. The mood of the moment is what matters. The fear." He leaned forward, pinning the banker with his gaze. "Once whatever is to happen has happened, there is no longer uncertainty . . . or fear."

"Señor," Luz whispered. "Please, do not misunderstand me . . ."

"I'm trying not to." Michael finished his coffee and replaced the bowl on the tray. "Listen, my friend, you and I have an opportunity for profit. That opportunity will not wait. Now, what do you propose to do?"

The banker drew a deep breath. "I will arrange to go to Lares today or tomorrow. I will begin speaking to the owners of the haciendas you wish to purchase."

"Glad to hear it, Luz," Michael said softly. The two men looked at each other for a moment. Finally Michael nodded. "How long is the journey to Lares?" Michael asked, breaking the tension with an ordinary question.

"Nowadays, only a matter of hours. Since the railroad came we can circle Puerto Rico in so little time that—"

"Excellent," Michael interrupted brusquely. "Now, there's something else you can do for me."

Luz raised his sad eyes to those of the Irishman and waited.

"Doña Nuria. I want you to tell me about her background."

"Her background, señor?"

"Yes. Where was she born for a start? And is it true she's never been to school, that she can't read or write?"

Luz relaxed a little. Discussing the affairs of the keeper of San Juan's most popular bordello did not make him as nervous as talking about the disposition of a million pounds sterling. "As to where she was born, I believe it was in the country, somewhere on the other side of the island. The country people, the campesinos, are many of them very poor, Don Michael. It is not surprising that Doña Nuria has no education."

"You're telling me it's true, then? She can't read or write?"

The Irishman's fixation on this point was beginning to sound insane, but then, Luz thought, many of his dealings with Señor Curran smacked of lunacy. Profitable lunacy. "I know for a fact that she cannot, señor. When there are papers to be signed, anything official, she comes to me in the bank. I witness her mark."

Michael walked to the open door of his balcony and

leaned against it, staring out at the sea. He seemed to be speaking as much to himself as to Luz. "What kind of official papers are there in the life of a mistress of whores?"

"The former slaves, if they are picked up for vagrancy or any other trouble, it's often Doña Nuria who takes responsibility for them. Then there are papers to sign."

Michael turned his head and looked at the banker. "What does she do with them? They can't all be suitable candidates for whoredom."

"She finds work for them, Don Michael." Luz stood up. "Now, you must excuse me. The bank is open and I—"

"Yes, go ahead. You'll go to Lares today?"

"Today or tomorrow, señor. As soon as I can make arrangements."

Michael nodded and allowed the man to see himself out.

The Calle Cruz drew Michael like a magnet. Soon after noon he was walking along the short street, looking at the house with the wrought-iron railings festooned with bougainvillea. Assunta would be on guard, and she'd tell him he couldn't get in until "de darktime." He could bribe her with another wad of pesetas, but if she said Nuria wasn't in, what would he gain?

There was a small lane next to the house, built in steps like so many of the narrow, rising streets of the town. It angled away to someplace behind the Calle Cruz. He remembered thinking the night before that Nuria had brought him to a separate house. Michael turned into the lane.

It led him around a corner and on to another street, this one unmarked. There was a small house—low, square-built, of the ubiquitous white stucco—that could be the one. He paused, trying to orient himself, and while he stood there an elegant little black carriage rounded a corner and drew up by the front door. The driver was in bright blue livery, and incredibly there was a liveried footman clinging to a perch in the rear. Michael hadn't seen such a rig since he was a small boy, and even then it had been quaint and old-fashioned.

The door of the house opened and Nuria came out. She wore red and black today, a length of printed native cloth wrapped round her in some intricate fashion, and like yesterday, a matching turban. She saw him at almost the same instant he saw her, and they stood in the blazing sun staring at each other.

"What are you doing here?" Nuria demanded.

"I was taking a walk."

"It's very stupid to walk in San Juan at this hour. The heat is bad for you."

"Thank you for your concern with my health."

She tossed her head, dismissing his attempt at irony. "I'll give you a ride back to the inn if you like."

He agreed, and they approached the carriage together. The footman went ahead of them and placed a small stool beside the carriage so his mistress could step into it with ease. At first Michael thought the footman was Obadiah, but this lad was older than the one who had served him rum punch. He held open the door until Nuria was seated, then waited for Michael to get in beside her before running around to take his place behind.

"I haven't seen anyone ride with a footman in the rear since I was a child."

"It gives me pleasure and it gives him a job," she said shortly. "Where was that?"

"What?"

"The place you were a child."

He hesitated, then decided there was no reason to lie. "In Córdoba first. That's in Spain. But I was taken to Dublin when I was thirteen."

"Ah, I see, you're really Spanish. That's why you speak our language so well."

"Half Spanish," he corrected. "My mother is Irish."

They were out in the main road by this time, on the Calle Tetuan. "What does the name mean?" Michael asked.

"It's an Indian word. When El Colón came; the Tainos tribe of Indians were here."

"I suppose they're all dead. Columbus has a lot to answer for."

"The Spaniards didn't kill all the Indians. They preferred to make them slaves."

"Not much different, was it?" Michael asked.

Nuria shrugged. "Alive is better than dead. But the Indians made poor workers. They were replaced by black slaves from Africa."

"What happened to the Indians?"

"They mostly died out because there was no longer any place on the island for their way of life. But they're not all gone. I'm going to see an Indian man right now. Would you like to come?"

"I'd like that very much."

She leaned out the window and gave the driver some instructions. The carriage didn't turn toward the inn but headed out of town. They drove without speaking for about ten minutes. He kept watching her out of the corner of his eye. Her profile was remarkable; she was a stunning woman. "I went back to the convent this morning," he said, breaking the silence.

"Oh. Did you expect to find me there?"

"I don't know what I expected. Anyway, I couldn't get in. Not without force. The place is still locked up tighter than a drum, and there are two men guarding the gates."

"What men?"

"I don't know. The only thing they'd say is that they were there on the orders of the bishop."

"But why should the bishop send men to guard a convent?"

"I don't know that either. But I mean to find out."

"Good, perhaps then you will know that I am not—how did you put it?—leading a double life."

"Perhaps." Part of him believed her, the largest part. But if she were telling the truth, then who was the woman he'd spoken to the first day? He didn't want to deal with that disturbing mystery. "Where are we going?"

"We're here."

The carriage drew to a halt as she spoke. They were in front of a large open-air market, roofed over with bamboo poles and tattered palm fronds. "The Indians who trade in this place don't take *siesta*. This is the best time to see them."

The footman performed his rituals, and they climbed down from the carriage and stepped into the welcome shade of the market.

From what Michael could see, there wasn't much to buy. What was available was spread on blankets on the ground: a few gourds carved into useful shapes, some dried herbs and spices, a couple of handfuls of coffee beans. Nuria ignored these displays and made her way purposefully along the aisles.

The man she'd come to see dealt in birds. A falcon and an eagle were beside him, tethered in place by wires twisted round their ankles and attached to a stake driven into the hard, dry earth. The big birds shrieked shrilly when Nuria and Michael approached.

"*Buenos días*, Santiago."

The Indian nodded. "*Muy buenos*, señorita."

"I'm told you have macaws. Show them to me."

He nodded again and removed a piece of burlap draped over a mound on his right. A pair of birds were crammed into a rough cage made of splintered wood and chicken wire that was barely big enough to contain them. The birds were huddled on the floor, there was no perch, and their blue-and-yellow plumage was sparse and soiled by their own excrement. The constant friction of their confinement had left ugly bald patches on their bodies. "A breeding pair," the Indian said.

"Only Señor Jesus knows that." Nuria bent over the cage. The macaws were too miserable to object to her scrutiny. They merely looked at her with dull bleary eyes.

"It's the truth," the Indian insisted. "They will make you many babies."

"They're half dead."

The man smiled, showing a few yellow teeth. "You will make them well." He leaned down to his captives. "I told you the Señorita Sanchez would come and take you to live like royalty, my little friends. Now she is here." He turned to Nuria. "Two hundred pesetas for the pair."

Michael did some rapid calculating. The Indian was asking an outrageous price, nearly three pounds sterling.

"Fifty pesetas," Nuria said. "And if they die before I get them home, you will give me back my money."

The Indian snorted in derision and replaced the burlap covering of the makeshift cage. "You waste my time, señorita."

Nuria made some disparaging remark about his ancestors. The birdman's only reply was to repeat his price. "Two hundred pesetas for the pair."

Michael watched them haggle, only half listening to the insults and prices they traded, mostly aware of the look on Nuria's face. She was shrewd and tough, but she wanted the birds. It surprised him how much she wanted them. Surely there were other birds to be had in Puerto Rico. Besides, she already had the dozens he'd glimpsed the previous night. Eventually she counted ninety pesetas into the Indian's hand, and the young footman seemed to appear from nowhere to scoop up the cage.

"Will your birds live?" Michael asked when they were back in the carriage heading away from the market.

"I hope so. I think I can make them live, yes."

"And then what? They'll spend the rest of their lives in a cage anyway."

"But a big cage," she said with feeling, turning her brown eyes to him. "A beautiful cage. They will have everything they want."

"They won't be free."

She stopped speaking, looking not at him but at her hands folded in her lap. She painted her fingernails red. Michael had never seen that before. He wondered what she used.

"Freedom is a strange thing, isn't it?" she asked at last.

"No, I don't think so. It means being able to do as you wish."

Nuria shook her head. "You're wrong. Or at least if you're right, then most of the world is not free. Very few people can do exactly as they wish, señor."

"Call me Michael. Maybe not exactly as they wish, but you know what I mean." She didn't answer. He waited a moment, then asked, "Have you found the girl you were searching for in the alley? The one you asked Señor Luz about. What was her name, Carmen?"

"Yes, Carmen. No, I haven't found her."

"And is that going to be bad for your discipline with the other women who work for you? That's what you told Luz."

She made a disparaging motion with one red-tipped hand. "Luz. I only tell him what he expects to hear. You think I am wicked, don't you? A wicked woman forcing other women to sell their bodies."

"You said it, I didn't."

"No, but you are thinking it." She turned to him, her eyes yet darker than they'd been. "It is not the way you imagine. You come here from Europe with all your European ideas. What do you know of the way life on this island?"

"Not much," Michael admitted. "But whoring is whoring, anywhere in the world."

"Listen, I will tell you something. Carmen is twelve years old. She was a virgin when she left my house."

"Sweet Jesus," he murmured softly, the breath knocked out of him by the bald words. "What were you planning to do? Get a special price for her because she was so young and innocent?"

"You . . ." Her voice sputtered away, unable to find words to tell him what she thought of his assumption. Instead she rapped on the window that separated them from the driver. He reined in the horses immediately. "Get out," she told Michael through clenched teeth. "Get out of my carriage. You are an animal."

Michael started to protest, then thought better of it. He was letting this woman distract him from the mission that had brought him to San Juan. He looked at her silently for a moment, then opened the door and jumped to the street without waiting for any help from the liveried footman.

London, Late Evening

The Hansom drew up in front of the Law Courts, silent and deserted at this hour. Norman Mendoza climbed down from the cab and stood on empty Fleet Street, indecision apparent in his stance.

"Wait for you, shall I, governor?" the driver asked.

Norman straightened his shoulders. "No, that won't be necessary."

"As you like, gov." The cab pulled away. The swinging lanterns hanging in the rear became two red dots, then quickly disappeared.

The day had been unseasonably warm; the night was cold. The combination always meant fog and mist, and this evening was no exception. Norman could see little, but he knew the way. It was whether or not to take it that disturbed him. The business was unsavory. Hang it all, he thought, it's too late to back out now. He walked a few yards, then turned into the passage known as Bell Yard.

The Three Herrings public house had stood in the same place for nearly three hundred years. It was a sagging, squat half-timbered structure, now dwarfed by newer buildings squeezing it from either side. Norman had a fleeting sense of déjà vu. The old Mendoza place on Creechurch Lane had looked a lot like this. He pushed open the door and went inside.

"Evening, sir. Can I get you something?"

He nodded a curt greeting to the barman. "I'll have a brandy."

"Certainly, sir." The man reached for a bottle of French cognac.

"Not that. The Spanish stuff. You've some right there."

The publican nodded and took down a heavy bottle with a label that said Gitana and sported a picture of a Gypsy. He poured a generous tot into a snifter and passed it to his customer. Norman took a long swallow, then placed a shilling on the bar. Ridiculous to pay for his own brandy, but the fact that the spirit had been named by Robert the Turncoat in 1825, was distilled in the Mendoza bodegas in Jerez, and was imported to England by himself and his brothers would make no odds with the barman. "Sell much of this?" he asked.

"A fair bit, sir." The publican put nine pence change on the bar. "It's good drink, though there's some as say French cognac's more refined."

"Some," Norman agreed. "But they're wrong. Spanish brandy has guts. Slow tonight?" he added.

"You might say." The publican was a man of experience. He could read the face of any customer, this one included. "Looking for someone in particular?"

"I did think perhaps I'd see Mr. Lacey."

"Oh, he's here, right enough. In the private room in the back. Shall I tell him you've come?"

"Thanks, there's no need. I'll go myself." Norman picked

up the brandy snifter and carried it to the rear of the pub, past a door so low he had to duck.

The man called Lacey was sitting beside a small coal fire, his short legs stretched in front of him. He spotted Norman as soon as he came in. "Over here," he said softly.

Norman pulled another of the leather armchairs to the edge of the hearth and sat down. "What do you have for me?"

"A bit, Mr. Mendoza. A fair bit."

"I think we'd best dispense with names."

Lacey waved a pudgy hand. "Not to worry. There's no one here but us. They know me well at the Three Herrings. Sort of an extension of my office, you might say. My club."

He was a solicitor, not particularly successful, not the sort of man to belong to any proper club in Saint James's or Pall Mall. Norman disliked him intensely, but Hiram Lacey was, he knew, the perfect man for the job he'd given him. "Tell me what you've found out."

The solicitor moved his broad rump into a slightly more comfortable position in the chair. "A question first, if I may. Tell me, sir, what do you know of these Fenians?"

"Not much," Norman admitted.

"Yes, I thought not. A gentleman like yourself isn't likely to have much truck with Irish rabble."

"Is that what they are, merely rabble? I'm told there are a number of gentlemen involved in this insane quest for Irish independence."

"Right enough, there are. But they're not Fenians. The Irish Republican Brotherhood, that's their official name. They were founded simultaneously in New York and Dublin in 1858. They've one tenet and one only: to free Ireland from Britain by force."

"Why in hell should we—"

"Please." Mr. Lacey held up his hand. "Allow me to finish. Point is, there are Irishmen who see independence coming through Parliament, and others who believe they'll get it only at the point of a gun. The IRB, the Fenians, belong to the latter persuasion."

"Armed rebels, more of that thuggery we had thirty years ago."

"Indeed. The rebellion of 1867 was entirely the doing of the Fenians. A lot of American Irish went over after their Civil War, and they brought their guns with them."

Norman was growing impatient. His brandy was finished for one thing, and the fire was dying for another. "Look here, this is all very interesting but—"

"It's germaine, Mr. Mendoza, I assure you. You hired me to discover the nature of Mrs. Lila Curran's connections to the Fenian movement. Before I tell you what I've learned, it seems wise that you know exactly what that movement is."

"Very well, continue." It was pointless to try and stop the man. Lacey was enjoying having a big fish on the line and playing with him. Norman resigned himself to giving the other man his moment of glory.

"One would have thought that the Fenians were finished after 1867," Lacey said. "But fanatics are never finished, are they?"

"Not in my experience."

"Quite. The Fenians are no exception. Their numbers are fairly small today, but those few are well disciplined, well organized, and committed."

"And am I to believe that Mrs. Curran is enlisted in this peculiar army?"

"Not exactly. She's a very clever lady is the Black Widow. Very clever."

"I don't need you to tell me that." Norman leaned forward and tried to poke a little life into the cinders of the fire.

Lacey too seemed at last to feel the cold settling in the room. He finally came to the point. "Her connection with the rebels is purely one of convenience. They always need money; she has it. She pays them, and being that they're the sort who get around to places where the lady would be conspicuous, they manage to keep her informed of things she might otherwise not know."

"I see. Then she's not interested in their cause?"

"That I can't say. It may be that Mrs. Curran would be quite pleased to see the union of Britain and Ireland dissolved, but it's certain that she supports the Fenians for what they can do for her."

Norman sighed and started to stand up. "Thank you, I suspected as much. Now if you'll send me your bill—"

"Sit down, Mr. Mendoza."

"There's really nothing more to say."

"There is. Please sit down."

Norman sat. "What is it?" he asked dully.

"A question first, if I may."

"You seem determined to say exactly what you wish, why stop now?"

"I shan't. The Mendoza Bank is issuing a public bond tomorrow, is it not? You have committed a very large loan to Paraguay, two million I believe. Investors are to be invited to purchase shares of the risk?"

"That's public knowledge."

"Yes, so it is," Lacey agreed.

"Well then?"

"I was only looking for links, things that might explain an extraordinary fact."

"And what fact is that?"

The solicitor took a small notebook from the pocket of his shabby suitcoat. "On the night of Monday the fourteenth of June, an English gentleman lodged in a Dublin public house known as the Swan. Not at all the sort of place that such a gentleman might be expected to choose. As well as being a very low class of establishment, the Swan is a hotbed of Fenian sentiments. Moreover, our English gentleman received a package delivered by a Mr. Fergus Kelly. Mr. Kelly is believed to be quite high up in Fenian councils."

"I see." Norman's voice was edged with controlled fury. "Well, get on with it, man. Who was the English gentleman? That's the point of this tale, isn't it?"

"Yes, I rather think it is. The gentleman who stayed at the Swan and took possession of Mr. Kelly's parcel was your younger son, Mr. Timothy Mendoza."

❧ 8 ❧

WEDNESDAY, JUNE 23, 1898
London, Five A.M.

Most of the city slept, but the heart of London was business and it beat unceasingly day and night.

"C'mon you fuckers, move yer arses or we'll all drown in fucking fish guts," a man called at Billingsgate Market where each week some three thousand tons of fish arrived. Every ounce was manhandled up narrow steps, often four hundred pounds to a load.

A short distance away at Covent Garden other men were unloading lettuce and cabbage and onions and potatoes, and a hundred other things that grew in the earth or on it. The crates and sacks dropped from shoulder to floor accompanied by a constant stream of obscenities, which somehow made the backbreaking work easier.

In the railway stations trains were being loaded with many thousands of copies of over two hundred daily newspapers. Not one of them approached the influence of the journal founded more than a century earlier, the *Times*.

In the pages of the *Times* the doings of the whole world

were reported and explained, and for men of power it was as important a part of the new day as breakfast.

On this Wednesday morning, page 4 was given over to a long essay by a man whose exploits always captured the imagination of the public. WHITHER GOEST LATIN AMERICA? questioned the head in sixteen-point type. And in only slightly smaller print—The Observations of Lord Sharrick After His Recent Journey South.

In Knightsbridge Timothy Mendoza's boiled egg congealed in its shell while he read that ". . . it is sad to have to report that political instability is prevalent, and corruption is rife."

Henry Mendoza lived in a suite of rooms that was part of James's town house in Gordon Square. Henry had his own dining room and staff of four servants. The steaming porridge they served him cooled while Henry studied Sharrick's assertion that ". . . finding a way to help countries such as Peru and Brazil and Argentina to a more stable and secure future requires utmost prudence and seems the job of Parliament. . . ."

James Mendoza, Lord Westlake, was not in residence at Gordon Square. He was at Westlake, a Tudor showplace in the lake district of Westmoreland. Jamie sat in the yellow-and-cream breakfast room that faced the east terrace and one of the rose gardens, the *Times* folded open before him. He had to read the sentence about Parliament twice before he understood its implications. But when he came to the bit about ". . . must personally question further investment . . . ," he recognized a message aimed straight at him, and written in letters of blood.

Charles Mendoza lived in a house across from Hampstead Heath. His wife, Sara, and his two-year-old son, Ian, were with him at breakfast, but Charles ignored them and concentrated on his food and his newspaper. Suddenly he choked on his buttered toast. He had come to the second column of Sharrick's article. "The problem is debt, and the servicing of that debt. It seems that many of these countries will not survive without further infusions of capital from those more fortunate, but how will it be repaid? How, in the conditions which prevail, can Latin America's immense natural resources be put to the production of wealth?"

In the exquisite Georgian house in Belgravia, where since his wife died Norman Mendoza had lived alone except for his servants, nothing was eaten at all. Norman made the mistake of reading Lord Sharrick's entire piece before he breakfasted. It quite destroyed his appetite.

San Juan, Three A.M.

In Puerto Rico it was "de darktime." In the bordello on the Calle Cruz business was thriving, but Nuria Sanchez slept alone in her cool and lovely room in the little house behind the big one.

Fernando Luz slept alone and badly in a bed belonging to his host Don Prudencio Alvarez of Lares. In the Posada de San Juan Bautista, Michael Curran's rest was disturbed by dreams of huge macaws descending on a woman wearing a flaming red turban. He couldn't fend off the claws and the beaks of the birds, and the creatures turned their attack on him.

The bishop of Puerto Rico did not sleep alone. Concha, his housekeeper of thirty years, lay beside him, snoring gently, the fragrant warmth of her body comforting him as it had for most of his adult life.

He was awake and worried, but it wasn't his broken promise of celibacy that bothered him. The bishop did not believe God would damn him to everlasting hell because of weakness. That was not evil, only sad. Besides, he had tried hard to be a good bishop. Now he was troubled by how to continue trying.

He wanted to dismiss Sister Magdalena's claims as the rantings of a hysterical woman, but the evidence was against it. In the past fifteen years he had known at least four occasions when she'd said something was going to happen and it did. Two of them were unforgettable: the terrible hurricane of '86 when, if he'd believed her he might have issued a warning and saved countless lives, and the incident of the rotten timber which brought down the roof of his dining room on an evening when he was entertaining five guests. If the nun hadn't sent her message, they would all be long dead.

Moreover, Sister Magdalena had cured at least a dozen people he was aware of, and God alone knew how many others. And the sisters who lived with her worshipped her, swearing she was a living saint. That alone was a testament to something extraordinary. Women living cooped up like that usually detested anyone who was different, who showed up their own faults by her virtues.

So what to do?

Warn the people, she'd told him. Something was going to happen and they mustn't resist. But what was going to happen? An invasion? Something to do with this insane war between Spain and North America? Probably. How in the name of *el Señor* could he tell the people of San Juan that such a thing was going to happen, but that they should accept it? The ordinary folk might agree, but the leaders were already rattling their swords and screaming that they would die to protect the autonomy they'd only recently won. What they meant was that they would send others to die. All the same, if the bishop preached peaceful surrender, they'd find some way to get rid of him.

"Lord," he whispered, "you know I'm not a brave man, not a martyr or a hero. What do you want me to do? I can't let her march through the island issuing her warnings the way she wants to do. And I cannot do it for her. What will be gained by panic? How can it be good if I set myself in opposition to the leaders and force them to silence me? And what, dear Lord, do you want me to do with that Irishman who insists on seeing me later this morning? It is said he is enormously wealthy, that he is planning to buy up the entire island. What do I know about the ways of such men, Lord?"

Sighing, the bishop reached for the string of rosary beads lying on the table beside him. He told his Hail Marys and Our Fathers to the rhythm of Concha's stertorous breaths.

"Good morning, Your Excellency."

"Ah, Mr. Curran. Good morning." The bishop offered his ring to be kissed, but Michael ignored it. Let the man assume he was a Protestant. The bishop gestured to the chair opposite his. "Please, sit down."

"Thank you. I've come to pay my respects, Excellency. I anticipate taking up residence in Puerto Rico."

"So I'm told."

Michael raised his eyebrows. "Is it common knowledge so quickly?"

"Not common perhaps. But I know it."

Give the cleric the first score. Michael acknowledged the other man's victory with a small smile. "I'm delighted to find you so well informed, sir. Doubtless you know, too, that I intend to go into the coffee business."

"Coffee has been profitable of late. A wise choice, Señor Curran."

"I hope so. I hope too that I will be a useful member of the community."

The bishop nodded. "An admirable aim, señor. I'm sure you will be welcome here, but . . . permit me to be blunt, you are not a Catholic?"

"No, Excellency."

"I see. Well, no doubt you know that almost everyone on the island, nearly a million people, is a son or daughter of Holy Church. Perhaps if you live among us you will someday abjure your Protestant heresy."

Michael saw his opening. "Nothing is impossible, Excellency. There is something that has provoked my curiosity."

"With God, indeed nothing is impossible." The bishop leaned forward. He had the face of a bird dog and a prominent hooked nose that seemed to be sniffing its way into Michael's soul. "If there is some doctrine of the faith which puzzles you, I will do my best to explain."

"Not a doctrine exactly. The first day I was here I met a remarkable woman, a Sister Magdalena, who lives in the Convent of Las Nieves—"

"How did you happen to go to the convent, Señor Curran?"

Michael could see the agitation behind the bishop's light brown eyes. "I had heard of the sister, the one called Magdalena. I was told she was very holy and had visions. I wanted to see for myself."

"And what did she tell you?"

The bishop's hands were clasped on the arms of his chair. Michael flicked one glance at that white-knuckled grip, then looked away. "Personal things, about my family. Nothing very important. All the same, it was remarkable that she knew them."

"Yes, Sister Magdalena is remarkable."

Michael noted that the bishop had relaxed somewhat. "She fascinates me. I wanted to see her again, but when I returned to Las Nieves the place was locked and there were guards. They said they were there on your orders, and that no one could visit Sister Magdalena."

"For the moment that is true."

"I see. Am I permitted to ask why?"

"Ah, it is nothing unusual, señor. But of course you do not know our customs. Catholic nuns, indeed all Catholics, sometimes enter into a time of deep silence and prayer. We call it a retreat. Sister Magdalena and the nuns of Las Nieves are on retreat."

"And it requires guards to make them adhere to this retreat?"

The bishop stood up and went to a table across the room and rang a small silver bell. "We must have some coffee. No, of course guards aren't required to keep the nuns to their holy duties. No one is in the convent except of her own free will, Señor Curran. I know the kinds of tales told by Protestants, but I assure you they are all absurd lies. The guards are there to make sure the sisters are not disturbed. Many people from the outside world visit them to ask for prayers or to bring alms. And Sister Magdalena is quite famous on our island."

A butler entered before Michael could reply. The bishop ordered refreshments, then turned back to his guest. "In Ireland you drink mostly tea, do you not?"

"We do. There are numerous coffeehouses as well, but I don't think you'd recognize the brew they serve. It's pretty weak stuff."

"I see. And have you developed a taste for proper coffee, Señor Curran?"

"I like it very much."

"Good, good. Ah, here we are."

The butler returned with a tray and poured the thick black liquid into little glasses set in silver holders. The bishop turned to his guest. "Will you take *café cortado* or *café solo,* señor?"

"*Café solo*, Excellency."

The butler put three lumps of pale brown sugar into Michael's glass of black coffee and brought it to him on yet another silver tray. The bishop took his *cortado,* with a portion of cream as well as brown sugar. He waited for it to be prepared, then raised the glass in Michael's direction. "To the success of your venture, señor."

"Thank you." Then, when the butler had gone, he continued, "Excellency, I'm still very curious about Sister Magdalena. How did she come by her unusual abilities?"

"They are a gift from God. There can be no other explanation. Where are you planning to establish your hacienda, Señor Curran?"

"I'm interested in the land west of Adjuntas."

"Yes, of course. That is the best coffee land. It is sad that so much of Arabia is troubled by war and disaster, but we are the beneficiaries since Europe now imports much of its coffee from the Indies and Latin America."

"Yes, Excellency. Can you tell me how Sister—"

"The land west of Adjuntas . . . ," the bishop mused aloud, as if he hadn't heard his guest's last words. "It is all in established haciendas, I believe. Do you plan to buy a plantation that already exists, Señor Curran, or to create a new one?"

"I'm interested in mature trees that are already bearing. Your Excellency, why don't you wish to discuss the nun?"

The frontal attack caught the old man off guard. "You mistake me. I have no objection. The good sister is remarkable, as we both said. But such phenomena are not really unusual among us, Señor Curran. Holy Church has produced many saints."

"Is Sister Magdalena a saint?"

The bishop shrugged. "Thank God, I do not have to make that decision. After she dies, if the Holy Ghost so inspires, the Congregation for Sacred Rites will examine the claim."

"Doesn't the request to the congregation come first from the local bishop?"

"You are better versed in our laws than I expected, señor," the bishop said softly.

Michael had a swift memory of the brothers who taught religion in his boyhood school in Córdoba. "Am I correct, Excellency?"

"You are." The bishop put his empty glass on the table. "But I am an old man, and Sister Magdalena will doubtless outlive me. The problem will not be mine to deal with."

"She is younger than you then?"

"Yes. Much younger."

"I see. Of course it's not possible to tell because of the darkness of that little room and the veil she wears." Michael watched the other man's eyes.

"All those things are part of her vows, señor. That is the manner in which anchoresses, hermit women, always live."

"And did she require your permission to begin such a life?"

The bishop nodded.

"Was she very young at the time? What kind of family is she from?"

"She was very young, yes. And she had no family. Sister Magdalena was an orphan. Now, Señor Curran, if you will forgive me, I am due at a meeting."

Michael stood up. "Of course, thank you for giving me so much of your time, Excellency." He took an envelope from his breast pocket and laid it on the table beside the coffee tray. "A contribution to your good works, sir. Perhaps it can be used to support your orphanage, the one where Sister Magdalena was raised. Where was it, by the way?"

"In Ponce, on the other side of the island. May Our Lord bless your generosity, Señor Curran."

Later, after the *estranjero* had left, the bishop counted the notes inside the envelope. The Irishman had given a thousand pesetas to the church he claimed not to believe in. A man could support a family for five years on that amount—maybe six or seven years if his wife was frugal. In all his life the bishop could not remember receiving such a large contribution from a single donor.

Lares, Ten A.M.

It was cool in the high limestone hills. Fernando Luz was shivering on the raised veranda of the house of Prudencio Alvarez. The five people Alvarez had summoned by messenger the night before were accustomed to the climate and did not seem cold.

Luz looked at them, trying not to be obvious. To his right was the youngest of the group. Manolo Trïgera couldn't be more than twenty-five or twenty-six, last year had inherited the abutting hacienda, and now was relaxed, confident. Cocky, Luz thought.

Beside Manolo was Felipe Rodriguez, who had a big plantation in the hills above the Rio Guaba. Then came Alvarez himself, and across from him two more coffee growers with significant spreads, Coco Morales—Luz thought he looked like a snake—and a man Luz scarcely knew, Jesus Fontana.

Between Fontana and Morales was a woman so old and so frail she looked as if the next breeze must blow her away. Doña Maria de los Angeles bent forward, leaning on her gold-topped walking stick. "*Ahora, Don Prudencio, ¿por qué estamos aquí?*"

It was the question they all wanted to ask: Why are we here?

Alvarez nodded in Luz's direction. "Our friend Don Fernando asked me to gather you together." He turned expectantly to the banker.

It was time. He must tell them. Luz's tongue felt thick and the words wouldn't come. "I am—I am happy to see you all here," he stammered.

Maria de los Angeles gave him a reprieve. "Happy? The only thing that makes bankers happy is to screw money out of the poor and to foreclose." She cackled with laughter.

The others laughed too, but the sound had a hollow ring.

"I assure you, Doña Maria—"

"Assure me of nothing, Señor Luz, I'm not interested. I owe you not one centavo, so what can you have to say that concerns me? Or any of us?" Her old eyes traveled the circle and stopped at young Manolo. "Except, of course . . ."

He rose to her bait. "You owe nothing, Doña Maria, because you have made no improvements to your hacienda in forty years. The rest of us borrow when borrowing is good for business."

"Debt!" The old woman stamped her stick on the wooden floor of the porch. "Debt will be the ruin of Puerto Rico, of all of you. You are fools and you give vermin like him—"

Alvarez jumped out of his chair. "Please, Doña Maria, don't excite yourself. There is no need. We haven't come together to talk about debts. Let me get you some more coffee."

He went quickly to the table near the door. Retrieving a silver coffeepot, he brought it to the old woman and refilled her tiny cup. Fontana held out his own, waited for a few more drops of the thick black brew to be added to it, then said, "So why are we here?"

Once more Alvarez looked at Luz.

"There is a man—" Luz broke off. He'd been crazy to tackle so many of Curran's major targets together like this. He should have seen them separately. Too late for that now. He swallowed hard twice, then tried again. "There is a man, an *estranjero,* who wishes to buy your land. I mean the haciendas of each of you. All of them." Luz let the words tumble out of his mouth, knowing that if he didn't he'd never say them.

The old woman's cackle was the only sound in the stunned silence. "I will never sell my land. You are crazy, Don Fernando. All bankers are crazy as well as evil."

"Never is a long time."

The words came from Rodriguez, and Luz turned to him. "Thank you, Don Felipe. A very long time. I was thinking the same thing."

Manolo Trigera drained the last of his coffee and set his cup on the railing of the porch. "Keep talking. It can't hurt us to hear what the Irishman proposes."

"What Irishman?" Jesus Fontana looked puzzled, as if most of the conversation had passed over his head.

"I never said anything about an Irishman," Luz protested.

"You don't need to say anything. What other *estranjero* can it be? Everyone knows that in San Juan now there is an Irish giant who has money to burn and who spends his time in the house of Nuria Sanchez."

Everyone also knew what kind of a house that was, even Doña Maria, though she would never admit it. "It is because of the slaves," she muttered. "Without the slaves there cannot be enough profit to pee on."

"The slaves are gone, so what is the point of talking about them?" Manolo took a fat cigar from his pocket and busied himself lighting it.

The old woman pointed her stick at him. The tip came within a few inches of his handsome face. "For a *niño* like you, a baby who only yesterday began wiping his own ass when he shits, there is no point in anything. But I remember how it was—"

"Please, Doña Maria . . ."

Luz knew why Alvarez tried again to placate her. He owed the bank more than he would earn in four years of perfect harvests, if such a miracle should occur. Besides, he had a mistress in Havana. Alvarez dreamed of convincing her to leave Cuba and go to New York with him. It would take a great deal of money to make her agree. Luz had expected Alvarez to be his strongest ally.

"I agree with young Manolo here," Alvarez said. "It costs us nothing to listen to Don Fernando's proposal."

Like a snake, Coco Morales had watched them all. Now he leaned forward. "How much?"

"Two pesetas per *cuerda*." Luz dropped the figure like a stone into a still pond and waited for the ripples. For some seconds no one said anything. Luz repeated the offer. "Two pesetas per *cuerda*."

It was not a bad price, even if only the opening bid. He could see the rapid calculations occurring behind the eyes of his listeners. *Madre de Dios,* Luz prayed, let me make this deal. Let me do it and I will give ten percent—no, one percent, that's more reasonable—one percent of my profit to the Church.

"And for the buildings?" Manolo asked.

"Why are we talking about this?" Doña Maria took a cigar from her drawstring bag and waved it in the direction of Morales. He dutifully struck a match and held it for her.

"For the buildings?" Manolo asked again, using the time the old woman's mouth was busy with her cigar.

"The price is inclusive," Luz said. "Two pesetas a *cuerda* for everything."

"But all land is not the same," Jesus Fontana protested. "All land is not equally productive."

Rodriguez made a noise in his throat. "You're right. All land is not the same. God doesn't do things that way. Besides, I think Doña Maria has a point. Why are we talking about selling the land that our families have bled over for a hundred years?"

Luz smiled. So Felipe Rodriguez was also on his side. The grandiose speech was a tactic, nothing more. His father had bought up the small holdings of dozens of *campesinos* and turned them off the land. That's how the Rodriguez hacienda came into existance. Devotion to a family home-stead didn't come into it. "Two pesetas a *cuerda*," Luz said again. "It is very generous."

"Speaking for myself," Manolo Trigera said, avoiding all their eyes, "I would never sell for less than five per *cuerda*. And the buildings and equipment would have to be assessed and paid for separately."

Maria de los Angeles was puffing so rapidly on her cigar the breeze couldn't carry the smoke away. She was wreathed in it. Smoke made a halo around her head and clung like a wispy shroud to her shriveled body. She waved it away from her face and stared at the young man. "Traitor." She spat at him. "Traitor!" She tried to stand up, but her legs failed her and she had to sit down again quickly.

"Doña Maria," Alvarez pleaded. "Please, you mustn't excite yourself. We are discussing a hypothetical situation."

Jesus Fontana was sweating; perspiration was pouring off his face. Luz was sweating too, for the same reason, but he would not give in and wipe himself with a large white handkerchief the way Fontana did. It was too obvious a sign of weakness. "Hypothetical," Fontana said. "Maybe for you. Me, I have a real hacienda. There's nothing hypothetical about it."

And real debts, Luz thought. At least five thousand in various loans. "There is something else—"

"Ah yes," Coco Morales interrupted softly. Luz realized what it was that made him look like a reptile: He never seemed to blink. The snake's eyes were staring into those of the banker and the lids never moved. "I was wondering when we would get to that," Morales said. "Go on, Don Fernando."

"I was simply going to point out that times are unsettled."

"Indeed. There is a war."

"We are not at war," Fontana protested.

Morales shrugged.

"We could be invaded at any time." Felipe Rodriguez waved away the cigar smoke drifting in his direction. "The *norteamericanos* could come and swallow us."

"What does that have to do with anything?" Fontana asked.

"Don Jesus," Coco Morales said patiently, "the *norte-americanos* drink a lot of coffee. If they take us over they could make us sell only to them, at a price they dictate."

"Yes," Rodriguez agreed. "Do you think there would be profits at a price set by the president and the Congress in Washington?"

Fontana looked helpless, unable to refute their arguments.

Doña Maria expertly tossed the stub of her cigar into a bowl of water by the stairs. It landed with a hissing sound. "Since my husband died there hasn't been a man on this island with *cojones*. None of you have any balls. Why aren't you talking about fighting the *gringos*?"

"It would be a very unequal battle," Don Prudencio murmured.

"Listen to me." Manolo Trigera stood up. His hair was very dark and slicked back with brilliantine. It glittered in the morning sun. "Listen, forget about the *norteamericanos*. We need to negotiate directly with the Irishman."

"I never said it was the Irishman," Luz protested. "An *estranjero*. That's all I'm saying."

"Where is he?" Jesus Fontana demanded. "Why isn't he here?"

"I am empowered to speak for him."

"You are fools." The snake again, letting those incredible eyes capture their attention before he continued. "You haven't asked the single important question. Whatever the final offer turns out to be, whoever the *estranjero* is, does he have the money to back up his words?"

They all turned to Luz. "Yes," he said. "You will be paid in cash. I personally guarantee it."

"Your personal guarantee is very welcome, Don Fernando," Morales said softly. "But whatever the final offer might be, we are talking about a very great deal of money. So, with all due respect, does the bank guarantee it?"

Luz mentally rehearsed the words of the cable from Coutts, then he nodded. "*Si*, señor. The Banco Mendoza guarantees the offer."

London, Three P.M.

The place Lord Sharrick thought of as home was his vast hard-edged granite manor in Glencree, in the windswept Wicklow hills of Ireland. His voluptuous cream-colored London town house designed by John Nash and set like a small diamond beside the larger jewel of Regent's Park he considered a seductive harlot in the land of the stranger. Still, harlots had their uses—and he used the London house now.

At the rear was a good sized conservatory where his lordship grew the tropical and semitropical plants he'd gathered from the wild in his many travels. Sharrick went there now, carrying the newspaper that had been waiting since breakfast. He paused a moment by a bench of cymbidium orchids, inspecting them with a critical eye. They were doing very well; the new head gardener was a good man. Satisfied, he sat in a wicker rocking chair beside a vining *passiflora edulis* and opened the paper.

He'd delayed reading the piece in the *Times* because it always pained him to see what editors made of his words. Last year in the *Spectator* . . . Ah, what difference did it make. This particular article had been written with a purpose beyond his usual aim of enlightening the Philistines. This time he was hunting big game.

He read quickly, his gaze running up and down the columns in search of wounds inflicted by the blue pencil. Not too many, he decided finally. The editor of the *Times* was perhaps ignorant of the distinction between *that* and *which*—he invariably preferred the latter—but never mind; the message had survived intact. Sharrick smiled. There was a particular pleasure to be gained by setting the cat among the pigeons. A terrible cliché. He'd never write it. The fox in the henhouse perhaps? No, equally bad.

He was still deliberating an original metaphor when his butler came into the conservatory, threading his way among the palms and the cacti, walking gingerly. The man was Welsh, and he sang rather then spoke his words. Every phrase ended on a rising note. "Telephone, milord. It's Mr. Drummond." It needed only one of those famous Welsh choirs to back up the butler's solo.

Sharrick sighed. Until a few years ago when the damned telephones became ubiquitous among a certain class here in London, Drummond would have come in person. He'd love to have had the opportunity of seeing the broker's face when they had this inevitable conversation. Nothing for it, they would speak through the ether. "Thank you, Jones. I'll take it in my study."

The study faced south to the park, and the curtains had been drawn against the afternoon sun. Sharrick waited a moment for his eyes to adjust, then reminded himself that it didn't matter and picked up the receiver. "Sharrick speaking," he said into the daffodil-shaped mouthpiece.

"Neil Drummond here, your lordship. Forgive my disturbing you, but—" A loud click made him pause.

"It's all right, that was just Jones ringing off downstairs. As you were saying, Drummond?"

"I wanted to speak with you about the piece in today's paper."

"Yes?"

"Well, hang it all, milord, do you really believe everything you wrote?"

The broker had to be very agitated indeed to use quite that tone of voice. Sharrick's smile widened. "Of course I believe it. I'd not have written it if I didn't."

"But surely—"

"Surely I've been there and seen for myself. I was simply reporting my opinion. I was at great pains to make that perfectly clear."

"I know. All the same . . ."

"All the same, what? You didn't ring simply to ask if I meant what I said, did you?"

"Yes, actually, I did. It's this new issue on behalf of Paraguay, milord. Mendozas put it on sale today. We were expecting to do quite well out of it."

"I didn't single out Paraguay."

"No, I realize that. But as far as your average Brit's concerned, one place in South America is much like another. Don't know the difference between Mexico and Chile most of 'em."

"Then I respectfully suggest they ought not to be putting their money on a blind horse."

"Milord . . ."

"Yes, Drummond, go on."

"A number of my clients were set to buy today. They've been placing orders for the last week. Now most of them have got cold feet. I was wondering, since you're also a client of the firm, if you would give me permission to say you didn't include Paraguay in your remarks about Latin America."

"If you mean to remind them that Paraguay isn't mentioned by name in the article, go right ahead. It isn't. But if you're suggesting that I think Paraguay is different from the rest, that it's a safer place for investment, no, Drummond, I'm sorry. You may say no such thing."

There was a long pause on the other end of the line. "Very well, milord. Thank you for clarifying your position."

"Not at all. By the way, do you think the other brokers have had the same experience? I mean with the Mendoza bond."

"I'm afraid so. It's been the chief source of talk in the City all day."

"I see. Well, sorry about your lost commissions, Drummond. But there it is."

Sharrick caught himself rubbing his hands after he hung up. Like the villain in a melodrama. It made him chuckle. He was still laughing when Jones came in. "Will you take tea in here, sir?"

"Yes, why not? I think I will."

The dimness of the room was pleasant; it induced daydreams. He'd always loved to daydream, ever since he was a small boy. That's what three hundred years in Ireland had added to his Saxon character. It was the Irish legacy that had produced a dreamer and an adventurer. Damn, his leg was aching, must be that the weather was going to change. Sharrick sat down and rubbed it idly and waited for his tea.

In minutes the butler returned with the tray. His lordship always took China tea, never Indian, a fragrant tarry blend called Lapsang souchong that he drank with only a touch of sugar. Beside the pot of tea was a small plate containing one scone, already sliced and buttered, nestled on a napkin. That too was exactly what his lordship required every day at exactly this time.

Sharrick eyed the tray and nodded approvingly. "Very good, thank you, Jones."

"My pleasure, sir. And this came in the afternoon post." The butler produced an envelope.

Sharrick took it, noting the handwriting with a frisson of pleasure. "That will be all."

He waited until the butler left before limping over to his desk and fetching an ivory-handled letter opener. The note within was brief. "I accept with pleasure," it said. There was no signature because none was required.

It was five P.M. when Philip Johnson entered his employer's office carrying a sheaf of papers. "Here are the reports, sir."

Norman had turned his chair round so his back was to his desk. He was staring out the window at the customary activity on Lower Sloane Street. "Thank you, Philip. Just leave them."

"Yes, sir."

"Oh, Philip, have the others been bothering you?" Norman jerked his thumb in the direction of the upstairs. He'd closeted himself in here all day, told his secretary he would take no calls and see no one. But doubtless that hadn't stopped Henry and Charles and Timothy from trying to break into his solitude. It would have been more difficult to refuse to talk to the senior partner, but Jamie wasn't here, thank God. He was still up at Westlake. Where, also thank God, they hadn't yet installed a telephone. Tomorrow's post would bring whatever was going to come from Jamie. Today there were only Henry and Charles and Timothy to be held off.

"Nothing I couldn't deal with, sir," Philip Johnson said.

"No, of course not. You're extraordinarily competent, Philip. I'm grateful."

"Thank you, sir."

"Don't mention it. Go on home, no point in hanging about. There's nothing to be done. Not today at any rate."

"Very good, sir, if you're sure you don't need me."

"Quite sure. Good evening to you."

"And to you, Mr. Norman."

That was a necessity, not familiarity. There were too many Mendozas in this place for the surname to make any sense; half a dozen distant relations worked in the bank in minor capacities. If one wanted to identify a particular Mendoza one had to use his Christian name. It had become common practice for everyone to do so.

"I'll come in early tomorrow, Mr. Norman," the secretary said before he left. "By seven if you wish. To deal with . . . Well, whatever requires attention."

"Yes, a good idea."

In seconds Norman was again alone, aware of the reports on the desk behind him. He didn't have to read them. He'd known the basic facts by noon. Some ten percent of the shares had been sold. The bank would have to buy in at the market rate in order to support the issue. It had happened plenty of times before, but not perhaps when they were so short of ready cash, and not as a result of one man's spite.

That was the thing that stuck hardest in Norman's throat. He barely knew Sharrick. They saw each other at the club of which they were both members, occasionally at some social function. They'd had no other dealings at all that he could recall. Why in hell had the bloody bastard wanted to knife them? Not marely wanted to, he'd done it. Brilliantly. Norman knew he had to figure out what was behind that before he could begin to repair the damage.

The habit of caution was ingrained. Lila rapped on the window and stopped the cab as it left Kensington Gardens. She went by foot from the Alexandria Gate to the Royal Albert Hall. It was only a short distance, but she wasn't dressed for walking and she was aware of a haze of perspiration on her face when she mounted the steps of the monumental building. It was a bit silly to be sneaking around now, she told herself. The cat had been set among the pigeons, and it was too late for anyone to stop the massacre. Still . . .

Sharrick watched her approach. The Black Widow was a vision this evening. Her silver hair was piled high on her head. She wore no hat, only a black silk rose held in place with a jeweled clip of some kind. Her frock was understated and simple, and doubtless wildly expensive. Black silk organza sleeves and bodice, ornamented with jet beading, and a swept-back silk skirt that hugged her hips and released all its fullness into a small train she carried gathered up on one wrist. The evening was warm and she'd added only a black feather boa to the outfit. "Charming," he said when she'd joined him. "You look lovely."

"Thank you. Your note said the opera and supper. It seemed that something a bit grand was suitable."

"Forgive my not calling for you at the hotel. Somehow it didn't seem wise."

"Nor would it have to me," she agreed. "We're still acting as if we had secrets, but we don't after today." She smiled, inclining her head to look into his face. "At least not so many of them."

Up close he could see that the silk rose in her hair was anchored with a spray of diamonds, and he was fairly certain the gown was by Worth. Lila Curran's tastes and expectations had changed considerably since she was a girl in the Dublin slums. Knowing her background didn't disturb him at all. In fact it added considerably to her appeal. "I'm so glad you could come."

Lila put her hand lightly on his arm, feeling the fine wool of his summer-weight tailcoat, admiring the starched whiteness of his shirtfront and the small pearl studs that closed it. "You're looking quite elegant yourself. Your note was signed only Fergus, I wasn't sure if I was meeting Mr. Kelly or Lord Sharrick."

"One and the same," he reminded her, linking her arm through his and turning toward the stairway to the stalls. "Though Kelly's brogue's rather broad, and his tastes don't run to Wagner."

She laughed softly. "As I said last time we met, your double life gives you an indecent amount of pleasure."

"Is there any other reason to do anything?"

"Yes, sometimes there is."

They'd reached their seats. Sharrick made sure she was comfortable, then leaned over to whisper the story of his call from Drummond the broker, but the lights dimmed and there was no time.

The sustained single note of the horns introduced *Götterdämmerung*.

"Did you think Wagner a strange choice for our little advance celebration?" Sharrick asked later.

They were at supper in the Café Royal on Regent Street. Lila twisted the stem of her champagne glass between her long fingers. The many rings she wore sparkled in the rosy glow of a pink-shaded gas lamp. "Not at all."

"No, I thought you wouldn't."

"Revenge isn't strange to me." She spoke in a whisper.

"There are dark secrets in your eyes."

"Are there, Fergus? Do you mind?"

He shook his head. "No, that's one of your charms for me," he admitted. "Your past."

"Compared to yours, it's a very short past. How many scores have been left for settling in your ancient lineage, my lord Sharrick of Glencree?"

"Nary a one. No, don't laugh, it's true. A very boring lot the Saxon side. My mother's people, the Kellys, they're something else again."

"So that's why you call yourself Kelly in your other incarnation."

"That's why."

"Forgive me, but it sounds rather a common name for the wife of a nobleman." She smiled, knowing Fergus well enough to realize he wouldn't be offended.

"My mother's family were rather common, at least in the sense of being ordinary. She and my father were a love match. That's the way the Kellys aren't common. They all have a great deal of pride and they're not afraid to aim high."

"High enough to want to be free. Independent of England. That's what you're saying, isn't it?"

"I guess I am, in a way."

"And is that why you got into this with me? Revenge on the English oppressors, on behalf of the Kellys?"

"Not really."

"Why then?"

"Does it matter?"

She shrugged. "It might."

"It's not because of the Kellys. Except that they made me what I am, more than half of what I am at any rate. I was thinking about it this afternoon. It's the Irish in me that craves adventure."

"So that's what you're after, adventure."

"No." He covered her hand with his. One of her rings was a huge emerald. The green stone seemed to burn the flesh of his palm. "No, I'm not after adventure the way you mean. I'm after you."

Lila drew her hand away. "I'm not sure, Fergus. I've told you that many times. I've been on my own so long—"

"You said you'd be more sure after you had established your son in Córdoba."

"Yes, I know I did."

"Well?"

"He's not there yet."

"As good as," he said.

"It's too soon to be certain. But you're not doing all this for Michael, and I don't believe you're doing it to win me. It's too much."

"Not for Michael, I hardly know him. But do you value yourself so cheaply?"

"I value myself very highly indeed. I think you know that." She leaned forward, speaking so only he could hear. "I know men, Fergus. I've spent my life studying them. A man will do many things for a woman, but to ruin another man, a series of other men, for that he must have a man-type reason. Women will kill for love, men kill for power and money."

"Is that what we're doing, killing?"

"As good as. There'll be very little left of the London

Mendozas when we're through. You know that. I never pretended it would be otherwise."

"What about young Timothy? Haven't you promised him the bank on a plate?"

"Timothy's a venal fool. He couldn't run the bank if it were given to him."

Lord Sharrick leaned back in his seat, studying her over the rim of his champagne glass. "As a matter of fact, you're quite correct," he said finally. "I suspected that from the first, that's why I insisted on giving him that report last week in Dublin."

"I don't follow you. I never understood exactly what you intended with that."

"I was testing the chap who'd decided he was the heir apparent."

"Meaning?"

"Meaning that I told him exactly what I told the general public in that article published today. Anonymously to be sure, but in even clearer and more specific terms."

Lila raised her eyebrows. "You never told me you were going to do that. I thought you were simply reassuring him—"

"I knew you'd disapprove," he interrupted.

"But why—"

"I had to see for myself. I gave the boy the chance to do the right thing, to warn his brother and his father and his uncles that they were heading for disaster. Apparently he did not."

"Obviously he didn't. If he had, they'd have found some way to wiggle out of today's issue." She was trembling and her hands felt clammy. She'd had no idea that Fergus had taken her so close to the edge of ruin. Lila drained the last of her glass of champagne.

Sharrick motioned to the waiter. He approached and refilled it. Another waiter appeared, bringing their grilled turbot. "You're not eating," his lordship said after a few moments. "Is something the matter?"

"I'm still reeling," she admitted. "Why did you do it, Fergus? How could you put everything at such risk?"

"My dear Lila, you yourself have likened what we're doing to murder. I had to know if the victims deserved their fate."

"And you decided that Timothy did. What about the others?"

"I already knew about the others."

She pounced on that. "So you do have a motive, something you haven't told me about."

"Not the way you mean. None of the Mendozas have done me any personal harm."

She waited, knowing he would go on if she gave him enough time. He was staring at his plate, a few seconds later he motioned for the waiter again. "We've decided we're not hungry," he told the man. "Take these away and bring some coffee. And a bottle of cognac, the Courvoisier '81," he added. Then to Lila he said, "I've seen what bankers do all over the world, not least in Ireland. I don't like it. It's as simple as that."

Lila suspected it was not in the least simple. He was lying, she could feel it in her bones. But it didn't matter. "The issue must have failed today, mustn't it?"

"Yes, it must have and it did. My broker called me about four. He was crying for mercy."

"And did you show any?"

"None."

"Ah," she said softly. "I know why I love you—whether you're calling yourself Fergus Kelly or Sharrick of Glencree."

"Do you?"

"Do I know?"

"No, do you love me?"

"In a manner of speaking," Lila admitted. "In a manner of speaking, I suppose I do."

❧ 9 ❧

THURSDAY, JUNE 24, 1898
London, Ten A.M.

The fine weather had disappeared. Rain sheeted down the windows of the Partners' Room in a gurgling flood. The damp seemed to penetrate the walls. "Bloody rain," Charles murmured. "Sodding, bloody rain."

The others did not comment. He was cursing their bad luck as much as the weather and there was nothing to add.

Norman pulled the cork on a bottle of sherry. It made an oddly loud sound in the grim silence. The bank employed a butler to serve whatever refreshments a principal might choose to offer a favored client, but it was a strict rule that when they met in the Partner's Room no one but themselves was present.

"Henry," Norman murmured, passing his brother a schooner of the pale gold amontillado. Henry took the drink and waited for the others to be served. Norman gave Charles and Timothy theirs, then filled his own glass and raised it. "Cheers."

"It's not a very cheerful occasion," Timothy said.

Neither Charles nor Henry took up the challenge. They echoed Norman's toast. "Cheers."

The sherry was a new bottling, a blend the master of their vineyards in Jerez had put down in barrels specially imported from California, and nursed with loving care for fifteen years. It was mellow and infinitely smooth, with a long aftertaste of walnuts. "Excellent," Norman murmured. "Ruez has outdone himself. I must write to him at once." He turned to his younger son. "Now, Timothy, what were you saying?"

"Simply that our present circumstances aren't particularly cheerful, this amontillado notwithstanding."

"You agree with me then?" Norman asked mildly. Timothy looked blank. "I mean about the sherry," his father explained. "Ruez is on to a winner, don't you think?"

"The sherry is superb," Timothy agreed. "But that's hardly the point of this meeting, is it?"

"Oh, I see. Tell me what you believe the point to be."

"Our situation, Father. I might say our dire situation."

"Ah yes." Norman tucked his thumbs in the pockets of his waistcoat and leaned back in his chair. "We've been in similar straits before this. We always pull through."

Charles looked from his brother to his father. The hostility between them was a knife-sharp thing, a weapon waiting to be unsheathed. By comparison the failure of the Paraguayan issue was less dangerous. "Have you spoken with Uncle Jamie?" he asked.

"No," Norman said. "You're forgetting there's no telephone at Westlake."

"I thought he might have returned to town."

"Why?" Norman drank the remainder of his sherry thoughtfully, with lingering sips, then poured himself a refill. "What earthly good could Jamie be? Or imagine he'd be."

"I just thought . . ." Charles's voice trailed away.

"Yes, well he's not here and he's not going to be. I had

a note in this morning's first post. Jamie will be staying up north with his roses."

Henry was shuffling through the stack of papers he'd brought to the meeting. "Eleven and a half percent of the shares that went on offer," he murmured. "That's what's been taken up."

"Yes, Henry. We all know that."

Henry looked at his younger brother. Norman had assumed the place at the head of the table. By common consent he always did that if Jamie was absent. Technically Henry was the next in line, but neither he nor anyone else paid attention to the accident of birth that gave him seniority over Norman. "What are we to do?" he asked, his eyes liquid with grief.

"For the love of Christ, man!" Norman exploded. "We'll do whatever we must. Stop looking as if you're facing a firing squad."

"But I knew," Henry whispered. "I knew in my bones the issue would go bad. I should have argued against it more forcefully. I should have persuaded all of you——"

"It's not your fault, Henry." Norman put out his hand and lightly touched the other man's shoulder. "You made your point and we outvoted you. Forget it."

Timothy reached for the sherry bottle and topped up his uncle's glass, but he spoke to his father. "What are you proposing we do?"

"Nothing."

Three pairs of incredulous eyes turned to him.

"Nothing, Father?" Charles asked. "Nothing?"

"That's right, nothing."

"But——"

"*But* doesn't come into it," Norman interrupted. "For one thing, the offer remains outstanding, more of it may be taken up, perhaps a good deal more if some new will-o-the-wisp attracts the great god public opinion. For another, the bond is payable in four six-month debentures. The first isn't due in Paraguay for thirty days."

"Half a million in sterling, less discounted interest of twelve percent, which is sixty thousand..." Timothy was scratching figures on a sheet of paper in front of him, as if they hadn't all done these sums long since. "So we'll owe four hundred and forty thousand in thirty days." He turned to his brother. "What's our cash position, Charles? How liquid are we?"

"Not very."

"How much is not very? Come, Charlie my boy, what exactly are the numbers?"

Norman didn't say anything, his gaze didn't move from Timothy's face. What's your game, lad? he wondered. You have one, I know you do. You're not messing about with the Fenians because you want Irish independence. Ireland could sink into the sea for all you care. So what's your game?

Charles was murmuring some figures.

"Speak up," Timothy commanded. "I can't hear you."

"I said we have seventy-seven thousand in reserve. And," Charles dropped his voice, "and the two million. I mean if we—"

Timothy leaned forward interrupting him. "The gold we're holding for the Imperial Treasury of the Czar can't be counted as part of our reserves."

No one said anything. They all knew that technically Tim was correct, but they knew too that the two million in gold bullion in their vaults was a source they could borrow against for the very short term. If absolutely necessary.

The Mendozas had begun doing business with the Russians half a century earlier, when the Imperial Treasury needed to raise forty million to finance the building of a railway. Barings was the czar's chief agent, but nearly every bank in Europe had dealings with the Russians, and occasionally floated their bonds. "The two million in Russian-owned gold imperials," Timothy murmured. "They're against a line of credit of five million. Correct?" He waited, but no one contradicted him. "As I see it, the way things are now, they're more of a liability than an asset. That leaves us with seventy-seven thousand of real liquidity."

"That's correct," Charles murmured.

Timothy turned to Norman. His voice was scathing. "Seventy-seven thousand pounds, Father? Against liabilities of what?" He glanced at the paper in front of him. "Sixteen million plus, I make it. Not counting the Paraguayan bond. Fairly slim, isn't it? Dangerously slim I'd say."

"Are you calling me to account?" Norman asked very softly.

Timothy's tone changed instantly. "No, sir, of course not. But we're under your stewardship, we all know that. So I'm asking what you suggest we do in this crisis?"

"Nothing," Norman said again. He leaned forward, both hands on the table, dominating the meeting by the sheer force of his personality. "Listen to me, all of you." He looked directly at his younger son. "You especially, Timothy. There is no crisis unless we say there is. There'll be talk, of course. Everyone in the City knows our issue failed. But it won't occur to any of them that Mendozas can't cover the debenture. Not unless we run around like bloody headless chickens and put the bloody idea in their bloody minds."

"But when the thirty days are up, sir?" Charles didn't seem to be able to raise his voice above a whisper this morning. "What then?"

"I'll get to that. First I want you to understand exactly what's at stake here. Henry and I have been through tight places before. It's you two who need to get it into your heads that any sign, the least hint of weakness, and the vultures will be all over us." He was still looking at Timothy. "It's your entire inheritance that's at risk, not merely a piece of it. You do understand that?"

"I do. Very well, sir." Timothy's voice was also low, but unlike his brother's, it was cool and self-possessed.

"Good." Norman turned to Henry. "Now, what exactly is the cargo situation?"

Henry ruffled through his papers once more. "The *Queens* aren't due back from the east until the first week in August." He spoke of the two ships that had replaced the *Queen Esther* and *Queen Judith* of their great grandfather's time. The old ships had been merchantmen, both new ones were wind-jammers. They plied the Orient trading for the Mendozas' own account.

"Both due at the same time?" Timothy asked.

"Yes," Henry said mildly. "We've always done it that way; double cargos coming to the floor of the exchange at the same time stir up the traders. The price is better."

Timothy nodded. He could feel his father's eyes on him. He knew the old man was aware of his objections to the double-cargo policy. They'd had a discussion about it some months before. "Yes, thank you, Uncle Henry. Please go on."

"Then there's the *Sarah Star* and the *Susannah Star*. The *Sarah* reached New York last week. She goes on to Caracas from there and won't be back in England until early September. The *Susannah*'s almost at the end of her run. She should call in at San Juan again in a few days and be in London some twelve days after that. By the eighth of July possibly." Henry finished his recital and turned to Norman. The two younger men did the same.

"Thank you," Norman murmured. "So with any luck we'll have the cargo of the *Susannah* to sell before the first debenture comes due. Coffee, sugar, and rum, isn't it, Henry?"

Henry nodded. "Yes, plus a couple of tons of copra."

"Then, speaking conservatively, we should see something in the range of a hundred thousand in profits from the *Susannah*'s hold." Norman looked into the three faces turned to his. "And there's Puerto Rico," he added, waiting until he was sure they'd absorbed the implication. "I cabled Luz this morning. Told him on no account was he to touch his reserves until he heard further from me."

Timothy stifled a sharply indrawn breath. Puerto Rico was a unique holding, unlike any other Mendoza interest. Nowhere else in the world did they have a true branch operation, let alone a bank not operated by members of the family. Timothy wondered why he'd left Puerto Rico out of all his calculations. That might have been a bad misjudgment.

Henry's eyes had lost some of their haunted look. "Yes, of course. Puerto Rico. And, Norman, if it were necessary, surely we could look to Córdoba for temporary support?"

"I'm sure we could. I've already alerted Francisco." Norman stood up, glanced at his fob watch, then tucked it back in the pocket of his silk waistcoat. "Now, gentlemen, there is still the day's business to transact. I suggest we each lunch out today. Separately. It won't be a bad thing if the various principals of this establishment are seen to be enjoying their food and looking quite unworried." He paused to be sure the three men had understood, then left the room.

Martha Clancy listened at the door of the upstairs front bedroom for a moment, then let herself in without knocking. It was nearly noon, but loud snores told her the two men were still asleep. Small wonder. They'd not arrived until three in the morning, and both of them looked exhausted. She'd shown them to their room without even taking the time to ask about her sons.

She was carrying two tin mugs of steaming tea on a tray and she set it on the stand with the mirror that had been a dressing table for the Black Widow. Lord, the different characters who passed through her little house! Who would believe that the two lumps now sharing the only bed in the room would have anything in common with the great lady who had warmed it before them.

"Sure and it's gone noon," she said, shaking the older man because he was sleeping on the outside. "You said to wake you."

Paddy Shea snored louder in protest, but the younger one, whom she knew only as O'Leary, sat bolt upright in the bed. "What time is it, mam?"

Martha smiled at being taken for his mother. "I'm not your mam, lad," she said gently. "I'm Mrs. Clancy, and your in me house on Thorparch Road in London. And it's five past twelve now. This one said you were to be called at noon." She pointed to the still-sleeping Paddy Shea.

O'Leary was rubbing the sleep from his eyes. He couldn't be more than sixteen, Martha thought. Sweet Mother of God, what kind of a world was it when boys of sixteen had to join a secret army and fight for what should be theirs by right? "I've brought you some tea," she said. "Get him up and come down to the kitchen for your breakfast. It'll be waiting for ye. And there's a pitcher of water and a basin behind that curtain, so's you can have a bit of a wash first."

Fifteen minutes later the men were in Martha's kitchen eating bacon and eggs and soda bread, and drinking yet more of her tea. " 'Tis, a wet day," Paddy Shea murmured.

Martha glanced out the window. "Aye, 'tis that. Yesterday was fine. Pity you weren't here yesterday." She finished washing the pan she'd used to fry the bacon. "Would you care for a bit more butter?"

"I would, thanks," Shea said. "And don't think we'll eat ye out of house and home and leave the larder bare." He put a shilling on the scrubbed table. "This is for our bed and board."

"There's no need," Martha said, taking a crock of butter from the shelf above the sink and scooping out another egg-sized lump. "It's for the cause and we manage." She could think of no better way to spend the two pounds a month her husband brought home from the railroad.

"It's the rules of the brotherhood," Shea insisted, pushing the shilling toward her. "No takin' from the mouths of our own if it can be avoided."

Martha shrugged and took the coin and put it in the pocket of her apron. "How long will you be staying?"

"Sure and I don't know exactly. We're to get a message here."

Martha understood the Fenian's way of doing things. If they weren't so brilliantly disciplined, they'd have been finished long ago. "Will you wait in today, or go out?"

Shea glanced again at the window. "Not much of a day for going out."

O'Leary had been too occupied with his breakfast to talk. Now he wiped the last bit of egg from his plate with a thick slab of soda bread and slathered some of the fresh butter on top of it. "Sure and wouldn't I want to see a bit of London, since we're here?"

"You'll do as your told," Shea said sharply.

"I never said I wouldn't, just that I'd like to see the City if I could," the boy muttered.

"What's your Christian name, lad?" Martha asked.

"Donald, ma'am."

"Well, Donald O'Leary, I expect you'll have a chance to see London one of these days. Maybe you'll even get the chance to burn some little part of it." Her eyes misted with the vision of meting out to the English what they'd dealt to Ireland, then she shook her head and brought herself back to the present. "Do you by chance know any of me boys? I've three of 'em fighting for the cause. Frankie and Kevin and Sean. Do you know any of 'em?"

O'Leary shook his head. "Can't say as I do, ma'am."

"I know Frankie," Paddy Shea said. "Saw him less than a week past. Right as rain he was."

Martha blessed herself. "Thank God and all the saints. It's been—" The front door knocker interrupted her words. "Wait here and be quiet. I'll see who it is."

She returned to the kitchen two minutes later, carrying a note. "For yourself, Mr. Shea."

Paddy took the piece of paper and read it quickly. "There's someone coming to see us here tonight after dark."

"Fine," she said. "Then you know what's expected of you. So there's no reason the boy can't go out and walk about if he doesn't mind the rain, is there?"

"No," Shea admitted grudgingly. "I expect there isn't."

O'Leary smiled his thanks at Martha.

"There's a mackintosh in the front hall cupboard that will fit you," she told him. "You're welcome to the loan of it."

Shea watched the boy leave, then turned to her. "Are you all alone here since your lads are over across?"

It didn't occur to her to be frightened of him. They shared too much for that. "Me old man's with the railroad. He does long runs sometimes. He'll be back tomorrow morning."

Shea nodded. "Good, then he'll not mind me taking his chair and having a look at his newspaper, will he?" He settled himself into the cretonne-covered armchair beside the stove and picked up the folded copy of the *Daily News*. "Is there a match for me pipe, missus? And would ye be having another cup of tea in that pot?"

San Juan, Nine A.M.

The Church of San José was very old and very beautiful. Michael looked up at the elaborate vaulted roof, then switched his gaze to the splendid marble tomb of the explorer Ponce de León, and finally looked left to where an exquisitely carved Jesus hung in agony on an enormous cross. It was all an exercise in avoiding the obvious, the black-draped bier in front of the altar on which there was a heartbreakingly small coffin.

The body of Carmen, the twelve-year-old who had run away from Nuria's two weeks ago, had been found. Her corpse had washed ashore in San Juan Bay. Both her eyes had been gouged out and the nipples of her young breasts hacked away.

"*Requiesca in pace,*" the black-vested priest intoned. He was a Jesuit, somewhere in his forties, tall and slim, with the stance and the bearing of an aristocrat. Jesuits had been a presence on the island since the sixties, Michael had learned. He wasn't surprised to hear them accused of being deeply involved in Puerto Rico's muddled politics. Jesuits had been making a second career of politics for three centuries.

"Amen." The young server sang the two syllables in a long intonation that matched the priest's, and then he rose from his knees. The Mass was over, but the congregation waited for the priest to arm himself with holy water and lead the coffin and the mourners to the cemetery. When it came to ritual and symbolism, Michael thought, nobody did it better than the Catholics. But to what end?

The church was less than a quarter full. Michael stood at the rear, drawn to the funeral when he'd heard the story but aware of having no real place among the bereaved and grieving. Apart from him there were some twenty people present; the women from the house on the Calle Cruz accounted for half the number.

Nuria Sanchez stood near the bier in the position of chief mourner. She was wearing black and had wrapped a black turban around her head. Nuria was surrounded by nine females who didn't look like the whores they were by night. They could have been respectable Puerto Rican housewives. Some wore black; the rest had chosen subdued colors. There was a marked gap between the prostitutes and the handful of others in the congregation. A space had been left around them, as if they were contagious.

The priest and his acolyte walked up the center aisle and took their place in front of the bier. The pallbearers assembled, all black men, men who worked for Nuria, Michael noted. He recognized young Obadiah and the footman and

Samsón, the ancient driver, and three others. The mourners fell into place behind the coffin. Again those who weren't from the Calle Cruz separated themselves from the whores.

Michael waited for the procession to file past and go out into the hot sun of the plaza, then he too left. He'd not accompany them to the interment; it wasn't necessary and he had no desire to prolong his contact with this ugly, pointless sacrifice of a child to evil.

"Señor Curran," a voice said quietly on his left.

Michael turned. A man stood beside him, his skin leathery and creased, his body shrunken with age. Gnarled hands gripped a cane and the man leaned forward, putting all his slight weight on the stick. "Señor Curran," the man repeated. "I think we should talk."

Michael started to reply, but he was distracted. Something was detaining the procession in the plaza. Old Samsón was clutching his chest and gasping for breath. He'd had to release his grip on the coffin. There was a flurry of activity while they looked for a substitute. Michael whipped his gaze from the drama taking place a few yards away to the stranger at his side. "Who are you? What do you want to speak to me about?"

"I am Rosa, señor."

"Rosa! I've been looking for you."

"*Sí, señor, yo sé.* I came today because I was sure I would find you."

"Yes, well you have, but—wait here a minute. Don't leave, for God's sake. I need to talk to you. Wait," Michael repeated.

He did not like what was happening in the plaza. There was a bigger crowd out there, curious ghouls who'd appeared because of the terrible way the child had died. They were watching the proceedings with avidity, but now, one after another, men were peeling off from the throng and disappearing into side streets lest they be asked to take the place of the old coachman who was too ill to help carry the coffin.

Curran strode across the plaza, elbowing his way through

the crowd. He hadn't seen Nuria for two days, not since their argument on the way back from the market, but now he went directly to her. "*Doy mis pésames.* Can I help?"

She looked at him coldly for a moment, then apparently decided to forget her anger. She nodded acknowledgment of his condolences. "Thank you, it is only that Samsón is too old to carry anything in this heat. I told him but he insisted."

Michael hesitated a moment, casting one quick look back to where he'd left the man called Rosa. He couldn't see him over the heads of the crowd. "I'll take Samsón's place." He moved to join the pallbearers.

Nuria put her hand on his arm. "No. Thank you, but it isn't necessary. They've gone to fetch someone else from my house. Besides, you are too tall, you would unbalance the others." Her eyes were red rimmed, but she produced a smile. "And one white face among so many black ones would spoil the symmetry, wouldn't it?"

Michael grinned. He started to say something else, but yet another black man appeared, running quickly down the street they called the Cristo and pushing aside the people in his path. The newcomer nodded in Nuria's direction, then took Samsón's position among the pallbearers.

Nuria pressed Michael's arm in a gesture of gratitude, then moved into place behind the coffin. The Jesuit opened his prayer book and signaled to a young boy who raised a long pole topped with a crucifix and led them from the plaza.

Michael watched the procession until it disappeared up the Cristo. When at last he turned back, the crowd had dispersed. The cobbled space in front of the church was deserted. Rosa too was gone.

"Damn!" Michael cursed aloud. He'd been looking for the fellow since he arrived, but there were hundreds of people named Rosa in Puerto Rico and he'd had to be careful.

So far he'd found nothing. Well at least now he knew what the man looked like.

"Psst . . . Señor . . ."

The summons came from an arched doorway on his right. Michael saw the shadow of the old man lurking in its interior, glanced about him to be sure he was unobserved, then sauntered toward it casually. He didn't pause until he drew level with the place where Rosa was sheltering.

Michael ran his gaze around the windows overlooking the plaza. No one seemed to be watching. "Is all this secrecy necessary?" he asked without turning his head to look at the man called Rosa.

"Sí, señor. I think so. I think I must be very careful."

Michael bent down. The sun was reflected back into his eyes by the ubiquitous blue cobblestones. There were none like them indigenous to the island. People said they'd been brought here as ballast in the Spanish ships. He pretended to be examining the lacing of his shoe. "I have to talk to you."

"I know. Come to the *taverna* of the rooster in the Callejon de las Monjas tonight at ten. *Adiós*, señor."

Michael grunted assent, then straightened and walked on.

London, Eleven P.M.

Jesus God almighty, wasn't it ever going to stop pissing down rain? Paddy Shea listened to the drumming sound on the windows of the kitchen on Thorparch Road. English rain was different, he decided. In Ireland rain was a gentle thing he was well used to, this was an angry outburst from the heavens which had continued all day without let up. "Is there another drop in that bottle, lad?"

O'Leary passed him the whiskey. "What time did the note say?"

"No time. Only after dark."

"Well, it's long past that."

"Sure, don't I know it? There's nothing for it. We have to wait, that's all."

"Who are we waiting for?"

"I don't know."

O'Leary got up from his chair; it was hard and cushion-less. Paddy had commandeered the only comfortable seat in the room. The boy took a small shovel of coal from the scuttle and tipped it into the maw of the stove. "We should give Mrs. Clancy another six pence for the fuel we're using."

"Aye. If I had a spare tanner I'd consider it. But I don't."

O'Leary knew that was a lie. Shea had been given ten shillings to cover the costs of the journey. If he hadn't spent a shilling on a bottle of whiskey he could pay a bit more to the woman. The boy didn't voice his thoughts as Paddy was his senior in Fenian rank as well as age. "Coal doesn't smell good like peat, does it?" he asked instead.

"Nothing smells good in London. The whole town stinks of the English."

"If we—" O'Leary broke off at the sound of footsteps in the hall. The door to the kitchen swung open and Mrs. Clancy came in. There was a man behind her.

"Here's your visitor then. I'll be waiting in the front room to lock up when you've done."

There was no fire in the front room. O'Leary had noticed the empty grate when he came back from his walk around Vauxhall and Nine Elms. Nice Mrs. Clancy would be cold. Damn Paddy Shea! Good thing if he choked to death on his bloody whiskey.

"A good evening to you, gentleman," the newcomer said, throwing back the hood of his flowing oilskin cape. "It's happy I am to see you arrived safe and sound."

He was dead bald, that was the thing O'Leary noticed first. But tall, and handsome with it. He'd never have be-lieved a man could look fine without hair. And didn't he have a gimpy leg, and now that he had the cape off, wasn't he dressed like a workman? Aye, all of that, but he was important. You could tell it by the smell of him, by the way his eyes took in everything in the room, all at once and sort of without moving. And the way Paddy Shea jumped to his feet.

"Sure and it's yourself is it, Fergus Kelly? I didn't know ye were one of us when I saw ye in Dublin."

"You don't have to know more than you need," Kelly said.

He perched on the corner of Mrs. Clancy's table, taking the weight off his bad leg. Paddy rushed to pour a tot of the whiskey into one of the tin mugs. The bald man took it without a word and tossed it back. "Sure and that's welcome on a night like this. Now lads, I've your instructions and they're plain as can be. You'll have no trouble."

O'Leary caught his breath, waiting to hear what they'd been sent to London to do. He'd been thinking about it all day while he roamed the district around Thorparch Road. It was a poor area until he went as far as Vauxhall Pleasure Gardens. Now that had seemed a fine target. They could blow it up at night when no one was there, if only someone would give them some dynamite and the order to proceed.

The older Fenians kept saying they must wait, that there was no point in doing anything until the time was right for them all to rise together and throw the bastard British out of Ireland once and for all. But sure, hadn't some of the others advised differently, and wasn't he all but certain that he and Paddy Shea had been chosen to strike the first blow?

Kelly took a small parcel from his pocket. O'Leary eyed it. Did dynamite come in as small a package as that? Enough to do any real damage? Sure, how could he know? He'd never seen even one stick of the stuff.

Fergus Kelly handled the parcel without any particular care, gesturing with it as he explained. "You're to leave London in a few hours by the early Liverpool train, then take the ferry over across. Day after tomorrow, when you're back in Dublin, the lad here is to bring this to Mountjoy Street." Another wave of the parcel. "Ten sharp in the morning. Don't be late or I'll see you hung from the nearest tree. There'll be a man at the bottom of the road. He'll have a bicycle and be kneeling beside it fixing the wheel." Kelly turned to O'Leary. "You say, 'Did you run over a cat?' Can you remember that?"

O'Leary stared at him. Holy mother of God, was this all there was to be, a foolish errand any nipper could do as well? "Did you run over a cat?" he repeated woodenly. "It's not much to remember."

Kelly nodded. "Good. The fellow with the bike, he'll say, 'Yes, there are far too many cats in Dublin these days.' When he says it, if he says it, you'll know you've got the right man."

"Then what?" O'Leary asked, hoping the next bit would be more dramatic.

"Then you give him this packet and take yourself off."

"That's all?" Paddy Shea asked. He was trying hard not to show his amazement and his relief. His belly had been quivering with fear since the council said he must go to London. The thought that he might actually have to do something to prove his Fenian loyalties, something that could land him in jail or worse, had terrified him. If he'd known any way to get out of it he'd have done so. But he didn't, so he came. And now this. It was simple enough for a baby to do. Best of all, he didn't have to do it. Whatever risks there might be were the lad's. "Is that all?" he repeated.

"Aye, that's all. There was something else possible, but—" Kelly shrugged. "It did not develop as I expected."

Shea blessed his luck. Still, it couldn't be that easy; he didn't believe in miracles. "What's in there, then?" He gestured to the package. "What are we carrying back?"

"Sure and don't you know better than to ask," Kelly said

quietly. "And you one of the brothers these past twenty years."

"But—"

"Don't plague me with your *but*'s, Paddy Shea." Kelly got up from the table and put his empty mug in the sink. "Here's the packet. Take it and do exactly as you're told. There's nothing else you need be knowing."

Shea accepted the package. It was really nothing but a big envelope, a bit smaller than the one this same Fergus Kelly had left for the Englishman a couple of weeks past in Dublin, but it too was tied with string and sealed with blobs of red wax. He'd not be able to open it and have a peek inside because there was some kind of design pressed into the wax, and he'd never be able to reproduce that.

Kelly fastened the buttons of his long rain cape and slipped the hood over his head. It shadowed his face completely; O'Leary thought he looked like some kind of strange monk. "Good night to you, boys. God speed the journey."

Martha Clancy stood waiting by the door of the front room when the lame man came into the hall. "It's glad I am you're still here," Fergus Kelly said, reaching for her hand and pressing something into it.

She glanced down. What had been left in her palm was a folded bit of money. Martha recognized the five-pound note, though she'd never actually held one before. "Glory be to God and His mother! And what am I to do with this?"

"It's for your good work for the cause," Fergus said. "The council know full well that you're out of pocket looking after so many of our people. This will go some way to putting that right."

"Some way? Sure it's more money than ever I seen at one time in me life." She tried to give it back to him. "There must be some mistake. How can the council afford to give me better than me Joe earns in two months, and for nothing but doing me duty like a good Irishwoman?"

"And haven't you been giving us safe harbor for more than two years?" Kelly insisted. "It's only a bit of help. Take it and use it for whatever you need. Now, I'm late, so if you'll see me out I'll be grateful."

She took the key from her apron pocket and unlocked the front door, still staring in amazement at the lame man and clutching the five-pound note in a tight fist.

"Ach, the rain's stopped," Kelly murmured as he stepped into the street. "That's a good omen I think."

Across the way and out of sight another man was also grateful for the end of the storm.

San Juan, Ten P.M.

A short distance from one of the gates that pierced the seventeenth-century walls of the town was the Callejon de las Monjas, the Alley of the Nuns. It was another of San Juan's step streets, climbing a steep hill by the device of broad stairs.

Whatever nuns had given the alley its name were gone, but at the top of the passage was a door decorated with a crude but colorful drawing of a rooster. Michael pushed the door open and entered the Taverna El Gallo. There was a lot of smoke and noise. The place was crowded, and in true Puerto Rican fashion everyone was talking at once. Two men sat in one corner; one strumming a guitar, the other playing the Puerto Rican güiro, a kind of maracas. Apparently they were unperturbed by the fact that no one was listening.

Michael too ignored the music. He elbowed through the throng to the bar and ordered a rum punch. The barman gave it to him and took his money, but didn't move away. "You are looking for someone, señor?"

"I might be," Curran said easily. "It depends on who's here."

"Many interesting people, señor. Perhaps the most interesting is down those stairs." He jerked his head toward a narrow flight of steps half-hidden by stacked baskets containing the ubiquitous dried fish the islanders prized.

"Thanks, I'll see for myself."

Michael waited a moment then carried his drink toward the stairs. The smell of fish became overwhelming. His stomach lurched. He ducked his head quickly and hurried down the narrow steps. When he reached the bottom he was in a long narrow cellar, lit by flickering candles impaled on upturned nails punched at random into the thick walls of the building.

"Over here, Mr. Curran," a voice called in English. "I have been waiting for you."

The old man was sitting on an upturned keg. His feet didn't reach the floor. Michael moved closer, then raised his glass. "Good evening, Señor Rosa. To your very good health. I didn't realize you spoke English."

"And to your health, Mr. Curran." Rosa too had a glass. He lifted it in response to Michael's toast. "My English. Yes. But I am showing off, reminding myself of earlier times. And . . ." He shrugged. "It doesn't matter, now is now. We should live in the present, eh?"

"So the philosophers tell us."

"Sí. And I think we will speak in Spanish and I will stop being a vain old man. ¿Qué pasa con su madre?"

"As far as I know she's well. I left Ireland some weeks ago and I haven't seen her since."

"Difficult times," the old man said softly, "when families must be separated. But necessary sometimes, eh?"

Michael nodded and waited.

"So you are here," Rosa said after a few seconds pause. "I was not sure it would come to pass, despite the señora's assurances."

"My mother usually does exactly what she says she'll do."

"Yes, I know. And me?" he asked. "What has the lady told you about me?"

"Not a great deal. Only that you were here and that I should find you. That you would be an ally."

Rosa nodded, then gestured toward another of the up-turned kegs. "Sit down, señor. We have much to discuss."

Michael accepted the invitation while studying the other man. Today in the plaza he'd thought Rosa a simple Puerto Rican campesino, a peasant. Obviously he wasn't that. His clothes were unremarkable, but there was something distinguished about him. Moreover, he didn't have a Puerto Rican accent. Now that Michael had heard him do more than whisper a few words he recognized that the old man's Spanish was pure Castilian. "You are originally from the peninsula, are you not, Señor Rosa?"

"*Sí.* From Madrid. I have been here about ten years. My wife died before I came, but my son is with me. I expect you have met my son. He is the barman upstairs."

"Yes. He hinted rather broadly that I'd find you down here."

Rosa laughed. "It's a good thing you are so easy to identify, Señor Curran. Pedro is not particularly subtle. That was one of the reasons I brought him here."

"Oh, is Puerto Rico better than Madrid for those without the gift of subtlety?"

"In some cases. Do you know my full name, señor?"

"No. If I had, I'd have found you before this."

"She didn't tell you," the old man mused. "That is strange, and perhaps interesting."

"Unlike your son, my mother is very subtle. She probably had her reasons. What is your full name?"

"Ah yes. It is Israel Rosa Salzedo. What does that tell you?"

Israel was self explanatory; *Rosa* so common as to be meaningless; *Salzedo,* which would have been the old man's mother's name, was also that of well-known textile manufacturers originally from France, now ensconced in the north of Spain. Michael could see no point in fencing. "If you're mother was a Salzedo I presume you're a Jew."

"You are correct."

"And is that the basis of your alliance with my mother?"

"Let us say it is the starting point. Things have changed in Spain. Since 1854 it is legal for a Jew to be in the country. Not to build a synagogue, mind, or to hold a public wedding or funeral. We can be there, but no one must see us. Do you imagine they think we are contagious?" The old man chuckled and didn't wait for an answer. "Still, it is better than banishment, isn't it? It must be. In Madrid there are now a large number of Jews. But not me. Me, I am here in Puerto Rico."

Michael waited for some further explanation, but there was none. "Listen," Rosa said, "over there behind you is some more of this excellent local rum. Perhaps you could get it."

Michael found the jug and refilled their glasses. Rosa sipped a bit, as if he were tasting wine, then nodded his head in approval and took a large swallow. "Was the map satisfactory?"

"Very. I found the convent."

"Good. And did you see Sister Magdalena?"

"I saw her."

"And?"

Michael didn't answer immediately. "How much of my mother's story do you know?" he asked finally.

"I know that she is a very wealthy lady, and that she plans to use that wealth to achieve something for our people."

Could you interpret Lila's intentions that way? Michael wondered. Perhaps. But if Lila struck some kind of blow for universal Judaism, it would be by accident. Her plans had to do with vengeance, and with regaining what she considered hers—and his. The commitment to restoring a Jewish house of Mendoza in Córdoba was important to others. To

Lila, and to him, it was simply part of the bargain she'd made. Rosa was watching him; Michael had to say something. "Yes, that will be one outcome of the plan," he admitted.

"Good. And Sister Magdalena's role?"

"Frankly, I'm not sure. What do you know about her?"

"About the nun? Very little. Let me explain. Your mother and I met some years ago, before I came here. Then we happened to see each other again in London. I was on my way to Puerto Rico at the time and the señora asked me to locate a woman. She knew only her first name, Nieves. But an extraordinary woman, a seer." He shrugged. "There are never too many seers in one place. Eventually I discovered that this Nieves was now Sister Magdalena of the convent in the hills. I wrote and gave Doña Lila those facts. That's as much as I know."

Michael's stomach was churning, but he kept the excitement from showing. "When you were tracing her, what did you discover?"

Rosa was puzzled. "What I have told you, what I told your mother."

"Yes, I know. But the line you followed, what else did it reveal?"

The old man shrugged. "Nothing particularly interesting. She was an orphan in Ponce, then she became a nun. Now they say she is a seer. But such rumors appear in the air on this island. The Puerto Ricans are very credulous people. That child they buried today, do you know what her death meant?"

"What can such a death mean?"

"Witchcraft." Rosa spat out the word. "The way her body was mutilated was because she was used in a ceremony having to do with witchcraft. Voodoo." Curran saw him shiver. "Do you know about voodoo?"

"Not really. Something to do with fetishes, isn't it? A lot of superstition."

"Superstition? Not entirely. The fetishes, for example. If someone makes a doll and puts your name on it, I suggest you be very careful, Señor Curran. Black magic is not something you should trifle with."

"And is there a lot of black magic, of voodoo, here in Puerto Rico?"

"I am told that there was not until recently. But now, with the slaves freed, moving from island to island in the Indies, it is everywhere. Haiti has always been the worst, and some of the Haitians have come here."

Michael was fascinated, but this wasn't what he'd come here to discuss. "Señor Rosa, if I have need of more help, can I count on you?"

"Of course. A month ago I had another letter from your mother, the first in some time. She said you were coming, that perhaps I could be of some assistance to you. That is why I made myself known."

There was more to it than that. Rosa was no altruist worrying only about his religion. There would have to be other rewards, but if he earned them, Michael wouldn't be reluctant to grant them.

The old man wore a filthy and misshapen straw hat. Now he took it off and revealed a stained sweatband from which he removed a small piece of paper. "Here is the address of my house. You can always find me, either there or here in the *taverna*. But please, señor, I beg you to be discreet. The things you are doing on this island, I do not think it is very wise to be seen to be too friendly with you."

Michael was startled. "What things?"

"The coffee haciendas, señor. Rumors breed in the air in Puerto Rico, as I told you. And your friendship with the *doña de las putas*."

"Is that what they call Nuria Sanchez, the lady of the whores?"

"Some people do. Other people have worse names. Of

course there are also a few better ones. There are some who say she's an angel of mercy."

"And you? What do you think?"

"Me, I think that we all do what we have to do to survive, Señor Curran. It says in the Talmud—" He broke off with another shrug. "I am rambling, the Talmud is not one of your interests. But I will tell you something, señor. You and me and Señorita Sanchez, even the holy nun up in the hills, we're none of us any different. First we survive—doing good or doing evil comes after that."

Upstairs Pedro was busy at the bar. He barely glanced at the tall Irishman. The *taverna* was full of men, all drinking and talking. The güiro player had disappeared and the guitarist had been joined by a pair of flamenco singers. They were shouting out the Gypsy rhythms of Andalusia, making up in volume what they lacked in skill.

Michael paused and listened a moment, but the musicians were neither good nor authentic. He thought about his great-grandparents, Robert the Turncoat and La Gitanita, the legendary Gypsy singer whose music had united a war-torn nation.

What a woman she must have been. His aunt Beatriz had told him the story. How after Sofía and Robert were married she went to France and found her family but discovered that the Jews of Bordeaux had lost nearly everything in the Reign of Terror. Sofía sang for them too, the old religious melodies she'd never truly forgotten and her Gypsy songs were for the people. Her concerts raised enough money to restore the little synagogue where her grandfather had taken her as a child. Then, when she returned to Andalusia, she'd been summoned by the Inquisition—and denied everything and faced them down.

"She told them she wasn't a Jew, she denied her God, because she knew it was a war," Beatriz had told him. "That she was doing battle for her people, and if you have to lie to win, then that is what you do."

"What about me?" he'd asked. "Am I a Jew too?"

Beatriz hadn't answered right away. Then she'd put her hand over his heart. "Here, maybe. Because you are a Mendoza. But you must never tell your father I have said so. Juan Luis is . . . different. Perhaps if my father had lived longer it would not be so. My mother said that he—my father, Rafael, the son of Robert and Sofía—had a secret to tell Juan Luis when he was old enough. Whatever it was, Papa died before he could pass it on. In a tragic accident. He left only the medallion."

Michael had been eight years old when that conversation took place. He had been puzzled about the medallion, and the motto that reminded them never to forget Jerusalem, and the secret that had perished with his grandfather, but he had never forgotten the conversation. Neither had he forgotten the time Beatriz took him to Seville to hear the Gypsies sing in their caves in the Triana.

For a few more seconds Michael listened to the music in the *taverna*, then walked away. He knew the difference between good and bad flamenco. But the man called Rosa was right: good and bad people were a more difficult proposition.

PART TWO

The Final
Three Weeks

❧ 10 ❧

SATURDAY, JULY 3, 1898
San Juan, Noon

Sweet bloody Jesus, it was hot. Michael had spent the morning roaming the streets of San Juan. Everywhere the talk was the same. People huddled on street corners and spoke in agitated whispers about the news published that morning. The first land battle of the war with the Americans had been fought in Cuba, and lost. San Juan Hill had been taken. The victors were no longer navy men the Puerto Ricans had never heard of. The names Roosevelt and Rough-riders punctuated the excited Spanish chatter.

When Michael heard enough people tell him that Puerto Rico was still not a target of the *norteamericanos*, he was convinced that nothing much had changed on the island. Moreover, the heat was a stifling blanket. He decided to return to the inn.

Ten minutes later he walked into his room with his suit-coat over his arm. He'd removed his collar and tie while he climbed the stairs, and now he began unbuttoning his shirt.

"Hello, Michael."

Briggs had drawn the curtains against the morning sun

and the room was dark. Michael stood in the doorway and blinked, trying to see who had spoken. The voice was familiar, but he rejected as impossible the name that sprang to mind. "Who's there?"

"Have you forgotten me so quickly, Michael?" The question wasn't serious. It had laughter behind it, the pleasure of someone who knows quite well they're not forgotten, who expects to be welcomed with joy. Beth Mendoza reached over and pulled the cord that parted the drapes at the window, opening them just enough for the midday glare to throw a searching shaft of white light into the room.

"Jesus bloody God," Michael murmured. "I don't believe it. In the name of all the hounds of hell, how did you get here?"

"On a ship. Two ships in fact. It was the most terrible journey. But that doesn't matter now. I've left Timothy."

"You've what?"

"Left him. He went to Dublin for a few days and I saw my chance and took it. I'd already made up my mind, of course. I did that the last time we were together in London."

"Your mind. . . . Did you think to talk to me about it?"

"Naturally not. You'd have made a lot of noises about not wanting to be dishonorable, about not having enough to offer me."

"Not having a settled place in society to offer you, yes. But—"

"Michael, you are happy to see me, aren't you?"

She sounded like a little girl. He was helpless to resist her when she used that tone. Besides, she looked exhausted. Lovely, but pale—and thinner than he remembered. He was still standing by the door holding his jacket and collar and tie; he flung them on the bed and crossed to her. "Of course I'm glad to see you. I was taken aback, that's all. Your coming here is pretty much the last thing I expected."

"I suppose that's true. But I am here. At least I think I

am." She lifted her face to his. "Kiss me, Michael, so I'll be convinced."

She smelled of lavender, as always, and he experienced her daintiness pressed to his brawn with the same shock of pleasure the contact always provided. It was as it had been for the past year of clandestine meetings in London and Dublin. But it wasn't. Michael didn't know what was different, only that something was. She moved closer, nestling against him with a sigh of contentment. He dismissed the question and bent himself to the task at hand.

It was after one when Beth rose from the bed. "Is there a bath?" she asked, wrapping her nakedness in the thin cotton blanket they'd discarded.

He lay on the sweaty sheet in nothing but his skin, arms folded behind his head. His earlier discomfort at her surprise arrival had faded in the delight of bedding her. The sensation of being satisfied was extremely pleasant, rather like the way he felt rising from the table after an especially good dinner. Only better. "Yes, of course, right down the hall. I'll have Briggs—" Michael broke off, he couldn't very well ask his valet to prepare a bath for her. "Listen," he said instead. "Where are you staying?"

"Here. Tillie's with me. We docked this morning and I asked for the best inn in the town and was sent here. So I took two rooms. I wanted a suite, but the innkeeper looked at me as if I had two heads."

"I don't doubt it. This place doesn't run to suites. How did you communicate with the landlord? I didn't think he spoke any English."

"He doesn't. I brought one of the ship's crew with me to translate." She had walked to the balcony doors and was peeping through the curtains. "Not very prepossessing, is it?"

"San Juan? I suppose it isn't. It has its points, though."

"What are they?"

He knew what she was actually asking, What are you doing here? Michael cursed the unguarded moment when he'd told her he was going to Puerto Rico—and was amazed at his own reaction. Why wasn't he thrilled to see her, to have her come all this way in pursuit of him? It was a question that didn't bear examining. "If Tillie's with you, hadn't you best go back to your own room and arrange a bath from there?"

"I suppose that would be more discreet. Do we still have to be discreet, Michael?"

"I think so, yes. At least until my business is completed."

She shrugged and, being Beth, made the gesture look elegant. "Very well, if we must."

"Did the landlord tell you the number of my room?"

"Of course. How would I have discovered it otherwise?"

"I don't know."

"I asked for the room of the tall Irishman and he told me, it was as simple as that."

"Through the interpreter?"

"Michael, you are asking the most extraordinary questions. Of course through the interpreter. How else?"

"I don't know," he repeated. What he did know was that it was now all over the island that a beautiful señorita *estranjera* had come to join the Irishman. It probably didn't make any difference to the negotiations, but it was a new and unplanned element and that made him nervous.

Beth had wandered to the single table in the room. A white envelope was propped in one corner. "What's this? It looks like an invitation."

"It is. The governor general of the island is giving a ball at his mansion. It's known as La Fortaleza."

"How exciting. When?"

"Tonight as it happens."

"Really? A ball, how wonderful. You'll take me, won't you? You can introduce me as your fiancée."

He couldn't think of any polite way to refuse. "Yes, if

you wish. But right now . . . Beth, don't you think you'd best get dressed?"

She dropped the invitation and turned to her hastily discarded pile of clothes with a frown of distaste. "I can't bear to put those back on before I bathe."

Michael swung his legs over the side of the bed and stood up. "What's your room number?"

"Eleven. It's on this same floor."

"That's easy then." He was putting on his trousers, pulling the braces up over his bare shoulders. "We'll wait until the coast is clear, then I'll whisk you down there."

A moment later he had opened the door and stuck his head into the corridor. "Fine, no one's around. It's *siesta* time; nobody moves again until after four." He left the door ajar and gathered her into his arms, blanket and all. "This way you won't have to walk down the hall in your bare feet."

"My clothes," she murmured, wrapping her arms around his neck and nuzzling his cheek. "You know, I think you're bigger and stronger than ever."

Michael held her with one arm and picked up the pile of silk and cotton and lace with his free hand. The scent of lavender grew suddenly intense. "Here we go."

It took less than a minute to transport Beth and all her finery to her own quarters. The door was unlocked and the room was, if anything, poorer than his. "Look, you can't possibly be comfortable here," he said looking around.

"Well, it is not the Paris Ritz. But if there was somewhere better, surely you'd have moved there."

"You're right, I would have and there isn't. But I have to stay on the island; you don't. I'd best book you passage to New York as soon as I can. You can wait for me there. I'll come the minute my business here is finished."

Beth didn't seem to be listening to him. She was knocking on the wall and calling for her maid. "Tillie's room is right next door, but she doesn't answer." She turned to him with a pout. "Where can she have gone?"

"I can't say. Listen, darling, did you hear what I suggested about New York?"

"Of course I heard. But I'm not going anywhere without you. Michael, I have really done it. You don't seem to realize that yet. I've burned all my bridges behind me so that we can be together the way we've dreamed of being. Now you're suggesting that we be separated again. That simply doesn't make sense. I can survive here as long as necessary. I'm sure you're not anxious to remain one minute more than you must."

He sighed, then said, "I'll go see if I can find Tillie and send her to you."

It took him five minutes of searching to discover Beth's maid. Tillie was sitting in the inn's kitchen with Briggs. The former cook had made friends with the kitchen staff, and now he used the place as if it were his private club. At the moment the locals were taking their siestas and the English pair was alone.

Briggs jumped to his feet as soon as he saw his employer. "Were you wanting me, sir? Right sorry I am, but you usually don't need me during siesta time. And you'll never guess what's happened, Mr. Curran."

"No, I suppose I won't unless you tell me." Michael looked at the man and the woman and at the two mugs of tea on the table. "I see you two have met."

"That's just it, sir. We didn't have to meet. Tillie's me sister."

"Your sister?"

"Yes, sir. She went into service round the same time I went to sea."

"And haven't you and Tillie seen each other since then?"

Tillie answered before Briggs could. "'Course we have, Mr. Curran. Not seen exactly, but we wrote letters."

Tillie knew Curran well. From the first she'd been party

to what was going on between him and Beth. Most of the messages that passed between them had been carried by the maid. Looking at her now Michael felt as if a deep quagmire was opening up in front of him, a squirming pit he'd thought he left behind. Tillie didn't seem to read anything at all in his face.

"Sends each other a letter we do, me and Tom here, every Christmas. Have done since I went away to be nurse to Mrs. Mendoza, when she was little Miss Turner I mean. Did you never know my surname was Briggs, Mr. Curran?"

"No, Tillie, I didn't." And if he had he'd have forgotten it. The names of servants were not among his chief priorities.

"Isn't it strange and wonderful though," Tillie continued. "Me and Tom fetching up here in this foreign place? Both of us at the same time? Right marvelous I calls it."

"Marvelous indeed, something to wonder at. But now, Tillie, your mistress wants you. She's in her room."

"Off I go," Tillie said cheerily. She paused long enough to give the beaming Briggs a big kiss on one seamed cheek, and to drop a curtsy in Curran's direction. He might be imagining things, but he thought the politeness was accompanied by something like a smirk. No, he decided, it's just a conspiratorial smile. "Right marvelous," Tillie murmured as she hurried away.

Michael remained in the kitchen, staring at Briggs, not knowing exactly how to explain, or why he should find it necessary to explain anything. "Tom," he said finally. "So that's your Christian name."

"Yes, sir. Thomas Archibald Briggs. That was me christening name. Ain't hardly anybody what calls me anything but Briggs now, though. 'Ceptin' Tillie."

"Well, Thomas Archibald Briggs, I think I would like a cup of tea. What's the condition of that pot?" Michael gestured to the teapot on the table. Like the tea itself, the pot was a rarity on Puerto Rico. Briggs had wheedled both luxuries from the quartermaster of the *Susannah Star* when they first arrived in Puerto Rico.

"Stewed it'll be, sir. Been sittin' there more'n an hour while Tillie and me had our natter. I'll make you some fresh right away. Won't take but a minute; kettle's boiling on the back of the stove. I'll bring it right up."

"Don't bother." Michael sat down on the rough three-legged stool Tillie had been using a moment earlier, groaning inwardly at the thought of the details of his private life that she must have shared with her brother during the course of an hour's talk. "I'll take it right here."

Somehow at this moment the kitchen felt safer than his room upstairs.

Westlake, Five P.M.

Beatriz Mendoza was bored with life in the country. She'd been a guest at Jamie's estate for ten days, and her cousin and his wife had pressed her to remain at least another week. "Pity you can't see my girls, but they're touring the Continent until the end of the month," Jamie had said, referring to his four daughters. "Still, if you stay on you can see the lilies. They'll be at their best in a few days. You mustn't miss the lilies."

"Mustn't I, why not?"

"Hang it all, Beatriz, you ask the damndest questions. Because they're beautiful."

"And beauty is its own reward." She'd quoted the English saying with a sigh. "I suppose I cannot be expected to understand, since I am not beautiful."

"Why do you always denegrate yourself, Beatriz? You're really very attractive." That had come from Jamie's wife, Caroline. Naturally Caroline was as exquisite as a porcelain figurine; Jamie wouldn't have married her otherwise.

Beatriz did not remind her that as a beautiful woman she

knew nothing of the feelings of one less favored. Instead she merely said, "Thank you, Caroline. And yes, if you will have me, I would be delighted to remain and see your lilies."

So she was still here, but the decision to remain had nothing to do with flowers; it was because she'd had a note from Lila the day before. In carefully masked terms Lila had said that the Cordobés part of the operation was to begin very shortly. Beatriz wanted to be somewhere entirely apart from that *zarzuela* when the pot began to be stirred.

"How big is this place exactly?" she asked now, sipping her China tea.

She and Caroline were alone on the terrace. Jamie's wife refilled their cups, then glanced at the south lawn, which rolled gently toward massed rhododendrons circling a man-made pond. The fells, those bare green hills surrounding the natural lakes that abounded in this region could be seen over the top of the shrubbery. "Do you mean how many acres? I'm not really sure. Hundreds and hundreds."

"No," Beatriz corrected. "I meant the house."

"Oh. Two hundred and forty rooms. It's horrific isn't it? A horrific old pile." The look on Caroline's face made it obvious that she didn't consider the tudor house horrific in the least.

"More than twice as many rooms as we have at the *palacio* in Córdoba. But you don't refer to Westlake as a palace."

"English understatement," Caroline said with a smile.

Beatriz shifted her position in the white wrought-iron chair. She had ample natural padding and there was a cushion on the chair, still its hardness was beginning to tell on her. "Where is Jamie?" If her cousin came and had his tea they could all go inside and disappear to their separate haunts until it was time for drinks before dinner. Beatriz could go to her room and lie in her bed and read for an hour or two.

"I'm not sure," Caroline said. "He seems to be disappearing rather a lot these days, doesn't he? He's always writing long letters to Norman in London."

"Oh? Is there trouble at the bank?" Beatriz regretted the words the instant she spoke them. She was trying hard to look innocent, but it would be far better to pretend total ignorance of all things financial.

Caroline waved the question away with an airy gesture. "I haven't the faintest idea, darling. I leave all such matters to the gentlemen. Don't you?"

"Of course." Beatriz helped herself to a third strawberry tart. There was absolutely nothing to do in this place except eat. She'd need a new wardrobe by the time she left Westlake.

"There you are, my dears. I've been looking for you. Tea on the terrace, I should have guessed. Where else on a day like this? Sorry to be late." Jamie kissed both his wife's cheek and his cousin's. "Well, Beatriz, what have you been doing this afternoon?"

I have been wondering what is going to happen to this place when you are ruined. No, of course she would not say that. "I looked at purple flowers. Not lilies, what do you call them, eeris?"

"Iris." Jamie corrected her pronunciation automatically and took the cup of tea his wife offered him. It was one of the rules of living he'd established as soon as Westlake became his; no butler to serve at teatime, not if there was a lady present. One of the prettiest things to watch in the world was a graceful lady pouring tea. He allowed himself a second to appreciate Caroline's mastery of the art, then turned back to Beatriz. "They're not all purple. Some of the irises are white and some yellow."

"Oh, I suppose I did not notice." She did, however, notice her cousin. Jamie looked ghastly lately; his smile was beginning to resemble a death's-head grimace. But Beatriz took her cue from Caroline, who pretended not to see the condition her husband was in.

Jamie seemed unaware of any scrutiny. "You don't understand my fascination with flowers, do you Beatriz?"

"I am afraid I do not."

He sipped the last the of his tea, refused more, and put the cup on the table. "Have you seen the yellow climbing rose over near the stables and in the Greek Garden?"

"I hate horses. I never go near the stables. The Greek Garden is the one with all the broken statues, no?"

"You might say. My father imported that statuary from Greece. There are some real rarities in that garden."

They'd all looked like castoffs to Beatriz. Each one was missing something—a head, a hand, an arm—and some were only fragments. To make peace she said, "I did notice a yellow flower. It was a rose?"

"Indeed. The most famous rose on the place, Cecil's Folly." Beatriz looked blank. "A folly's a mistake," Jamie explained. "Something you do that you shouldn't." He paused. "Follies generally produce quite terrible consequences."

He was suddenly cutting very close to the bone. Beatriz stared at him. Jamie stared back. They held the pose for a few seconds.

Caroline looked from her husband to her cousin-in-law, then leaned forward and took up a small silver bell. "I'll have the tea things cleared."

Jamie stayed her hand. "Let's not go in just yet, darling. It's so lovely out here. I'll tell Beatriz the story of Cecil's Folly."

Caroline had dark gray eyes, many people likened them to black pearls. When she was disturbed they grew even darker. They were almost opaque now. "If you wish." She fought back a rising sense of panic. It had been threatening her for days. Something terrible was afoot. Something about which she could only guess, but she knew it had placed them all on the edge of a disaster. "If you're sure Beatriz won't be bored by old family stories."

"No, of course not," Beatriz insisted. "It is my family too." She wouldn't drop her gaze from Jamie's face. He must be the first to look away.

Jamie obliged her by taking a gold case from his breast pocket and breaking the tension by lighting one of the oval Turkish cigarettes his tobacconist imported from Cairo only for him. "My father bought Westlake in 1825," he began. "It was a total ruin; no one had lived in it for over a hundred years. He acquired Gordon Square at the same time, incidentally. Commissioned it and had it built for less than three hundred pounds. A very far-sighted man my father. He chose Gordon Square because he anticipated how important the railway terminus at Euston Street be would would be and as it turned out he was the first Englishman to have a private railway car."

"How clever of him. Was that before or after he got his title? Jamie, may I try one of your cigarettes?"

"What? Oh, of course, if you wish. I never thought . . ." He handed one to her and lit it. Beatriz held it awkwardly but she puffed with some expertise, and she didn't cough. Damned woman must be a secret smoker as well as ugly as sin. She probably went to bed reeking of tobacco and wearing a cotton nightdress buttoned to the neck. Poor Francisco. "To answer your question, both houses were bought before Papa was made a peer."

"Yes," she said. "I thought so."

He ignored her tone, and the way Caroline was looking at them, and plunged ahead with the story. "Anyway, Papa had to be in London most of the time. Because of the business. So he installed Cecil, his young brother, up here in Westlake. The place was in ruins then. Papa meant Cecil to oversee the restoration, but my uncle was only interested in the grounds."

Beatriz made a face. "That's something I'll never understand about the English, this fascination with digging in the dirt."

Jamie chuckled softly. "Perhaps you won't. But this case was rather different. Papa was an only child until he was fifteen. Then grandmother suddenly produced twins, Cecil and Roger. Cecil was always very shy and strange. Loved flowers, but thought a good deal less of people. Anyway, he created most of the gardens you see now. And he went in for hybridizing roses in a big way. Papa had supplied him with a staff of twenty-six gardeners, but Uncle Cecil insisted on doing a lot of the physical labor himself. He worked on the hybridizing program out of doors in the rain all one week, and caught pneumonia and died." Jamie spoke the words with extraordinary emphasis, never taking his eyes from his cousin's face.

"Poor man," Beatriz said automatically while she thought, you suspect me, cousin James. I don't know how or why, but you do. "Is there a point I am not seeing?" she asked.

"I haven't explained it yet. Thing is, the rose Cecil was working on when he died turned out to be the first scented yellow climber in cultivation. Naturally enough, my father named it Cecil's Folly."

"Oh, I understand."

Jamie stubbed out his cigarette in a silver ashtray. "No, I doubt that you do yet. It's become extraordinarily popular, that yellow rose. You see it everywhere in the British Isles, from workmen's cottages to great estates. And that's the point. With us beautiful and successful things always rise from the ruins. That's our gift, Beatriz. That's the Mendoza legacy."

"But if you betray the legacy?" she asked. "If you do something to shame the family?"

Jamie smiled. "Being one of the Cordobés Mendozas," he said softly, "I expect you'd know more about the consequences of that than I would. Your side has been at it much longer, haven't they?"

San Juan, Late Afternoon

Michael tapped lightly on the door of room number 11. It was Tillie who answered his summons. She glanced over her shoulder at the bed, then stepped into the corridor and pulled the door shut behind her. "Mrs. Mendoza is sleeping, sir. She had a most trying journey. Do you want me to wake her?"

"No, not at all. I merely wanted to say I had to go out for a few hours. There's a ball tonight and I promised to take her, but it's only quarter to five and we won't be going much before eleven. That's how they do things here."

"Very well, sir. I'll tell Mrs. Mendoza."

Michael winced. "Tillie, do you know what name your mistress gave the landlord?"

"'Course I do. Miss Elizabeth Turner, same as we used when we was on them boats as brought us here."

"Good, very wise. Now I think it best if the fact that your employer is a married lady and a member of the Mendoza family remains our little secret. Do you think you could leave off using her legal name while you're here?"

The maid sniffed. "I can leave off whatever I'm told to leave off, Mr. Curran. Very discreet I am. And begging your pardon, sir, I'd expect you to know that."

"Yes, indeed I do. So we'll call the lady Miss Turner while she's in San Juan, all right?"

"All right. And she's to be ready for the ball at eleven this evening. Is that what I'm to tell her, sir?"

"Yes, that's it."

Tillie's curtsy was entirely perfunctory, and he thought he heard another sniff when she turned to go back to Beth's room. Damn, he'd have to make his peace with the woman.

She knew far too much to be made an enemy. A pox on all servants, Briggs included.

The sprightly black rig was waiting for him on the corner of the Calle Cruz. Michael saluted the footman with a wave but opened the door himself. His long legs required no assistance to bridge the gap between the carriage and the road.

"¡Hola! Michael." Nuria seemed genuinely pleased to see him. Her smile was warm and friendly. "You are exactly on time. I think it is quite amazing, this Irish habit of being punctual."

Michael laughed. "Any Englishman or Continental would be amazed to hear you say that. We're called the Spaniards of the British Isles. It's only compared to the real thing that we seem punctual."

The horses trotted off and the carriage moved through the town. There had been no need for Nuria to issue any instructions. Samsón knew exactly where they were going. This was an outing that had been planned for some time. Obviously Nuria had been looking forward to it. She was excited and lively, quick to smile and to laugh, unaware that Michael was barely listening.

Her attitude toward him had changed these past ten days. Michael had to force himself on her at first. Again and again he'd sought her out, driven to explore the mystery that he felt around her. Nothing he'd learned had explained how she could be both Nuria Sanchez and Sister Magdalena, but whether she was or she wasn't, somehow they'd become friends. His public offer to help carry the coffin on the day of Carmen's funeral had doubtless helped. And that was the one thing Michael had done without calculation.

Nuria broke off in the middle of an animated description of the skills of the man they were to meet, conscious at last that his thoughts were elsewhere. "What is it, Michael? Why do you look so grim?"

"Nothing really. I had a bit of a shock this afternoon, that's all."

"What kind of a shock? Something to do with your business?"

"Not exactly."

She waited, but he said no more. "So never mind, you do not wish to tell me. I don't care."

He knew from her expression that she did care. Nuria's moods were quixotic, mercurial. She would see his reticence as a lack of trust and thus a betrayal of friendship. But how the hell could he tell her about Beth? He and Nuria were not lovers—yet. Still, they both knew they'd been moving slowly but inexorably toward that point. Michael certainly couldn't deny that he wanted very much to bed her. He'd been biding his time, waiting for the right moment. But now—no, he couldn't figure out how to tell her about Beth. She'd find out eventually, and when she did it would be the end of things between them. Better to delay that rupture as long as possible.

"You look very fetching," he said.

Nuria adjusted the curved front of her black bolero jacket. "You think you will make up with me by compliments? I'm not that silly."

"I didn't realize we had to make up. Have we quarreled?"

"You know what I mean."

"I suppose I do. But I wasn't complimenting you merely for something to say. You do look fetching. I've never seen you in such an outfit."

She was dressed like a Sevillana horsewoman. Her hair was sleeked back under a broad-brimmed hat, and she had a red hibiscus blossom pinned above her ear. The short black jacket exposed part of a red silk blouse, and she wore a long black skirt that wrapped and tied on the left. "In Spain women wear such clothes to ride horseback," he said. "Do you ride?"

"Of course. But not sidesaddle like a *peninsulara*. I am a

country woman of Puerto Rico. I ride like a man, and without a saddle."

"I'd enjoy seeing that," Michael said softly. Sweet Jesus, he could hardly believe himself! Only a few hours out of bed with one woman and his crotch was aching with hunger for another.

"Maybe you will." Nuria's tone told him she'd picked up the vibrations of his lust, but she didn't openly acknowledge it. That's how it had been between them for days. The promise was there and recognized. Eventually they both expected it to be fulfilled, but so far neither of them had made that first inevitable move. "We're going deep into the forest," she continued. "Too deep to take the carriage. Perhaps we will ride."

"Where will we get mounts?"

"José will bring them."

"Is that the name of the man we're to meet, José?"

She nodded. "Sí, he is the best *cazador* in the islands. I sent for him as soon as I heard about the *papagayo*."

"You're sure this parrot is there?"

"I'm sure. Obadiah was gathering coconuts and he saw him and told me about it."

"But couldn't the bird be anywhere by now?"

"He is there," Nuria said. "The *papagayo* is waiting for me. That is why he has come to Puerto Rico. Normally this kind of parrot lives only in Brazil."

He couldn't say anything when she lapsed into this mystical-superstitious vein. The bishop had told him that almost all Puerto Ricans were Catholics. It was true as far as it went, but Michael had learned that many of them were something else besides. The former slaves and the Indians had simply added a layer of Christianity to their own beliefs. Nuria was dark. He guessed she was Octaroon, one-eighth part Negro. Her attitudes, however, her ways of looking at the world, were more strongly African. Perhaps she'd been affected by the many former slaves she employed.

They drove on in silence, and when they turned onto a path cut between dense trees, the city of San Juan, any city, might not exist. The track they followed was overhung by branchs, and the footman had to leave his perch in the rear of the carriage and climb up to sit beside Samsón. Michael leaned out the window and smelled the scent of something primitive, an aroma of animal and earth that was growing stronger with each passing second.

After a quarter of an hour the driver reined in his horses. "Dis be all de ways we can *verdad* go, Missy Doña. What for I should be *verdad* doing now?"

"Stay here," Nuria said. For once she was too impatient to wait for her footman's assistance. She jumped down from the carriage with an athletic agility that surprised Michael.

"Where's your friend José?" Michael asked.

"He's meeting us a little way farther in, by the river." She set off without saying more and Michael followed her.

The trapper appeared when they'd been walking for ten minutes. He was sitting beneath a tree, a large burlap sack beside him and three horses tethered nearby. He got lazily to his feet when Michael and Nuria came into view. "*Buenas tardes, señorita.*"

"*Muy buenas,* José. This is my friend, Señor Curran. I have told him how skilled you are, and he wanted to see for himself."

José bowed in Michael's direction. He was a small man, wearing a tattered shirt and trousers held up by a knotted rope, but his whole body rippled with muscles. When he smiled he displayed four gold teeth. Gold teeth were a mark of wealth in the Indies, Michael knew. Trapping must be a lucrative business. The man's features were strongly Indian, but not entirely so. Mixed blood, and not all of it black. There was a healthy dose of white Spaniard in this *mestizo.* Aloud Michael said, "So, José, have you spotted our quarry?"

"No, señor. Only the señorita knows where the *papagayo* is. I am waiting for her to take me to him."

"By Las Tres Niñas," Nuria said. "I didn't tell you before because I didn't want you catching my bird and selling him to someone else."

"How can you know where the damned parrot is?" Michael demanded incredulously.

Nuria shrugged.

"The señorita has much good magic," the trapper said. "She knows." He glanced at the horses. "But from here to Las Tres Niñas the way is too overgrown for horses. We must walk."

Nuria started to protest, then changed her mind. "Very well, we'll walk." She struck off, leading the way. Both men followed her silently in the deepening dusk.

Soon it's going to be too dark to find our way out of this bloody place, Michael thought. This whole excercise is mad, and I'm mad to have come along. Nonetheless he kept walking. The lure was irresistible. It was moving ahead of him now with long strides and swinging hips, like some Amazonian woman of old. He thought he could smell her excitement mingling with the forest smell, and the combination was like temple incense in another world.

"Here," Nuria said at last, pointing to three boulders that stuck up out of the earth in a small clearing. "Las Tres Niñas. The *papagayo* is here."

José had left the horses tethered by the river but carried his burlap sack over his shoulder. Now he unslung it, pulled out a cage, and set it on the ground.

Nuria took a step closer to inspect the bird captive inside. Michael did the same. It was a parrot about a foot long, gray with a crimson tail. José bent over it. "*Ven, mi chica guapa,*" he crooned softly, "*ven. Tenemos trabajo.*"

The trapper hitched up his trousers and wiped his palms on his hips, then bent down and opened the door of the parrot's cage. The bird stepped out onto the moss-covered earth of the clearing.

"Won't he escape?" Michael asked, astounded.

"Not he, señor," José corrected. "She. This bird is *hembra,* a señorita. That is why we do such good work together. And she does not choose to run away from me. We are good friends." He reached into his pocket and produced a brazil nut. "*Toma, mi niña.* Show the señor how we are friends."

The gray parrot extended one foot and daintily grasped the nut in two of its three talons. It lifted the prize to its curved beak and began gnawing, not moving from the position it had taken up when it walked out of the cage.

Nuria had circled round to stand beside Michael. "Its wings are clipped," she explained.

Michael felt a wave of distaste at the thought of the mutilation. He looked up at the sky. He could see more of it here in the clearing than in the forest itself. It glowed with the orange fire of sunset. "It will be dark soon."

Nuria nodded. "*Sí,* sundown is the best time for what we have to do."

The parrot had opened the nut; it was munching on the sweet white kernel. "Now you must do your work," José said. He gathered up the sack and the cage and walked to where the two onlookers stood. "Go back over there, into the trees. You will be a distraction if you stay so close. And don't talk."

"What's going to happen?" Michael asked.

"You will see, señor. But please, not a sound."

They took up the positions the trapper had indicated. José positioned himself somewhere on the other side of the three boulders. Neither Michael nor Nuria could see the trapper, only the gray parrot, ruffling its feathers and spreading its useless wings, and making a sound that Michael had never before heard. The caged parrots in Nuria's patio had raucous cries, this was a cooing call that reminded him of doves.

They waited. For some minutes nothing happened. Then there was a flash of movement in one of the trees across the way. Nuria drew one short breath. Michael heard and followed her gaze to the top of a palm tree on the edge of the clearing.

Sitting just above the cooing gray parrot was something so beautiful he didn't think it was real; a parrot that glowed with an iridescent color somewhere between purple and blue. This was the bird Obadiah had seen and told his mistress about, one of the rarest parrots in the world, a hyacinth. Sweet Jesus, no wonder Nuria had made up her mind to have it. The creature was incredible.

The hyacinth was looking down on the gray, and the flightless bird was still cooing. It's a mating call, Michael realized. The gray is seducing the hyacinth. On command. And the damned blue bird was there, close enough to hear the call or smell the female. Exactly the way Nuria said it would be. Cold chills traveled down Michael's spine. At that moment he wished he was very far away from Puerto Rico. But only with part of him, the rational part. Some atavistic hunter's instinct was stirred by the scene he was watching, and he couldn't look away.

The hyacinth stayed in the tree for many minutes. The gray walked a few paces closer to it, cooing more rapidly, sticking out its chest and ruffling its feathers. Like the whores of Amsterdam who sit in the windows and display their charms, Michael thought.

At last the hyacinth made its move. It swooped down in one graceful motion and hovered above the gray for a moment that seemed out of time. The female raised her head beckoning the male closer, the hyacinth closed its purple-blue wings and dropped to earth. And at that same instant José appeared from nowhere and dropped a net over the second bird.

Later, in the carriage heading toward San Juan through the dark, Michael asked, "How did you know the wild parrot was a male, that it would be attracted by the female?"

"I knew," Nuria said, pressing her hand over her heart. "I knew."

The hyacinth was riding above them, in a cage on the driver's seat, wedged between the old man and the footman. Michael could hear the beating of the bird's wings as it fought fruitlessly against its captivity. He wanted to argue with Nuria, beg her to release the bird back into the wild, but he knew it would be pointless. "Listen," he said instead, needing to break the spell the capture of the bird had worked, to remind himself of the real world and his part in it. "There's something I've been meaning to ask you."

"What?"

"Is there any chance you have a twin sister?"

She erupted into laughter. "*Ay mi madre!* I think the Irish are not just *loco* and punctual, they are like fighting cocks that never give up. You still think I am the nun in the convent, the one who has visions?"

"I know you look exactly like her. I'm simply trying to figure out how it's possible."

"Well, I have no twin. I am sorry, *querido,* but I was the only girl in my family. I had six brothers and my mother and I cooked and cleaned for all of them."

"I see. What about your father?"

She pulled the black hat off her head, laying it on her knee and tracing the line of the brim with one red-tipped finger. "I have no idea who was my father. My brothers and I, we had many fathers. Does that shock you?"

"Not really. I know this is a world different from mine."

"Poor is always different from rich, wherever you are in the world."

"I know that too."

"Do you?" she asked.

"Yes."

"Then maybe you are wiser than I give you credit for, *querido*."

For a few seconds neither of them said anything. The captive bird was cawing frantically now, announcing its misery to the world.

"Let it go," Michael said through clenched teeth.

"Let the hyacinth go? You are insane. It is a prize beyond price, that parrot. Oh, what's the use of talking to you, you don't understand anything."

"You said I was wise."

"I said maybe you were wise. But you're not, you're a fool." Again they rode in silence. Then Nuria spoke. "I want to tell you something. Sometimes I get crazy too. Crazier than you. I have bad dreams. And not only when I'm sleeping. Sometimes during the day a great blackness comes and I don't know what is happening for hours. So maybe I am two people, like you think."

It was a wilder idea than any he'd thought of. An idea that could only be entertained here in this tropical place with its many different layers of life superimposed one atop the other. "No one can be two people," he said. "Have you seen a doctor?"

"I have been to three *curadores* and even a *bruja*."

Faith healers and witches, just what he'd expect her to choose. She didn't see his expression of disgust. "No one can help me," she said. "Except . . . perhaps if I were not afraid . . ."

"Afraid of what?"

"Of really strong magic. The kind Assunta has."

"Assunta is a witch?"

Nuria shook her head. "Not a witch. She is a priestess."

"A priestess of what, for God's sake?"

"You do not understand." She pursed her lips in disapproval. "It is stupid of me to talk to you. I keep forgetting that you are a European. You know nothing."

Michael thought about what Rosa had told him. And he remembered the first night Nuria had taken him to her house behind the bordello, the thing on the table she'd snatched away before he could see it. "Is Assunta a voodoo priestess?" he asked.

"I will tell you nothing because you know nothing," she said sullenly.

The conversation was going in useless circles. Besides, he needed another piece of information. "Are you going to the governer's mansion tonight?"

She laughed softly. "I don't think *la doña de las putas* would be welcome at La Fortaleza. My house serves a necessary purpose in San Juan, but people prefer to pretend it doesn't exist."

Damn, he should have known that without asking. He'd been stupid and probably wounded her. "Do you mind that?" he asked, preferring to get the undercurrents into the open.

She shrugged. "It doesn't matter whether I mind. It's the way things are. Will you be at the ball?"

"Yes." There was no point in lying. On an island as small as this everything was known almost as soon as it happened. And what wasn't known was invented, rumors were born in the air, as old man Rosa had said. "Nuria, listen, I meant to tell you earlier. I have a guest. A young woman I knew in London."

"A guest? Did this young woman come all the way from England to Puerto Rico only to visit you?"

"No . . . or perhaps she did. I'm not sure."

It was completely dark now. He couldn't see Nuria's face, but he could feel her eyes staring at him.

❦ 11 ❦

London, Nine P.M.

It had been cold and foggy the first time Norman came to the Three Herrings public house. Tonight was hot and humid, but the place looked exactly the same. There were no customers in the bar and he was alone with the publican.

"Evening, sir. What's your pleasure?"

Norman remembered paying the man to serve him his own brandy. Too hot for brandy tonight. "A pint of your best bitter."

The beer was drawn and passed to him in a pewter tankard. Norman took a long swallow, then glanced toward the private room in the rear.

"The other gentleman's waiting for you, sir."

Norman nodded and walked off carrying his drink.

This time Hiram Lacey was sitting by the window, leaning on the broad wooden sill and fanning himself with a folded newspaper. "Good evening, Mr. Mendoza. Bit warm, isn't it? Forgive my not rising. My gout's playing up again." He gestured with the newspaper, drawing attention to his swollen leg. He was resting it on a worn leather hassock from which half the stuffing was trying to escape.

Norman offered no sympathy. "No names. I've told you that repeatedly."

"So you have, so you have." Lacey didn't apologize. He waited for Norman to move a second chair into place beside the window. "Interesting news, isn't it? Cuba, I mean. Roosevelt's Roughrider's seem to have given the dagos a thrashing."

"That little war seems as good as over," Norman agreed.

"I don't expect it matters much to you. Bankers make money whoever wins or loses, isn't that so?"

"More or less. Now, can we get to our business?"

"Of course, sir." Lacey wedged the newspaper between two perky potted geraniums. Obviously somebody watered them, but the rest of the room smelled of dust and decay.

"Are you quite comfortable?" Lacey asked. "The tale I have to tell is a bit long."

"I'm fine. Get on with it."

"Yes. Well, you'll recall that you came back to see me the night after we met, the night of Wednesday, the twenty-third of June." Lacey looked up, expecting confirmation. Norman nodded.

"Not a date you're likely to forget, I imagine," the lawyer added. "What with having just floated a new issue and—"

"Come to the point, for God's sake."

"I am, sir, I am. The point is, I was incredibly lucky. Or perhaps the luck was yours. At any rate, following your instructions I began my surveillance of his lordship the following morning and kept it up until last evening. That's ten full days, you realize. I couldn't go out this morning because of my leg, but—"

"I'm not going to quibble about the number of hours you put in. You're quite sure Sharrick never saw you?"

"Quite sure. I'm something of an expert in these matters, Mr. Mendoza—excuse me, no names, I forgot. Now, as I was saying, the biggest stroke of luck came that first Thursday. His lordship spent the daylight hours at home, only went out to his club for a brief visit during the morning. Whites. The same as yours, I believe."

Norman nodded. The lawyer smiled and shifted his gouty leg into a slightly more comfortable position. "Nothing unusual in a man calling at his club before lunch, is there? Well, he returned home and though I watched all day he didn't go out again. By eleven P.M. I assumed the gentleman had gone to his bed. I was about to leave my post and do the same, when I saw someone coming round the corner from the back of the house. I could tell by his limp it was his lordship, but he was wearing most extraordinary clothes."

"Extraordinary in what way?"

"Workmen's clothes. Heavy trousers and boots and—it was raining quite hard as you may recall—an oilskin cape with a hood, such as a fisherman might use. His lordship's carriage hadn't left the stables since noon, and obviously he hadn't called for a cab because he started walking across Regent's Park. Naturally I followed." Lacey reached for a glass of sherry lodged on the windowsill and stopped talking long enough to sip it.

"And?" Norman demanded.

"And he went to Nine Elms. Do you know the district?"

"I've never been there."

"No, I'm not surprised. Not your sort of place at all. Not his lordship's either, if one were to guess. A poor neighborhood, a slum you might say."

Lacey paused again, as if waiting for a reaction. Norman shifted his position in the uncomfortable chair. "Get on with it, man. At this rate we'll be here until next Sunday."

The lawyer smiled. "Perhaps you'd prefer I just give you a summary of my findings. The details are all here in this folder." He reached down and produced a buff-colored paper case of the sort solicitors often used.

"That would be helpful," Norman agreed. "If you can bear to skip the dramatic rendition."

Lacey seemed oblivious to sarcasm. "Only my conclusions then, as long as that will satisfy you." He paused once more but held up his hand before Norman could speak. "I'm simply organizing my thoughts. Here then are the bald facts." Lacey chuckled. "No pun intended. Lord Sharrick of Glencree has a secret identity. In some circles he's known as Fergus Kelly. Kelly is deeply involved with the Fenians. I've been unable to ascertain whether any of that rabble are aware of who he really is."

The lawyer paused again, watching the effect of his statement on the other man. He wasn't disappointed.

Norman stared at Lacey, opened his mouth to say something, then closed it. A few seconds later he tried again. This time he managed to croak, "Sharrick? A Fenian? For the love of Christ, are you sure?"

"Quite sure." Lacey pointed once more to his paper document case. "All the details that verify my conclusions are in my report."

"But, for God's sake, why? What earthly reason could a man of Sharrick's wealth and position have for wanting Irish independence?"

"I've no idea, sir. Unless of course he's using the Fenians for some end of his own."

Norman leaned back and closed his eyes, letting his brain absorb the facts and paw among the myriad possibilities and connections. "Yes," he said after a moment. "That has to be it. But what are his ends?"

"I'm afraid I've no information about that either, except—"

"Yes?"

"Except one other piece of information I think may be important to you." The lawyer was speaking very softly now, lingering over every word, obviously relishing each one. "His lordship has seen Mrs. Lila Curran four times in the past week."

"Ah," Norman said softly. He closed his eyes and was silent for a moment, then he said again, "Ah." Lacey waited for something more. "I take it Lila's here in London?" Norman asked finally.

"She is. At that new hotel over on Carlos Place. The Connaught."

Norman stood up and reached for the document case. Lacey did not release it. Norman put his hand in his breast pocket and withdrew an envelope. "It's all there. Twenty-five guineas, as agreed. You may count it if you wish."

"There's no need to do that, Mr. Mendoza. The integrity of your house is legend." Lacey took the envelope and let go of the file. There was something very unpleasant about his smile. "One other thought has occurred to me. It's beyond my brief, of course, and I merely mention it in case you may have forgotten. The last job you gave me, the one involving Mrs. Curran directly. You do remember what I said about the place Mr. Timothy Mendoza stayed whilst in Dublin?"

"Of course I remember."

Lacey continued as if he hadn't heard. "It was the Swan on Bachelors Walk. A hotbed of Fenian sympathies, as I said at the time."

A few miles away Lila lay on her bed in the Hotel Connaught, sleepless, excited, and yet somehow frightened by her own eagerness, by the singing sense of joy building within her. Why, she asked herself for the hundredth time, why did she so mistrust her own emotions? Because they were inappropriate, premature. Had her life taught her no caution, no prudence? How could she feel this way when her plans, though ripe and ready, had not yet come to fruition.

It's not the plan, whispered a small interior voice she could not silence. It's not because soon you will repay the

Mendozas for all they've done to you, or because Michael will have what is rightfully his. That's not why you're singing inside. It's because of Fergus.

She rolled over and punched the pillow in frustration. How could she be so stupid, how could she betray her own rules like this? "I do not need a man." Lila whispered the words aloud in the empty room. "I do not have to be any man's wife, much less his mistress, to be whole and happy." She had repeated this motto many times in the sixteen years since she escaped her living death. As week after week and month after month she had clawed out a place for herself and her son in a world where single women were judged to be either whores or idiots, she had established the rule. I need no man to validate my existence. I can and will survive alone.

Remember, she prodded her rebelling heart, remember Papa, so poor, so helpless, so ineffectual. Remember Juan Luis who wooed you with sweetness and honeyed kisses— and became a monster. Remember . . . remember . . . remember . . .

But when at last she slept, Lila dreamed of sparkling dark eyes, of quick wit, of a warm smile and a ready laugh. In her dream she was running across an Irish meadow, a young girl again, her hair blowing free, her heart pounding with joy. And waiting for her, holding open his arms, was Fergus.

San Juan, Eleven-Thirty P.M.

Soon after Columbus made his second voyage and stumbled on what was then a virgin island, the world changed. Spain had to defend her claim to the fabulous Indies with more than words, and newly discovered Puerto Rico became a strategic prize. By 1540 the Spanish had erected on the island a brooding stone edifice known as La Fortaleza. It was impregnable, but the military decided it was in the wrong place.

They built a second fort, El Morro, at the mouth of the harbor, and turned the first over to the colonial governors. For three and a half centuries these governors had lived in La Fortaleza and ruled Puerto Rico with absolute authority; now it was the turn of General Manuel Devega.

Beth looked up in astonishment when Michael helped out her out of the carriage he'd hired for the evening. "Is this where we're going? It looks like a prison."

"You're in for a surprise. La Fortaleza is not what she seems."

Beth smiled and took his arm. She wore a gown of white lace and pale lavender satin with matching satin evening slippers. No jewels, she'd sold them all. "It was the only way I could get the money to come to you," she'd told him simply. Now he looked at her and felt guilty as hell. All the same, she looked wonderful.

Beth followed his glance, looked down at herself, then once more at the forbidding hulk of La Fortaleza. "Let's go in, shall we? I hope my lack of diamonds and pearls won't shame you." She summoned a bright smile. "Lead on, sire. I'm at your command."

The surprise he'd promised her was a cunning addition made fifty years earlier, which managed to add the refinements of the nineteenth century to the interior of the fort. The governor general could entertain his guests in elegant style. They took their place in the receiving line, and Beth looked with delight at the ballroom. "But it's really quite enchanting."

"Told you so," Michael murmured.

"You've been here before?"

"Not in the ballroom, but I came to pay my respects to the governor."

"You're not going to tell me why, are you?" Beth asked softly. "Or what you're really doing here."

"Not at this precise moment."

They had reached the first of the official receivers. Michael shook hands and bowed, Beth curtsied. Greetings were murmured, introductions exchanged. Beth spoke no Spanish, but it didn't matter. This was a ritual she'd been through countless times, the ordinary courtesy of daily life—at least in some circles. Michael translated when necessary; she kept smiling and nodding.

It took nearly twenty minutes for them to reach Devega. "*Excelencia,*" Michael said, "*Yo le presento la Señorita Isabela Turner de Londres.*" He'd already explained to Beth that *Isabela* was the Spanish form of *Elizabeth*. She smiled and curtsied. "I'm afraid the señorita doesn't speak Spanish," Michael added.

The governor bowed low over Beth's hand and held it a second or two longer than necessary. "But such a beautiful young woman need say nothing at all." His sibilant Spanish was full of the lisping sounds that marked him as a Castiliano, born in Madrid. "Merely to look at her is communication enough. Please tell the señorita she is welcome to Puerto Rico. And you, Señor Curran, you are still enjoying your time among us?"

"Still happy to be here, *Excelencia.*"

Devega smiled knowingly. "Yes, I expect you are. Your plans are proceeding, I hear."

"They are, sir. And so, may I say, are yours."

The governor laughed. "*Sí,* you are correct. That is why we are having this party. To celebrate the fact that in two weeks time the new autonomous government of Puerto Rico will take office. Now, my friends, go, enjoy yourselves. Perhaps we may speak again later, Señor Curran."

Michael led Beth from the receiving line toward a table where white-gloved waiters were serving rum punch. "What was all that about?" she asked.

"He was welcoming you to Puerto Rico, and explaining that the ball is to celebrate a new government soon to take office. It's supposed to be independent of the mother country, but the governor's still going to be calling most of the shots."

Beth wrinkled her nose. "Politics. How boring."

"Even more so here. They wrangle endlessly." He gestured toward a tall, impressive-looking man on their right. "See that chap over there, the one with the big handlebar mustache? That's Muñoz Rivera. Owns a newspaper called *La Democracia*. If he hadn't finally agreed to it, the so-called autonomous government still wouldn't be taking over. They were supposed to be in office last May, but they've been warring so bitterly among themselves it couldn't happen."

Beth glanced at the man Michael had indicated, then looked away. "He doesn't appeal to me; too old. But the ladies look charming! Perhaps this isn't such a backwater after all. I'm not being outshone, am I?" she added anxiously.

He knew he was expected to respond with a pretty compliment, but another man had caught his eye. A short, stocky gentleman was standing near the serving table, watching their approach. Michael identified him instantly as a planter. Something about the way the man's dinner jacket sat on his fleshy form made it seem he'd be more comfortable on a horse, riding his acres with his overseer at his side.

The planter inclined his head in a slight bow. Michael did likewise. He waited for the stranger to speak, but the planter merely kept staring at him. Extraordinary eyes. Like those of a reptile. Michael turned to Beth. "Rum's the local tipple. This is rum punch. It's quite good. Will you try some?"

"Whatever the custom may be, darling," she said offhandedly. She was busy examining the clothes of every woman in the room.

He was amused. For a moment he too appraised the guests. Chalk up another score for Lila. She'd given him a discerning eye where ladies' finery was concerned. There were many lovely gowns, but none bore the stamp of Paris so obviously as Beth's. "Yours is the prettiest frock here," he told her. The required compliment at last. Beth beamed.

The waiter stood by patiently to serve them drinks. *"Hay cava si la señorita prefiere, señor,"* he murmured.

"Devega has done himself proud," Michael explained. "They've Spanish champagne. Would you rather have that than rum?"

"Whatever." She waved her fan in a dismissive gesture, still occupied with her study of the ballroom and its occupants.

"Perhaps you'd best then. Rum's probably considered too strong for ladies." Michael gave their order, thinking all the while that Nuria drank rum. Tiny glasses of it, which she served neat in her austerely simple sitting room behind the whorehouse. He took the drinks from the waiter's hand and gave Beth her champagne. "To your very good health, my dear."

Beth removed her attention from the throng long enough to toast him. "To us, Michael darling," she said softly. "To our future."

Michael drank his rum in one long swallow and asked for another.

"Señor . . ." It was the stocky man, the one he'd identified as a planter. He'd moved closer and was speaking very quietly, as if he were greatly concerned about being overheard. "I have been hoping to meet you, Señor Curran."

"You have the advantage of me, sir."

"I know. But you are very identifiable, señor."

"So everyone keeps telling me."

"Permit me to introduce myself. I am called Coco Morales. I have a hacienda near Lares."

"Ah yes, I see." Michael turned to introduce Beth, and saw Fernando Luz approaching, almost shoving his way through the crowd in his anxiety to get to the punch table. "Here comes someone else we both know," he said.

"The banker," Morales agreed. "At the moment he has

all our attention, yours and mine, does he not, Señor Curran?"

"Bankers always attract attention. Money has that effect on people."

"I've noticed the same," Morales agreed.

Luz joined them and bowed to both men, then turned his back on the planter. He began speaking before Michael had a chance to present Beth. "I was hoping to see you this evening, Don Michael. It is very important. I stopped by the inn on my way here, but you'd already left."

"Since you've found me, that can hardly matter." Christ almighty! Luz was sweating like a pig. Didn't the damned fool know better than to display such public anxiety? "Allow me to introduce my charming guest," Michael said before Luz could make things worse. "This is Doña Isabela from London."

Beth included both the banker and the planter in her curtsy and warm smile. "Delighted, gentlemen. I've only arrived today, but I'm quite taken by your charming island. So quaint, and so different from anything I've seen before. I'm only sorry that I don't speak your language."

Michael translated rapidly. Luz and Morales made appropriate responses, and he translated those as well.

"Listen," Beth said, clapping her hands in glee. "The orchestra is playing an old-fashioned gavotte. How charming, I haven't danced a gavotte in years."

Michael flashed her a look of thanks. "Don Fernando, you must oblige me by dancing with the señorita. I don't dance myself, and she's longing to."

Beth didn't understand the words, but she devined his intention from his gestures. She smiled winningly at Luz. The banker could hardly refuse. He held out his arm. Beth took it, smiling at Michael over the top of her fan, and she and Luz glided to the floor.

"Very well done," Morales said softly. "You are an accomplished manipulator of men, Señor Curran, and the lovely señorita is a clever accomplice."

"I believe you wish to speak with me?"

"I do. But not here. Please, let us go to the terrace."

They went outside. The night was balmy and the breezes that wafted over the garden were scented with oleander and jasmine. "Now, Señor Morales?"

"Yes, now, Señor Curran." But having said that, the man said no more.

Michael watched the snakelike eyes watching him. He knew he had to take control of the situation, that somehow he had to convince this Coco Morales of his strength. "You said you were from Lares, señor."

"I believe you know that. And many other things besides."

"Yes," Michael agreed. "Many things. What do you do, señor?"

The man's eyes narrowed slightly, searching for a clue to the Irishman's meaning.

"What do you do?" Michael repeated.

"I am a coffee planter."

Michael shook his head. "No, that's not the right answer. Ask me what I do, Señor Morales."

There was a pause. "What do you do?" the planter asked at last.

"Useful things," Michael said.

Morales smiled a knowing smile. "Give me a letter," he said, an undertone of irony in his voice.

"L," Curran replied instantly.

"And I say M."

"Yes. *Libertad o muerte,* liberty or death."

"So you know about the secret societies," Morales said.

"Yes, and about the Lares uprising in sixty-eight, *el grito de Lares,* the Lares cry. I know about all of it."

"You are well informed, señor."

"And so are you, Señor Morales."

"But for me it is not so surprising. I am a Puerto Rican, a man of Lares. You are an *estranjero*."

"But we are neither of us revolutionaries," Michael said. "That's the point, isn't it? If the Lares uprising had been successful, if any of the secret societies around the island had done more than have meetings and make up codes and dream dreams, then we would not be standing here today."

"Perhaps not exactly as we are," Morales agreed.

"Not as two men of affairs contemplating a venture, no. Revolutions are not good for business, as I'm sure you know."

"But now?" Morales gestured toward the ballroom. "Now we are to have a revolution of sorts. We are to be autonomous."

"If it comes to pass," Michael said softly.

"You have doubts?"

"I don't think Puerto Rico's destiny is entirely in the hands of the Puerto Ricans, or of Spain for that matter."

"In the hands of the *norteamericanos* perhaps?" Morales took a cigar case from the pocket of his evening coat and offered one to the Irishman.

Michael accepted with a nod of thanks, waited until both cigars were lit, then repeated the other man's words. "The *norteamericanos*." He did not make it a question.

Morales leaned against the railing of the balcony, puffing deeply on the pungent tobacco. "You are sure they will come?"

"Let's say I think it's likely."

"Very well, we will say that. There is no longer the need for your fiction that Luz is acting for an unknown principal, is there Señor Curran?"

Michael shrugged. "I don't think many people are fooled by what you call my fiction."

"Not many. So that is out of the way. And the *norteamericanos*, they are in the way. Yet still you wish to make this investment, I may say this huge investment, in our island."

"Because of, not in spite of, Señor Morales. I am, as we say in English, backing my hunch."

"Why?" Morales leaned forward, pinning Michael with his unblinking stare. "Why, Señor Curran? Tell me that. Explain it to my satisfaction, and I will not only agree to sell you my land, I can promise you the agreement of at least nine other planters."

Michael had not supposed Morales was conducting this interrogation for himself alone. "Ten is not sufficient, señor. I must have all seventeen of the haciendas in which I'm interested—or I will have none of them."

"Why?" Morales demanded again.

"Because what is a threat to you, the coming of the gringos, is an opportunity for me. I am not Spanish, señor. I'm an Irishman. I speak your language, but English is my mother tongue. And not being a Latin I can think the way the Americans do. I understand them, and they will understand me." Michael flicked a long tail of ash over the railing into the garden. "Tonight I am perhaps the only man on this island who can say as much."

He was still waiting for Morales to answer when Luz arrived with Beth on his arm. "Ah, here you are. We have been looking for you."

"We stepped outside to smoke Señor Morales's excellent cigars," Michael said easily. And in English, to Beth, "Did you enjoy your dance?"

"Not particularly. Your friend reeks of garlic." She smiled and nodded while she spoke. Both Spanish speakers assumed she was complimenting her dancing partner, Luz even bowed slightly in acknowledgment.

Michael took a deep puff to cover his laughter. "Once more, please," he murmured quickly. "Not the banker, the other one."

Beth moved closer to Morales, fluttering her fan and smiling at him. "They are playing a Spanish tune now, señor. Will you show me how to do the dance? I'm afraid I don't know it."

Michael translated. Morales instantly bowed. "The señorita does me honor. It will be my pleasure, Doña Isabela." He gave her his arm and they went back inside.

"Don Michael," Luz said at once. "What did Morales say?"

"Quite a bit. I almost got a commitment out of him, but you came back a moment too soon."

"*Lo siento, discúlpame . . .*"

"No need to apologize. You couldn't know the timing. But you were nervous as a cat before I had my little talk with the planter. What's the matter, Luz?"

"It is the ship, the *Susannah Star,* Don Michael."

"What about her?"

"She called in to Puerto Rico a week ago, headed for London. I gave the captain your letter to Coutts, the way we agreed. The first available ship you said."

"Exactly. I still don't see the problem."

"There may not be one, I'm not sure. But . . ." Luz's voice failed, and he took a large handkerchief from his pocket and wiped the sweat from his face.

"But what? Come on, man, get a grip on yourself. What's troubling you?"

"There was a bad storm at sea the beginning of the week, Don Michael, and the *Susannah* was due in Bermuda two days ago. As of nine o'clock this evening there was still no sign of her."

There was a long silence. Michael thought of canny, capable Judson Hughes, and of the crew, and felt sick to his stomach. "Jesus Christ. What foul luck."

Luz nodded. "*Mala suerte, sí. Para ellos, y para nosotros.*"

"For us? I don't—Ah yes, I do understand. The demand letter to Coutts. It could be at the bottom of the sea as well."

"*Sí, señor.*"

"Well, I'll just have to write another, won't I?"

Luz sighed with palpable relief. "I hoped you would say that, Don Michael."

"What else would I say? How long until we can get it off the island?"

"With luck, tomorrow morning. There's a ship in the harbor at this moment, a steam-driven freighter called the *Lady Jane*. I believe the same ship that brought your charming guest. The *Lady Jane* leaves at dawn and will be in New York in two days. I was thinking, perhaps Coutts's agent there.... It would make up some of the time we've lost, Don Michael."

"Excellent. Arrange it." Michael flung away the stub of his cigar. "Come, Luz, we'll find Devega or one of his underlings and ask for paper and a place to write a letter."

Luz trotted after the Irish giant, offering silent prayers of thanksgiving to *nuestra señora* and all the saints. It was terrible to think he might have lost the profit of doing business with Judson Hughes, but far worse if the *estranjero* had taken the opportunity to back out of the deal with the haciendas. Far worse. He must light a candle in church tomorrow. For the souls of the crew of the *Susannah Star*, and for his own good fortune.

A buffet supper was set out on the balcony, which ran round the ballroom. Michael and Beth were there together in the small hours of the morning. He had eaten heartily; Beth merely nibbled on some of the tiny quail in aspic. Michael was about to suggest it was time to leave when a flurry of activity on the floor below caught his eye.

He leaned forward to see better. Most of the dancers had stopped moving in any prescribed formation; they were merely milling about. The orchestra was still playing, but no one was paying attention. Almost the entire company was looking toward their host. Devega had been genial and charming all night, passing from one guest to another with compliments and kind words. Now he was drawn up to his full height and bristling with authority.

A woman dressed entirely in black was the focus of the governor general's attention. She had her back to Michael. All he could see was her black turbanned head and the haughty sweep of her long black satin evening cape. Nuria had told him the lady of the whores wouldn't be welcome in La Fortaleza, but she was there.

Devega shook his head angrily. Nuria raised both her hands. From where he stood Michael could hear nothing, but he could see Nuria's red tipped nails. Her hand movements indicated to Michael that she was pleading with the governor. She was trying to convince him of something. Devega half turned. It looked as if he was about to summon his guards, then he apparently changed his mind. He turned back to Nuria and said something. She nodded.

Devega sagged, stood very still a moment, then walked toward the podium where the leader of the orchestra had finally stopped waving his baton in an ineffectual attempt to divert the crowd with music.

A hush fell over the room. The governor took his time, nearly a full minute of silence elapsing before he spoke. Michael was gripping the railing of the balcony, leaning forward. If what he guessed was correct, everything was ruined. His Puerto Rican strategy would have failed through a miscalculation of timing.

"*Amigos míos,*" Devega began. "I have sad and terrible news. It is not confirmed yet, but I have decided not to keep from you the possibility that . . ." His voice faltered and he broke off. The silence was absolute. The governor cleared his throat and began again. "I believe you have the right to be informed, even without official word. As most of you already know, two days ago the *norteamericanos* took control of San Juan Hill in Santiago in Cuba. Admiral Cervera and our fleet were blockaded in the harbor. Apparently—" Devega paused again. This time he looked directly at Nuria, standing on the edge of the crowd. Michael was also watching her. He saw her nod firmly. Devega seemed to shudder, then he continued. "Apparently the brave admiral chose to do battle with the enemy. I must sadly tell you that first reports are that he lost. It appears that Cuba has fallen to the Americans."

Michael exhaled a deep sigh of relief. Cuba, not Puerto Rico. At least not yet. He grabbed Beth's hand without waiting for the reaction of the crowd. "Come. Quickly."

Beth hadn't understood a word of the announcement, but she followed him without a murmur or a question, trotting to keep up with his long strides. Michael's bulk cleared a way through the excited crowd. They sped down the broad stairs and on to the floor of the ballroom.

Michael didn't thrust himself into the agitated press of people surrounding Devega but went to the shadowy corner of the room where Nuria stood alone. He didn't greet her and he didn't introduce Beth. "How did you find out?" he demanded.

Nuria's dusky skin was drained of color. The gold flecks in her brown eyes seemed to spark. She looked at Beth, studying her openly for countable seconds, then turned to Michael. "I hear things. I listen to people the governor general doesn't know exist. People who have ways of their own of communicating. Is this the visitor you told me about?"

Michael ignored the question. He was thinking of the former slaves who surrounded Nuria, of Samsón and Assunta and the rest. People said that the blacks had mysterious links of their own, that somehow throughout the Indies they stayed in touch, that their witchcraft and voodoo made it possible. The way she looked tonight, Nuria herself could be a witch. Or the nun in the hills—

"Assuming it's true," he said. "How bad is it? Are the Americans completely in control?"

"It's true. Cervera's fleet is completely destroyed and Spain has lost Cuba." She stopped and looked at Beth again, then at Michael. Without another word Nuria turned and walked away, her long black cape belling out behind her in the wind of her passage.

Beth didn't press him for explanations. She said almost nothing until they were in a carriage on their way back to the inn. Then, "She's very beautiful, isn't she?"

"Who? Nuria?"

"I don't know her name, you never introduced us. I mean the woman in black."

"She's Nuria Sanchez. And I may as well tell you because you're bound to find out sooner or later. She's a friend of mine and she runs the local bordello."

"I see. Have you been spending a lot of time in the local bordello, Michael?"

"Not the way you mean."

She took his hand. "I don't mean anything. Tell me what happened. What was all the panic about?"

"There's a war on between Spain and the Americans."

"I know that."

"Well, it seems that Spain's lost Cuba, a small island not far from here."

She cocked her head and studied him, raising her eyebrows. "I know where Cuba is. It was your friend Nuria who brought the news to the governor?"

"Yes, that's right."

"Extraordinary. How come she was the first to know?"

"I'm not quite sure. And if I told you what I suspected you'd think I was mad."

Beth laughed softly. "I doubt that. But it doesn't matter." She paused. "Michael, there's something else I don't understand. Why did the governor make so public an announcement of such bad news?"

"That's a good question. I've been wondering about it

myself. The only explanation that occurs to me is that he preferred to have the panic take place while he had so many of the island's leading citizens in one place and could calm them down."

She mulled that over for a moment. "Yes. I'm sure you're right. And it makes him seem honest and straightforward, even if he isn't always. That must be important if he's going to have to live with an autonomous government."

Michael turned to her. She was remarkably lovely in the moonlight. "I thought you said politics bored you."

"Of themselves they do, but I suspect this is all tied up with your mysterious business here, and nothing about you bores me, Michael Curran."

He looked at her with new respect. "I forgot to tell you what Señor Morales said about you."

"Morales is the one with the lizard eyes, isn't he?"

"That's right. The planter. When you took Luz off to dance so Morales and I could talk, he said I was a good manipulator of men, and that you were a perfect accomplice."

She laughed softly. "Not as perfect as I could be. Listen, if we're going to be here for any length of time perhaps I should learn Spanish."

"Do you want to? Wouldn't it bore you to tears?" A few seconds passed and she didn't answer. "What's the matter?" Michael asked. "Why are you frowning?"

"I'm thinking that you sound like Timmy. Don't be like Timmy. Michael. I couldn't bear it."

"How do you mean, like Timmy?"

"He always considered me a decoration. Always acted as if I hadn't a brain in my head. I know I'm only a woman, and everyone thinks I'm willful and selfish. They'll think so more than ever now that I've run away from my husband. Maybe I am all those things, but I'm not stupid, Michael."

"I'm beginning to appreciate that," he admitted.

Córdoba, Seven A.M.

In Spain the church bells were calling the faithful to the first masses of Sunday morning. The news of the loss of San Juan Hill was forty-eight hours old; that concerning the destruction of Admiral Cervera's fleet was beginning to come over the transatlantic cable but was not yet common knowledge. Those who talked about Cuba were not ready to admit that Spain had lost one of her last colonies and that they were witnessing the death throes of a once mighty empire.

In the southern province of Andalusia the sun rose a brilliant ball of fire in a searing blue sky. The humidity began climbing immediately, and Córdoba shimmered in the heat's haze. Behind high walls, which turned a blank face to the street, the exquisite Palacio Mendoza glittered like a secret jewel in the sunshine.

Don Francisco Valdez de Gias, titular head of the Spanish Mendozas, had designed a ceiling fan and installed several of them in the palace rooms, including the old counting room.

These days the Banco Mendoza conducted its business from a modern building on the Calle Real, the main street of the city. Francisco almost never went to the bank, but each Sunday morning before going to mass he closeted himself in the counting room to look over the week's reports. That's why he'd put one of the fans in there.

It was a clever innovation operated by a series of weights and pulleys. Francisco could activate the fan by tugging occasionally on a cord beside his chair. A spring coil kept the blades turning for five or ten minutes, then he had to yank on the cord again.

The fan had been turning continuously for over an hour this morning, but the counting room felt like an oven. However, it wasn't the weather that made him so hot; the sweat pouring off Francisco's body was a response to the document he was reading.

"*Madre de Dios,*" he whispered into the empty room. "Why did this happen? What in the name of God am I supposed to do about it?"

He was looking at a demand for payment. It was covered with multicolored seals and stamps and ribbons and was official notice that the Imperial Russian Treasury, which lodged vast sums of money with numerous European bankers besides himself, wished to withdraw the funds they were keeping in Córdoba. The amount represented many, many millions of pesetas.

Francisco kept scratching sums on a scrap of paper. He got the same results each time. It was exactly as the manager of the bank indicated in his report. When in ten days' time they released the czar's money as they must, the reserves of the Banco Mendoza de Cordoba would be dangerously low. In the five years of Francisco's stewardship, such a huge single withdrawal had never occurred. Now that it had, he hadn't the remotest idea of what he should do.

Nothing had prepared him for the role he'd been forced to play these last five years. It had never been envisioned that he would have to become a banker when twenty years earlier Francisco's father had decided his son should marry Beatriz Mendoza. He had been negotiating with the bank for an enormous loan on his tanneries when Juan Luis, afraid he might not find a better husband for his plain sister, suggested the match.

Everything should have worked out well. Juan Luis settled a generous allowance on Beatriz and invited the couple to live in one of the many private apartments in the palace. Both men were satisfied with the arrangement. Juan Luis didn't have to worry about the management of his household because Beatriz could continue to oversee it, as she had since their mother died. Francisco had more money at his disposal than ever before, plus the delights of Córdoba and nearby Seville to amuse him. But things did not proceed as expected.

Beatriz never conceived; not even a still birth or a miscarriage attested to Francisco's performance of his duty. And two years after his sister married, Juan Luis brought an extraordinary bride home from Ireland. Soon after that he went crazy.

Francisco never understood what drove his brother-in-law into the abyss of insane jealousy. Lila gave him a son within a year of their wedding, and he should have been content. Instead Juan Luis turned into a lunatic, and for years there was no peace in the house.

That episode ended when in some mysterious fashion Lila got the upper hand and forced her husband to let her go. Francisco knew she'd taken a great deal of money with her. Fair enough, he'd thought. She's earned it after the hell Juan Luis put her through. But he never understood why Lila had been allowed to take her son with her. Still, she had. Whatever hold she had over Juan Luis had been strong enough to make him release the child as well as the woman.

When Juan Luis died, his will revealed that he had disinherited his son, and named Francisco his successor. So the responsibility of this unprecedented Russian demand for payment was Francisco's.

He held his head in his hands. He was not a bad custodian of the Mendoza millions. He'd realized in the first days of his tenure that he knew almost nothing about finance. He allowed the bank manager trained by Juan Luis to run the day-to-day affairs. Still, he kept a careful eye on the fortune in the time left after his own pursuits. And since Beatriz had produced no heir, he didn't have to worry about what would happen once he was dead. Doubtless after an unequal fight with numerous Mendoza cousins and distant relations here in Spain, the Cordobés interests would be swallowed by London.

That was all right with Francisco, but he preferred that

the English should assume power after he died, not interfere with his life while he was living it. So he was a careful and cautious steward, and until this morning he'd seemed to be managing well enough.

Dublin, Two P.M.

On Sundays the General Post Office on O'Connell Street was closed for everything but emergency business. When Lila Curran's butler arrived, he went to a small desk near the entrance. A sign above it said Urgent Business.

"Afternoon, sir," the clerk said. He was dressed in a uniform of drab gray wool, and he was perspiring profusely. The clerk wiped his face with a soiled handkerchief. "Would your business be after waiting until tomorrow, sir? We only deal with urgent matters on Sundays."

"I know. These are urgent." Winston placed a packet of envelopes on the desk.

The clerk eyed them suspiciously, then picked them up and counted them. There were twenty separate pieces. "Sure and are you telling me all of these are urgent?"

"I am."

"Can't be. Are they letters, or what?"

"Cables. To Spain."

"Twenty different cables to Spain, and all of 'em an emergency? Now look here—"

"They're all the same, only the addresses are different." Placating people he considered beneath him didn't come naturally to Winston, but he made a great effort. "It's a brief message."

"And it has to go today? Tomorrow won't do?"

"It really won't. My employer insists they be sent this afternoon."

"Your employer," the clerk repeated. "Then you didn't write these yourself?"

"No. My employer wrote them. Mrs. Lila Curran."

"Ach, so it's the Black—" The clerk stopped himself. "Wants 'em sent right now, does she?" he asked again, as if that hadn't been made clear.

"Immediately," Winston said. "Mrs. Curran won't forget the favor."

The clerk picked the first envelope off the pile. It was addressed to a señora somebody in Córdoba. A quick check indicated that each cable was being sent to Córdoba. Mother of God, it would be an almighty job tapping them foreign addresses into the machine. "A brief message you said?"

"That's right. You can see for yourself."

The clerk opened the top envelope and withdrew an official telegraph form, properly and carefully completed. The message was written in block capitals on the lines indicated for it. PARTY ON 26 JULY.

"An invitation to one of herself's parties. That's what's so urgent?"

"Yes," Winston insisted. "Mrs. Curran is most eager . . ." He let his voice trail away, but he placed another envelope on the corner of the desk. This one was not addressed.

Both men pretended nothing had happened. "Ach, I suppose if Mrs. Curran says it's urgent, sure it must be." The clerk stole a quick look at the twenty-first envelope. "Right, I'll send 'em. Cost you a penny a word." He gathered up the pile of messages, slipping the extra one to the bottom with a deft motion. "I'll just go in the back and tot up the charges."

❧ 12 ❧

TUESDAY, JULY 6, 1898
London, Eleven A.M.

In the Partners' Room on Lower Sloane Street the fate of the *Susannah Star* was discussed with little emotion. Only Henry seemed visibly affected. His skin was ashen and he kept muttering about the captain and the crew. Jamie wasn't saying much of anything, but he too looked gray and drawn.

Norman ignored Henry's distress and Jamie's appearance and spoke to his sons. "She's five days overdue, so we have to assume she went down in the storm. Nothing to worry about. The ship is insured for a hundred and twenty thousand pounds, the cargo for ninety. We'll do all right. The problem is simply one of time."

"How long will it take to get the money?" It was Timothy's first encounter with this type of disaster. The last ship the Mendozas lost had gone down when he was two years old. A remarkable record, but that was irrelevant now. "Will Lloyd's hang about or pay up promptly?"

"Promptly enough by their standards. Thirty days after settlement," Norman said.

"The settlement's the sticky part." Henry shuffled the papers in front of him. "It's a question of agreeing on the amount of the loss." He swallowed visibly. "They don't make any allowance for the loss of life."

Jamie's cadaverlike appearance apparently had nothing to do with the human element of the tragedy. He waved Henry's comment aside with one hand. "It's hard to see how there can be any quarrel. If everything's gone that's about it, isn't it?"

Norman was filling his pipe, watching his younger son over the rim of the bowl. He'd been looking steadily at Tim since the meeting began, but the lad hadn't once met his eyes. "Insurers always quibble, that's their game. What do you think, Tim? Will we weather the storm?"

Timothy still didn't look up. "I expect you know more about that than I do."

"I expect I do too. But I'm asking your opinion. How's it going to turn out when all the chips are counted? Curtains for Mendozas? Finished? The end of a great banking institution? C'mon, if you were a gambling man which way would you bet?"

The attack was too savage and sudden to be ignored. Tim looked directly at his father. "I doubt very much if Mendozas is finished, sir. Not because of the loss of one ship."

Norman wouldn't let it rest. "But there's more involved, isn't there? We're very short on liquidity, aren't we? And there's this damned undersubscribed Paraguayan bond to be dealt with. The first payment's due in sixteen days' time. How are we going to survive that?"

"I'm waiting for you to tell me how, Father. I've been waiting for weeks."

Norman held a match to his pipe and didn't reply.

Jamie cleared his throat. The others turned to him. "There is something else," he began slowly. "A gentleman came to see me at my club yesterday evening. A Russian. He said he wanted to let me know informally, before the matter became official."

He stopped speaking. The others watched him and waited. Jamie seemed not to understand that something more was required of him.

"C'mon," Norman demanded. "What's the rest of it? What did he want to tell you? Unofficially."

Jamie drew a long breath. "That the Imperial Russian Treasury is going to withdraw its deposits before the end of the month."

The announcement had a shape and a feel, like something physical. It dropped into the quiet room and lay among the five men, an obscene and revolting thing none of them could bear to look at.

Seconds went by. Finally Charles broke the silence. "Sodding bloody hell."

Henry, Jamie, and Charles began talking at the same time, none of them pausing to listen. Norman didn't say anything, but he continued to watch Tim. This time Timothy stared back.

At last Norman broke the eye contact. He turned to the others. "For God's sake, shut up. Stop all this clatter. Jamie, how do you know the man was telling the truth? Who is he?"

"I don't know really," Jamie admitted. "But he seemed convincing. Here's his card." He handed it to Norman.

Norman studied the string of names. "Unpronounceable. What exactly did he say?"

"That he used to work for the Imperial Treasury. That he still has contacts." Jamie was perspiring now, wiping his face with a large white handkerchief.

"I suppose he expects to be paid for this advance information." Norman slipped the card into the pocket of his waistcoat.

"We didn't discuss it. He was quite gentlemanly really. But naturally I assumed—"

"Quite." Norman looked at his eldest son. "Charles, get

a packet of five-pound notes ready. Shall we say twenty of them? That should be adequate for a start I think."

"Are you going to see him?" Jamie asked.

"Yes, of course. I'll do a bit of checking first, but I'll have to see him."

Jamie stood up, obviously intending to declare the meeting ended.

"Wait," Henry murmured. "About the ship, we haven't settled anything concerning the survivors."

"There weren't any survivors, not that we know of," Tim said.

"Uncle Henry means the widows and children." Charles looked at his father. "I agree. We should compensate them."

Tim spoke before Norman could. "We're not exactly in a position to be throwing money around."

"Don't be an ass." Charles spat out the words. "If we can pay some supposed Russian for dubious intelligence, we can put a few bob in the way of people who have a right to it. People who depend on us."

Jamie and Henry nodded agreement.

"You're sentimental, son," Norman said. "It's not fitting for a banker. But in this case you're right. See to it. Twenty-five pounds for each widow. A fiver more for each minor child she's left with." He stood up. "That's it then. Henry, keep after Lloyd's. Don't let them shilly shally. I'll take care of the Russian. Charles, will look after the cash outlays."

Nobody expected Jamie to have any specific task, but Tim looked at his father expectantly. Norman said nothing more. "What about me? Nothing you want me to do, Father?"

Norman stared at him. "I can't think of a thing," he said finally. "Seems to me you've done quite enough."

Philip Johnson didn't say anything when his employer returned to the office. Johnson knew about the loss of the *Susannah*; everyone in the bank had heard about it. The secretary intended to offer condolences; losing a ship was like a death in the family, but seeing the barely suppressed rage on Mr. Norman's face deterred him.

Norman strode past Johnson as if he weren't there, and went into his office and slammed the door. Johnson looked after him a moment, then went back to his papers. Three minutes later the door to the private office opened again.

"Get my son Timothy down here. Right away."

"Yes, sir."

"No, wait. Don't do anything. I'll go up to him."

The secretary watched in amazement as Norman hurried past him and headed toward the stairs to the third floor. He couldn't recall a single instance when Mr. Norman went up to one of the others rather than sending for them. Except for his lordship, of course. But Mr. Norman seldom wanted to speak with Mr. James.

Norman took the stairs two at a time, rage boiling inside him, growing more intense as he neared his son's office. Bloody fool. Sodding little ingrate. Somehow Timothy was behind all this trouble, had his fingers in it and was stirring the pot. How? Why? He meant to have the answers to those questions right now.

Without a word he walked past the three clerks seated outside the pair of rooms occupied by Charles and Timothy, and entered the one on the left.

Tim had his back to the door. His feet were propped up on the windowsill and his hands clasped behind his head. It was the pose of a man content with his universe.

"Turn around, I want to talk to you."

Tim hesitated a second, then lowered his feet to the floor and spun the desk chair around. "Yes?"

"Yes, sir. I've had enough of your insolence. And your troublemaking. I know about the Fenians."

Timothy studied his father's red face. The fury in his eyes was terrible. In spite of himself, the younger man's stomach started to churn. "I don't know what you're talking about. What Fenians?"

Norman took a step closer to the desk and leaned both his hands on it. "I'm your father as well as your employer. You call me sir. And get on your feet when you speak to me."

Timothy stood up. "You're getting yourself in a state, Father. You'll be ill if you don't calm down."

"I'll calm down when it bloody well suits me. When I know what stupid mess you've got yourself and the rest of us into. Stop looking at me like that. I'm not going to have a convenient stroke or a heart attack to make it easier for you. My health's fine. So whatever you and Lila Curran have cooked up, I'm not going to die and leave you a clear field."

"What's she to do with anything?" Timothy added a belated, barely audible, "sir."

"That's what you're going to tell me."

"I can't. I don't know what you're talking about."

"Yes, you do. She's at the Connaught Hotel, here in London. You've seen her." That was a shot in the dark; he hadn't found any way to confirm that Lila and Tim had met, he'd just guessed they had.

Timothy began gathering his wits. It would be stupid to deny seeing Lila. "I had tea with her a week or so ago. Because of my wife and that bastard Michael. But I still don't see what that has to do with anything. You yourself told me to speak with Lila."

Norman knew he had, but he didn't intend to let Timothy off the hook so easily. "I'm not talking about that tart you're married to. Lila wants power. She wants Córdoba for Michael, even though Juan Luis's will expressly forbade it. She's using you to get what she wants. The only thing I don't know is how she means to do it, or what she's promised you. And how the Fenians fit in. You're going to tell me."

There was a small table beneath one of the windows; it held a decanter of sherry. Timothy went over and poured a drink, feeling his father's eyes boring into his back all the while. "Here, have this. You'll feel better."

Norman reached up as if he were going to take the glass, instead he swept it out his son's hand. The schooner made very little sound as it fell to the carpeted floor. The puddle of spilled wine quickly soaked into the wool.

"Pity," Timothy said softly. "That was some of that excellent amontillado Ruez sent last month. There's not a lot of it."

"Don't play games with me. I'm not fooled by your sanguine facade, boy." Norman's voice was very low now. It was deadly. "You're shitting in your pants right this minute. Like when you were little. You never had any real courage, Timmy. Not the kind it takes to be a man. Always a mama's boy, until she died and you couldn't hide behind her skirts anymore. Every time you earned a whipping, and got it, you ran to your mother or your nurse. You're using Lila Curran the same way now. Need a woman to give you balls, always have."

Rage was a lump in Timothy's throat. It was choking him. He had to struggle to speak past it. "You haven't the right to mention my mother's name. You killed her. You and your whoring around after every cunt in London. You weren't fit to lick her shoes. You still aren't."

Norman's arm came up with the speed of a snake's tongue. He lashed out once, fist balled and ready to smash. Tim was even faster. He caught his father's wrist and held it.

The boy was surprisingly strong. In seconds Norman realized that he couldn't lick him, not physically. He stopped trying to free himself and relaxed the muscles in his arm.

Timothy felt the slackness and released his grip. He flushed with elation at the victory. "You despotic old tyrant, you never understood a damned thing. You don't now. You're dead, you and your two idiot brothers, and you haven't the sense to lie down." He was drunk with a sense of power, his voice rising on every word. "I'll be there to dance on your grave, don't you forget it."

"I'll see you in hell first." Norman's breath was coming in hard gasps. "In hell!" he shouted.

The door to the office burst open. "What in God's name's going on in here? Are you mad, the pair of you? The whole bank can hear." Charles looked from Timothy to Norman. It was his father who alarmed him. He was dripping with sweat and breathing as if he'd been running for hours.

Charles pulled a chair from its place beside the desk. "Sit down, sir. Please, you must. You're looking quite ill."

Norman turned to Charles and the contempt he felt for both his sons poured out of his eyes. "Not worth a tinker's damn. Neither of you. Never were." He was mumbling, speaking to himself, not to them. "Not worth the fuck it took to make you. You'll not win, neither of you."

He stumbled past them, dodging Charles's outstretched hand and walked out of the office.

Charles stood staring after his father, then turned to Timothy. "What happened? What did you do to make him so angry?"

"Be born. Same as you."

Tim raised the decanter to his lips and took a long swig of the sherry.

"You're mad. Both of you are mad. This is the worst possible time to quarrel among ourselves. Don't you understand anything of what's happening?"

Timothy put the wine back on the table and wiped his lips with the back of his hand. "I understand exactly what's happening. But that old bastard doesn't. Not yet. Neither do you, brother mine. But you will."

San Juan, Ten A.M.

"There's no choice," Michael said calmly. "We have to move now."

Luz didn't answer immediately. Each time the big Irishman came into his office it was the same thing: he got deeper and deeper into this venture. Part of him was overjoyed, ecstatic at the thought of all that money. Another part remained cautious and skeptical—and frightened. "I'm not sure. There are many things that still aren't clear and—"

"What's clear is that the *norteamericanos* may be here any day."

Luz shrugged. "Even if that is so, and I must admit it now seems as if it could happen, what difference does that make, Don Michael? You have expected them from the first."

Michael took a long pull on his cigar and exhaled the smoke in a slow satisfying stream. "Indeed I have. But what position I'm in when they get here—that makes a big difference."

Michael hadn't anticipated these developments. Neither he nor Lila had moved when they did because they knew the future. It was Lord Sharrick talking to his mother about Mendozas floating another bond for Paraguay, about the idiocy of pumping good money after bad, which had set the train in motion. America and Spain going to war had simply convinced them to include Puerto Rico in their scheme. Now events were playing exactly into his hands, and Michael had trouble hiding his elation.

He had to hide it though; Luz was looking at him like a puppy who's been kicked by his master. The banker had taken the loss of the *Susannah Star* very hard. It confirmed Michael's suspicion that the man had a private deal with that poor sod Judson Hughes. Now Hughes was at the bottom of the sea and Luz's backbone was near crumbling. Michael wasn't ready for that. Not yet.

He leaned forward. "Look, from our point of view there's never going to be a better time. Everyone's running scared, not least the planters. They're all expecting the Americans to take over, and dictate the terms on which they'll be allowed to trade."

"And you, Don Michael, you do not expect the Americans to dictate such terms?"

"Frankly, no. They're good capitalists, believe in market forces. I'll strike my own deal and do very well out of it. But I have to be in control when they get here. Not arrive later like some bit player who's been waiting in the wings."

It was logical, Luz couldn't deny that. Still he hesitated. "But what you wish me to do . . . it is most unprecedented, señor. For a banker it is almost illegal."

"Almost, not quite. Look at it this way: you're making me a loan."

"A very large loan, enormous. Nearly two hundred thousand pounds sterling." A drop of sweat fell from Luz's chin to the desk.

"Secured by well over a million," Michael reminded him.

"But the bulk of that, the money with Coutts, hasn't been paid into your account yet."

Michael shrugged. "You have their cable."

That was true, like everything else the Irishman said. But Luz had another cable as well, though no one else knew about it. In the safe behind the picture of Doña Maria Ortega was an advice he'd received two and half weeks ago from his employer, Norman Mendoza. Using the code long established for such procedures, Mendoza had told Luz to be prepared for a demand from London on the reserves in Puerto Rico. "If I make this loan, señor, I will probably lose my job," Luz whispered.

Michael laughed. "You don't give a hoot in hell about your job. Not if you see a way to get off this damned island with a small fortune of your own. Where's it going to be, Luz? Europe or North America?"

Luz didn't answer.

Michael leaned back, chewing on the cigar. "North America, I bet. New York, right? Yes, that's mecca for this part of the world. New York, isn't it?"

"I admit I would love to go to New York, Don Michael. If I had the opportunity."

Michael leaned forward again, fixing the other man with his direct gaze. "I'm giving you the opportunity. The only thing you have to do now is make sure you don't piss it away. Men have lost a lot less for lack of *cojones*."

Luz pursed his lips, thought for a few more seconds, then rose. "*¡Bueno!¡De acuerdo!* It will be as you say." His heart was pounding. He was afraid the Irishman would hear it. The *cojones* in his trousers felt very small indeed. He could only croak the words, but he managed to say them. "I will do it."

Michael pretended to be unaware of the Puerto Rican's nerves. "Good. Sit down and we'll work out the details. It will have to be in cash. You approach each of the planters with seventy-five thousand pesetas, fifteen thousand pounds. A cash down payment when they sign on the dotted line. And—"

"I cannot, señor." Luz had grown more pale. He looked as if he might faint.

"Dammit, man! You just agreed."

"To make the loan, yes. Against the security of your account. But I cannot go running around the island seeing all the planters. Not now. You said it yourself, there is panic here, Don Michael. If I leave, if I'm gone for days, it will make everyone more jittery. And word is bound to get back to London. We are the only bank in San Juan. I must stay. If I do not, the governor general—" Luz threw up his hands, unable to continue.

Michael leaned back and narrowed his eyes. A new development but not perhaps a major setback. "Very well," he said after a few seconds. "I'll do it myself."

Beth was not pleased. "I've only just got here and you're going off and leaving me."

"You know I've business on this island. Why else would

I be here?" It was on the tip of his tongue to add that he hadn't asked her to come to Puerto Rico, but he didn't say it.

They were in the dining room of the inn, eating the final course of an indifferent lunch. The dessert was intensely sweet guava paste served with the pungent local goat's cheese. The combination was surprisingly good, better than the dishes that had preceded it. Michael poured more of the astringent red wine for both of them. "Be a good girl. You can be, I know you can."

She was in no mood to be gentled out of her temper. "You're doing it again."

"Doing what again?"

"Treating me as if I were a child or a moron. You never used to do that, Michael. That's why I fell in love with you. You talked to me as if I had a brain."

"You do have a brain."

"Yes. So why won't you take me with you? Remember what Señor Morales said, that I was a clever accomplice? I could help you. You'd be surprised how useful I could be."

"It's out of the question. The whole island would talk about the scandal of us traveling together."

Her chin came up. "I don't care. I don't see why you should care either." Suddenly she had a new thought. "Michael, do you intend to remain here? To live in Puerto Rico."

"God forbid! Whatever gave you that idea?"

"Because if you plan to leave when your business is finished, as you said, I don't see why it matters what the islanders think."

"First of all, they don't know I plan to leave. Secondly, it matters precisely because I'm doing business. I have to be seen as someone responsible. A gentleman who can be trusted. Gentlemen do not take respectable young ladies on jaunts into the mountains."

"We could take Tillie and your man Briggs. They could be our chaperones."

"They're servants, not companions. It won't do, Beth. In these circumstances it's out of the question."

God how she wished she was single. If she didn't already have a husband, she'd win this argument easily. She'd simply insist that they get married immediately, then the problem would be solved. They could combine Michael's business trip with a honeymoon. Since that wasn't possible she had to take a different tack.

"Is it always going to be like this?" Her voice had a hint of tears.

Michael was surprised; she'd never been the sort of woman who cried to get her own way. He wasn't sure what to make of her distress. "Like what?"

She pressed a handkerchief to her eyes. "Are we going to have to live the rest of our lives pretending?"

His gut knotted. "Beth, listen, darling, we've got to get some things straight. I—" He broke off, not knowing how to continue. How could he explain that under no circumstances could he spend the rest of his life with her? He was going to Córdoba to claim what belonged to him. At least he was doing everything he knew how to make sure he went there. He needed a wife, sons. A Jewish wife. Even if Beth got rid of Tim, it would make no difference. Certainly he couldn't bring a divorced woman to the Palacio Mendoza in Córdoba.

"What things do we have to get straight?" she asked.

"You and me, our future."

"Yes?"

He couldn't find the courage to say more. Not when he already had so much on his plate. "What I mean is that we've a thousand plans to make and I can't give them my full attention right now. Please, can't it all wait until I've done what I came here to do?"

He felt rotten, like a gutless liar, but Beth gave him her sunniest smile.

"Of course it can wait. I'm sorry, darling. I shouldn't be

distracting you now. We have our whole lives to look forward to. I suppose I can stand to let you go for a few days."

Beth had taken readily to the custom of the siesta. She disappeared to her room when they finished lunch. Michael wasn't interested in a nap. He hesitated a moment, debating the wisdom of what he intended to do. Probably a mistake, but he was going to do it anyway.

He left the inn and headed on foot for the Calle Cruz.

He didn't have to brave Assunta and her admonitions about "de darktime" any longer. These days when he wanted to see Nuria he went directly to her little house behind the bordello.

The afternoon was hot and still, the street empty. He mounted the single step to the door and lifted the brass knocker and let it fall. After a few moments the door opened. Samsón greeted him with a formal bow and invited him in. "The señor be *verdad* welcome. We been not seeing you many together days."

"Hello, Samsón. I wish to see Doña Nuria. Is she sleeping?"

"Missy Doña no sleep," the old coachman said. "She *verdad* no sleep at all. Very bad."

Michael wasn't sure he'd understood. "You mean she doesn't have a siesta in the afternoon?"

"Is not only siesta, señor. Missy Doña, she no sleep in de darktime."

"And you're worried about her I gather." Michael eyed the black man. "Well, I'll see if I can pursuade her to change her ways. Where is she?"

"Missy Doña be with de birds. Always she be with de birds."

"Out on the patio at this hour? Is she mad? It must be over a hundred degrees." He strode past the servant toward the patio.

The hundreds of caged birds made soft, cooing sounds.

Afternoon sounds, Nuria had once called them. Michael saw the creatures only as a blur of color against the stuccoed patio walls because his focus was on Nuria. She was sitting beside the fountain, dark hair hanging free. He'd never seen it like that before. A length of plain white fabric was wrapped around her body, and her feet were bare. Nuria's only ornament was the hyacinth parrot. The bird was perched on her wrist, its brilliant blue-purple plumage glittering in the harsh glare of the tropical sun.

Michael walked closer, but she didn't acknowledge his presence. "What are you doing out here in this heat?" he asked. "You don't even have your head covered. You'll get sunstroke."

"Hello, Michael." Her voice was dull, uninterested in him, and she kept her eyes fixed on the parrot.

The bird turned its beady glance on the newcomer, looked once at Michael, then let out a shrill cry.

"Quiet, my beauty," Nuria whispered. "It's all right, he's a friend."

"How have you tamed that damned bird so fast? He was a wild creature so short a time ago."

"I didn't tame him."

"What do you mean? He looks tame enough to me. He's sitting there on your wrist and not moving, isn't he? Do you have him chained?"

Nuria shook her head. Michael looked more closely. There was no chain. "Bloody amazing," he murmured.

"This *papagayo* was meant for me. I told you that the first day. He came to the island to find me."

"More mystical gobbledygook." He sat down beside her. The sun was intense, its fire barely mitigated by the splashing water of the fountain. Michael didn't remove his panama hat, but the heat seemed to find its way inside his skull. "You'll get sunstroke," he said again. "We both will if we stay out here."

She didn't reply. He reached over and put his hand beneath her chin, turning her face to him. "Let me look at you. Samsón says you're not sleeping. He's worried about you."

Nuria looked at him silently, their eyes met and held. Hers were as they'd been Saturday night at the ball, dark holes in a face devoid of color. "You look terrible," he said frankly. "What's the matter?"

Nuria pushed his hand away and tossed her head, shaking back the heavy curtain of black hair. "I'm fine." She stroked the bird's feathers. "Isn't he beautiful?"

"Forget the damn bird, I'm talking about you."

The parrot uttered its shrill cry again, as if it understood. Nuria stroked it and the bird calmed. "The dreams are worse," she said, not looking at Michael. "They're terrible. How can I sleep when I have such awful dreams?"

"What do you dream about?"

"I can't tell you. Terrible things."

"Is that how you were the first to know about Cuba? A dream?"

"No. It was after one of the black times. They come when I'm awake. I told you about them."

"Yes, so you did. Nuria, you should see a doctor."

"I have. I told you that too. I was right about Cuba, wasn't I?"

"Of course you were right. The news came by cable a few hours after you told it to Devega. Look, I don't know how you found out, maybe I'd rather not know, but it's not a surprise, Nuria. The Americans were always destined to win this war. I think they're going to take over Puerto Rico as well. Have you thought about that? About what you'd do?"

She shrugged. "I will do what I do. American men are the same as all other men, aren't they?"

"I suppose so. Can we go inside? I'm feeling this heat even if you're not."

She stood up, the bird still on her wrist, and took a step

toward the entrance to the house. The parrot set up a fierce squawking and took flight. "He hates to go inside," Nuria said. She stopped walking and looked up. The patio was unroofed, the blue sky beckoning wide overhead. The hyacinth flew in widening circles, sometimes hitting its wings against the walls, but it never rose toward freedom.

"Why doesn't it fly away?" Michael demanded.

Nuria looked at him. "I keep telling you, but you don't believe me. I can't go inside, the *papagayo* doesn't want me to." She returned to the fountain and sat on the edge again. The bird circled twice then dived toward her. Nuria raised her arm and the creature perched on her wrist.

Michael watched the scene with a growing sense of dismay. "I don't know what you've done to the parrot, what's between you, but you're making yourself ill, Nuria. You're letting go of reality."

"What is reality? You think I'm living two lives, that I'm a nun in a convent as well as the *doña de las putas*. Is that real?"

"I don't think that anymore."

"Why not?"

"I'm not sure. It simply doesn't make sense. I know you better now and I know it doesn't make sense."

"Sense. Reality. You are a prisoner of your own ideas, Michael."

They were going round in circles. He'd say what he'd come here to say and have done with it. "I'm going out of town for a few days, maybe a week. I didn't want to leave without telling you."

She turned toward him. "Is she going with you?"

"Beth? No, of course not. It's a business trip."

"She is your business."

"What are you talking about?"

"The other night, when I saw you together, I knew. Inside she is hard like you. She is your woman." In Spanish the phrase your woman, *tu mujer,* had many meanings. Your lover, your wife, your creature.

"She's not," Michael said.

Nuria didn't seem to have heard him. "It is as it should be. You have her and I have my beautiful *papagayo.*"

"Oh, for God's sake, Nuria! This business with the bird is insane. Put him in his cage and come inside and lie down. A few hours sleep and a decent meal is what you need. You're thin as a rail. When I come back we'll talk again. There's a lot you don't understand. I want to explain, but there isn't time now."

"I understand everything," she said softly. "Good-bye, Michael."

He stared at her hopelessly for a few moments, then left because there was nothing more to say.

Michael stood in the street in front of the bordello, gazing at the big house, thinking of Nuria in the small one behind it. He hated leaving her like this. She was walking some kind of tightrope. He was fairly sure it was of her own making, but also that she was bound to fall off. And he'd be away. There was Beth to consider too. Damn! He should never have got himself in the position of feeling responsible for these two women when he had so much else to do. Too late for that now.

A man walked past him, looked from Michael to the door of the whorehouse, and smiled. The man looked familiar. Michael couldn't place him at first, then he remembered. He took a step in the stranger's direction. It brought him close enough to see his mistake. It wasn't Rosa. Now there was a thought. He could ask Rosa to keep an eye on Beth, maybe on Nuria as well. It wasn't clear what the old man might do for them, but the idea gave Michael some respite from worry. He fished in his pocket and found Rosa's address.

Córdoba, One P.M.

The message had come for Francisco half an hour earlier. A young boy dispatched by the bank manager had knocked on the door of the palace and said he had an urgent communication for Don Francisco.

The note had been brief. He must go to the bank, and if he had any substantial amounts of cash he must bring it.

It was the first such summons Francisco had ever received, and it didn't occur to him to take offense or ignore it. He took a leather valise into the counting room, unlocked the secret door in the ancient cupboard, and from the hole behind it took fifty packets of notes. Each packet was worth five hundred pesetas. When he arrived at the marble-fronted building on the Calle Real he was carrying the modest fortune he'd secreted against some unforseen circumstance.

Juan Luis had built the new bank in 1890, three years before he was killed. It was part of his plan for modernizing their operations in Spain. "We got rich on the gold from the colonies and we've always relied on traders and merchants," he'd told his brother-in-law. "But the day of the colonies is past. The future of banking is elsewhere."

According to Juan Luis that future was in the hands of small depositors. "Lots of little fish weigh as much as a few big fish, and they're easier to catch."

As far as Francisco was concerned it had all been idle chatter. In those days it had never occurred to him that someday he'd be responsible for the bank. He'd chuckled indulgently when he first heard about the plan to catch the little fish. Francisco was going after women.

"They all gamble like crazy, every woman in Spain. The rich ones have nothing to do but gossip and play cards. *La Escoba, La Ronda, La Brisca.* Those games occupy their lives. And they save up coins to bet with."

"A few coins from women's purses, Juan Luis? That's what

you're building your big new bank for?" It was hard for Francisco to keep from laughing.

"Many women make lots of coins."

It hadn't turned out to be such a crazy idea. Juan Luis had Beatriz tell all her friends that the Banco Mendoza welcomed small accounts from ladies. "Tell them we'll keep everything in strict confidence. Their husbands don't have to know a thing. And every woman who opens an account with a deposit of ten pesetas or more gets a present. A fan."

He had the fans made by some Gypsies in Seville, bright-colored paper with painted pictures and lace frills. They cost him only a few centimos each. Juan Luis gave away quite a few fans, because a number of Córdoba's fine ladies were intrigued by the idea of having their own bank account.

This afternoon it looked to Francisco as if every one of them had arrived at the bank at the same time. The hall was crowded with jabbering women. They stood in long queues, which seemed to reach into infinity because they were reflected in the long mirrors that lined the big room, and their voices were like the droning of a million bees.

"*Madre de Dios*," Francisco breathed into the ear of the bank manager. They were standing in the manager's office, peeking at the scene outside through a crack in the door. "What's going on? Why are they here?"

"*Yo no sé.* I only know that a few of them came this morning, then more of them every hour. Each one of these women is withdrawing all her money. It's true that none of the accounts is very large, but all of them at one time.... There is very little money left in the vault, Don Francisco. Did you bring more?"

Francisco held up his valise. "All I have, but the Russian withdrawal . . . I cannot cover the withdrawal of the Imperial Treasury out of my private resources." His face was a sick shade of gray.

The bank manager bit back the curse that came to his lips. Working for an idiot who knew nothing about banking was impossible. He'd have to find another job. "I'm not talking about the total reserves of the bank, Don Francisco. Only the operating cash we keep in the vault. By tomorrow I can get more, but there's half an hour to go before closing." He glanced over his shoulder at the clock on his desk. "Only twenty-five minutes now. Please, Don Francisco." The manager gestured toward the valise.

Francisco shoved it into his hands. "Yes, yes, take it. But why did all these women come today, they—"

"Perhaps you will figure it out and tell me, Don Francisco. Now I must bring this money to the tellers."

Francisco watched as the manager distributed the stacks of notes to the three men standing behind a long counter. Each man had a thick ledger beside him, and every time he served a customer he made lengthy notes on the lined pages. The tellers were writing slowly, with infinite care. Francisco assumed they were following orders. The longer it took to deal with each withdrawal, the fewer there would be before closing time.

But it was a delaying tactic, nothing more. God alone knew what had caused these women to swarm on his bank, but if they carried whatever story they'd heard home to their husbands . . . *¡Jesus!* it could be a disaster.

He recognized many of the ladies in the long lines. Quite a few of them were friends of Beatriz's. Francisco felt a surge of anger. Why wasn't Beatriz here where for once she could be useful? She could call on these women, find out what they'd heard, where. She could put their minds at ease. But no, once more she was failing in her duty to him. She was gallivanting around England when she should have been at home.

Somewhere a bell rang. One thirty. Closing time. Each of the tellers slammed his ledger shut and locked the cash drawer he'd been plundering.

The women crowded into the bank set up a wail. It was like the scolding of a hundred magpies. No, a thousand.

The manager was moving among them, reassuring them that the bank would open at eight-thirty the following morning. If they wished to withdraw their money, they could do it then. But really, there was no reason. He knew for a fact that the Mendoza family were contemplating a raise in the rate of interest . . . Rumors were nothing but mischief . . .

The manager cast a longing look toward the slightly open door behind which his employer was hiding. Francisco knew it was a plea for him to go out and face the women. The presence of the owner, at least the man people thought of as the owner, would be calming. It would convince the women that everything was well.

The thought of going among those harpies made him shake with fear.

Francisco slammed the door of the office and dashed out the rear exit. In the alley behind the bank he doubled over with cramps. He started to retch and couldn't stop. In minutes he'd vomited everything he'd eaten for the past two days.

The Hills above San Juan, Four P.M.

Sister Paloma knocked on the door of the mother superior's office, then went in without waiting for a reply. "You wished to see me, Madre?"

"*Sí, mi niña. Siéntate.*"

Paloma sat on the wooden stool beside the superior's table.

The older nun was writing a letter. She took a moment to finish it and sign her name with a flourish, then transferred her attention to Paloma. "You have been taking Sister Magdalena her meals?"

"*Sí, Madre.* That honor has been mine for many months."

"But sister cook tells me that the trays come back untouched. Is that true?"

Paloma nodded. "It is true. I keep telling the holy sister she must eat, but she doesn't listen to me. She is very weak, Madre. And even in the dark I can see how thin she is. I think she is doing penance."

"Penance is one thing," the mother superior said firmly. "Suicide is quite another. It is a sin. How long has this been going on?"

"Since the visit of His Excellency the bishop," Paloma explained. "Ever since the day he padlocked the door to her cell she has eaten almost nothing."

The superior sighed. When that remarkable child was thrust upon her community but not actually made part of it, she'd known it would bring trouble. Now the child was a woman, a saint probably, but the basic problem remained. Sister Magdalena was not vowed to obey the mother superior in all things, the way the other nuns were. She gave her obedience directly to the bishop. Still, everyone thought of her as part of this convent. And if she died under questionable circumstances, of starvation perhaps, it was the convent that would be blamed. The nun glanced at the letter she'd written, then picked up her pen again and added a postscript. *Please come quickly, Excellency. It is most urgent.*

She initialed the sentence she'd written below her signature and folded the letter. "I believe it's tomorrow, Paloma, that you are to go into San Juan to buy material for new habits?"

The little nun nodded enthusiastically. As the extern she was permitted such jaunts, but there were few opportunities for them. She was looking forward to this one.

The mother superior smiled. "Do you ever long to fly free, little dove? To leave this place? Then you could go to San Juan whenever you wished."

"Leave! Oh, Holy Mother, do not tell me to leave. I could not bear to be separated from the convent. I will—"

"Ssh. Don't excite yourself. I was asking a question, not making a suggestion. Now, about tomorrow. Before you leave you are to come to me. I will have this letter ready to go. You are to bring it to the bishop's palace and wait for a reply. And be very discreet, Paloma. There is much excitement in San Juan at the moment, much distress. See that you add nothing to the general uproar. No one is to know that Sister Magdalena is following such a severe fast."

❧ 13 ❧

THURSDAY, JULY 8, 1898
London, Seven A.M.

Charles walked quickly, turning into narrow Basil Street just as a clock somewhere chimed seven times. Knightsbridge was all but deserted. The only other person on the street was a man polishing the wheels of a Harrods delivery carriage. It was parked a few doors from Tim's house. There was a rumor that Harrods wanted to expand yet again, that they'd offered as much as a thousand pounds for some of the houses that backed up on their already enormous premises. If Tim had been approached by Harrods, he hadn't told Charles about it. Nothing unusual in that.

Charles climbed the few stairs to the front door and rapped sharply. The maid who appeared was very young, fourteen or fifteen perhaps. Her apron was wrinkled and she had a polishing cloth in her hand. "Yes?"

A badly managed household. Sara would never allow their door to be answered in such a fashion, not even first thing in the morning. "I'm Charles Mendoza. I wish to see my brother."

The girl cocked her head. There was something insolent in her expression. "Mr. Mendoza ain't up yet."

"Very well, wake him."

Charles started to step inside; the girl didn't move. Over her shoulder he saw Harcourt, Tim's butler, coming into the front hall. He was pulling on his tailcoat. "Who is it, Flossie?"

"A gentleman, Mr. Harcourt. Asking for Mr. Mendoza."

"I'm sorry, sir, Mr. Mendoza—Oh, it's you, Mr. Charles. I didn't realize. Flossie, why didn't you say it was Mr. Charles? Come in, sir."

Charles gave Harcourt his hat but refused to hand over his briefcase. "Thank you, but I'll keep this. Please wake my brother and tell him I'm here. It's urgent or I wouldn't disturb him at this hour."

"Of course, sir. Right away." The butler showed Charles into the morning room, sent the maid for tea, and disappeared.

Charles sat down at an elegant mahogany writing table, fidgeted a moment with the pristine blotter and the silver desk set, then got up. He wandered around the room, gazing at the pictures on the walls—mostly hunting scenes—and examining the rugs and the furniture. He'd been here before, but not all that frequently. Beth and Sara were no fonder of each other than he and Tim. Sara would never admit it, but she was jealous of the other woman's astounding good looks. For his part Charles liked Beth well enough. At least he had until she'd pulled this ghastly trick of running off with Michael Curran. Tim was probably well rid of her. The house missed her, though. The absence of a woman's touch was evident. No flowers in the morning room for a start.

"What the hell are you doing here at this hour?"

"Good morning. Sorry to get you up." Charles spoke the apology through habit; he wasn't really sorry. The sight of Tim started him seething again, the way he had all night.

Tim had pulled on trousers and a brocaded silk dressing gown but hadn't taken the time to shave. His face was shadowed by dark stubble. He ran his fingers through his hair, but the gesture didn't do much for his appearance. "I don't accept your apology. Not yet. What was so urgent it couldn't wait a few hours until I see you at the bank?"

He went to the door before Charles could answer. "Harcourt! Where's that tea?" He turned back to his brother. "I can't think before tea."

"I'd better wait until it arrives then. You'll have to think." The words came out clipped and hard, edged with anger.

"About what? What you've come here to say? Is it about the old bastard?"

"About Father, yes, in a way."

"I thought so. Anybody seen him yet?"

Norman had left the bank immediately after his shouting match with Tim on Tuesday and not appeared since. Philip Johnson had gone to the house yesterday afternoon, but Norman's servants hadn't seen him either.

"We still haven't found him," Charles said. "And it's been thirty-six hours. I rang Whites last evening, but he's not there."

"Well, I'm not—" Tim stopped speaking when Flossie came in.

The house was some two hundred years old and the door to the morning room was a massive slab of carved oak. The maid didn't knock, merely pushed the door open with her knee because both hands were occupied carrying a heavy silver tray. "Your tea, sir." She put the tray on a small table near Tim. "Will the gentleman be staying to breakfast, sir?"

"I expect so. Tell cook we'll have it as soon as possible."

Flossie dropped an indifferent curtsy and left them alone.

"All right about breakfast?" Tim asked. "Haven't lost your appetite because the old bastard's gone missing, have you, Charles?"

"You shouldn't talk about him that way."

"Why the hell not? Bastard's too tame a word for him."
He poured the tea. "Milk and sugar?"

"Yes, please. Listen, now you've got your tea, are you
ready to hear what I've come to say?"

"I thought you'd already said it. We're supposed to be
weeping bitter tears and combing London for the man who
gave us life and breath."

"I've already started inquiries," Charles said. "I don't need
to involve you in that."

"Discreet inquiries, I hope. It wouldn't do for the City to
get wind of some foul stink around our doors. Not at the
moment."

"No, it wouldn't," Charles agreed. "But I've been wondering if you care."

"Of course I bloody well care. I don't want to bring the
whole bank tumbling down around our ears."

"Don't you?"

"What the hell's that supposed to mean?" Tim demanded.

"What I asked. Do you or do you not wish to cause
Mendozas to fail?"

"That's the craziest damned question I've ever heard. My
bread's buttered on the same side as yours. Who have you
got looking for Father?"

"Philip Johnson. He was the natural candidate for the
task."

"Yes, I suppose you're right. He's checking doctors' sur-
geries, hospitals, places like that?"

"Among other possibilities, yes."

"Good. And I agree, Philip will be discreet."

Charles drained his cup and put it on the writing table.
"You have been too, haven't you? Very discreet."

"I don't follow."

"Yes, you do. As I said, you've been very discreet about
your affairs. You might say secretive."

"If you're talking about my wife, there's no point in making a public fuss, is there?"

"I don't mean Beth."

"What do you mean then?"

"I mean that you're a bloody liar."

Charles didn't raise his voice, but the words came out hard and fast, as if they'd been contained under pressure. Timothy didn't respond immediately. The two brothers appraised each other. "Mind telling me the basis of that insult?" Tim asked at last.

"No, I don't mind. The basis, as you call it, is in there." Charles pointed to his briefcase on the table.

"I see. And the next act in this melodrama is that you show me whatever it is you've got in there."

"That seems like a good move, yes." Charles crossed to the writing table and flipped the catches on the leather satchel. He withdrew a sheaf of papers and passed them to his brother. "These are copies. I have the originals in a safe place."

"Copies of what? I don't understand—" Timothy stopped speaking as soon as he saw the first page. "Where did you get this?" His voice had changed, the bantering, sarcastic undertone had disappeared.

"That's not important. You know what it is, I see."

Timothy realized his mistake, but it was too late to backtrack. He should have pretended not to know that this was a report of the financial and political conditions prevailing in Paraguay, identical to the one he'd received in Dublin. "I know what it claims to be," he admitted.

"You knew weeks ago. That's the point. You got this on the fifteenth of June. It was delivered to you at a pub called the Swan, on Bachelors Walk in Dublin."

"You have a lot of information. Are you sure it's accurate?"

"I'm sure."

"How can you be? Who told you all this rubbish?"

"Who told me isn't important. What matters is that you knew about the mess in Paraguay eight days before we floated the issue. When he had that meeting you knew what Uncle

Henry was so unhappy about. Father asked us then, you and me, if we knew anything to back up Henry's position. You didn't say a word."

Tim had been ruffling through the pages of the report. Now he dropped it casually on the table. "I'm less trusting than you are, brother mine. I wasn't prepared to believe everything I read in an anonymous report."

"Liar," Charles said again.

"Careful," Tim said softly. "Careful, Charlie my boy, you're treading on dangerous ground. Keep up the insults and I'll be forced to respond. Demand satisfaction. Slap my glove across your face, or whatever it is that gentlemen do."

"I don't think you know a damned thing about what gentlemen do. For a start, they don't conceal vital information from their own flesh and blood. They don't sit by and watch a situation develop that could bankrupt everyone around them."

"Bankrupt's a pretty strong term."

"Not too strong. Here's something else you don't know about." Charles handed a pale yellow envelope to his brother. "This cable came late last night, after you'd left the bank."

For a moment Tim wondered if it was from Russia, notice of withdrawal of the funds of the Imperial Treasury. Could Lila really wield that much influence? He was sure she was behind the Russian who'd cornered Jamie at his club, but he'd assumed it was a ploy, a tactic to make them nervous. If the Russian funds really were withdrawn . . . Christ, what a mess that would be. Certainly more than he bargained for.

"Stop standing there wasting time," Charles said. "Read it."

Timothy opened the envelope and withdrew the half-page message.

URGENTLY REQUEST THAT YOU SEND SOMEONE TO TAKE OVER MY DUTIES IN CORDOBA STOP DIFFICULT

SITUATION DEVELOPING WITH THE RESERVES STOP
CANNOT BE RESPONSIBLE FOR SAME DUE TO FAILING
HEALTH SIGNED FRANCISCO VALDEZ DE GIAS.

"Jesus Christ almighty," Tim whispered. "He sent this by
public telegraph?"

"He did."

"That's it. It's bound to leak. He's dropped us in the
manure pile, has old Francisco."

The tone infuriated Charles, snapped his control. Tim
sounded as if he were discussing something outside himself,
something for which he bore no responsibility.

"You bloody sodding liar." He took a step toward Tim,
both hands balled into fists, his voice rising on every word.
"You're the one who's dropped us in the manure pile. You
could have prevented all this. You knew things weeks ago
that none of the rest of us knew and you didn't say a bloody
word. You let Father go on when you could have stopped
him."

"Nothing can stop Father once he's made up his mind.
You know that perfectly well. What the hell's the point of
putting facts in front of a bloody mindless bull? He just
charges on."

Both men were shouting now. Charles pitched his voice
above his brother's. "I know that you're behind all this. That's
what Father was so angry about the other day. It's true.
You've some scheme of your own, a plan to take over. You've
been so goddammed worried that I'd get the bank and not
you, that you—" Charles lunged for Tim at the same moment that Flossie came in.

Stepping backward to avoid his brother, Tim took the
weight of the heavy oak door full in the back. The crack of
the wood connecting with his head and spine was audible.
Tim lurched forward one step, then collapsed. There was
another sound, that of his forehead hitting the brass fender
surrounding the fireplace.

"Breakfast is—Oh, my God! Oh, my God, sir, what's happened?"

Charles looked from the terrified maid to Tim's body crumpled on the floor. A spreading pool of red was dripping from the fender railing onto the pale cream hearth rug. "Get Harcourt. Tell him to ring for a doctor."

"Yes, sir, I will sir. But it wasn't me, honest. I didn't do nothin' but open the door to say about breakfast bein' ready and—"

"Stop babbling. Go do as you're told."

The maid fled. Charles crouched beside his brother. Tim lay facedown and unmoving. Charles tried to decide whether he should attempt to feel beneath him to see if his heart was beating. He stretched out a tentative hand. That's when he realized it was still balled into the fist he'd made seconds before when he'd begun his aborted attack.

San Juan, Eleven A.M.

The man shuffled across the inn's courtyard, walking with difficulty and leaning on a cane. The landlord was sitting in a woven cane chair near the door, chewing on the stub of an unlit cigar, and he watched the stranger's approach without interest.

"*Buenos días, señor,*" the newcomer said.

"*Muy buenos.*" The innkeeper didn't take the cigar out of his mouth when he spoke. "*¿Qué quieres, abuelo?*"

Rosa grimaced at being addressed as grandfather. He'd been lame for a week, since he got drunk and fell down the steps of the *taverna*'s wine cellar. That didn't make him old. This one was without manners, stupid and overfamiliar, like all the islanders. "I wish to see the English señorita. Send word to her at once." Rosa spoke with contrasting formality, standing as erect as the support of the cane allowed.

"We have many guests, *abuelo*. What is the señorita's name?"

"You have only one English lady staying in this pigsty. Now get her, or when he returns I will tell the Irish *caballero* that you are charging him double what you would charge any local."

The innkeeper stood up, removing the cigar from his mouth and aiming an accurate jet of yellow spittle at a brass bowl on the floor. "Wait here." He started toward the stairs, then paused. "What name do I tell her?"

"A friend of Señor Curran's, that is enough."

Beth arrived in five minutes. Rosa had seated himself in one of the half-rotten wicker chairs; now he struggled to get up.

"Please, don't trouble yourself. You wished to see me?"

Rosa ignored her request and pulled himself to his feet. "*Sí*, señorita. I hope I am not disturbing you."

"Not at all. And your English is very good. I don't speak Spanish, I'm sorry."

"It is not important. You are young. I have lived long enough to learn many languages. Perhaps you will do me the honor to step outside to the patio where we may speak with more privacy."

Beth walked slowly beside him, matching her gait to his. The man looked like a peasant, but he was clean, and his manners were those of a gentleman. "I understand you have a message from Mr. Curran," she said as soon as they'd reached the courtyard.

"In a manner of speaking. We can sit over there if it pleases you, señorita." Rosa gestured with his cane to a bench in the partial shade of a palm tree. "The sun is very hot, no? You do not have such hot sun in London."

"No, we do not. Have you been in London, señor?"

"Many years ago, when I was a much younger man. A wonderful city; I liked it a great deal. Except for the rain."

They'd reached the bench and sat down. "You are comfortable, señorita?"

"Quite comfortable. Now, please. Mr. Curran . . ."

"Ah, yes. You get to business directly, you English. Forgive my Spanish custom of rambling. Mr. Curran asked me to call on you. Before he left."

"Oh. You haven't heard from him since he went away?"

Her hair was an incredible color. He couldn't take his eyes off it. The color of a pale yellow rose. And only English women had skin like that. No wonder the Irishman was anxious about her welfare. "I have heard nothing since Señor Curran came to me the day before yesterday. He asked me to come here and to see if you needed anything."

She was disappointed, but pleased at Michael's concern. "That is very kind, señor. No, there's nothing I need."

"Good. This pig of a Puerto Rican, the innkeeper, he is treating you well?"

"Perfectly well. You are not from the island, señor?"

Rosa smiled. He was missing a number of teeth. "No, señorita. I am a *madrileño,* from Madrid."

"And did you know Señor Curran when you were in Spain? Before he left there?"

"He was a young boy when he left. I didn't know him, but I knew Doña Lila, his mother."

Beth fingered the fringes of her silk shawl and didn't look at him. "Lila Curran is a most remarkable woman."

"She is," Rosa agreed. "Most remarkable. And her son seems to be—how do you say it in English?—cut from the same cloth."

"Yes." She turned to him, her green eyes studying his face. "Michael Curran is destined for great things. I wish I knew more about his boyhood in Córdoba. I envy you that you knew the family there."

"The family." Rosa paused. "They are more than a family;

the Mendozas are—" He stopped speaking, afraid he'd said too much.

"I know the Mendozas very well," Beth assured him. "You might say I know them intimately. At least the English Mendozas."

The Spaniard shrugged. "I doubt if there is much difference between the English and the Spanish Mendozas. If you know them, you must know what I mean."

Beth's mind was racing. Did she dare push this conversation further? It was risky. If Michael found out he might be furious. But this old man knew things she longed to know. Things no one else could tell her. And he'd arrived unannounced, like a gift from fate. Michael hadn't mentioned sending someone to see her. She leaned over, laying her hand on his. "Señor, I feel I can trust you. I want to ask you something."

"Whatever you wish, señorita. I am at your command."

"In England it is well known that the Mendozas were Jews before they became Christians. Is it true that in Spain that isn't known?"

"In Spain," he began hesitantly, "it is different. In England you did not have the Inquisition."

"No, but—"

"It is different," he repeated. More firmly this time. "There are plenty of people in Spain who know of the Mendoza origins. But they do not discuss it. To talk about such a thing is considered—" he hesitated again, seeking the English word, "evil. Filthy. I do not know if those are the correct terms, but I think so."

"And do you think," she asked very softly, "that it is filthy and evil to talk about Jews?"

His dark eyes searched her face. "No, señorita. I do not think so."

The shade of the palm tree wasn't sufficient to protect them from the steadily rising temperature. It was almost noon and the sun was directly overhead and remorseless.

Beth moistened her lips with her tongue and fanned herself. "Señor . . . may I know your name?"

"Forgive me, it was rude not to introduce myself. I am Rosa."

"Señor Rosa, do you believe that Señor Curran is . . . that he believes in Judaism?"

"It is not possible to say what any other man believes, señorita. Why do you think that may be so?"

"My servant and Mr. Curran's servant, they're brother and sister. It's just a coincidence, but—"

Rosa bent forward, leaning on his cane. "Yes?"

"—but I am told that Señor Curran will eat no pork. Isn't it true that Jews do not eat pork?"

"That is true. But to say that a man is a Jew because he doesn't eat a certain food . . ." He shrugged.

"It sounds ridiculous, I know. It's only because of everything else—"

"What else?"

"I'm not sure," Beth admitted. "But Lila, Mrs. Curran, they say . . ." She broke off. It was too complicated and she was getting in too deep. Michael really would be furious if he found out.

"People say many things, señorita. In the old days, for instance, in Spain during the time of the Inquisition, if it was reported that a man changed his underclothes on Saturday he was accused of being a marrano, a secret Jew. Because Saturday is the Jewish sabbath. If he refused to eat pork they were sure of it. So you are perhaps not being so ridiculous."

"But Michael doesn't seem to believe in any religion. So why—"

"You know, señorita, that he was born in Córdoba. Perhaps that is all you need to know."

"And that he's a Mendoza," Beth added.

Rosa stood up. "Yes, that too. Now, señorita, if you are sure there is nothing I can do for you . . ."

"Nothing, Señor Rosa. Thank you very much for calling on me."

The Spaniard bowed gracefully. "It has been an honor to meet you. I hope we will see each other again."

Beth rose, the folds of her pale blue cotton dress fell gracefully around her small form. "I think we will, Señor Rosa. In fact I'm sure of it."

London, Two P.M.

Philip Johnson had exhausted all the likely places; it was time to think about unlikely possibilities. Mr. Norman wasn't at home, he wasn't at his club, there was nothing to indicate that he'd had an accident or was ill. So where was he?

The secretary was walking up Baker Street. He'd been in and out of every public house in Marylebone, as well as Mayfair and Belgravia and half a dozen other districts. If Mr. Norman had gone to drink himself into a stupor, he wasn't doing it in any taproom he could be expected to frequent. And he wasn't on Baker Street.

Philip reached the end of the road and paused. There was something nagging at the back of his mind, something he thought might be important but that he couldn't quite dredge up.

Passersby jostled him on every side. The fine summer weather had given way to thick gray clouds half an hour ago. Now a soft rain began to fall. Umbrellas appeared instantly. Londoners knew their climate too well to venture far without them. Philip also carried one but he didn't open it. He was too preoccupied to realize that the rain was getting heavier and he'd soon be soaked.

A man hurrying along bumped into him. "Sorry, gov," he murmured. It required only those two words to identify him as a Cockney. The man started to walk on, then paused. "Need any 'elp, gov? Not sick or nuffin', are you?"

"What . . . ? Oh, very kind of you. I'm fine."

The stranger tugged at the brim of his cap and moved on. Damned nice of him Philip thought. The East Enders were like that. A hard lot, but—Christ, that was it! Creechurch Lane in the East End. That was the thought that had been nagging at him—the old house where the Mendozas had lived for centuries, where they had conducted all their business until his lordship sold up and moved the bank to Lower Sloane Street.

Philip unfurled his umbrella, opened it with a decisive snap, and began walking.

"How did you think to look for me here?" Norman asked.

"It struck me as likely, sir. Being upset about what had upset you, it seemed natural that you'd gravitate to the old place."

"Well, you were right." They were sitting by the window of a pub. Norman could look directly across Mitre Street to the intersection with Creechurch Lane. Number seven was straight ahead. "Look at it, Philip. That narrow little house with its crooked half timbers, it's been standing there some four hundred years. How it escaped the Great Fire, or a hundred lesser fires, is a mystery."

"Yes, it is, sir. Who lives there now?"

"The man my brother James sold it to, I imagine. A German baker come to England to make his fortune."

"Maybe the house will be lucky for him too, sir."

Norman snorted. "Lucky? I suppose it looks that way from the outside." He raised his empty glass in the direction of the bar. "Terence, another. And one for this gentleman with me."

The clock said two minutes to three, almost closing time, but the publican didn't glance at it. He drew two more glasses of bitter and brought them to the table.

"Thank you, Terence. Do you know my guest?"

"Course I do, sir. Afternoon, Mr. Johnson. Hope you've been well."

In the old days, before they'd moved, Philip had often stopped in here for a drink on his way home. "Very well, Terence. And you?"

"The same, sir. Always the same."

The publican left them, pausing to lock the front door and draw the curtains. "You gentlemen sit as long as you like. No one will bother you. I'll be in the back when you want me, Mr. Norman."

"He's been here since before I was born." Norman said. Philip's employer looked ghastly: his suit was wrinkled and filthy and he hadn't shaved in two days, but his words weren't slurred. Maybe he'd wanted to get drunk, but he hadn't achieved it.

"You weren't born in the old place, were you, sir?"

"No. My father had moved to Gordon Square by then. But the business was still conducted from Creechurch Lane. Sometimes he'd bring me here when I was little. To see how the bank worked. I was bred for that bank, Philip. All the Mendoza men are. At least they used to be."

"They still are," Johnson said quietly. "Young men need to prove themselves, sir. They don't mean to be disrespectful—"

"Some young men," Norman interrupted. "But sometimes the breeding goes wrong. A rogue element creeps in. That's what I've been thinking about these past couple of days. How if there's a rogue element, you have to get rid of it. However ruthless you have to be, it's got to be done." He paused and took a deep breath. "Drink up. It's time we left."

A few seconds later Norman asked, "Who sent you to look for me? Was it Henry?"

"No, sir. Mr. Charles. He was very concerned."

"Charles. I see."

They finished their beer and called for Terence to unlock the door of the pub. It had stopped raining and the puddles were evaporating in bright sun. "So it was Charles," Norman murmured, more to himself than to Philip. The thought made him feel a bit warmer. He'd been shivering the entire two days since he'd stormed out of the bank. Felt as if he'd never be warm again. A bit better now. Norman waved his hand to attract a passing cab.

Charles stood to one side, watching the doctor who was watching the still figure in the bed. Timothy didn't move. He looked deathly pale against the white linen sheets. The doctor leaned down and pulled back each eyelid in turn, then sighed and stood up. "There's no change."

"Should there be? I mean it's very soon, isn't it? It's only been a few hours since the accident."

The doctor looked at his watch. It was after three. "Eight hours. And he's lost a lot of blood." He touched the bandages wrapped around Timothy's head. "I've done all I can. Now we must simply wait."

"Yes, I understand."

"I hope you do, sir. I don't wish to sound harsh, but in my experience it's best if someone in the family understands the implications from the first. Your brother has a very severe concussion. I cannot tell whether his brain is damaged, but—" he hesitated, then went on, "it may be."

"He could be a vegetable, that's what you're telling me? Even after he wakes up."

"If he wakes up. Yes."

Charles shivered. He'd been having chills since he and Harcourt and the physician had managed to carry Timothy's limp body up to his bedroom. The doctor had suggested a hospital but Charles had vetoed the idea. Anything that happened in a hospital was bound to be known by a large number of people. Rumors spread like wildfire in such places. The last thing Mendozas needed was fresh gossip and speculation. Now he thought about the doctor's words.

"You mean he may not wake up? He could go on like this . . . for years?"

"Precisely."

"I see. I suppose I must thank you for being frank." Charles swallowed hard. "When will the nurse arrive?"

"Any minute now. Miss Dancer promised to come before three-thirty, and she's—"

A soft tapping at the door interrupted his words. Both men expected the nurse. Instead it was Harcourt. "Mr. Charles," he whispered.

"Yes, Harcourt, what is it?"

"Telephone, sir. It's the bank. They said it was urgent."

"Thank you. I'll come immediately." And when they were on the way downstairs, "Harcourt, you didn't say anything—"

"About the master's accident? Of course not, sir. You told me it wasn't to be mentioned to anyone."

"Yes, right. Good man."

Charles followed the butler into Tim's study. A portrait of Beth hung over the fireplace. He glanced at it, wondering briefly why Tim had left it in place considering the way she'd walked out on him, then picked up the telephone. "Charles Mendoza here."

"It's Lawson, Mr. Charles. Sorry to disturb you, but you said I was to ring if there was anything urgent."

Charles had not yet informed either of his uncles about the accident, but he'd telephoned his clerk at eight this morning and said that he and his brother would be working at Timothy's house all day. They were to be disturbed only in the event of an emergency.

"Well, what's the urgency, Lawson?"

"A telephone call, sir. Gentleman said it was of vital importance that he speak with you today. Asked if you'd ring him back."

"What gentleman?"

"Lord Sharrick, sir. That's why I thought I'd best pass

the message on right away. Given that he wrote that piece in the *Times* last month, I mean."

"Yes, I know what you mean. Good, you've done the right thing, Lawson."

Charles was thoughtful when he hung up. It was a damned strange development. What could Sharrick want now? Hadn't he done all the mischief possible? And why didn't he want to speak to James, or at least to Norman or Henry? Men like Sharrick usually expected to deal with those at the very top. He shook his head. No point in standing here worrying about it; he'd call Sharrick and get the answers.

Still, he didn't pick up the telephone. He felt guilty about Tim and weighed down by all the trouble, by the feeling that suddenly everything was his responsibility. Christ, Philip Johnson had better find his father soon. If he didn't, only God knew what was going to happen.

He heard a visitor arrive in the front hall, Harcourt's voice, and that of a strange woman. Must be the nurse. Charles debated going out to meet her, then decided it could wait. Resolutely he lifted the receiver.

Lares, Four P.M.

The house of Coco Morales was a magnificent ruin. Once it had been a showplace set like a jewel in the hills above the town. Now the paint was peeling, the gardens were overgrown, the roof sagged, and most of the furniture looked as if it would crumble to dust if you touched it. The only exception to the general decay was the large room where Michael now sat with the planter.

It was well furnished and freshly painted. The carpets spread over the tile floor were orientals that must have come from the Spanish mainland in better days. The windows looked out on rows of coffee trees, the near edge of the actual working plantation. The day was overcast and hazy, the short thin trunks of the trees melded into a blur in the dim light.

Like his guest, Morales was intent on the view. "I shall be sorry to leave here."

"Where will you go?" Michael asked.

Morales shrugged. "I'm not sure. Panama perhaps, or Mexico."

"Not Madrid? The mother country doesn't call you?"

"I am a man of the islands, Señor Curran. Spain is not my mother. Spain has bled the Indies dry."

"But without her you wouldn't be here. You're not an Indian or a black, Morales. Your blood is Spanish. If they hadn't come, you wouldn't exist."

The planter shrugged. "Your argument is logical. But it doesn't mean anything here." He thumped his chest. "Here I know that when Spain took away our slaves she cut out our heart. Everything you see, what this place has become, it is because in Europe they made a decision without consulting us, without considering what it would do to what we'd spent years building."

Michael had been in arguments like this before. He knew it was useless to try and persuade people who had been impoverished by losing their slaves that they'd never had any right to them. Perhaps he'd feel the same way in their position. "I take your point," he said easily. "Now, I must go or I'll miss the train."

Michael walked across the room and hefted his valise. It was light now, empty of the stacks of peseta notes he'd brought with him.

A stab of elation ran through him, but he did not allow it to show. His thoughts were racing. He'd done exactly what he'd come here to do. Sixteen of his original targets had agreed to his terms. Only Doña Maria de los Angeles had refused, and though he'd made a great show of regret, Michael could afford to lose her. As yet no one but he knew it, but from this moment the Banco Mendoza de Puerto Rico was in his control. It was all over bar the shouting. There would be plenty of that, but it wouldn't make a penny's worth of difference. Nonetheless, he had to continue the charade a little longer.

"Thank you for your hospitality," he told Morales. "It was good of you to let me make your home my base, and good of the other planters to come here to see me."

The lidless eyes studied him. "Most men will travel a considerable distance for seventy-five thousand pesetas in cash money, Señor Curran. That was not remarkable."

Michael knew what the other man had left unsaid: that it was the Irishman's desire to buy seventeen plantations—to pay a premium for them at a time like this—that was remarkable. He grinned at the planter. "We all have our own ideas of how to make our fortunes, Señor Morales. Only time will tell if we're right or wrong. Speaking of which . . ." Michael took the fob watch from his waistcoat pocket and looked at it.

"Yes, you must go," Morales agreed. "Come, my carriage is waiting to drive you to the station."

The two men walked together toward the door of the room. Morales stopped and looked back over his shoulder. "Señor Curran, I believe you are forgetting something vital." He returned to where his guest had been sitting and retrieved a briefcase. It contained the documents the sixteen planters had signed.

Morales carried the case to Michael, and the Irishman took it. He wanted to laugh out loud, but Coco Morales wouldn't understand the joke.

❧ 14 ❧

London, Eight P.M.

"Good of you to come," Sharrick said. "Please sit down."

He indicated a chair by the fire and Charles took it. Sharrick seated himself on the other side of the hearth. They were in the study. The smell of burning peat filled the air.

"Not too warm for you, is it?" Sharrick asked. "I'm afraid the tropics have spoiled me. I like a fire even in an English summer."

"It's very pleasant. The evening's turned quite cool. Peat isn't it? You don't often smell a peat fire in London."

"An extravagance of mine. The peat's cut at Glencree, my place in Wicklow. I have it shipped here by the boatload . . . reminds me of home."

Charles wasn't surprised that the other man thought of Ireland as home. His blood was probably Saxon or Norman or both, but God alone knew how many generations of his family had lived across the water. Doubtless they considered themselves Irish by now.

Between the men was a small table with a decanter and two glasses. "Whiskey?" Sharrick asked.

"Thank you, I'd appreciate that."

The whiskey was Irish as well, very old and very smooth. "Delicious," Charles said.

"I'm glad you like it. It's a private label. We distill it ourselves at Glencree. And I might tell you that my next favorite tipple is Mendoza sherry. The fino's wonderful stuff."

Charles smiled and lifted his glass in a toast. He sipped the drink slowly, as it deserved, watching his host over the rim of his glass. An extraordinary man. Almost a legend. Charles had been hearing of the exploits of Sharrick of Glencree since he was a child. This was the first time he'd met him. It was also the first time he'd realized that baldness could be attractive. He smoothed back his own thinning hair. Maybe he should stop worrying so much about it. A clock ticked on the mantelpiece; it was the only sound in the room.

Sharrick's voice broke the silence. "Well, what did you think of my message?"

"I was surprised that you wished to speak with me and not my father or my uncles," Charles said frankly.

"I'm not referring to the telephone call."

"Oh? Then I'm afraid I don't know what you mean."

"The package you got last night. I presume you've read the material."

Charles's hand started to tremble. He put his glass on the table. "I'm still not sure I—"

"Let's not waste time," Sharrick interrupted. "The Mendozas don't have much of it at the moment."

Still Charles hesitated, then he made up his mind. "Are you telling me that you're Kelly?"

That's how the covering note had been signed. It had said, "Please read attached at once. Same was delivered to your brother Timothy in the Swan pub, Bachelors Walk, Dublin, on fifteen June." And it was signed with the single name, Kelly.

"I am," Sharrick admitted. "It was my mother's name. I use it when it suits the occasion."

Things were falling into place. "You were in South America a short time ago. The *Times* said so. I presume you went to Paraguay, though you didn't mention it in your article."

"Correct. I mentioned it to your brother Timothy, however. As I told you, I sent him a copy of that report almost a month ago. He chose not to do anything about it. What do you choose?"

"It's too late for me to choose anything. The bond was issued. As I'm sure you know."

"Yes. But it's not too late. There's still time for you to keep Mendozas from going down the drain."

"Now look here. We're in a sticky patch, I don't deny it. But there's no question of the bank failing. It's absurd to suggest there is. I assure you we—"

Sharrick waved away the protests. "Look, Timothy's finished. Even if he comes out of the coma he'll be a mindless vegetable. As for—"

Charles turned very white. "How do you know about Tim?"

"I have my sources. Not that it's necessary to protect this one any longer. So, since you'll have to look after your brother's affairs now, I'll give you some free advice. Sack Willis, the valet. The man's a swine; he can be bought for a few bob."

"But why should you want to spy on Tim? What's any of this to do with you?" Charles was trying to control himself, but his voice had the hint of a quiver. It had been such a long and awful day.

"Until this morning Timothy was a key player. I had to know what he was doing."

"A key player in what? What's Mendozas to you? That's the part that still doesn't make any sense."

Sharrick leaned forward and refilled both their glasses.

"My connection is admittedly tenuous. And completely personal. A lady."

"A lady? Do you mean Beth? But it's Michael she—" Charles broke off. "It's not Beth, is it? She wouldn't interest a man like you. It's Lila Curran, the Black Widow. She's Irish too. It figures."

"Mrs. Curran is not, I assure you, the only attractive woman in Ireland. Drink up. You look as if you need it."

"It has to be her," Charles insisted. "She's one of us, at least by marriage. She's the only possible link between you and the bank." He took the glass of whiskey and downed it in one swallow. This time the alcohol hit his gut with a thump and spread its warmth through his belly and up into his chest. It felt good.

"Another?" Sharrick asked.

"No, thank you. I think I need a clear head for this chat."

His lordship smiled. "Perhaps you do. It's all up to you now, as I said before."

"I don't see how you reach that conclusion. My uncles and my father—"

"Are finished." The Irishman leaned forward. "Listen to me, young man. The Mendoza Bank is within a quarter inch of falling off the edge into an abyss. It's going to fall. James and Henry and Norman will fall with it. They must; everything is in their names. Their private holdings—property, cash, everything they possess—are going to tumble into the pit with them. The authorities will have it no other way."

"I don't know what you're talking about. Forgive me, but I think you must be mad." Charles was aghast, but inside him a little voice was saying that every word he was hearing was true.

"You know I'm not. How old are you, thirty? Do you remember the Barings crisis? You must, it happened eight years ago, in ninety."

"I remember," Charles pronounced the words with difficulty, his voice weak and uneven. "But Barings came out fine. They reorganized and—"

"Exactly. The reorganization required an entirely new structure. Barings became a limited company, with young John Baring at the head. He was in much the same position you are now; he'd not been a senior partner, so he couldn't be held responsible for the bad judgment that created the mess."

Sharrick went on, speaking slowly, knowing the other man needed time to absorb the implications of his words. "It was Argentina that got Barings into trouble. Funny how both Barings and Mendozas met their Waterloo in South America. It's an extraordinary place, but none of us here in Europe seem to understand it. Something tells me you won't be the last bankers to slide down that particular slope."

"Nor are we the first," Charles said at last. He'd stopped shaking and his voice was firm again. "There have been a number of defaults over the past fifty or so years."

Sharrick nodded. "You'll have to restructure the loan when you take over. But I imagine you know how to do that better than I."

"It could be done," Charles said slowly, thinking it out as he spoke. "We could give them a more realistic repayment schedule, set aside a larger contingency fund to cover any losses incurred down there. And I think it would be best to buy back the shares we've sold. Better for public confidence I mean." He was warming to the subject now. "You see, if you treat the debt as bad to begin with, you don't have any surprises. So you don't get into hot water. And you retain confidence, as I said. Confidence is the sine qua non of banking."

He stopped, aware that he'd sounded as if everything would transpire exactly as the Irishman predicted. As if he were willing to take over from his father and his uncles immediately. Anxious to do so, in fact.

Sharrick read his thoughts in his face. "Don't be embarrassed. It's natural for you to want the power, to plan how to use it. You'd be useless if you didn't feel that way."

"I don't," Charles said vehemently. "I'm not going to be part of any plot to throw my father and my uncles to the wolves. I was merely commenting on the scenario as you set it out."

"Pity," Sharrick said. "I thought you could save them. If you don't want to . . ."

Charles's fingers were laced together, his knuckles white. "I never said I didn't want to. Just that I wouldn't plot."

"Listen to me, young man. You cannot have it both ways. Either you play Pilate and refuse to accept responsibility, or you recognize the opportunity and take the risks and the pain that go with it. The choice is yours, but you have to choose."

"Who are you to tell me what I have to do?"

"A man who's been involved in this from the start. Before any of you knew what was happening. A man who has seen a great deal more of life than you have. I give you my word, everything is going to happen exactly as I've said it will. Eventually you'll get the title, whatever happens. But there'll be damned little of substance to go with it. Perhaps you'll manage to salvage some investments from the ruins. Unless . . . As I said, you have to choose. The Mendoza empire, or a cottage somewhere in the country. You can retire and lick your wounds on an income of about five hundred a year."

The clock on the mantel ticked on. Charles didn't say a word. Sharrick waited. Finally the younger man looked up. "I can't let Mendozas die," he said quietly. "It would be spitting on everything my family's been, everything they've done for generations."

Sharrick nodded. "Very good," he said quietly. "I approve your decision, for what that's worth. Now, before we say any more, I must ask you something. How do you get on with your cousin Michael?"

"Michael Curran? I've only met him a few times. Seems

like rather a flamboyant sort to me. A lot of the Spaniard in him."

"I don't know him well either, but I think that's true. Not a bad thing perhaps. He's going to take over in Córdoba."

"But Francisco . . ." Charles stopped speaking, remembering the cable.

"Ah yes," Sharrick said softly. "What about Francisco?"

"Nothing."

"Come, don't play with me. Not now. I know things have been happening in Córdoba. Have you heard from Francisco?"

"How do you know—" Charles stopped speaking again, knowing the answer to his own question, understanding for the first time the breadth and depth of the net that had been spread to catch them. "You had something to do with that too, didn't you? The troubles in Córdoba, whatever they are, you're behind them."

"In a manner of speaking," Sharrick admitted cooly.

"Oh, my God." The enormity of it appalled him, then Charles saw the next logical link. "It's because of Michael, because the Black Widow wants him to have Spain. But Juan Luis's will—"

"Can't be binding on a new entity. The will won't have any effect on the limited company that's going to rise like a phoenix from the ashes of this one. I have it on good authority that Spanish law is the same as ours in that regard."

"Whose authority? Lila Curran's?"

"Yes. And don't for a moment doubt that she's done her research very thoroughly. She's an extraordinary woman. You underestimate her at your peril. Timothy did, and it was a great mistake."

"Tim was colluding with her, wasn't he?"

"He thought he was. Mrs. Curran used him. She'll use you too if you let her."

"How do I prevent it?"

"By keeping your wits, being as smart as she is. And never letting her think that you think you're fooling her. About anything."

"Does she know about this? The things you're telling me tonight, I mean."

"No. She has reason to be far more emotional than I am about this affair. She thinks she wants to bring London down. To destroy the bank here. It's the one weak point in her reasoning. But I'll deal with that at the proper time. Let's get back to Michael Curran. Can you work with him?"

"I don't know. I suppose so. If he thinks like a banker."

"You've had more experience of that than he has. But I expect he can be trained to think that way. And he has strengths of his own which will make up for your deficiencies. Imagination, flair. Yes, you'll be a good team."

Charles was still trying to absorb it all. He reached for the decanter. "I think I'd like another one of these now. May I?"

"Of course. I'll join you."

The two men toasted each other again.

They talked for a while longer, but Sharrick gave Charles no more facts. The details would come later. There were things this young man still did not know, but Sharrick wasn't ready to enlighten him.

Eventually Charles realized his host was only making polite conversation, waiting for him to leave. "I suppose there's not a lot more to say at present," he ventured.

"Not just now," his lordship agreed.

Sharrick got to his feet, so did Charles. "I can see myself out, no need to trouble yourself."

"It's no trouble." Sharrick led the way down the long corridor that led to the front door. Charles watched his limping gait and wondered how a man with a game leg could do the things this one did. Apparently he could do anything he damned well pleased.

The clock in the foyer struck nine-thirty. "Will you be

going home?" Sharrick asked. "You must have put in a long day, what with one thing and another."

Charles realized that the other man knew he'd been at Tim's at seven in the morning. The valet Willis would have told him. And told him as well that Charles was there when the accident occurred. He found some small satisfaction in thinking of what he'd do to Willis. "No," he said, his voice not betraying his dark thoughts. "Not straight home yet. I'll call in at my brother's to see how he is."

"Yes, very bad luck that. I hope it turns out . . . well, perhaps better than it looks at the moment."

Charles acknowledged the good wishes with a wordless nod. "When will I—I mean, shall we speak again?"

"Of course. Soon I expect. I'll be in touch."

Charles stepped out into the night.

Sharrick watched him go, closed the door, and stood thinking a moment. The butler appeared at his elbow.

"Sorry sir, I didn't realize the gentleman was leaving," Jones said in his Welsh singsong.

"It's all right. We didn't need you and I didn't ring."

"Very good, milord. Is there anything more you require?"

"Nothing thank you, Jones. Go to bed. I'll put out the lights before I go up."

The butler went away.

What to do now was the question. Sharrick glanced at the grandfather clock. It was a wonderful timepiece, built during the reign of Queen Anne. It told the phases of the moon and the configuration of the constellations, as well as the hour. Sharrick wasn't interested in the heavens, only the time. It was twenty to ten. Too late to ring Lila at the Connaught? More important, did he want to?

He returned to the study. Jones had been there before him. The used glasses were gone and fresh ones had been put in their place. The cushions had been plumped and the peat fire tended. It burned with a steady glow, the rich, sweet smell filling the room. Suddenly he was consumed with longing for Ireland, for the green hills and blue-gray mountains and the soft air, for the sound and the feel of home.

Not yet. He hadn't won the race, and the prize remained to be captured.

How to tell Lila that he'd decided the scepter was to be passed to Charles Mendoza? She wanted it broken into bits, buried for all time. He knew enough of her story to understand the hatred in her, but she was directing it at the wrong source. Córdoba was the cause of her suffering, not London. She couldn't destroy Córdoba because of her son, so she'd transferred her wrath to the target closer at hand. Brilliant and beautiful Lila, even she made mistakes sometimes. Well, he wasn't going to let her make this one. But how to tell her? When?

Not now, he decided. It was too late. And he couldn't deliver such explosive information on the telephone. He'd see her tomorrow. His heart lifted at the thought, though he knew it would be a stormy interview.

Sharrick poured himself another whiskey and stood by the fire sipping it, thinking of Lila. Amazing that she still didn't realize he'd done it all for her. She still believed he had another motive, some secret score of his own to settle. She was wrong. The simple truth was that after all these years he'd found the woman he wanted and decided to have her. Whatever it took. But his way. If he let Lila dictate all the terms, make all the rules, she'd never respect him. He couldn't live with her under those conditions. And eventually she'd hate it as much as he.

He tossed back the last of his whiskey and smiled. "You'll thank me for it in the end, my lovely Lila," he murmured aloud, his thoughts running on into the future. What a great end it will be. You and I, lord and lady of Glencree, filling our Irish hearts with the beauty of the place for as long as we need, then roaming the world as we choose. A great end. No, a great beginning.

But first this affair to see through. And no ugly regrets at the finish. I'll save you from yourself, Lila Curran. I'll save you for me.

Except for Norman Mendoza's office on the ground floor, the bank was silent and locked. Norman and the night watchman were the only two people in the place. He was conscious of that; it intensified the aloneness he'd been feeling all day. He wanted to get away, but there was more work to be done. He couldn't leave yet. Still he needed a breath of air.

Norman got up from his desk and walked to the private door that led from his office to the street. The night was unseasonably chilly but fine; the sky blazoned with stars. Lower Sloane Street was deserted except for a hansom cab parked a short distance away. Waiting for a fare no doubt. He'd ordered his own carriage to return at quarter to eleven, forty-five minutes yet. But a lot of work remained. He'd best go back and get at it.

The folder Philip had put on his desk in the late afternoon still bulged with documents requiring his signature and memorandums to which he must reply. And at the bottom was the copy of the cable and the envelope. He had to deal with those as well.

It had been nearly four before Norman got to the bank. He'd not come straight back with Philip after they left the East End. First he'd gone home to bathe and change, to wash some of the stink of the past two days off his body, even if he couldn't wash it out of his soul. Then, when he finally arrived, ready to do what he knew he must, he'd discovered that fate or God or what have you had taken the decision out of his hands. Jamie had come to him immediately.

"Charles has just given me the most appalling news. I'm so sorry, Norman."

"Sorry about what?" It was so like Jamie to plunge in at the middle. So like him not to ask where his brother had been, or why, but respond to the emotion of the moment. That was Jamie's great flaw: he couldn't separate emotion and business. "C'mon, tell me and get it over with," Norman demanded. "What's happened? What did Charles tell you?"

"It's Timothy. He's had an accident. I'm afraid it's serious."

Then the hurried visit to Timothy's house—and standing beside the boy's bed, seeing him lying there, not moving, barely breathing, his head swathed in bandages. Looking like some kind of Egyptian mummy. And the swirling, shifting morass of his own emotions. Hating his son, and loving him at the same time. And feeling glad because it had been done and he hadn't had to do it. And ashamed because he was glad.

The nurse was called Miss Dancer. A joke, that name. She was a huge elephant of a woman, not likely to dance. But she seemed competent. "He's in no pain, sir," she'd assured him. "I promise you, the young gentleman is quite peaceful."

Norman had stood there a moment longer, looking at his son and reviewing the thoughts that had haunted him for the past forty-eight hours. He thought about the Mendoza legacy and how it passed from father to son, about how some of the sons were worthy and some were rogues. He had two sons—one brilliant but untrustworthy, one loyal but incompetent. How to choose between them had always been his problem. Now it seemed the decision had been made for him. He was left with the worst of a bad bargain.

In the silent office lit only by the lamp on his desk, Norman began to think about it again, his hand on a letter that needed signing, his mind a million miles away. Could Charles carry the load, be trusted with the secrets, bear the burden, protect the house? Christ almighty, he still wasn't sure. Maybe one of the others, the distant cousins or in-laws . . . Never mind. Plenty of time before he had to decide. He was young enough and vigorous enough to go on for quite a while yet.

He pushed the thoughts away and picked up his pen and signed his name. Then did it again. And again. Twenty minutes later the last of the ordinary business had been dealt with. He was left with the two matters that were not ordinary.

Francisco's cable first.

He wasn't looking at the original; someone had copied it for him. Charles's hand. The boy had not trusted even Philip with information like this. That was a good sign. Some things were only for the eyes of the family. Jamie knew about it, of course, and Henry. Charles had done his best to see that the message was known to no one else. But what about the telegrapher who sent it, the one who received it, the messenger who delivered it—and maybe a dozen leaks in between? Christ! How could Francisco be so stupid.

There was a code for secret communications between Córdoba and London. It had been established by Robert the Turncoat and Liam, back in the days when both houses were run by Englishmen. It had never been used often. They chose to discuss really important matters viva voce whenever possible. That was even truer these days, when travel between Spain and England was so much easier than it had been. But if ever there was a circumstance when the code was called for, this was it. Maybe Francisco didn't know it. Given the peculiar way he'd been catapulted into the leadership, that was possible.

Too late to worry about any leaks now. Or maybe too early. Those particular pigeons would come home to roost soon enough if they were out there. The thing now was to discover the nature of the trouble in Córdoba and sort it out. Somebody would have to go over. But who? He daren't leave; there were too many unsolved problems right here in London. Jamie was out of the question. Henry was too emotional and too timid for something that would probably require decisive action. Two months ago he'd not have hesitated; he'd have sent Timothy. But now...

It would have to be Charles, Norman decided after another few seconds' thought. And pray God he was up to the task. He'd see the lad first thing in the morning. With any luck he could be on the boat train for the Continent by evening.

One thing more required his attention; a cream-colored envelope bearing no return address, only his name and the words *Personal and private*.

The note had been hand-delivered sometime in the late afternoon. It was on his desk, still sealed, when he returned from seeing Tim. "The messenger said he wasn't instructed to wait for a reply, sir," Philip had explained.

"Yes, thank you." Norman had started to slit the envelope, then stopped. Why? God alone knew. Some instinct. Some feeling that whatever it contained would have to wait, that he couldn't deal with it until he'd cleared away the other urgent matters. Now it was time.

He opened the envelope and withdrew a single sheet of paper. The hand was unfamiliar. "I believe it would be advantageous if we meet privately sometime in the next forty-eight hours. I shall be at evensong at St. Magnus the Martyr on Friday at five. Perhaps you too will feel a need for prayer." It was signed Johnathon Hammersmith.

Norman knew Hammersmith, but not well. He was a senior man at Coutts. They'd dealt with each other from time to time. That was inevitable in the complex gavotte danced by the major private banks. Sometimes demands were too great to be borne by one house alone, and they shared the burden, and the profit or the loss. But it had been at least six years since Mendoza did a deal with Coutts. So what did Hammersmith want now? And why choose such an extraordinary venue? Well, he'd find out tomorrow. He would, of course, go to evensong. And that would be the first time he'd been in a church since Timothy's wedding. Tim . . .

Norman sighed, opened a drawer, put in everything he'd

been working on, and locked it with a key that hung from his watch chain.

Ten forty-five. The carriage would be waiting outside the main door.

The night watchman let him out. His driver was standing beside the carriage. Norman nodded to him, suddenly too tired to speak.

"Home, sir?"

Norman hesitated. Great God but he wanted to sleep. The past two days were demanding their toll. Despite that he shook his head. "Not directly. I want to call at Mr. Timothy's first."

"Very good, sir."

The distance to Basil Street was short. They were at the house in ten minutes. Harcourt let him in.

"Mr. Charles came a while ago, sir, but he's just left. The doctor's upstairs."

"Yes, thank you." Norman didn't wait for the butler to show the way. He climbed the stairs and went into Tim's room without knocking. The nurse stood on one side of the bed, the doctor on the other.

Miss Dancer moved her great bulk in something that passed for a curtsy. "Good evening, sir." Then, to the doctor whom Norman had yet to meet, she said, "This is the gentleman's father, sir. He came earlier today when you weren't here."

The doctor nodded in acknowledgment of the introduction but didn't turn to look at Norman, his attention concentrated on his patient.

Norman watched him listening to Tim's heart, probing his stomach, opening his eyelids with a practiced thumb. "Well?" he demanded.

The doctor raised his head. "No change. None at all."

"And what does that mean?" He already knew what it meant. Charles had told him in the few minutes they'd spent together earlier in the evening, when he explained what had happened. At least a version of events. Norman didn't imagine that he'd heard the whole story. He'd read guilt behind his elder son's eyes. There hadn't been time to probe deeper. Charles had claimed an urgent appointment and hurried away, promising to call once more at Tim's before he went home.

"What does no change mean?" Norman asked again, needing to hear the words from the medical man.

"Exactly what it sounds like. Your son shows no sign of coming out of the coma."

"And how long might that continue?"

The doctor looked hard at the other man, appraising his ability to accept the unadorned truth. He made up his mind. "Possibly years. Such cases are not unknown."

"Bloody hell," Norman said softly. "And the alternative?"

The doctor shrugged. "He could die. A blockage could develop and affect the lungs or the heart. In these cases that's not unheard of either."

"I see. And how likely is it that he'll recover? Come out of this in a few days time and be as he was before?"

"Not very likely. No chance at all, in my opinion."

"You don't mince words, do you?"

"Would you rather I did?"

"No, I wouldn't."

After another long look at his son Norman left the room.

❧ 15 ❧

The Hills above San Juan, Seven P.M.

There was a strange smell in Sister Magdalena's tiny cell—not unpleasant, but unidentifiable. The bishop sniffed loudly twice but couldn't put a name to the odor. He leaned over the body of the nun. The mother superior lifted her candle so that His Excellency might see better.

Magdalena was dressed in her habit and stretched out on a narrow straw mattress atop a stone slab. Both visitors watched her. She lay so still they thought she might be dead. The mother superior crossed herself and murmured a prayer. Sister Magdalena opened her eyes, blinked once or twice in the unaccustomed glow of the candle, then tried to struggle to her feet.

"Your Excellency, I did not know—"

The bishop put out a restraining hand. "Please, you must not try and get up. It is not necessary. They tell me you are very ill, my child."

"No, no, I'm not. It is just that—"

"Clearly you are ill. You have been most disobedient to allow your health to deteriorate in this fashion. Mother Superior tells me you refuse to eat. That is not part of your vows, Sister."

"I hear you as the voice of God Himself," Magdalena murmured. "I have done so since I came here. Except—"

"Except that you are angry with me for not allowing you to go among the populace and cause a panic. So you starve yourself to death in protest."

"No. Forgive me, Excellency, you do not understand. I wish to do only what Our Lord charges me to do. Only his will."

"His will is that you honor your vow of obedience to me."

Magdalena's face had lost none of it's beauty, thin as it was. Now it contorted into a grimace of pain. "That is the mystery that is tearing my soul apart," she confessed. "If the voice I hear is that of God, and if my vows are of God, how can the two be in conflict?"

The bishop knew that the nun's problem was not unique; through the ages such puzzles had exercised the minds of many holy men and women. He knew too that the saints usually chose the direct voice of God over that of authority, but he had no intention of saying so to Magdalena.

"You must put all this from your mind and do as I say, my child. Only when you honor your vows will you know peace. Now, I want you to leave this isolated cell and move into the convent, so Mother Superior can look after you better. And you must rest, and eat everything you are given."

Magdalena had heard only the first order. "Leave my cell! No, Excellency, I beg you. Do not ask it of me—"

"Only for a short time. Until you are well again. Then we will see."

"I cannot! May God and His Holy Mother be my judges, I cannot leave this place. Unless it is to go among the people and tell them of what is to come. Our Lord has told me so over and over."

The nun looked at the two faces still peering into hers—

the older woman who carried so much authority in her own right, and the bishop who had behind him the entire weight of the universal Church. "Please," she murmured.

"We will look after you well, little sister," the mother superior promised. "You know how much we all love you."

Magdalena's eyes were dark with torment. "Please, Excellency," she whispered. "Will you hear my confession?"

The bishop nodded. He could not refuse such a request; it would be a violation of every tenet of his priesthood.

The mother superior immediately put the candle on the rough wooden table beside Magdalena's bed. "I will be outside when you need me," she said as she left the cell.

Magdalena had known the other woman would leave as soon as the sacrament of penance was mentioned. Canon law decreed it. All confessions were strictly between penitent and confessor.

The bishop reached into the pocket of his robe and withdrew the short, narrow stole that like most priests he always carried. It was the outward sign of his most sacred function, that of administering the sacraments. The stole was satin— purple on one side, white on the other. He pressed it to his lips and started to put it around his neck.

"Wait," Magdalena whispered.

"Yes?"

"Before I confess myself, I wish to say something."

The bishop held the stole loosely in his two hands and waited.

"I wish to speak with you about Concha."

It had come at last: the judgment he'd hoped would be delayed until he faced his Lord. The bishop's heart was thumping and sweat ran down his back, but his voice was calm. "My housekeeper? What about her?"

"You must not be so afraid," Magdalena said simply.

He was not sure he had heard her correctly. He leaned closer. "What? What did you say?"

"I said that you must not live in such fear. This sin of

yours, this small sin, it will be only between you and God. No one will find out. Not in your lifetime or hers. God is very tolerant of our weaknesses, Excellency. He understands our fears and our loneliness."

"But you," he whispered, knowing it was futile to deny the truth, "you know."

"I was told only that I might comfort you. Now, in these last days."

"The last days of what?"

"Of my life."

"But you are a young woman. These are your last days only if you so will. And to will such a thing is a sin. Surely you know that."

"It is not my will but his."

"How can it be God's will that you starve yourself?" In spite of how humbled he felt by her mere presence, by the holiness he recognized, the bishop couldn't keep the impatience from his voice. "You must eat. Our bodies are the temple of the Holy Spirit. We are required to take care of them."

"*Sí*, Excellency. Until such time as God wills otherwise."

Sister Magdalena fumbled among the bedclothes on the side farthest from the bishop, then brought out a crumpled piece of rough cotton that had once been white. She raised her shoulders slightly from the bed and leaned toward the candle. "Look, Excellency. Please."

He looked at the cloth, then started back. "Blood!"

"*Sí*. I have been coughing blood for over two weeks. That is why I do not eat, Excellency. I cannot; my throat is closed. A little liquid, nothing else will pass."

The bishop made the sign of the cross. "*Madre de Dios,* then it is more necessary than ever that you go into the convent and be properly cared for."

Magdalena shook her head. "No, there is no need. Here I have my Lord with me always. I require nothing else. Except..."

"Except what?"

"Two things, if you can do them for me, Excellency."

"Tell me."

"First, the people, this thing which is to happen—"

"The Americans. They are probably going to come," the bishop admitted. "They have Cuba now. It is logical to assume they will also take Puerto Rico."

"But there must be no bloodshed."

He hesitated, deep in thought. "I can speak with some people. Not the official leaders, but the men who have influence in the pueblos. Perhaps . . ."

"*Sí!* That is a wonderful idea. They will listen to you."

"Now perhaps they will," he admitted. "A few weeks ago when you first mentioned this thing, there was still bravado and the crazy notion that this small island could somehow resist the *norteamericanos*. Now, I think people are growing more realistic. I give you my solemn word that I will try," he promised. "You said two things, what is the second?"

"The man who calls himself Michael Curran," Sister Magdalena said without hesitation. "I must speak to him once more before I die. There is something I must tell him. Can you send him to me?"

"I will try to do that too. I don't think it will be difficult. Señor Curran is very interested in you."

Sister Magdalena smiled. "Thank you, Excellency. May God reward your goodness to me. Now, please . . ." She gestured to his stole.

The bishop put it on and knelt beside the stone slab. Magdalena made the sign of the cross and began her confession. "Bless me, Father, for I have sinned. . . ."

Ten minutes later the bishop came out of the cell, carrying the candle into the small dark parlor where the mother superior waited. He conferred with her for a few moments, issuing instructions. All the while he was speaking he was thinking about the smell that hung in the air around Sister

Magdalena. He'd identified it at last; there were no flowers anywhere nearby, but it was the scent of roses.

Ponce, Eleven-Thirty P.M.

Michael stood on the main street of the town, cursing the impulse that had brought him here. He'd been at the station in Aguadilla waiting for the train to San Juan, when one arrived that was going in the opposite direction, toward the island's second city on the southern coast. Without more than five seconds' thought he'd boarded it. Now, three hours later, he was standing in the usual crowd of noisy Puerto Ricans and wondering what in hell he was doing here.

He stopped a passerby. *"Discúlpame, señor, pero . . ."*

"Sí, señor?" The man stared at Michael, obviously fascinated by his appearance.

"I'm looking for the orphanage," Michael explained.

"¿Qué orfanato, señor?"

"The one supported by the bishop in San Juan."

The man spat on the ground at Michael's feet. "Nothing in Ponce is supported from San Juan."

Michael wanted no part of their rivalries and political factions, only information. "Very well, but the orphanage . . ."

"I don't know of any orphanage."

The stranger started to move away, but Michael put out a hand to stop him. "Please, I really must find the place. I know there's a place near here where they care for children who have no families."

Suddenly the man snapped his fingers. *"Yo sé.* I know what you are thinking of, señor. The woman called La Bruja, out by the de Vives hacienda, she looks after children sometimes."

"La Bruja. Doesn't she have any name other than the Witch?"

"*Sí, señor,*" he admitted. "I suppose she must have. I think it may be Dolores, but I'm not sure. We call her only La Bruja."

It was not an auspicious beginning. Michael got directions to a place some six miles north of the town, then hefted his luggage and began walking.

The moon was nearly full again. It lit the track he followed. The going was fairly easy, but it would be a lot faster if he left his things hidden in the underbrush. He hesitated, trying to make up his mind, then decided to risk it. He hid the valise and the briefcase and marked the spot with a stone so he could identify it on his way back, then pushed on.

A small river ran beside the road. He could hear it while he walked. Once Michael stopped and fought his way through the brush to kneel beside the river and wash his face and drink. The water was icy cold. It must come down from the high mountains that crossed the center of the island. Those mountains separated Ponce from San Juan. In former times they'd have been all but impassable. Until a few years ago when they opened some roads and started the train service, the people of the two towns probably never saw one other.

While he walked he thought about the way things were likely to change once the Americans came. It was idle speculation, he didn't really care, but it occupied his mind. It kept him from thinking about the insanity of tramping through the deserted countryside at midnight. He was looking for a woman everyone referred to as a witch, who would doubtless have nothing to tell him, even if he managed to find her.

The cabin appeared after he'd been walking for an hour and a half. It was small and so much whitewash had been applied for so many years that it looked like an iced cake. Behind it land had been cleared and a garden ran in neat rows down to the river. Michael examined the house. There were no windows. Only a low door painted green broke the blank facade the place turned to the road.

He was here; now what should he do? He couldn't knock on the door at this hour. But if he didn't intend to do that, why had he come?

He was still trying to decide on his next move when the door opened. "Come in, señor."

The woman who'd addressed him was small and old. Her skin was olive toned, deeply furrowed and etched with lines. Her gray hair was cut short and clung to her skull in tight curls. There was a lot of Indian in her, judging from the cheekbones, and some black as well. She could pass for a man except for her long dress and apron. Michael stepped forward. "I'm sorry to disturb you at this hour," he began.

The woman shrugged. "People come when they need to come. The time doesn't matter." She stepped aside and motioned him inside.

The house was built in the ubiquitous form the Spaniards had carried to every corner of the Indies and Latin America. He found himself in a small square patio with rooms opening off on three sides. There was a bench against the wall that guarded the patio from the street. The woman motioned him toward it. "Sit down, then tell me how I can help you."

Michael didn't know how to begin. The story he had to tell, the questions he wanted to ask, it all seemed preposterous now that he was here. Besides, this didn't look like an orphanage. The bishop had said that Sister Magdalena had been raised in an orphanage.

"A woman?" La Bruja asked, when he didn't say anything. "You want her and she doesn't want you? You have come to me for a potion that will change her mind?"

"No, nothing like that."

"Very well. What then? You are unable to get stiff," she said after another pause. "Ah, don't be ashamed, señor. Many men come to me with the same problem. I have something that will make you so big and hard you will not believe your eyes. And your wife, she will run screaming in terror from the bedroom—" Seeing Michael's expression, she broke off. "You have a wife?"

"No, I'm not married."

"But a girlfriend? Whores? You can satisfy them?"

"I do my best," he admitted. "So far I haven't had any complaints."

The woman looked genuinely puzzled. "Then why, señor, have you come to me in the middle of the night?"

"I want to ask you a question. At least I think I do. I'm not sure you're the right person to ask."

"But you think I may be?"

"Yes. At least when I asked in the town for an *orfanato*, they sent me here."

The woman nodded her head. "Sometimes I take care of children whose mothers cannot care for them, that is true. But an *orfanato* . . ." She gestured to the simple house. "This is only my home, señor."

"Have you had many such children?"

"Over the years, quite a few." She was peering at him closely. "Are you looking for a lost child, señor? Someone you think maybe was left with me."

Michael shook his head. "Not the way you mean. The woman in the convent, Sister Magdalena, she was with you, wasn't she?"

La Bruja did not reply. Her hands were folded in her lap. She stared at them a while, then stood up abruptly. "Wait," she commanded.

A few minutes passed and she didn't return. Michael wondered if she was simply going to leave him out here until he gave up and left. But eventually she came back carrying a bottle and two tin cups.

"Here, I brew this myself. You will like it." She poured a dark brown viscous liquid into the cups and drank hers down immediately. Michael did the same. The liquor had been brewed from sugar cane, but it was stronger than any rum he'd tasted on the island. The drink brought tears to his eyes and made his throat feel as if he'd swallowed fire. His belly liked it fine, however. The rum warmed him and made him feel less like a fool for sitting here and talking to an old witch woman when he should be in San Juan tending to his business.

La Bruja poured them each a second drink. They downed them in one swallow, as they had before. He felt a little light-headed now. But much better.

"Sister Magdalena," the woman said as she corked the bottle and set it at her feet. "Ah yes, she was with me."

"Who was her mother?" Michael demanded. "Did she have any other children?"

"If Maria Nieves, the one you call Sister Magdalena, had a mother, she wouldn't have been with me."

Michael knew she was fencing with him, still trying to decide how much to tell him. "That's ridiculous, everyone has a mother, even if they're abandoned."

"Nieves wasn't abandoned. She was left with me. Because—"

"Because why?"

"The mother had her reasons." La Bruja wouldn't look at him.

"What reasons?" Michael reached into his pocket and withdrew a handful of pesetas. "Here, take this for your good works. I'm sure you can use it. What reasons?" he asked again.

She hesitated a moment, then took the money and put it in the pocket of her apron. "I will take the money because you can afford it, and as you say, I can put it to good use. But my tongue is not for sale, señor."

"I'm sorry." Christ, he'd offended her. That would ruin everything. "I didn't mean to buy information. Only to help you, because, as you said, I can afford to."

"Sometimes women come to me, they have great trouble, many problems. I do what I can to help them."

"Did the mother of Maria Nieves have many problems?" he asked softly.

La Bruja spoke slowly, as if explaining things she did not expect him to understand. "It was a very difficult birth. The labor went on for days. She dragged herself to me. While she was in labor, she walked here. Can you believe that?"

"I can believe it. People do incredible things when they are desperate. And the labor was so hard because she was having twins, isn't that right?"

He waited. She didn't say anything.

"Twins," Michael repeated. "She gave birth to two little girls, didn't she?"

La Bruja nodded.

He felt a surge of triumph. "And she left one and took the other. That's what happened, isn't it?"

"At first she meant to leave them both," the old woman admitted. "The man she was living with, he wasn't the father of the babies. She knew he wouldn't accept two more mouths to feed that were not his. She loved him, and there were other children at home. She had to make a choice. So she meant to leave them both."

"But she didn't?"

"No. At the last minute, when she was leaving, she ran back and looked at the two infants, and picked one up and ran out that door with her."

She gestured to the door to the road. The moon was high overhead now, it cast a bright light on the faded green paint. The moonlight was a path beckoning Michael to leave, to go back to his own world and his own concerns.

"I don't think she knew which one she was taking," La Bruja continued. "But I knew. From the first minute I'd been able to tell them apart. She had named them herself, as soon as they were born. One she called Nieves—"

"And the other Nuria," Michael supplied.

La Bruja looked at him. "You know a great deal, señor. For an *estranjero*, a very great deal indeed. But you are right, she took Nuria and left Nieves. I had to tell her. 'Nuria,' I shouted after her, 'You've taken Nuria.'" She paused, remembering, then asked. "How did you know?"

"It was an accident, my realizing how alike they were. Only an accident."

"I don't think anyone knows but you. Because Nieves was such an extraordinary *niña*. She was touched by God, that one. Even I could not understand how she knew the things she knew, could do what she did."

She put her head back, talking more to herself than to him. "*Mira,* there are things that are impossible, but all the same true. Here there are no schools, and unless you walk for many hours, no teachers. But when Nieves was seven years old she could read and she could write. I cannot do either, but she could."

"Where did she learn?" Michael demanded. "How?"

La Bruja shrugged. "I do not know, señor. Maybe God taught her." She leaned forward, studying him. "So it shouldn't surprise you that when she told me I must take her to San Juan I did it. When she said something, you knew you must do it. There was no railroad then. We walked across the mountains. It took us a week."

"What happened when you got there?"

"She went to the bank. To that evil old woman, Maria Ortega. I do not know what happened between them. Only that Nieves was satisfied with whatever it was. Then she said I must take her to the bishop."

"And he put her in the convent."

"Yes. He too had to do whatever she said. He knew it from the first minute, as I had always known it. She explained that she must be a hermit, not live with the other nuns, that she must keep her face always behind a veil. And when she said that I thought, ah, so no one will ever know that you have a twin." La Bruja cocked her head. "So how did you know, señor?"

"An accident," he repeated. "As I told you. It's not important. Tell me what the bishop said when Nieves told him what she wanted."

La Bruja laughed; it was a soft cackling sound. "The bishop listened to her and nodded his head and did exactly what she told him to do. So no one has seen both of them and no one knows. Except you."

The two of them were silent for some time. "Do you know what happened to Nuria?" Michael asked at last.

The old woman shrugged. "I have heard stories. Whether they are true, or whether it is the same Nuria, that I do not know. I do not wish to know, señor. Sometimes not knowing is better."

Michael got up and she rose with him. Her gray head came barely to his shoulders. Curran leaned down and kissed her gravely on both cheeks. "*Gracias*, Doña Dolores. You have helped me a great deal. And I will tell no one what I know or where I learned it."

"No one has called me Dolores since I was a child," the old woman whispered. "And I know you are a good man, señor. I can smell the goodness in you. And the danger. Be careful señor. I think you must be very careful."

❧ 16 ❧

The morning was beautiful in Regent's Park; the sun shone and the flowers of high summer bloomed. Displayed in precise geometric beds, they were blocks of vivid color set in intricate patterns on a faultless carpet of green grass.

"I love marigolds," Lila said.

"I hate them like that." Sharrick lifted his gold-topped walking stick and pointed to a planting of orange marigolds and bright red zinnias, edged with blue lobelia. "Nature doesn't force everything into strict forms that way."

"You have a taste for rarer things, Fergus. Like orchids and passion flowers."

"Simple ordinary things too, but treated with respect."

There was a vacant bench beneath a large chestnut tree. Lila took his arm and steered him toward it. "Shall we sit down? If I'm to keep up with you I need to be in the country. And wearing sensible shoes." She lifted one foot and showed him the pointed tip and slender heel of a patent-leather boot. The gesture disturbed the ribbon-trimmed hem of her black skirt and allowed a brief glimpse of silk-clad ankle.

Sharrick was aware of the sap rising in him. In her presence he was a willow burgeoning green in the spring. "I'd like to see you like that." His voice was husky. "In the country, I mean . . . perhaps in tweeds. At Glencree. It's a beautiful place, Lila. Exquisite."

She heard the longing behind the words and fought to keep her own from showing. "I'm sure it is. Maybe someday."

"Someday soon."

They sat down, both of them retreating from the brink of feelings inappropriate to the time and the place. Lila fanned herself briefly. Sharrick crossed his bad leg over his good and propped the walking stick beside him. "Amazing how hot the sun can be even as far north as London," he said.

"Yes." Then, after a long pause. "We seem to be avoiding the obvious topic, Fergus. What's wrong?"

"Why should there be anything wrong? It's all going exactly as you planned, isn't it?"

"So far it seems to be. But I have the feeling you've something to tell me."

"A little something perhaps. Francisco's caved in. Exactly the way your sister-in-law said he would. Sent a cable to London forty-eight hours ago. He's begging them to send someone to take over."

"Fergus! Why didn't you tell me right away?"

"I tried to see you yesterday, but you put me off with tales of hairdressers and dressmakers."

"But I didn't know it was so important. You never said—" She broke off. Fergus always challenged her for control, and that was what she both loved and feared in him. "How did Norman and the others react? Do you know?"

"Apparently Norman was as cool as always. The rest of them ran around wringing their hands and waiting for him to tell them what to do."

Lila chuckled. "I'm sorry, I can't help thinking of poor

Francisco put to flight by fifty or so women who wanted to take their few pesetas out of his bank."

"And the Russians, of course. He must have been worried about the Imperial Treasury calling in its deposits."

"Yes, doubtless that softened him up. But it has to have been the women who delivered the coup de grâce. I can imagine how Juan Luis would have handled them, but not Francisco."

"How many women did you say you set on him? Fifty?"

"That's a guess. I cabled twenty different ladies. Inviting them to a party on the twenty-sixth. That was the arrangement Beatriz made—whatever the date of the message, they were to subtract twenty. Then they would know the target day."

"And on that day they were all to go to the bank and demand their money?"

"Yes. And each of the twenty was to tell a few of her lady friends that she'd had word the Banco Mendoza was in difficulty, that their money might be lost."

"Do you think some of the ladies might have passed on the rumor to their husbands? Their deposits must be a great deal larger."

"Of course they are, and I suppose some of the ladies may have said something. But you don't know Spanish men, Fergus. They're not likely to run off and take action because of something a woman says. And if they checked a bit they'd know it was only gossip. There's no evidence to support it. No, I doubt there's been a real run on Córdoba, only a female frenzy. Which was quite enough to panic Francisco."

"So you protected Córdoba."

"Naturally. I don't want Michael confronted with a genuine crisis the minute he takes over."

"How's he going to manage?" Sharrick asked, as if the thought had just occurred to him. "He has no experience of banking, has he?"

"Only what I've been able to tell him over the years, and

what he's observed at the banks where I do business. It will be enough. Michael is brilliant. The scheme with the coffee plantations was entirely his idea."

"Brilliant, yes, perhaps. Look at his mother." Sharrick reached out and put his hand over hers. "But he's bound to need help, my dear."

"He'll learn," Lila said, a slight defensiveness creeping into her tone. "Michael was born to take over Córdoba, destined for it. You'll see, he'll learn very quickly." She didn't want to continue this line of discussion. "What did Norman decide to do about Francisco's cable?"

"He sent his son Charles. Last night, on the boat train to Calais—and from there to Spain in a private railway carriage. He'll be arriving in Córdoba about now."

Lila cocked her head and studied him. "You seem to know a lot of the details. I didn't know your contacts inside Mendozas were quite so good."

"It could have been a problem, particularly after Timothy had his accident. You know about that?"

She nodded. "Yes, Beatriz managed to ring and tell me the story. There's no telephone at Westlake, but she found a way to use one in the next village." She paused. Sharrick didn't say anything. "Do you expect me to make hypocritical noises of sympathy, Fergus?"

"Not you. You're a good hater, Lila Curran. Perhaps too good."

"What does that mean?"

"Only that sometimes you forget whom you should be hating. If you can't find one target, you choose another."

"I still don't know what you're getting at."

She'd withdrawn her hand from his. He could see the long elegant fingers folded in her lap, jeweled rings sparkling beneath her net gloves. "What I'm getting at," he said softly, "is that you are, if you'll forgive a hackneyed expression, cutting off your nose to spite your face."

Lila waited, knowing he'd explain when it suited him,

aware of the strength of him, the iron determination she'd long ago recognized as a match for hers. Fergus was the first man she'd ever known whom she believed to be smarter than she was.

"You need London," he said now. "Your son needs London."

She saw the implication of his words and this entire discussion. "Are you weakening, feeling sorry for them?"

"Not a bit sorry. Jamie and Henry and Norman deserve what they'll get. Timothy's out of it, poor sod. That leaves Charles."

"Leaves him where?"

He twirled his walking stick between two fingers, watching the gold top spin in the dappled sunlight. "As successor to the present management of Mendozas. He's got the right bloodlines, he's out of the right stock." He might be discussing one of the Arabian horses he raised at Glencree. "The best thing is for Charles to become chief officer of a new limited company here in London. A new legal entity, just as you've planned for Córdoba."

She sprang up, shaking with a rage that destroyed her facade of calm. "No. No, no, no! I won't have it, Fergus. I won't have you plotting behind my back and making new rules of your own. They're going to fail, all of them. Be left with nothing."

"Sit down." His voice was cool and hard. "Sit down, Lila. You're going to listen to me because you must, so sit down."

She lowered herself back to the bench, sitting gingerly on the edge of it, not letting any part of herself touch any part of him. "Go on," she said bitterly. "Say what you have to say and have done with it."

"You can't unbury a corpse, you have to realize that. Your enemy is dead, beyond your vengeance. Now you're striking out blindly, and doing yourself and your son an enormous disservice. Mendozas great strength is its dual nature. At least—"

"Córdoba existed for centuries before London was even thought of," she interrupted.

"I know. But that was then. Now banking is infinitely more complex. And having two organizations so intimately connected, that's what gives the Mendozas their edge. Rothschild has it as well. France and England. But no one else has a finger in Spain, another in the Indies, and one here. It's a unique advantage, and you're prepared to throw it away because a man abused you."

"Abuse? Is that your word for—for what happened to me? If so, I assure you it's not strong enough."

He heard the anguish, recognized the ugliness of the memories, the pain. "I know," he said more gently. "But whatever horrors you lived through, they're over. Juan Luis is dead. But you're alive, and Michael's alive. That's your triumph, my dearest Lila. Please, don't turn it into a Pyrrhic victory. That would be the greatest tragedy of all."

"Are you quite through?"

"For the moment. That's all I have to say right now. I think it's enough."

"It's more than enough, Fergus. It's sufficient to show me the turncoat you really are."

Lila rose and walked away.

Sharrick didn't go after her. He knew it would be useless. The time to comfort her, to convince her of his motives, would come, but it wasn't now. He felt a deep, cold pit opening in his gut, the pain of loss—even though he believed the loss was temporary. And if it wasn't? He did not want to think about that.

He rose from the bench and began walking home, thinking all the while how much he hated the pristine flower beds that decorated Regent's Park. Life wasn't regimented and predictable. Those who pretended it was were idiots who fooled only themselves.

•   •   •

Norman Mendoza was also looking at flowers. He was staring at a circular bed of geraniums that decorated the small square of lawn beyond his drawing-room window. The house didn't have a real garden—merely a small patch of grass with two trees and a few shrubs out back, and two smaller bits of lawn either side of the front door. Nonetheless, he paid a gardner twenty pounds a year. All life was insane these days. Things seemed less and less to be what they seemed.

Yesterday—the meeting with Hammersmith—that had been the most insane thing of all.

Norman had arrived at Saint Magnus the Martyr as the lesson was being read. "To everything there is a season," the curate had intoned from the lectern beside the altar. "A time to be born and a time to die, a time to plant and a time to pluck up that which is planted. . . ."

It was a large church, the nave broad and well lit by hanging brass chandeliers. Norman had spotted the back of Hammersmith's head in the sparse congregation, and walked down the aisle and slid in beside him. "Good afternoon, Johnathon."

"Afternoon, Norman. We'd best wait to talk until this is over."

Norman had nodded. The reader had come to the end of the long and famous passage from Ecclesiastes. "'. . . a time to love and a time to hate, a time of war and a time of peace.' Thus saith the Lord God, Amen."

Norman had added his "amen" to the rest. Hammersmith's seemed a little louder and more forceful than was required. Maybe the man was a sincere believer. Damned few of those about. Perhaps Johnathon conducted a large part of his business in church. Bloody peculiar if it were so.

The service had droned on, psalms and hymns and another reading. Norman had squirmed a bit, gazing at Wren's white-and-gold columns and the elaborately carved wooden altar screen, and wondering why Hammersmith didn't signal that they should slip away. But both men stood and knelt with the rest and in the end obeyed the command to bow their heads and ask for God's blessing.

"In the name of the Father and the Son and the Holy Spirit, Amen," the curate finished.

"Amen." Norman and Hammersmith had said together, like a pair of trained parrots.

"Now can we go somewhere and talk?" Norman had whispered through clenched teeth.

"Yes, of course."

Norman had followed the Coutts's man out of the church. Hammersmith led the way down Lower Thames Street, past the Billingsgate Market and its all-permeating stench of fish. Some twenty yards along he turned into an alley leading to the docks beside the river.

They had come to a pub identified by a swinging sign that said The Jew's Gold. Norman stopped short.

Hammersmith followed his gaze. "Sorry," he had muttered, "I didn't think—No offense, old chap. Been here for donkey's years, before modern sensibilities and all that."

"Why the hell should I be offended? I was startled because it's unique, that's all. Come on, I'm parched."

The two men had seated themselves in the section known as the snug. It was a booth in the back, separated from the public bar by a high wooden partition and a dusty, faded cretonne curtain.

"I don't suppose there's any point in asking why we didn't meet at your club or mine," Norman had said. "Or come directly here rather than stopping for prayers first."

"I often go to evensong. It's soothing. And if you'll give me a chance to explain, I think you'll agree this was wiser."

"Fair enough. Is the beer drinkable?"

"Very good," Hammersmith had assured him.

They had ordered two pints of bitter and waited for the publican to bring them. Hammersmith kept his hands folded on the table. His eyes hadn't once met Norman's.

Three minutes later there were two tankards in front of

them, the beer smelling rich and yeasty, the foam exactly right. Norman had taken a long swallow. "Excellent. Your taste in pubs is vindicated." He leaned forward. "Now, what's this all about?"

"I've given the ethics very careful thought, I do want you to realize that. Very careful consideration—weighing up the morality, the rights and wrongs."

"I'm sure you have, Johnathon," Norman had said patiently. "And I'm sure you're doing the right thing. A man like you, who goes to church, you're not going to do anything unethical, are you? But for the life of me, I still can't figure out what the hell you're talking about."

"No, I know that. It's difficult, you see."

"For both of us," Norman had assured him. The bench was hard and he was sore and uncomfortable, still not entirely recovered from his forty-eight hours of wandering the London streets. He had wanted to squirm, but he restrained himself.

"I've been with the bank all my life," Hammersmith had said. "I owe it everything I have. You understand how that is."

"Of course I do. We're two of a kind in that respect. Both of us born into banking families, always knowing we'd carry the responsibility someday. It shapes a man."

"Yes, it does. I'm not exactly in your position, however. You more or less make all the decisions on your own, don't you, Norman?"

"No, I don't. Jamie's the senior partner, as you know. And there's Henry."

"His lordship is the titular head, I know that. But everyone also knows he's not particularly interested in banking, that you're the one who makes the running at Mendozas."

"Do they? Well, who am I to contradict the conventional wisdom. Very well, Johnathon, have it your way. I'm the chief at Mendozas, and you're not in a position of quite so much freedom at Coutts. Where does that leave us?"

Hammersmith had drawn a long breath, let it out noisily, then took another swallow of his beer. "I suppose the best thing is to say it straight out." Still he hesitated, visibly gathering his courage. "You're about to face a demand for one million sterling. In cash. You'll have ten days to pay."

"A demand from whom?" Norman couldn't get out anything but those four words. A great lump of fear had risen in his throat and cold sweat was starting to drip down his back. None of what he was feeling showed. "From whom?" he'd managed to ask again.

"Well, from us actually. On behalf of our client Michael Curran."

Norman began to relax, the flood of relief almost harder to hide than the panic had been. "We don't owe Michael Curran a penny. It's absurd. You must have it wrong."

"No, I haven't," the other man had insisted. "You owe him one million pounds. The letter instructing us to demand payment is on its way to London right now. It will be here Tuesday. Wednesday at the latest."

Norman's emotions seesawed. One moment he wanted to laugh aloud because he knew the whole thing was ridiculous, the next he was sure that Hammersmith was telling the truth and that some skeleton had come tumbling out of a closet, rattling its bones at the worst possible moment. He had controlled himself because he knew he must. "I think you'd best explain the basis of this alledged debt."

"It's very simple really. A bearer bond issued in 1825. It carries no interest, but the principal is a million in sterling. There's a clause saying the instrument is exempt from any statute of limitations. As I said, it's redeemable on ten days notice."

Jesus almighty Christ. It couldn't be. Something had to be wrong. "You've actually seen this thing?"

Hammersmith had nodded. "Indeed. A number of times. I went into the vault and looked at it again before I came to meet you this afternoon. The bond appears to be absolutely legitimate. It's lodged in the account of Mr. Michael Curran; it's been there for six months. Toward the end of last month we had word that Mr. Curran planned to present it. We got that word by cable, but of course we wouldn't do anything without written instructions. Three days ago our agent in New York wired me that such instructions were on the way."

Norman had stared at Hammersmith, then tipped back his head and finished his beer, thinking all the while: Twenty-five was when Robert the Turncoat was in Córdoba and Liam was in London. They'd had their differences over the years, but they were quite close at the end. It was because Liam sent his son Joseph, Norman's father, to visit Spain that half the medallion came back to England. "Who signed this damned bond?" he'd demanded. "Can you tell me that?"

"Liam Mendoza."

"I see."

"He was your grandfather, wasn't he?"

"That's right."

"Yes, I thought so." Hammersmith had followed Norman's lead and emptied his tankard. He pushed aside the curtain and called, "Two more of the same, please."

"Right away, sir."

The beers came. Norman drank down half of his in one go—the cold frothy liquid cooling the fire inside him. Michael Curran, he kept thinking. Lila must be in it with him, she was bound to be, but . . . Something erupted in his brain. He realized the question he should have asked, but so far had not. "These instructions you say are on the way, they're coming from New York?"

"Yes, that's right."

Not good enough. New York told him nothing. There was no reason for New York to figure in any attack thought up by Lila and Michael Curran. "Did the original cable come from there as well?" he'd demanded.

Hammersmith had shaken his head. "No, not from America."

"Where then?"

It was a clear violation of a client's confidence but so was this entire conversation. Hammersmith had decided on the correct course to follow; he had no choice now but to continue down the same path. "The cable came from Puerto Rico."

Norman let out a long slow sigh. Unlike New York, Puerto Rico made sense. "And the funds, are they by any chance to be transferred to the Banco Mendoza in San Juan?"

"Yes, that's right."

Puerto Rico, the bastard child. Like most bastards, it was bound to give trouble. Puerto Rico. Damn, he should have guessed. Trust the Black Widow to sniff out a weakness. But what was she planning? "Any idea what the funds are to be used for?" Norman had kept his voice even.

"None," Hammersmith had mumbled. He hadn't touched his second beer, just kept staring at it as if it might have something to tell him. After a few seconds he cleared his throat. "I know it's quite irregular, giving you advance notice like this. I want you to realize that. It's simply that a million in cash, out of the blue . . . It wouldn't be easy for any of us. And for you, right now—"

"We won't have any difficulty making the payment," Norman said sharply. "Not that I don't appreciate your letting me know," he added. "I do. Very good of you. I shan't forget. Of course, it remains to be seen if this thing is legitimate."

"I understand your doubts," Hammersmith had said. "In your position I'd feel the same way. But perhaps it will clarify things if I tell you we've had the bond in our possession since before it was deposited in Mr. Curran's account."

"How so?"

"Mrs. Lila Curran also banks with us. She keeps accounts with Rothschilds and Barings as well, but she's been a Coutts customer since she returned from Spain sixteen years ago."

"Get to the point, man."

"The point is that she brought the bond with her when she came back from Spain, and lodged it with us for safe-keeping. About six months ago she came in and transferred it to her son."

Her son, her son, her son . . .

A day later the words kept repeating themselves in Norman's head as he stared unseeing at the bright red geraniums outside his window. Lila Curran's son, the boy disinherited by his father, the man whom his mother was determined to see regain his patrimony. Lila Curran's son.

The pieces of the puzzle were finally coming into place. Michael Curran was the key to the mystery of all that had happened this past month. And he hadn't seen it until now. No wonder he'd been groping in the dark. He hadn't figured Michael Curran into the equation, and that had been a dangerous mistake.

Norman found the next question obvious, but not the answer. What was Michael Curran planning to do?

San Juan, Eleven A.M.

"It was very good of you to send Señor Rosa to me." Beth and Michael were seated in the courtyard of the inn, on the bench beneath the palm tree.

"I thought you might need a bit of looking after by some-one who speaks English," he said. "How did you get on with him?"

Beth fanned herself vigorously. The day was oppressively hot and sultry, the humidity intense, the sky black with clouds. It felt as if a storm was on the way, but the locals said it was much too early in summer for a hurricane. "We got on very well. He's a most interesting man."

"Interesting?" Michael asked. "I wouldn't have thought you'd find Rosa interesting. Useful perhaps, but that's all."

"No, you're wrong. He's quite knowledgeable. We had a long chat on Thursday when he came to see me. So yesterday I went to see him."

Michael stared at her, astonished. "How did you find him? Where? Why did you want to?"

"I found him at the *taverna*, the one called El Gallo. He'd told me to send someone there to fetch him if I had need."

"Oh, I see. Did you send Tillie or Briggs?"

Beth shook her head. "Neither. I went myself."

"You did what? Good Lord, that must have turned a few heads."

"I expect it did. But it was quite safe really. I went after lunch and there was no one there except the barman, Pedro. Did you know he's Mr. Rosa's son?"

"Yes." God almighty, she was full of surprises. And determined as hell when she wanted something. Michael was seeing a side of Beth Mendoza's character that hadn't surfaced in the months they were clandestine lovers. "What did you and Señor Rosa talk about in the *taverna*?"

"We didn't stay there. He took me to the cliffs beyond the fort, not the Governor's Palace, the one they call El Morro. There wasn't a soul around. It was quite private really, and very pleasant."

"I see. Doesn't answer my question, though. Or perhaps you don't intend to tell me why you went looking for Rosa, or what you talked about."

She closed the fan with a snap of her wrist. It was useless; nothing could alleviate the heat of a day like this. "I do intend to tell you. I'm simply wondering how much you're going to understand."

"Try me," Michael said softly. Anger was rising in him. He thought it irrational—as far as he knew there was nothing to be angry about—nonetheless, the whole business annoyed the hell out of him. Beth prancing around San Juan on her own, attracting attention, poking her pretty little nose where undoubtedly it didn't belong. "You'd better tell me what happened," he said coldly.

"You're angry with me."

"No, of course I'm not."

"Well, you're going to be angry."

"For the love of Jesus! Sorry, I apologize for my bad language. But you're being very difficult."

"I'll try not to be." She hesitated, then plunged. "I discussed Judaism with Mr. Rosa. He's a son of Israel, did you know that?"

"A Jew," Michael corrected. "All these euphemisms are barely disguised insults. He's a Jew, plain and simple. And yes, I knew it."

"Your mother is a Jewess, isn't she? Or am I not supposed to use that word either."

"It's less offensive. And yes, Lila's parents, my Curran grandparents, were Jews. Look, what's all this leading up to?"

"You're tired, Michael. I don't think it was very wise of me to bring this up now."

He was tired. He'd returned from Ponce late yesterday afternoon. He'd wanted to go and see Nuria at once, but first he had to be sure Beth was all right, and to bathe and change. When he got to the inn he found a note from the bishop and one from Luz. Both men wished to see him on matters of urgency. He'd put Nuria out of his mind and told Beth he'd see her in the morning. His Excellency the bishop would also have to wait. Luz could still cause trouble if Michael didn't keep him under control, so he saw Luz first.

He'd spent the entire evening in the man's flat above the bank, reporting on the success of his journey, calming Luz's fears, letting him ramble on about how wonderful everything was going to be now that Don Michael had managed to buy the coffee plantations. How they were both going to be rich men. At least Don Michael would be richer, and he, Luz, would have enough for security in his old age.

Before he left Michael had paid Luz the equivalent of
fifteen thousand sterling. On account. The balance of eighty-
three thousand pounds would be turned over as soon as the
million was transferred from Coutts. Around the same time
that pigs sprouted wings, Curran told himself, unless there
had been some horrendous cock-up in London.

Michael wasn't thinking of Luz now, except as one reason
he felt so exhausted. He looked at Beth. "Maybe whatever
it is should have waited. But you've started, so you'd better
continue."

"Yes, I suppose I had. I really don't know why I hadn't
figured it out for myself. I mean everyone knows that the
Mendozas—" She broke off.

He didn't need to ask, but he did. "What about the
Mendozas?"

"They're Jews too. At least they always were until the first
lord Westlake converted."

"Some of them still are." Michael kept his tone calm and
conversational, not wanting her to see the fury building
inside him. He felt somehow shamed that this particular
topic could affect him in this way. "I have Mendoza cousins
who make no pretense of being Christians."

"I think it's a pretense with Jamie and Henry and my
father-in-law. I know it is with Tim."

"Do you mean that secretly they're Jews still? In their
heart of hearts, you might say."

"No, that's not it. They're not anything. It's all a show
for propriety's sake. The Mendoza men I know don't believe
in anything except themselves."

"Do you include me in that assessment?"

"I'm not sure," she whispered. "That's what I've been
trying to find out, but I still don't really know."

He couldn't keep it bottled up any longer. A little of what
he was feeling came out in his words. "Why didn't you ask
me, rather than discussing my family's private affairs with
a stranger?"

"I couldn't."

"What does that mean?"

"It means I knew you'd react the way you are now. That you'd be furious with me for trying to—to get beyond the screen you put up. You're a closed man, Michael Curran. The only time I feel I really know you is...in bed," she whispered at last, turning bright red.

"Some things are better left there," he said through clenched teeth. "And since you've pried this far, I'll tell you another piece of the story. In Córdoba it's different. My Spanish relatives have been Christians for a few hundred years. At least since the Inquisition. Maybe before. And I was baptised a Roman Catholic when I was born. That's how they do things."

"It doesn't matter." She spoke urgently, longing for him to understand, to see her real motives and know that they sprang from her love for him. "It doesn't matter about your father, because being Jewish is passed from the mother to her children. Mr. Rosa told me that."

"Bloody hell." This time he didn't apologize for cursing. "Would you mind telling me one more thing? What in the name of all that's holy has any of this got to do with you?"

"Not with me, with us. Don't you see, Michael? I know about your not eating pork: Briggs told Tillie and she told me. And I know that what you've always wanted is the inheritance your father cheated you out of—Córdoba. So I put and two and two together. And I realized that if I was going to help you I had to understand more. That's why I went to Mr. Rosa and made him tell me as much as he could."

"Help me how?" He bit out the words.

"Help you in our lives together."

He was almost angry enough to say it. We aren't going to have a life together. It's impossible. You were an interlude; you can never be anything more. Almost angry enough, but not quite. It was too hurtful, too cruel. She didn't deserve to be treated so viciously. Instead he stood up and started to walk away.

"Michael!" she called after him. "Michael, where are you going?"

"I don't know, but I know I have to get away for a while. I'm furious, Beth. You had no right whatever to poke around in matters that are none of your damned business. And if we keep talking I'm going to say things we'll both regret."

He strode through the courtyard to the street. She called his name again, but this time he didn't turn around.

Michael wandered at first, roamed aimlessly through the twisting narrow streets and small cobbled alleys of the town, giving himself time to cool off. San Juan was very quiet. He sensed that the island knew it was under threat.

But why did he feel threatened? Because Beth was . . . what? Beautiful, desirable, intelligent. All the things that had made him pursue her in the first place. Beth excited him, but she frightened him too. Because of what she could make him feel, her way of finding the heart of an issue and laying it bear. Because in some ways she was like Lila.

That was the basis of his anger today. Like his mother, Beth had been unafraid to take the initiative. Women weren't supposed to do that, but Lila did and so did Beth. He seemed always to have to meet the challenge of unusually strong women. And he was both attracted and repelled by them. Damn! A woman should soothe a man, give him comfort and ease, not always be pulling him up to the mark.

In half an hour he was calmer, his anger under control because he'd analyzed it. He'd go see Nuria now, Michael decided. He turned toward the Calle Cruz, thinking of the differences between Nuria and Beth, unsure what he made of them, when he heard someone shouting his name.

"Señor Curran, I have been looking for you!"

"Luz, what are you doing here?"

The banker put a hand on Curran's arm. The hand was

trembling and the fingers clutched at his sleeve as if it were a lifeline. "Don Michael, please we must talk."

"We talked for four hours last night."

"But now—" Luz broke off and looked about him, his eyes searching the road. "Please, come to my house, it will be safer," he said in a harsh whisper.

He couldn't refuse. Luz was still in too pivotal a role. They walked together to the Calle Fortaleza, neither man speaking. In ten minutes they were climbing the stairs to Luz's apartment. The Puerto Rican locked every door behind them, selecting the keys from a ring attached to his watch chain, checking each at least twice. "Now, we are alone, *gracias a Dios*. I have sent the servants away."

Michael took a chair without waiting to be asked. "Why'd you do that, Luz?"

"So I could think. So I could speak with you in absolute privacy. So—"

"So you'd better tell me what this is about. You were a happy man last night. Now you look as if your mother has just died."

"My mother, Don Michael? I do not understand, my mother has been—"

"Only a figure of speech, forget it. Tell me what's got you so upset."

Luz went to the desk and took another key from the ring. This one was small and fit into a carved wooden door that was unrecognizable as such until it was opened. He withdrew an envelope and passed it to Michael with shaking hands.

"A cable? From London, isn't it?" Curran looked at the other man. There was a sense of excitement building in him, which he took care to conceal.

"*Sí*, señor, from London."

Michael had the single sheet of paper in his hands by this time, but none of the words made any sense. "It's in code."

"*¡Ay mi Madre!* I forgot." Luz ran to another drawer in the desk and came back with a second sheet of paper. "Here is the translation I made."

The words were few and very simple.

"TRANSFER LONDON IMMEDIATELY EQUIVALENT THREE HUNDRED THOUSAND STERLING STOP SIGNED NORMAN MENDOZA."

"I cannot do as he asks," Luz whispered. "The reserves are gone. I gave them to you. What do I do now, Don Michael?"

Michael was jubilant, his blood singing. It was working. It was working exactly as they'd planned it! He kept the excitement inside, spoke cooly and with great confidence. "First, get yourself a drink, one for me too. And stop acting as if the world's caved in. It hasn't."

"But—"

"But there's nothing to worry about. You're entirely safe."

"How can I be safe? How can the bank be safe? What I did, I told you it was almost illegal, I told you—"

"And I told you it was a question of judgment, yours as the man on the spot, against those of your employer thousands of miles away. You made your call, Luz, and you did the right thing. There's nothing to worry about." He debated saying more, decided against it. Timing was everything and the timing wasn't perfect yet. More would have to wait—probably only another few days, a week at the most.

Luz had followed his instructions and poured two large portions of brandy. He gave Michael one and drank the other quickly. "What do I do?" he asked again.

"You send a cable to Mendozas in London. Get me a pen and some paper and I'll write it out for you."

Luz did as he was asked, then watched silently while the Irishman composed the message. "This will do it," Michael said when he was finished. He passed the paper to Luz.

"Reserves temporarily depleted for large venture that will reap considerable profit for bank," Luz read aloud, moving

THE FLAMES OF VENGEANCE   335

his lips slowly, lingering over each word. "If I send this, señor, it is the end of my employment here." He spoke more quietly, the brandy having calmed him.

"Perhaps, but not immediately. The Mendozas have other things to worry about."

"What do you mean? How do you know—"

Michael stood up. "Never mind that now. I'll explain later. Meanwhile, you put that message into your code and send it."

"Don Michael," Luz said pleadingly as his visitor headed for the door.

"Don't worry. You're going to come out of this in fine shape. A much richer man than you went into it. Aren't you already fifteen thousand pounds richer?"

"Yes. But that money, Señor Curran, I have been thinking about it. The money you gave me, it too came from the . . . the loan I made you, no? So it came from the reserves of the bank and it isn't really yours. Or mine," he added sadly.

"It's yours," Michael assured him. "I give you my word, it's yours."

Luz nodded, wanting to believe. "Yes, because when your one million is transferred you will repay—"

"Yes, that's right. Now get those keys out of your pocket and let me out."

Michael walked down the Calle Fortaleza with a new spring in his step. He hadn't felt this good in days. It was working, the whole complex scheme, exactly as he and Sharrick and Lila had laid it out. By Christ, it had to be working if Mendozas was calling in the relatively tiny reserves of this far-flung outpost. So coming here hadn't been a futile exercise. Puerto Rico really would lead him to Córdoba.

He turned onto the Calle Cruz, passed the big house, and went through the alley. He would save Nuria from her demons too. That was another bonus of his sojourn on this wretched little island. Michael rapped sharply on the door.

"*Buenos días,* Señor Curran," Samsón said.

"Good day to you too. I wish to see Doña Nuria."

"I am *verdad* sorry, señor. Missy Doña, she no see nobody."

"She'll see me. Tell her it's urgent. Tell her I've something important to say."

Samsón shook his head. "I am *verdad* sure I can no do nothing, señor. Missy Doña, she tell me *verdad* plain. She see nobody. Especially not big Irishman. Is *verdad* true, Señor Curran. Sorry."

Michael pleaded, but there was no getting past the old black man. He could shove him out of the way easily, of course, but there were half a dozen other younger men waiting to do whatever Nuria wanted done. Throw him out, in this case. And if he licked them all and got through to her? It was absurd. If the woman didn't want his help, then damn her to hell. It was no concern of his.

London, Five P.M.

"So, I leave you at the Connaught and I come back three weeks later and you are still here." Beatriz slipped a green silk cape from her shoulders and draped it over the back of one of the chairs in Lila's sitting room. "This place must be costing you a fortune."

"It's money well spent."

Lila came forward to greet her sister-in-law; they kissed on both cheeks in the Spanish fashion. "Let me look at you. Hmm, you've been eating very well at Westlake. Apart from the food, how was it?"

"Boring. Jamie's daughters might have been amusing, but they are making what you call the grand tour of the Continent. Visiting museums with their governess. There was only me and Jamie and Caroline. And their friends, of course." She raised her eyebrows and shuddered delicately.

"When they are not talking about flowers they talk about horses and killing little foxes. I was so bored I could not stop eating. That is how it was."

Beatriz dropped heavily into a chair and pointed to a tray on the table in front of the sofa. "The tea is still warm?"

"No. I'll order some fresh." Lila walked to the bell rope hanging beside the fireplace.

"And some of those lovely buttery things. What are they called? Crumpets!" Beatriz added, delighted with herself for remembering. "I love crumpets."

"Yes, I can see that. It would be better if you loved them a little less."

But when the maid came Lila asked for more tea and hot buttered crumpets. "Now," she said when the servant had gone. "Tell me all about it."

Beatriz shrugged. "I already have. Boring. And they eat a lot. There is nothing else to do except look at flowers."

"I'm told that Jamie looks terrible. He can't have been eating much."

"No, until he left for London a few days ago I thought he was going to get so thin he'd disappear. Caroline kept ordering his favorite things, but he only pushed the food around on his plate. Poor things, they don't know what's happening. It is hard not to feel sorry for them."

"Not you too!"

"I don't understand. Me too what?"

"Feeling sorry for the Mendozas," Lila said bitterly. "I wish I knew an antidote for unwarranted mercy."

Beatriz watched her through narrowed eyes. "I am not showing mercy, Lila. I don't know who is. And you forget, I too am a Mendoza. A real one. By blood, not marriage."

"I know. I'm sorry. I didn't mean you, only those damned men."

"Michael is a Mendoza."

"That's different."

"Because you say so? Not really. I th—"

She stopped speaking because the maid tapped softly on the door, then came in carrying a laden tray. "Shall I pour, madam?"

"No, leave it. I'll do it." When they were alone again, while Lila was pouring the tea, she said, "Tell me what you were going to say. What do you think?"

"That you are under too much strain. You are very nervous, *querida*. I have a tonic that will help you. An old Gypsy woman in Córdoba makes it for me. I will find it for you as soon as I unpack."

"Thank you, but I don't need a tonic." Lila passed the cup to Beatriz and put two crumpets on a small porcelain plate. "Here, these should fend off starvation."

"Thank you. So, if not a tonic, what do you need? I know, a man."

Lila flushed. "What nonsense."

"No, it is not nonsense. Me, I have never had a good man, and I do not miss the one I had. But you, Lila, you are different. We must find you the right man, *querida*. Then you will be calmer."

"I've been alone for sixteen years. And the ten before that were not exactly paradise, as you well know. I'm not eager for another man."

"What then? Look at you." Beatriz pinched her own chubby arm. "I wish I could give some of this fat to you. You are much too thin."

"What I need is to hear from Michael."

The other woman sat up straighter, suddenly alarmed. "Is something wrong? Something not as you expect it to be?"

"Not the way you mean. As far as I know everything is exactly as it should be. But it's nerve-racking not hearing from Michael directly."

"Was he supposed to write to you?"

Lila shook her head. "No, we decided there was no point. Letters take so long that whatever he had to say would be ancient history by the time I read it. And cables are very public, and therefore dangerous."

"So you did not expect to hear from him and nothing is wrong." Beatriz settled back to enjoying her tea and crumpets.

"I'm thinking about Timothy," Lila said quietly.

"*Ay mi Madre!* That is really terrible, to be dead is one thing, but like that, alive but dead . . . horrible."

"Yes. Beatriz, do you know about Beth?"

"The wife of Timothy? What about her?"

"No one told you?"

"Told me what? I was in that *carcel* in the country."

A *carcel* was a prison. Lila understood applying the term to Westlake; she felt like that about it too. She'd been there once with Juan Luis, in the early days of their marriage, before all the trouble. She'd found it beautiful, but cold. And Caroline had treated her like a leper. "Was she nice to you?" Lila asked now.

"Caroline? Oh, very nice. She flits around and laughs her little laugh that is like bells, and says amusing things, but there is no meat in her. With Caroline you cannot talk about anything real."

"I have barely said two words to her in my whole life," Lila admitted. "When Juan Luis took me to Westlake Caroline simply ignored me."

"Of course. You are not, what is the expression, out of the upper drawer."

"No, a very bottom drawer in fact. That never bothered you, did it, Beatriz?"

"Hah! Of course not. I am a Mendoza. My family is too old to have such false snobbery. Caroline I think has only one toe on the snob ladder. So she is worried about being pushed off."

"Even now that she's married to Jamie and has a title?"

"But she has no sons," Beatríz said with finality. "I am not surprised that Caroline hated you. You were as pretty as she was, and maybe you would have a son." She leaned forward and put her empty cup and plate on the tray. "Now, tell me what you were going to say before. What nobody has told me because I talked only with Caroline and Jamie and their boring friends."

"I suppose I may as well. Timothy's wife left him last month. She . . ." Her voice trailed away.

"Yes? Lila, please do not tell me half a story. I can't stand it. Why did she leave him? Where did she go?"

"She left him to join Michael. As far as I know, she's in Puerto Rico with him now."

Beatriz didn't say anything for a few moments. When she did her voice was hard. "She is a Christian, this Beth? A Protestant?"

"Naturally. Would Timothy have married her otherwise?"

"I suppose not. And soon she will be a divorced woman, no?"

"Before the accident Timothy planned to divorce her. I know because he told me so himself."

"It will not do." Beatriz shook her head firmly. "It is not acceptable, a divorced Protestant woman as mistress of the Palacio Mendoza. She would never be acceptable in Andalusia."

"And not acceptable to you."

"No. You know our bargain, Lila. You promised. You told me Michael had promised."

"I do know. So does Michael. Don't worry, he's only amusing himself. He won't do anything foolish."

Lila heard her own words and prayed they were true. "Now," she said, "I must tell you the really important thing. About Francisco. . . ."

The singsong accent of Lord Sharrick's butler grated on Norman's ears. He'd never much liked the Welsh. He gritted his teeth and told the man that yes, he'd be glad to wait. "Tell his lordship I apologize for calling without an appointment," he added. "But it's in both our interests for him to see me."

"Of course, sir. I shall give his lordship the message. In here if you please." The butler opened a door, waited for Norman to enter, then closed it softly.

He was in the morning room. It was paneled in ivory wood as far up as the chair rail, above that the walls were covered in some sort of silk printed with Chinese scenes. Damned expensive stuff. He remembered Penelope wanting to use it in their dining room in Belgravia. Out of the question, he'd told her. Costs a king's ransom. They had settled for ordinary flocked wallpaper. That was about six months before she died. He'd always felt a little guilty about it.

"Good afternoon, Mendoza. You're admiring my wall covering I see. Came from Canton. Brought it back myself."

"Afternoon, Sharrick. Yes, it's handsome stuff. My wife liked it. Before she died—" He broke off. Absurd to be chatting about decorating. "This isn't exactly a social call. I don't imagine you think it is, so we can both stop pretending."

"Pretending? I'm not pretending anything. You seem distraught. Here, have some sherry. Your own must be the one you prefer."

There was a series of decanters on a sidetable. Sharrick poured some Mendoza fino into a schooner and offered it to his guest.

Norman took the glass with a murmur of thanks, then returned to the attack. "Perhaps you'll want something stronger when you hear what I have to say."

"Will I? I can't think why. You're the one who apparently knows what this call is about. Perhaps you'd best enlighten me."

"Lila Curran," Norman said.

Sharrick's eyes narrowed, but his expression didn't change. "What about her?"

"You know the woman, don't you? Know she's a distant cousin by marriage."

"I'm afraid I don't follow. A cousin of mine or yours?"

Norman set down his glass and leaned toward the Irishman. "Don't play bloody games with me, Sharrick. I've not the time, neither have you."

"If you're going to use that tone, this meeting will be over quite quickly," Sharrick said. "Now either sit down and tell me what you want, or get out."

"I know you're involved with the Black Widow."

Sharrick started for the door. "My personal life is none of your business. Neither is hers. I'll have Jones show you out."

Norman didn't move. "I'll try another name," he said to Sharrick's back. "Fergus Kelly."

The Irishman stopped, but he didn't turn around. "And who might I ask is that?"

"You. When you're playing games with the bloody Fenians. There are quite a few people in London, in the government in fact, who'd be interested in that piece of information. Don't you agree?"

Sharrick turned slowly. "What in God's name are you talking about?"

Norman moved to a brocaded chair and sat down. "You did ask me to sit, didn't you, Sharrick? I think it might be best if you did the same."

Sharrick took a chair and waited.

"It began with the article in the *Times*," Norman said in conversational tones. "I didn't understand what you were after, why you'd chosen to savage us. So I did a bit of checking and—"

"What kind of checking?"

"Oh, the sort that's usual in matters like this. There are some rather unsavory people who can be employed to follow other people. But I'm sure you know that. It must be a fairly common practice in your line of work." Norman rose and went to the table. "Mind if I help myself to a bit more of this?" He lifted the decanter of fino, filled his glass, and took a sip before he continued speaking.

"Anyway, all the pieces have fallen into place nicely now. You and your alias, Lila Curran and her god-blasted son, even Timothy's treachery. I've figured it all out, Sharrick. That's why I came here to discuss it."

"I see." Sharrick had been thrown at first. Norman Mendoza knowing about Fergus Kelly had been a blow. Now he was regaining his composure, remembering how close to the pit the other man was, and how much more secure his own footing. "Yes, Mendoza, perhaps it is time we had this little talk."

Sharrick rose, limped to the table, and retrieved the decanter. Then he returned to his chair and set the sherry where they could both reach it.

↶ 17 ↷

WEDNESDAY, JULY 14, 1898
London, Eleven A.M.

Jamie looked from the cable lying on his desk to Norman, then back again. "I'm sorry, I can't remember how to decode this," he said hopelessly.

"I doubt you ever knew," Norman muttered. "Never mind, I've told you what it says."

"That there are no reserves in Puerto Rico for us to draw on. But..."

"But nothing. That's the long and the short of it. There isn't time to send someone over there to check. For the present we have to take Luz's word. Doubtless there'll be a fuller explanation by post."

That was a sop for Jamie. Norman knew the explanation. He'd been expecting more trouble from Puerto Rico since his meeting with Hammersmith. The demand for payment of a million in sterling was Michael Curran's opening salvo; this cable was his second volley. Damned clever, have to give him that. How in hell had he managed to empty the reserves of the bank?

Jamie was looking at his brother with a blank expression.

"Luz," Norman repeated. "The manager in Puerto Rico." Jamie nodded as if he understood.

"I'll sack him of course. But even that should probably wait until we see how this absurd war turns out and whether America or Spain winds up owning the island. Meanwhile, the fact is it's another closed door."

"Yes, another. Norman, did you see the man who came to me at my club, the Russian?"

"I saw him."

"And?" Jamie kept fidgeting with a jade-handled letter opener, pushing it around the desk like a child playing trains. "What did he say?"

"Pretty much what he told you. He's giving us advance warning that the Imperial Treasury is going to withdraw a large part of its deposit. Perhaps all of it."

"Do you believe him?" Jamie's voice was harsh with fatigue and worry, but for once he was paying attention to the matter at hand.

"I'm not sure," Norman admitted. "I've been able to find out that he did at one time work for the Russian Treasury. As for the rest of it . . ." He shrugged. "Who knows?"

"But—"

"Look, I think it may be a ploy, part of a scheme—" Norman stopped speaking. He couldn't muster the strength to explain his suspicions to Jamie, to outline the role of Lila Curran and her son in all their troubles. "All the same, we have to act as if the Russian's information is reliable," he said. "We have to prepare for the worst."

Jamie glanced up and a spark of hope lit his eyes. "Norman, do you have a plan? How can we prepare? I've been thinking about it, but I can't come up with any answers. Though I suppose we could borrow—"

"You're mad. Mendozas can't appear in the open market as borrowers. It would trigger the most appalling attack of nerves imaginable. The whole London financial market could crash. And take us with it."

"What then?"

"I've put out one or two very discreet feelers, and made some arrangements. We can count on half a million from a private lender. It's a drop in the bucket, but for the very short term—"

"What private lender? Who?"

"Never mind, it's not important that you know who," Norman said wearily. "Look, Jamie, leave the details to me. I've a question for you, though. Two in fact. First, if it becomes necessary, will you put up Westlake and Gordon Square as collateral?"

"Oh my God. I . . . Norman, do you think . . ."

"I think that if we go under every damned thing any of us owns goes with us," Norman said brutally. "I'm asking if you'll agree to use your property in a more orderly way. Assuming that's what's required."

"Of course I will if I must," Jamie whispered.

"Good. So will I and Henry and Charles, though the combined worth of what we have doesn't begin to compare with your holdings. Now, the second question. When Father handed over to you, did he say anything about an outstanding bond given to Córdoba by London in Grandfather's time?"

"A bond? What kind of a bond?"

"A promise to pay on demand one million pounds sterling. With no statute of limitations."

Jamie blanched. Norman wondered if he were going to faint. No, he decided, not yet. He had to keep pressing. God alone knew the next time he'd get Jamie to concentrate on business. "Well, did he?"

"Nothing. Never. At least I don't recall . . ."

No, that was the hell of it. Jamie might have been told all manner of things, their father had persisted in believing that his eldest son would grow to fit his role; it was unlikely that Jamie had listened then, and less likely that he'd remember now. But Norman felt he had to try. "You're sure?"

"No, I'm sorry, I'm not sure. But I don't remember anything. Norman, is there such a bond? Who has it?"

"I'm told there is. And that Lila Curran had it until she gave it to her son."

"Michael? But how did Lila get it?"

"It has to have been from Juan Luis. She held him up for a fortune before she left Córdoba. You know that."

"Yes, but I've never understood—"

Norman cut him off. "Neither have I. But that's unimportant now. I believe we're about to be asked to make good the debt."

Jamie seemed to shrink into his chair. He was shivering and he wrapped his arms around his torso and rocked back and forth like an injured child. Norman went to the table beside the window and poured a tot of brandy from a blown-glass decanter old enough and fine enough to be in a museum. "Here, drink this. And get hold of yourself. We're not dead yet, Jamie."

Jamie accepted the brandy with a murmur of thanks. He sipped it, then took a longer swallow.

"Better?" Norman asked.

"I think so, yes. Where is this bond? Do you have it?"

"No. If I had it I'd put a match to it. The thing's with Coutts. I'm to go to their offices this afternoon and see it, and presumably receive a formal demand for payment."

"But we can't—"

Norman leaned forward, propping himself on the desk with his two husky arms. "Don't say it. You know it and so do I. But don't say it. Don't even think it. If those words are ever uttered, if we ever actually default on a payment of any sort, it's all over, Jamie. Do you understand?" His brother nodded. "Good, it's very important that you do."

"Have you told Henry?"

"Yes."

"What did he say?"

"What you'd expect, but Henry's all right. He's tougher

in his way than we give him credit for. He's pretty miserable, but he won't break."

"It's all on your shoulders, isn't it, Norman? You're really the only one who understands, who can pull us through. You should have been . . . I mean, Father should have . . ."

"Yes, well he didn't. Look, you may as well get out of here. You're not doing any good and you could do harm. Don't go to your club; the look of you will start a panic. Go home to Gordon Square. Stay there until you hear from me. Don't take telephone calls from anyone but me or Henry. Say you're ill. Where's Caroline, by the way?"

"Not in town. She stayed in the country."

"Just as well. The girls?"

"They're still traveling on the Continent. Until the end of this month." Then, as if that reminded him, he said, "Have you heard from Charles?"

"A cable Sunday evening, saying he'd arrived in Córdoba. That's all so far. I expect a longer message tonight or tomorrow."

Jamie nodded, finished his brandy, and stood up. "I'll leave now, shall I?"

"Yes, Jamie. Go straight to Gordon Square. And once you're there think about this bond affair. See if you can recall anything Father may have said."

Jamie was at the door of his office, but he paused. "I'm sorry I forgot to ask until now. How's Tim?"

"The same. No change."

"Dear God . . ."

Norman opened the door and gently shepherded his brother through it.

Dublin, A Little after Noon

Paddy Shea was eating his lunch in the kitchen behind the pub. Dinner he called it—boiled potatoes and cabbage, and bread soaked in dripping. Shea was alone; his wife was out front tending the bar. He could hear the noisy voices of the many men crowded into the public room. Shea glanced at the clock above the stove. Most of the customers would be gone in half an hour or so, home to their dinners or back to work. He'd go out then and relieve her, let the woman come back here and eat.

He got up and checked the pot on the stove. Two large potatoes were swimming in the cooking water. Ah well, she seldom ate a lot. He speared one of the remaining potatoes and carried it back to his plate, belching loudly in the process. A good belch made more room; he tucked into the extra potato with relish.

"Are you by yourself, then?" a voice asked.

Shea looked up and saw young Donald O'Leary standing in the door. "Aye, I am. Sure and I'm having me dinner. A man should have his dinner in peace."

"I need to talk to you."

Shea put the last morsel of potato on his fork, added the last bit of cabbage, and put the food in his mouth. He chewed slowly, still watching the boy. O'Leary looked different. He'd changed since they'd been to London, got more sure of himself. Shea swallowed and shoved the plate away. "Well, come in and sit down, since you've a mind to."

"Have you a glass of beer? It's powerful thirsty I am. It's turned warm again."

"Beer's in the bar and we sell it." Shea got up and lay a hand against a teapot that had been pushed to the back of the stove. "There's a bit o' this you're welcome to."

He poured the tea into a mug. The brew had been sitting for hours and it was bitter and black and barely warm. O'Leary sipped it, then made a face. "Sure and I think you dry out your tea leaves and use 'em a second time, Paddy Shea."

"Seems to me I heard somethin' about beggars not bein' able to choose."

"Who's begging? In a civilized house you're offered a drink. You don't have to ask for it."

"Oh, is that so? Is that how they do things up on Dawson Street? Hand out drinks to all comers at Bellereve, do they?"

"That's what I came to see you about. I want to pack in the job." O'Leary pushed the mug of undrinkable tea to the other side of the scarred table.

"Do you now? And why, might I ask, do you want to do that?"

"It makes no sense me stayin'. The Black Widow's not been home for nearly a month. Nobody knows when she's coming back."

Shea leaned forward. "But she will. She'll come back as she always does, will Lila Curran. And the committee wants you there to tell us what she's doing."

"No, they don't, not anymore." O'Leary reached into the pocket of his shirt. "This note came two days past. It says I'm to go up to Wicklow, to Glencree. There's a job for me there."

Shea grabbed the paper out of his hands. "Let me see that. Who sent it?" He squinted at the signature. It was only the initials F.K. "I ain't heard nothin' about this, and I'm your captain."

"And isn't that why I'm here tellin' you about it, because you're me captain? But see that F.K.? That's himself, I'm sure of it."

"Himself who?"

"The man what came and gave us our orders when we was in London. Himself what gave us the package to bring back here. Fergus Kelly."

Shea still wasn't convinced. "Any change in posting is supposed to go through the committee to the captain, then get passed on. That's how it's done."

"Well, maybe it's been done different this time."

"And maybe it's some kind of trick."

"What kind of trick? Who besides ourselves cares if I work at Bellereve or Glencree? Or in hell, for that matter?"

"I'm not sure," Shea admitted. "But you never know with the bloody English. They're always tryin' to find us out, spyin' on us. Clever as snakes they are. And as deadly."

"It's not a trick." O'Leary took the note back and returned it to the pocket of his shirt. "Doesn't make no sense for it to be a trick."

"You're not goin' up there, not without I talk to the committee first."

"Sure and I am. Why shouldn't I? If it's a trick the agent will say he never heard of me. That's who I'm supposed to see. The agent." He tapped his chest. "That's what this here note says."

"And what kind of job do you think you might be getting?"

O'Leary shrugged. "And how could I know that? But whatever it is, it won't be any worse than bein' a footman under that bloody Winston."

Shea leaned forward, breathing fetid breath into the face of the younger man, staring at him. "You'll wait until I talk to the committee, or you'll be finished as far as we're concerned. Dead. One way or t'other."

"No, I—" O'Leary stopped and shook his head. There was real menace in Paddy Shea's eyes, but that wasn't what made him back down. He'd been a Fenian since he was twelve. He couldn't break faith now. "Aye," he said finally. "You talk to them, Paddy. Find out if I can go up to Glencree and see what's waitin' for me."

Córdoba, Three P.M.

Charles had been to Westlake any number of times. He'd wandered the great house and the endless grounds and considered the fact that unless his aunt Caroline produced

a male heir, something less likely to happen as each year
passed, the estate would be his someday. He and Tim were
Jamie's closest male relatives, and Charles was the eldest.
The title and the property would pass to him. He'd known
that since he was quite young, had learned to be comfortable
with the expectation; but his own potential grandeur had
not prepared Charles for the Palacio Mendoza in Córdoba.

The palace had something he'd never found in any English country house, however huge and venerable. Perhaps
because it was right in the middle of the city—hidden behind enormous walls—the house breathed mystery. It whispered secrets into his ears as he walked from one lavish
room to another. The patios were still more remarkable.
He'd been told there were fourteen of them, but he'd not
managed to see them all yet. Each was different; each suddenly appeared as you turned a corner or crossed a hall.

He was in what they called the Patio de los Naranjos
now. It was a long rectangle, with an exquisitely tiled reflecting pool flanked by a dozen orange trees. The trees were in
flower. He'd never in his life smelled anything so heady.

"Ah, Charles, you are here."

He turned at the sound of Francisco's voice. Thank God
the man spoke English, however thick his accent. "Has he
come?" Charles asked.

"The manager of the *banco*, yes, he has come. He is waiting
inside."

Charles took a last look at the orange trees, reluctant to
leave this peaceful place for business. "It's lovely," he murmured.

"Yes, yes. It is all very lovely, no? And you are a Mendoza,
so all the old stories have meanings for you."

"What old stories?"

"The legends. Every room and every patio in this *palacio*—each has another legend. Another story about the family. You do not know them?" Charles shook his head. "Then
it is a pity Beatriz is not here," the other man said. "She

knows them all, and delights in telling them. But I think now we must..." He gestured toward an arched door.

"Yes, of course." Reluctantly Charles followed Francisco inside.

He'd thought perhaps the bank manager was waiting in the counting room, which is where Francisco had taken him the first night he came. He had explained that it was the oldest room in the palace, and that the head of the family always used it for business. But they didn't go there now. Instead Francisco led him down a series of corridors with tiled floors overlaid with Turkish carpets, and tapestries hanging on the walls.

Charles thought they were in the east wing, but there were so many twists and turns he couldn't be sure. They came to a book-lined room where Francisco swung open the door and waited for the younger man to precede him.

A third man was waiting, seated beside a long oak table covered with yet another tapestry. He rose and inclined his head in a bow that included both Francisco and Charles.

"This is Señor Martín," Francisco said. "He does not speak English, so I will translate."

The two men shook hands. The bank manager's was sweaty, Charles noted. And the man didn't look at him directly.

There were many ledgers on the table. Martín gestured to them and said something in Spanish.

"He says that everything you need to know is in there," Francisco explained. Martín spoke again. "He says that he's sure once you've examined the figures you will realize that there is no cause for alarm."

Charles nodded. The three men arranged themselves around the table. Charles studied Francisco out of the corner of his eye.

Sunday evening his cousin-in-law had seemed close to a nervous collapse; today he was genial and very much in control. Francisco had grown calmer each day that they waited for the bank manager to prepare the records. Obviously he'd made up his mind to abdicate, to turn the whole thing over to London. The longer Charles stayed, the more convinced Francisco must be that it would really happen that way. He would escape this responsibility and live on whatever he'd squireled away.

"The current accounts first," Charles said, waiting for Francisco to translate.

The bank manager nodded as soon as he understood. He opened one of the ledgers and they set to work.

London, Four P.M.

Coutts was lodged in the same building they'd been in for over a century. It wasn't filled with exquisite antiques and rarities as were the Mendoza premises; this place smelled of old leather and old wood and old, very solid, investments. A hundred years earlier King George III had placed his "privy purse" account with Coutts; since then the bank had been manager of the private finances of the royals. It was a most secure base from which to operate.

"In here, Norman." Hammersmith opened the door to a spacious office. "Good of you to come."

"I'm hardly likely to have refused," Norman murmured. He glanced around the room; there was no one else there.

"I don't think it's necessary to widen the knowledge of this matter, do you?" Hammersmith asked.

"No. I appreciate that."

"Please, sit down."

They seated themselves on opposite sides of a large mahogany desk. The only things on its polished surface were a silver pen stand, an immaculate blotter, a crystal vase containing a single rose, and a blue folder tied with a black ribbon. Hammersmith put his hand on the folder.

"That's it, I take it?" Norman asked.

"Yes."

"May I see it?"

"Of course." Hammersmith untied the ribbon and opened the folder. The bond lay on top of some other papers. He removed it and passed it across the desk.

Norman took it, gratified to see that his hands weren't visibly trembling. He read slowly, not wanting to miss anything that might indicate the document was a clever forgery. Before his eyes were half way down the page he was convinced that it was not.

This was unquestionably his grandfather Liam's hand; he'd seen it many times in the old records. And the style was Liam's—straightforward. "In return for personal services and guarantees granted me I do promise and swear in the name of the house of Mendoza to pay to the bearer the sum of one million pounds sterling, whensoever said bearer presents this bond. There shall be no limit upon the time when payment may be demanded. The sum is to carry no charge of interest, nor be changed by any circumstance whatsoever. . . ."

"It's legitimate, isn't it?" Hammersmith asked after Norman had been studying the bond for nearly five silent minutes.

A second's pause. Another. Norman's palms were sweating, his mouth dry. "I believe so, yes," he said quietly.

He'd told Jamie that he'd burn the bond if he could, and he'd come here intending to bluff, to insist that the instrument was a fake, to stall. Now—reading his grandfather's plain words, holding the thing in his hands—he couldn't do it.

The bond was real; the debt was real. If he denied it, what the hell was it all for? Mendozas, the family, the legendary reputation for absolute reliability? What did any of it mean if he sat here and lied about what he knew in his bones was true?

Hammersmith watched the play of emotions on his visitor's face. He leaned forward. "Norman, for all our sakes, give me an honest answer. Can you pay? Is Mendozas solvent?"

Last month, last week, he would have answered with bluff and bravado. No hesitation. But now? After the hours he'd spent standing beside Tim's bed, trying to separate the boy's duplicity from his tragedy, after the hours of pondering Charles's abilities to take over, the hours of examining his own life, his part in the building or breaking of what generations before him had created—after all that he had no stomach for deceit. "No," he said softly. "No, we can't pay, not in ten days time. And no, we're not in very good shape."

Hammersmith leaned back and closed his eyes. "I thought not. The other day, in the pub, that was the first time I suspected the rumors might in fact be true. They started about the time the Paraguayan issue did so poorly, but I dismissed them. Mendozas, after all. For years it's been the greatest banking house in Europe. It didn't seem possible. But the other day there was something about you, something in your eyes . . ."

"If we go under you won't come out of it unscathed," Norman said.

He'd been honest; he'd kept faith. Now it was time to fight with every weapon he possessed, because that too was part of the legacy. What was that reading in church the other day? *For everything there is a season, and a time for every purpose under heaven.* Now was the time to claw his way out of the pit. "There will be an unholy panic. The whole City will face the greatest crisis of confidence it has ever known."

"We survived Barings," Hammersmith reminded him.

"Yes, but only just. And a second failure, coming less than ten years later? You won't survive that, Johnathon. Not without some very painful wounds. They could be fatal wounds."

Hammersmith eyed him. "I presume you're looking for a loan." Norman didn't answer. "How much?" Hammersmith pressed. "How much do you need? What's the gap between your acceptances and your bills?"

Acceptances was an old-fashioned word. It had come into being in the seventeenth century. Smith in Delhi could ship his tea to Edwards in London on the strength of a bill of exchange guaranteed by a banker in whom they both had confidence. The banker had "accepted" the responsibility. No one talked about acceptances anymore. Strange for Hammersmith to put the question that way. But everything about Coutts was determinedly old-fashioned. The men still wore swallow coats to work. Norman did not wish to play by those antique rules.

"Including that," he pointed to the bond now lying on the desk between them, "our liabilities are somewhere around eighteen million, our assets—" he paused.

"Yes?" Hammersmith urged.

"—the bank's assets have to be judged in numerous ways."

Norman wasn't prepared to let personal holdings come into it yet. But he thought of the cargoes still on the high seas, subject to the same possibility of bad luck that had sunk the *Susannah Star*. "Some are admittedly shaky; others are very solid indeed."

"I'm aware of that. It's always so. But I'm waiting for a number, Norman. I think it had best be the most conservative number that fits the case."

"Say five million." And pray God the Russians didn't withdraw their deposit.

Hammersmith nodded, his expression giving nothing away. "And of that five million, how much represents liquidity?"

Norman reached for his pipe and tobacco pouch. "Do you mind?"

"No, not at all." Hammersmith leaned over to the windowsill, retrieved a heavy brass ashtray, and pushed it across the desk. For a few seconds he watched the other man fuss with his pipe. "The liquid funds, Norman," he said finally. "What do they come to?"

"Less than a hundred thousand." Norman spoke the words with his teeth clenched around the stem of the pipe. They came out muffled.

"What? I'm not sure I heard you."

"About a hundred thousand, give or take." Clearer this time, and not flinching from the other man's stare.

"Jesus God almighty," Hammersmith breathed. Coming from him the words might be a prayer.

Norman had no intention of getting into a discussion about the responsibilities and failures of management. It was time for a diversionary tactic, part of the required dance in every negotiation. There was no need to ask for discretion; the entire point of this conversation was to find a way not to let Mendozas tumble and take the other private banks with them. Discretion was guaranteed because it was in Coutts's own best interest.

"Tell me something," Norman said. "Have you any idea what prompted Michael Curran to demand payment now?"

"None."

"It must be something to do with Puerto Rico, since he wants the funds sent there."

Hammersmith was obviously uncomfortable. "I think that's more your line of country than mine, Norman. The Indies have always been your bailiwick."

"For the moment they still are." Norman tapped ash from his pipe into the brass ashtray. "Of course with this idiotic war going on, it's hard to know what the future holds."

"Look, hadn't we better discuss a way of getting you out of this mess?"

"You mentioned a loan," Norman said softly.

"Not for thirteen million! My God, Norman, surely you can't expect—"

"Thirteen million's out of the question. It's an absurd

figure. We don't need thirteen million. We need enough to see us through the cash requirements of the next thirty to sixty days. Once our ships—"

"Trading on your own account is an outdated mechanism for a banker," Hammersmith said sharply. "It has to stop. It's doubtless what's got you into this position. At least in part."

"Now look here, Johnathon—" He started to tell the other man to mind his own goddammed business, then stopped because he had to. "What are you suggesting then?" A lump of ice was forming in his gut. If he'd played this wrong, made a mistake in trusting Hammersmith with so much truth, then in the name of Christ, where did that leave them?

Hammersmith hesitated, knowing how objectionable the other man would find his words. "I think I've only one course open," he said quietly. "I'll have to speak with Ransom. Suggest he meet with us at the very first opportunity."

It was the worst possible answer. Ransom was the governor of the Bank of England. Once so high an authority was involved there would be no turning back; the control would have passed out of Norman's hands. He felt a crashing in his head, a loud ringing in his ears. Nonetheless, his voice was steady. "If you feel you must."

San Juan, Three P.M.

"Ain't hardly said two words to her, he ain't. Not since Saturday." Tillie sniffed as if the insult had been delivered to her personally.

Her brother looked worried. "Thing I can't figure out is, are we stayin' here or goin'? What's Mr. Curran plan to do, that's what I don't know."

The brother and sister were in the kitchen of the inn.

They met there most afternoons while everyone else took *siesta*. "I don't know," Tillie said. "It's been worrying me too, but Miss Beth ain't told me nothin'. Right upset she is. Him acting so sniffy and all, after she come so far and burned all her bridges behind her, just for the love of him." She sighed. The romance of it had always thrilled her. That's why she'd been a willing accomplice since the beginning of the affair.

"She really cares for him then?" Briggs asked, refilling his sister's mug with tea.

"Course she does. She ain't a loose woman, my Beth. She was brought up proper. But that Mr. Timothy, her husband, a right blighter he was. Not good enough for her. Mr. Curran, now he's different. Leastwise I always figured he was. Lately I ain't so sure."

Briggs sipped his tea, deep in his own thoughts. "Tillie, you think the Americans is comin'?"

"Here to Puerto Rico? I don't know. Everyone says they probably is. Won't have nothing to do with us if they do. That's what Miss Beth told me. We're foreign nationals of a neutral power." She smiled, pleased with herself for remembering the official phrase. "That's what Miss Beth says. Right smart she is."

"Bullets don't ask who's British and who ain't," Briggs said glumly. "They just come."

"Bullets! Are you daft, Tom? Why should there be any shooting?"

"Use your head, woman. If one country invades another country there's always shooting. Always, since time began. Even back in the Bible days. You can read about it in the good book."

"They didn't have no guns back in the bible days."

He made an impatient gesture with his mug of tea. "That's not the point. Thing is, the Puerto Ricans will fight. Leastwise they may. That's what I can't decide. Will they or won't they?"

"Don't make no difference to us," Tillie said again. "We can stay here quiet as little church mice until it's over. Have to be over right quick. The Americans are bound to swallow them up like the whale swallowed Jonah."

"We could leave before it happened, if we was smart and lucky," Briggs said. "I hear tell there's a ship due in a few days. Seems to me smart folks will leave when she does."

"What ship?"

"The *Arabella,* British registry. Trades a lot in these islands. I know her. She's a steamer," he added, his face creased with disgust. "But she's good and sound despite that."

"You told Mr. Curran?"

"Not yet. Been grumpy as a sick cow he has these last few days. Ever since he and Miss Beth had that fight."

"I'll bet he's shamed of treating my lady so bad, but he's too proud to say. That's why he's been away so much. Can't face Miss Beth. He's hiding."

"Mr. Curran don't hide from nobody."

"Oh, doesn't he? Well, where is he now? Tell me that."

"I can't say," Briggs admitted glumly. "He's been runnin' here and there and not tellin' me where he was goin'."

"Hiding, like I said." Then, when her brother didn't answer, she added, "One thing I know, Tom: I don't want us to be separated again. Not like we was all them years. You and me, we're each other's only family."

Briggs nodded. "I know. I don't want to be separated neither."

"You think he'd leave without me and Miss Beth?" she asked, suddenly worried by a new threat.

"Never," Briggs said firmly. "Whatever they quarreled about, he's a gentleman is Mr. Curran. He wouldn't leave two helpless women behind in a war. Not two English-women."

Tillie sniffed. "I hear tales as how he has a taste for women who ain't English. Women who ain't as good as they might be neither."

Briggs didn't look at her. "Where'd you hear that?"

"Oh, here and there. There are some folks on this island what speak proper. Not many mind, most of the poor things only know that gobbledygook language. But you can talk to some as are proper Christian people what speaks English."

"And what kind of stories have these 'proper Christian people' been tellin' you?"

"Only snips and snaps of stories. Hints like. They say as how Mr. Curran's been spendin' a lot of his time in a certain house with a mighty bad reputation."

"Men do some things women don't understand," Briggs said loyally. "It's natural. And proper ladies don't ask too many questions. Though I daresay, proper ladies don't leave their husbands and run after a man they ain't married to neither."

"Mind your mouth, Thomas Archibald Briggs! And talking about not understanding, let me tell you something, my Beth is not a wicked woman. She's a fine lady. She's got courage, that's what she has. Right brave it was to choose love at any price. So don't you go putting a nasty face on what she done. Except for Mr. Curran, there ain't never been nobody else."

"Calm down," Briggs said easily. "Don't get in a stew, Tillie. I didn't mean nothin'. I'm worried about the future, that's all."

Tillie glanced out the window; the sun was a good deal lower than it had been when she came to the kitchen. "It's gettin' late. I got to go and see if my lady needs me. But listen, Tom, I think you should talk to Mr. Curran, tell him about the ship coming and all. I'll mention it to Miss Beth as well."

"Would she leave without him?"

"Not on your life she wouldn't. But I don't think that

comes into it. They love each other those two. I'm sure of it. Whatever the trouble between 'em now, it'll pass over. Mark my words."

Michael reined in his mare a few yards from the convent gate. Should he ring the bell at the main door or go round to the back and let himself in? His interview with the bishop hadn't touched on that small point.

"I hear you have done what you came to our island to do, señor," the bishop had said when the two men met at the episcopal palace the previous afternoon.

"Oh, what is it you hear, Excellency?"

"That you have bought every coffee plantation in Puerto Rico."

"I've contracted to buy a number of them," Michael had admitted. "But not every one."

"Every major plantation except that of Doña Maria de los Angeles," the bishop had corrected. "It is a most astounding venture, Señor Curran."

"I enjoy large gambles, Excellency. They give spice to life. And you are very well informed."

The bishop had shrugged delicately. "I am responsible for my flock. It is necessary that I be well informed."

"Yes, of course." Michael had said no more. The churchman had summoned him and it was up to the bishop to say why. One thing was certain: it wasn't likely to have anything to do with coffee. The bishop wouldn't have been so obvious about dabbling in temporal affairs.

"You will have some sherry, señor?" His Excellency had asked.

"That would be most welcome, thank you."

This time the bishop hadn't rung for a servant. He'd gone to a cupboard in the corner of the room and come back carrying two glasses and a bottle. "This is a special treat that was sent to me direct from Madrid. I think you will enjoy it."

He had put the bottle on the table beside Curran. The label said Leche de Jerez and carried the picture of a bird and below that the name Mendoza-Ruez. His great grandfather had introduced that sherry at the beginning of the century. The story was that Robert had designed the label himself.

"Do you know the wine?" the bishop asked as he poured. His voice gave nothing away.

"I've had it, yes. An excellent sherry." Michael had acted as cool as the other man.

"Remarkable people the Mendozas, a remarkable family."

Michael had lifted his glass and toasted the prelate. "Your very good health, Excellency."

"And yours."

They sipped the sherry, murmured appreciative comments, then there was silence.

The bishop had caved in first. And whatever he knew or suspected about Michael's relationship to the Mendozas, it apparently wasn't enough to make him probe further. "I had a number of reasons for asking you to come here." His tone of voice indicated that the subject was to be changed.

"I realize you must have," Michael had said, breathing a little easier.

"Yes. A number of important reasons. More sherry?"

"Thank you, but I'll wait."

The bishop had refilled his own glass. "Señor Curran, do you remember the things we discussed on your previous visit?"

"Indeed I do. We talked about the island. And about Sister Magdalena."

"Yes, about the island."

Michael's heart sank. He'd been sure he was here to talk about the nun. He needed to talk about her. It was no longer simple curiosity. Magdalena was the key to Nuria and Nuria was in some kind of desperate trouble. He'd tried to see her repeatedly since Saturday when Samson turned him away. Each time he was refused entrance to the small house behind the bordello. But Curran couldn't let it rest. There was some need in him to solve this thing, to bring the two women together. "Sister Magdalena," he began.

The bishop had held up his hand. "Later, señor. First I must do my duty and reiterate the things I told you the last time you were here. We Puerto Ricans are a Catholic people. We do not demand that you believe as we do. Those days are past in our Church, but you cannot flout our rules, señor. Shall I say our sensibilities."

"I'm not sure I understand."

"Oh, I think you do. There is a young English woman, Doña Isabela I believe she's called."

"In Spanish yes. In English we say Elizabeth." Sweet Jesus! He should have guessed. No matter how careful they'd been to keep up appearances, his relationship with Beth was bound to cause talk. Curran was furious with himself for not seeing this coming. He'd been so preoccupied lately that he'd missed an obvious trap.

"This lady came to Puerto Rico to be with you?" the bishop asked.

"Doña Isabela is an old friend. She was traveling in the Indies. Knowing I was here, naturally she stopped to visit your beautiful island."

"A—what is that new word?—a tourist. I see. I am perhaps old-fashioned. I find it strange that a young and beautiful woman should travel so far from home with only her maid for company. But I'm delighted to hear that the lady is a tourist, señor. She will be leaving?"

"Eventually, of course."

"Of course. Good. Because, Señor Curran, I must tell you that irregular alliances are not approved of here. We value family life, the sanctity of marriage."

Bloody hell! Was the man asking if he planned to marry

Beth, or worse, did he somehow know she was already married? "I too value the sanctity of marriage, Excellency."

"I am glad to hear that, my son."

Michael had not missed the switch to clerical paternalism. "And I am glad to meet a bishop so concerned for the moral well-being of his flock, Excellency. As I'm sure you know, it hasn't always been so."

"In history, no," the bishop had agreed. "But in these modern times things are different." He lifted the sherry bottle. Michael nodded agreement this time. "Now," the bishop said as he poured, "to the matter of Sister Magdalena. I am sorry to have to tell you that she is ill."

"Oh, nothing serious I hope."

"I am afraid it is very serious. That is why my request to you was urgent."

"I'm not sure I follow, Excellency."

"Sister Magdalena has expressed a strong desire to see you, señor. I promised to ask you to call on her."

"But I've tried to see her any number of times these last weeks and—"

"Let me speak frankly," the bishop had interrupted. "I did not approve of your efforts to speak with Sister Magdalena, but now the little sister does not have much time in this world. In such circumstances . . ." Another delicate shrug. "I think you must go to her as soon as you can, Señor Curran. I'm sure the visit will profit your soul."

Michael had stood up immediately. "With your permission I can go now."

The bishop had glanced at the clock. "Not now, the nuns retire early. By the time you arrived at Las Nieves it would be too late. Tomorrow, señor. If it is possible tomorrow afternoon. Perhaps you could arrange to arrive at the convent immediately after vespers. Shall we say at half past four?"

Now Michael held the reins loosely in one hand and took his watch from the pocket of his waistcoat. It was thirty-two minutes past four. And given the official nature of this visit, it was probably best if he announced himself at the front gate.

He cantered his mare forward, slipped out of the saddle, and tethered the horse to a nearby tree. Then he reached up and tugged forcefully on the bell rope of the convent. Peals of sound vibrated in the still, hot air.

❦ 18 ❧

Sister Paloma opened the gate at Curran's summons. "Ah, señor, we have been waiting for you."

"How is Sister Magdalena?" he asked at once.

"Very ill, señor, but she is still with us, God be praised."

"The bishop said she wished to see me. He said it was all right for me to come."

"Yes, I know. Please sit down here in the shade, señor. I must get Mother Superior."

She left before Curran could say more. Damn, he didn't want to exchange polite remarks with the superior. He wanted to see Magdalena. If she was as ill as they said, this was probably going to be his only chance to . . . to what? What did he really think Magdalena could contribute to curing the strange malaise afflicting the sister she'd never seen? He wasn't sure. But he felt in his bones that there was something. Some key that, if he could find it, would unlock all the mysteries in this bizarre affair.

"Señor Curran, I am Mother Evangelista. It was kind of you to come."

The two nuns, Paloma and the older woman, had arrived so silently Michael hadn't heard their approach. He jumped to his feet. "*Mucho gusto, Madre Reverenda.* I am delighted to meet you."

"And I am pleased to meet you, señor. You have been much on the mind of my little sister."

"I am very sorry to hear she is so ill, Reverend Mother. I hope she will recover."

The nun shook her head. "Only if God sends a miracle, señor, and I do not think the little sister has asked for such a miracle. She is anxious to go to heaven."

"I cannot say that I understand a desire to die," Michael admitted. "But I'm told that there are those who feel that way."

"I assure you that there are, señor. You are not a believer, are you?"

Michael couldn't look into her wise eyes and lie. "I'm not, Reverend Mother. Sometimes I wish I were."

The nun nodded. "Then you are halfway there, Señor Curran. In the matter of religion to seek is to find." She saw the doubt on his face and smiled. "But come, I will take you to Sister Magdalena. To be with her even for a short time will do more for your soul than any poor words of mine."

She led the way along the route Curran remembered from the last time, through the series of beautifully kept and tended courtyards to the final one, so much poorer and plainer than the rest. "You have been told that this patio is outside our convent, not technically part of it?" Mother Evangelista inquired.

"Yes. Sister Paloma explained."

The superior nodded with satisfaction. They crossed the rough paving stones to the small door.

Michael followed the nun inside, crouching because he remembered the low ceiling. As before, the darkness was profound.

"Wait," Mother Evangelista murmured. He heard her strike a match, then a lantern flared. "There, that is better. The bishop has given Sister Magdalena permission to receive you in her interior cell, señor. But she prefers to come here. If you will excuse me I will assist her to get out of bed."

She left, taking the light with her. Curran waited in the darkness. There was a delightful smell in the little room today. Roses. He didn't remember any such odor the last time he'd come. Perhaps the nuns were bringing flowers in here now that Magdalena was ill. Odd that it should be roses; he didn't recall ever seeing one in Puerto Rico.

"So you have come, Michael. Praise be to God."

Her voice was the first sign he had of her presence. The Mother Superior hadn't reappeared and neither had the lantern.

"Hello, Sister Magdalena. I've tried to come before, but I wasn't permitted."

"I know. It doesn't matter. That's all in the past." Her voice was incredibly weak; he had to strain to hear her. "Are you sitting down? Did you remember the stool? I haven't been in the parlor in many days, but I'm sure it must still be there."

"I'd forgotten. Wait a minute." Curran groped in the darkness. "Got it. Now, I'm sitting down. Why can't I see you? Aren't we going to have a candle today?"

"I prefer the darkness. My eyes have grown very tired since I've been ill."

"Whatever you wish. I'm sorry you're not well. Have you seen a doctor?"

"I do not need a doctor, Michael. Our Lord takes perfect care of me. And the sisters have been wonderfully kind."

"I thought there was a saying about God helping those who help themselves. Surely a doctor—"

"Please, do not worry on my account. And we must not waste words, Michael. I am not very strong."

"I understand. I have something to tell you, a remarkable story. Can I go ahead?"

"Yes, say what you wish."

"Look, I know you may find this hard to believe, but I've been in Ponce and seen the woman who raised you. Doña Dolores, the one they call La Bruja. She told me that you have a twin sister. I'd already guessed that because the first time I saw—"

"So Dolores told you about Nuria," Magdalena said softly. "She must have decided you were a very good man, otherwise she would not have trusted you with such information."

Curran didn't try to mask his astonishment. "You know about Nuria? But I thought you and she—"

"We've never seen each other. Not since our mother took her away."

"But how do you know? She doesn't know a thing about you. Have you had another one of your revelations?"

"You do not sound as skeptical as you did when you were here before."

"Perhaps I'm not. A great many things have happened."

"Whatever the reason, I'm glad. But the answer to your question is no, Our Lord has never told me about Nuria. Before I came here Dolores told me I had a twin sister."

He relaxed slightly, breathing more easily because the explanation was so ordinary. "Nuria's in a great deal of trouble. I'm not sure exactly what. But I think you can help her. At least knowing about you might help her. There are all sorts of strange stories about what happens when twins are separated. Perhaps—"

"I am very sorry to learn that Nuria has trouble," Magdalena interrupted. "I have prayed for her every day since I came here. But other than that I cannot help her. If I could, Our Lord would have told me about it."

"Look, I admit you get some information in a peculiar way I don't pretend to understand. But surely that doesn't mean you can't find out about things in an ordinary way. If you'll let me bring Nuria here, if the two of you can talk, I think—"

"Michael, I beg you. I have so little time and so little strength. I must tell you what I have been told to tell you."

He sighed. "Very well, let's get that out of the way first. What message do you have for me this time?"

"It is the only message I've ever had for you. I told you I'd had three revelations about the Mendozas. The first was the truth about Doña Maria Ortega and what she'd done, the second was for your mother, the third was simply to tell me to expect you."

"Yes, so you told me. And now?"

"Now I am to tell you that you cannot trifle with God. God will not be mocked, Michael."

He sat silent, incredulous. Finally he managed to ask, "What the hell is that supposed to mean?"

This time she didn't bother to reprimand him for cursing. "It means that this thing you think you will do on the outside only, you must do it with your whole heart and soul, or you will be mocking God."

"I don't know what you're talking about. What thing I'm thinking of doing?"

"I cannot say," Magdalena said simply. "That's not for me to know. But that is what I was told to tell you."

"I see." The words came out clipped and hard because sick as she was and extraordinary as were these circumstances, he was furious. "So, mysterious warnings for me about God knows what—but you won't perform a simple act of kindness and see your sister."

"I cannot."

He rose and the stool fell backward with a dull thud. Magdalena drew a sharp breath. "You are going?"

"There doesn't seem to be much point in my staying."

"No, please you mustn't. There is more to the message." He heard the strain in her voice, knew the effort it took her simply to speak, much less plead. "Very well, what else are you supposed to tell me?"

"Two things. That strength is holy, and the strength of a woman is the holiest thing of all. And that you are to remember the waters of Babylon."

Curran waited for some explanation. She didn't say anything more. "None of that makes any sense. Maybe you've got the wrong recipient for your message, Sister Magdalena. Maybe your heavenly messengers have made some kind of mistake."

"There is no mistake. When the time comes you will know. Michael, I will——" Her voice was swallowed by a long bout of coughing. "I think I must go," she said when she could speak again.

He heard the pain and fatigue in her voice. "Look, I'm sorry if I've tired you. Go and rest now. But if I can bring Nuria here tomorrow, or perhaps the next day, will you agree to see her?"

Silence was his only answer.

"Sister Magdalena, are you there?" He started forward, groping in the direction her voice had come from. At that moment the little room was lit once more with the flame of the lantern. Curran squinted against the sudden light.

"It is I, Señor Curran, Mother Evangelista. The little sister has returned to her bed. We must go now."

They went together into the courtyard, the nun leading the way as before. Curran wanted to ask her a million questions, but she never turned to face him and he couldn't bring himself to address them to her black and upright back.

When they arrived at the entrance patio she nodded farewell. "I must return to my duties, señor. Sister Paloma will bring you coffee and refreshments to fortify your long ride back to San Juan."

"Reverend Mother, please wait a moment. I must ask you something."

"Yes?"

"Before she came here, Sister Magdalena was living with an old woman, in a sort of orphanage, and—"

"With Dolores, the one they call La Bruja, I know."

"I spoke with Dolores, she told me—"

She put up her hand to cut off his words. "Our lives before we came here are as nothing, señor. A nun is born the day she puts on the habit. Good afternoon to you. May God grant you a safe journey." She paused a moment, but before Curran could say anything she added, "I think yours will be a very long journey, Señor Curran. I will keep you in my prayers."

Curran was halfway to San Juan before it hit him. By the waters of Babylon. Those were the opening words of the 137th psalm, the only part of the Bible he'd ever committed to memory. Because it was the psalm that contained the Mendoza family motto: *If I forget thee, O Jerusalem, let my right hand forget her cunning.* He touched the half moon of gold that hung round his neck, feeling its presence beneath his shirt. Magdalena's message, wherever it came from and whatever it meant, was truly intended for him.

London, Ten P.M.

"I expected Lord Westlake to be here." The governor of the Bank of England looked at Norman and at Johnathon Hammersmith, then let his eyes scan the room as if he suspected Jamie might be hiding behind the damask curtains.

"My brother isn't well, sir," Norman said. "I have complete authority to speak for him, indeed for the bank."

They were in Bayswater, in Johnathon Hammersmith's well-appointed study. Rain beat on the windows. A coal fire burned in the grate. Hammersmith gestured to a high-backed leather chair drawn up beside it and Ransom lowered his bulk to the seat.

He was a short, stocky man of about sixty, with light blond hair that showed no gray and unexpectedly dark eyes. He was beardless but had a drooping mustache and muttonchop whiskers. He looked like a throwback to fifty years earlier and the golden age of Victoria. Sounded like one too. Ransom had a brusque, clipped manner of speaking that was almost a caricature of an upper-class Englishman. In the past Norman had found the man comic, a kind of music hall character. He didn't feel that way tonight.

"Complete authority." Ransom repeated Norman's words, leaning toward the fire and rubbing his hands. "Yes, so you do I'm told. Which puts this entire mess rather in your lap, doesn't it, Mr. Mendoza?"

"In a manner of speaking."

Hammersmith stepped forward. "Whiskey, sir?" The question was pro forma. He'd already poured a generous amount of pale single malt into a heavy crystal tumbler.

"Thank you." Ransom took the drink. "I'm chilled to the bone. It feels like February out there."

"We're having a strange summer," Hammersmith said. "Hot as Hades one minute and freezing the next."

"An English summer," Ransom insisted. "Nothing strange about it. Not here." He turned to Norman. "Not much point in talking about the weather. You're in difficulty."

The governor spat out the words as if they were bullets. "Johnathon said it was exactly like that mess with Barings a few years ago. Can't go on, Mendoza. We can't have it. The City must be run on sound principals, and seen to be so."

"Yes, sir. I realize that."

Norman knew that Hammersmith was married to Ransom's goddaughter, in the small world of high finance everyone knew such details, so it was natural that the governor used his host's given name. Norman had met Ransom numerous times, but they'd never progressed to any pretense of friendship or intimacy. He leaned forward and spoke with as much sincerity as possible. "I assure you, sir at the core Mendozas is entirely sound. It's simply that we've run into some unexpected events and there's a short term—"

"Unexpected is not permissable. Damm it, man! You've a responsibility not to allow the unexpected."

God, what a bloody fool! Norman settled back in his chair and accepted a whiskey from Hammersmith. He took a long swallow of the excellent single malt. It soothed him, helped him guard his tongue. "Perhaps I should say unusual rather than unexpected. Not everything in life is predictable, not even everything in banking. I'm sure you realize that."

"Beside the point. What are we to do? That's the thing. How bad is it? I'm not sure I understand that yet."

The effect of the whiskey was short-lived. Norman's mouth was dry again; it tasted of ashes. "Well, sir, it seems that we—"

"Please, Norman, if you'll allow me." Hammersmith turned his frank blue-eyed gaze to his guest. He sounded like a man about to do something he hated doing but felt he must. "Perhaps it will be easier if I explain."

Norman nodded and said nothing.

Ransom looked at his host. "Well, go on then. How bad?"

"About as bad as it can be." The Coutts man shot another quick look at Norman. "I'm sorry, but really, there's no point, is there? I mean—" he paused to marshal his thoughts, "if some sort of rescue isn't worked out immediately, Mendozas must stop."

"Stop what?" Ransom seemed determined to play out the drama to its last scintilla of misery.

"Stop trading, sir."

"You mean fail? Default on all its obligations?"

"Yes, sir, or at least a great many of them. That's exactly what I mean."

"Good Lord," Ransom muttered. "It really is Barings all over again."

"Yes, sir."

Norman was white-faced, rage and agony warring for dominance in his head. "I do think that's putting too fine a point on it," he began.

Hammersmith stopped him. "No, Norman, I'm sorry, but it isn't. You've a gap of some thirteen million between your assets and your liabilities, and less than a hundred thousand in liquidity. I don't think I'm exaggerating the situation in the slightest."

Ransom leaned back, stroking his mustache with one finger, studying Norman through narrowed eyes. "What if there is no aid? What if this time we don't all scurry around cleaning up the mess incompetence has made? Say we let nature take its course, market forces prevail. What then?"

"Sir, you can't—"

Hammersmith's cry of anguish was interrupted by Norman's explosive curse. "Christ Almighty! With all due respect, sir, are you suggesting that the oldest and most powerful banking house in London could simply go under and no one but us would be any the worse for it?"

"That's exactly what I'm suggesting." The governor's dark eyes were opaque; they gave nothing away.

"Then I must tell you I believe you are—" He almost said that he thought the other man a bloody idiot, but he stopped himself in time. "I believe you are deluded, sir. Perhaps naive is the word."

The governor appeared to take no offense. "Why?" he asked mildly.

Norman understood the ploy now. Ransom knew damned well that he couldn't sit back and do nothing. But he wanted Norman to give him the reasons why, say all the things that shouldn't need to be said. That way the governor could repeat them as arguments that came not from him but from Mendozas. Ransom might look and sound like an ass, but he was obviously a master at protecting his flanks.

"Because, sir, if we fail, then every man of means in this empire is going to presume that no bank is safe, that the entire financial structure underlying the British economy is a fool's game. There will be mob scenes outside every change hall in London and the provinces, and it'll spread to the colonies within hours. The system will crumble like a house of cards." Norman leaned forward, hammering the words into the ears of the man sitting opposite him. "The French have an apt term for what will happen, a *"sauve qui peut."* In other words, every man for himself and the devil take the hindmost."

Ransom nodded. "I know another term for what you're describing," he said quietly. "Chaos."

"Yes, you might say."

Hammersmith looked from one to the other, sensing the fierce hostility flowing between them. For the moment at least, it was genuine hatred. "Look, we really won't get anywhere by dramatizing this. Forgive me if I seem impertinent, but surely, Governor, you agree that we must not allow Mendozas to fail?"

"Oh, I quite agree. One way or another, Mendozas must be saved."

Hammersmith breathed easier. "Well then—"

"I simply wish to make it clear that I do not consider it the responsibility of the Bank of England to be the savior."

Hammersmith drew back as if he'd been physically assaulted. "But if you—"

"The government refused to help Barings," Norman interrupted. There was a slight lessening of the tension in the room. He had given tongue to the unspoken truth lurking in the corners since the discussion began. The three men knew that this same scene had been played out less than ten years before, and they knew that the precedent once established would be difficult to ignore. Norman took another sip of his whiskey. "But . . ." he murmured softly.

"But?" Ransom asked.

"But Barings is not Mendozas."

"How so?" Ransom held his empty glass in his hands,

twisting it between his palms as he leaned forward. "In what way are they different?"

"The Barings are not Jews. That has always made a great deal of difference."

The gasps of the other two men came simultaneously. The offensive words lingered in the air like a bad smell.

Norman pressed his advantage. "I am well aware that the history of my family and my house is no secret. Neither of you is going to pretend that you don't know that my father converted to Christianity, and that the Mendozas were English Jews for centuries before that. Nor that a great many, I could say a majority, of the men of high finance in this nation remain Jews."

"I really don't see—" Ransom began, visibly uncomfortable.

"I'm sure you do," Norman interrupted again. "If help is refused Mendozas, that is not at all the same as refusing to help Barings. Unreasonable perhaps, but men can be sometimes. In this instance, a large and extremely influential segment of the financial community is going to take it as a personal affront. You might say an attack. An overt example of prejudice."

It was complete rubbish. Norman knew it even while he spoke. For one thing, the Jews in England were under no illusions about their status. For years the great baron Rothschild had been unable to take his seat in Parliament because he wouldn't take the oath "on the faith of a Christian." For another, Joseph Mendoza's conversion had alienated the Jewish community more thoroughly than anything the Bank of England could do.

That was irrelevant. What mattered was that neither Hammersmith nor Ransom had any confidence where Jews were concerned. They viewed them as something alien and exotic. They wouldn't have the least idea of how such men would react. And they would imagine what Norman Mendoza did:

that some mysterious heritage had given him a secret knowledge they didn't possess.

Ransom and Hammersmith looked at each other; they
both avoided looking at Norman. Johnathon remembered
his duties as host. He fetched the decanter of single malt
and poured some into each man's glass, still not meeting
Norman's eyes.

"Well," Ransom said finally. "I will speak with the chancellor. That's really all I can do."

It was close to midnight when Norman used his own key
to open the front door of the house in Belgravia. His servants
were under instructions never to wait up for him. It wasn't
charity on Norman's part; he simply preferred that his late-
night comings and goings be unobserved.

The lamp was lit on the foyer table and something was
propped below it. Norman ignored it while he removed his
hat and placed his sopping umbrella beside the door. Christ
he was tired. What a miserable day it had been. A whirlwind
of misery. How had he come out of it? He still wasn't sure.
Hammersmith had completely thrown him at their first
meeting that afternoon.

He'd been sure Johnathon would commit Coutts to a
secret short-term loan; that had been the object of being
straight with him. Instead he'd jumped immediately to involving Ransom. Norman felt that was his own fault. He
should have remembered the connection between the governor and Hammersmith's wife. It was logical that Johnathon
would be inclined to trust Ransom. But dammit all, he
couldn't remember everything, not these days, not with so
much happening so fast.

Maybe it hadn't turned out so badly. Throwing the Jewish
business in their faces wasn't a bad idea. True he'd done it
only because it had suddenly flashed into his mind. He'd
grabbed at the idea the way a drowning man grabs a floating
straw—knowing it isn't enough, but knowing there isn't

anything else available. And it might work. You never knew. He'd been in negotiations where the most outlandish ideas produced results. Perhaps this one—

Norman broke off his musings. The thing propped up beneath the table lamp was a yellow envelope. It had to be a cable. He grabbed it, ripping it open without bothering to go to his study for a letter opener. From Córdoba, by God! And properly coded.

Suddenly he didn't feel quite so wrung out. Good for Charles. Good thinking to send the cable to the house. And ten pence to a pound the lad had sent a copy to the bank as well, so his father would get it immediately, whatever time it arrived. Good lad. He felt immeasurably better.

There was a copy of the codebook in the safe at the bank, but the original was in Norman's study. He went there now and stood beneath the portrait of his wife, which hid the safe.

The picture had been painted by Sargent. Both his sons hated it. Penny herself had hated it. Norman liked it well enough. True, her eyes looked sad, but then they usually had. Great sad eyes, like a cocker spaniel's. All the same, Sargents were increasing in value by the day. He quite enjoyed having this one on his wall.

If the chancellor insisted that the Mendozas put up their private holdings as guarantee for a loan, what price would be fixed on the painting of Penny? The thought made him shudder. Norman swung the picture aside, spun the dial in the combination only he knew, and opened the safe. The codebook was in the back, and he removed it with a sense of relief.

He'd rather deal with the business in Córdoba than go on worrying about Hammersmith and Ransom. Better to concentrate on the business at hand, deal with problems one day at a time. Much better.

For a moment Norman held the small notebook in his hand without opening it. The cover was black cowhide, worn at the edges with use. The pages were heavy vellum. The notebook had been intended to last. The ink had faded from black to a yellowish brown, but Liam Mendoza had written with great care, and the words were entirely legible.

Herein a code arranged by myself and my brother Robert in this year of 1819. In these modern times life is so uncertain, and standards of behavior among ordinary people so much lowered, that we propose to use this code for all communications having to do with the important affairs of the family and the institution we represent, and to pass this code on only to the rulers of the houses of Mendoza in London and Córdoba. May the Holy One, blessed be His name, grant that the generations which come after us use the code with wisdom and safeguard the family in all things, whatever the cost.

The Holy One, blessed be His name. It was an entirely Jewish construction. Norman knew it was; his father had told him so. Old Liam hadn't been religious and God knows neither was Robert the Turncoat, but by a peculiar coincidence they'd both had wives intensely committed to Judaism. It must have rubbed off, at least it had on Liam. Joseph had waited for his parents to die before switching to the Church of England, and something of his Jewish heritage had always remained with him.

When he gave Norman the codebook Joseph had said, "This is the original, written in your grandfather's hand. There's a copy at Creechurch Lane; Jamie can use that."

He'd opened the book and painted to the inscription. "See what your grandfather wrote? The Holy One, blessed be His name. That's how it's done among Jews." Joseph's eyes had grown misty; that was the only time Norman had ever heard his father discuss religion, much less grow emotional about it.

Liam and Robert had been cool-headed, not emotional.

The code wasn't particularly intricate or brilliant, but it was clever. The value of the letters of the alphabet changed according to the month. They'd divided the year into four trimesters and each one had its own key. From January to March each *A* is plus three letters, each *B* plus four letters, and so on. April to June worked in reverse with the numerical values increasing by one, and you subtracted rather than added. It was too complex for anyone to remember. Before Charles left for Córdoba Norman had given him a copy of the code for July. He flipped open to that page now, put the notebook and the cable on his desk, and began.

N equalled *E*, so the first letter of the first word was *E*. The second was *P*, that was really *V* . . .

The cable was lengthy. It took him two hours to decode it but the task soothed him. By the time he'd deciphered Charles's report, Norman felt much better. He heard the clock on his mantel chime twice when he sat back to reread it. Two A.M., but he wasn't tired—exhilarated rather. On reflection, the 15th of July may have been quite a good day. He was sure he could handle Ransom and the chancellor, and Charles seemed able to deal with Francisco.

EVERYTHING BETTER THAN EXPECTED STOP APPROXIMATELY HALF A MILLION IN LIQUID RESERVES STOP BELIEVE IT SAFE TO TRANSFER HALF SAME LONDON STOP RUN ON BANK ACTIVITY BY SOME LADIES REASONS UNKNOWN STOP FOLLOWED PURPORTED OFFICIAL NOTICE RUSSIAN TREASURY INTENDS WITHDRAW SPANISH DEPOSIT IN THIRTY DAYS STOP TWO EVENTS SENT F INTO PANIC STOP F NOT CAPABLE RUNNING AFFAIRS HERE AND DOES NOT WANT TO STOP PRESENT MANAGER NOT COMPETENT FULL CHARGE STOP SUGGEST I TEMPORARILY REMAIN CORDOBA AND TAKE OVER STOP PLEASE ADVISE.

Norman chuckled. Charles must be besotted by Spain. The palace in Córdoba was something out of a dream, and the sun always shone in Andalusia. Any Englishman would fall for that. Out of the question, of course. Charles was the next Lord Westlake and the next head of the bank. His place was here in London although he wouldn't take over for some years to come. Norman himself would remain in charge and train the boy. So he had to find someone to take over in Córdoba. This was an excellent opportunity to be rid of Francisco, and to regain control of Córdoba by London.

Norman looked at the telephone and grimaced. He'd heard that the Americans had managed to link places as far apart as New York and Chicago, and in '92 a cable had been run under the Channel connecting Paris and London. Spain, however, was still as isolated as outer Mongolia. Damned backward sods.

He fitted a fresh nib to his pen, dipped it in ink, and began composing a cable to his son. After a few minutes he read it over and was satisfied.

GET SIGNED AND WITNESSED TRANSFER OF FULL POWERS TO US FROM F STOP ALSO SIGNED RESIG-NATION OF ANY CLAIM ON BANK STOP INSIST F STAY IN PLACE UNTIL WE MAKE OTHER ARRANGEMENTS STOP IMPERATIVE YOU RETURN AT ONCE.

Norman changed a couple of words, then began the laborious task of encoding the message.

Sharrick pulled his oilskin cape tighter against his body and walked faster. The driving rain beat on his shoulders and swirled in his face and his leg hurt. It always did in weather like this.

He'd had enough of the bloody British climate. Not that Ireland was much better. They'd spend a few weeks at Glencree as soon as everything was settled here, then he must take Lila somewhere hot and exotic and totally different. Africa perhaps. Or maybe India. He had a long standing invitation to hunt tigers with the maharaja of Jaipur. Lila would love it. He could just see her, sitting beside him in a bejeweled and tassled howdah atop some great and glorious elephant . . .

Sharrick did not allow himself to dwell on the fact that he'd not seen Lila since their quarrel in Regent's Park. Everything was going to work out as he'd planned it, because he wouldn't allow anything else.

He approached Tower Bridge from the City side of the river, glancing toward Saint Katherine's Dock to his left. No one around. Why should there be? It was midnight and raining bloody cats and dogs. Any sensible man would be home in bed.

"Over 'ere, gov."

Sharrick paused. The man waiting for him ought to have been an Irishman as always, but this one's accent was pure Cockney. He waited until the man huddling beneath the overhang of the bridge moved nearer. He was a big fellow. Sharrick had a theory that most Fenians were small men, slinky, able to slither into the interstices of life and politics.

"It's a fine night, ain't it?" the man asked as he came closer.

Sharrick kept his head down; the hood of the cape shadowed his face and the night was black. This fellow would never be able to identify him. "Not as fine as might be expected," he said.

"Will the moon rise?"

"It will. Finer days are coming."

The man nodded acknowledgment of the correct answers to the identification code. "I've a message for you, gov."

"Sure and what happened to t'other one?" Sharrick spoke with the broad brogue that distinguished Fergus Kelly.

"What other one?"

"And who would I mean but the lad I usually meet here?"

The Cockney shrugged. "Can't say. This time they sent me."

"And it's yourself I'm to deal with then?"

"Looks as if I'm the only one 'ere, don't it?"

"Aye, but you've not the music of over across in your speech," Sharrick said softly.

The man chuckled. "Better to fool the bloody English, ain't it? Born with Bow's bells in me ears, but I'm Irish all the same."

Londoners said you were a Cockney if you were born within the sound of the bells of Saint Mary-le-Bow. It wasn't always true. This man's Irish parents had made him what they believed themselves to be, a son of Ireland in temporary exile. It often happened.

"Sure and it's glad I am to hear it," Sharrick said. "Now then, lad, let's do our business and get out of this bloody English rain. What do you have for me?" Sharrick kept his face in the shadows, but he put out his hand.

"Nothin' in writin'," the Cockney said quietly.

The hairs rose on the back of Sharrick's neck, every sense alert for trouble. Any departure from routine was extraordinary. This brief meeting had produced two abnormal events in the space of five minutes. His eyes measured the distance between the other man's back and the river. If it came to a fight, that would be his best chance. The Cockney was younger and heavier, and he didn't have a game leg. Surprise and an almighty shove toward the Thames, that was his best defense. Sharrick braced himself, ready to lunge.

"It's a message in words wot the council gave me," the Cockney said. "Verbal like I think you calls it."

Sharrick noted the other man's stance. The Cockney was relaxed and easy, didn't seem ready to spring. He waited.

"Seems as how it's a question," the Cockney added.

"Sure and you'd best ask it then."

"The council wants to know why there's a lad in Dublin

wot got a note signed by you tellin' 'im to do somethin' wot the council ain't agreed for 'im to do."

So young Donald O'Leary hadn't taken the opportunity to extract himself from Dublin and the Fenians—probably a mistake to think he would. Certainly it was a mistake for Sharrick to be sentimental about a boy he'd only seen once, however much he'd liked the look of him. "What lad would that be?" Sharrick asked.

"Now 'ow would I know that, gov? I only knows wot the council tells me. Wot I need to know like. Same as you."

"And if you don't know what we're supposed to be talking about, how am I to answer you?"

"By tellin' me the answer to the question wot the council sent me to ask, gov. 'Ow come?"

"Now I'll have to think about that," Sharrick said slowly, playing for time. "It's two questions, or maybe three. Who's the lad? What message did he receive? And why should the council think I sent it?"

The wind suddenly changed direction. It swung round to Sharrick's back and at once the air felt warmer. The Cockney felt it too. "Wind's changed," he muttered. "All sudden like. Can't trust nothin' these days, can you?"

"Not the weather, that's for sure, lad."

"The council's trusted you. For years they 'ave. Now they ain't sure things is wot they seem."

"The council has to decide for itself who it trusts and who it doesn't," Sharrick said mildly. "But sure and I've never done 'em a wrong. And it's many a right they've had from me."

"Wot's the answer to me question, gov?" The Cockney seemed weary of fencing, ready to admit that Fergus Kelly could beat him at that game.

"My three questions in reply. Sure and I think that's as much as I can tell ye to take back to 'em. Except maybe one thing more."

The man's face was barely visible, but his disgust was

evident in his voice. "Questions won't satisfy 'em when they want answers, gov." Then, knowing he'd get no more, "Wot's the last thing?"

"Ach, it's nothing much, lad. Only to remind the council that it's always been my way to work alone," Sharrick said softly. "Outside the organization, as you might say. That's suited them and it's suited me. And if in future they want to do things differently, then sure it may be time we came to a parting of the ways."

❧ 19 ❧

THURSDAY, JULY 15, 1898
San Juan, Nine P.M.

Beth's room at the Posada de San Juan Bautista overlooked the shabby courtyard that fronted on the street. The moon was full. Standing at her window she could see Michael clearly.

They hadn't spoken for five days. A few times she'd glimpsed Michael coming or going, but he never looked up at her room. Tillie reported that he was away a lot and seldom ate at the inn. Nonetheless, Beth had taken all her meals on a tray to avoid meeting him in the dining room. Tonight he must have dined early, whether here or elsewhere. Now he was sitting beneath the palm tree smoking a cigar.

He looked thoughtful and rather sad. She watched him for a long time, debating what to do, as she had been since their quarrel on Saturday. She could be soft and sweet and easy, play the female role she'd been taught to play. She could go to him right now and apologize, say it was all her fault, beg his forgiveness.

Beth knew what would happen if she did. Michael could

be very hard, very stern—but almost never with her. No, he wouldn't reject her tonight. She could sense his mood. If she went to him now he'd take her in his arms, they'd slip away to his room or hers and make love. Afterward nothing would have changed. The problem had become brutally clear once she'd made herself examine it with logic rather than emotion.

In the nearly three weeks since she arrived in Puerto Rico and threw herself at him, Michael had been dropping hints. No, not hints exactly. It was what he hadn't said that spoke so loudly. Not once had he referred to the future. And that had to be because he did not envision a future with her.

She had blithely presumed he'd be overjoyed that she'd left Tim and was prepared to spend the rest of her life with him. Hadn't he told her over and over again how he adored her, how he longed to have her all to himself? Yes, but he'd said those things in what seemed another life—when they were in London, excited by the clandestine nature of their love. She only recognized it in hindsight, but things had changed from the time he'd told her he was going away on an extended business journey. And since she came here he hadn't mentioned their future.

It was transparently obvious now that she'd let herself see it. Michael didn't want her, not in any permanent sense. Whatever he was up to here, whatever his plans, she didn't fit into them. Why? That was the question she couldn't answer. He did love her, she was sure he did. But—

Michael stirred. Beth stepped back into the shadows of her room, but he only tossed the stub of his cigar into a broken clay pot serving as an ashtray and settled again to his thoughts.

What was he thinking about? Herself probably, how to find some kind way to send her away, to free himself of the burden of her presence in Puerto Rico. But doubtless she wasn't his chief preoccupation. That must be whatever elaborate scheme had brought him to the island. Since Saturday

Beth had been adding up the facts she knew. Michael Mendoza Curran was in Puerto Rico because he wanted to be in Córdoba. This place was a stop on his journey to Spain, roundabout though it seemed. And if Michael thought he had a chance of getting back what his father had denied him, it was because Lila Curran said he had.

Beth bit her lip, still tempted to run down the stairs to Michael and force the issue. If she didn't move soon the opportunity would pass. He wasn't the sort of man to sit in thought for long. Soon he'd get up and stride away to do whatever it was he did these days. Go to Nuria Sanchez probably.

She frowned, but it wasn't really Nuria she was worried about; it was Lila Curran. She put her hand in her pocket and withdrew the cable she'd received the previous day. She'd told no one about the message, not even Tillie.

REGRET TO INFORM YOU TIMOTHY BADLY INJURED
STOP SUGGEST YOU RETURN AT ONCE STOP SIGNED
L C.

Beth read it again and sighed. Poor Timmy. She felt sorry for him, she really did. He had loved her in his way, and once upon a time she'd thought she loved him. Until she met Michael and discovered the true meaning of the word. That's what she'd hoped would happen with Timothy, that he'd meet someone else and learn about real love and have a happy life. But now . . .

Beth looked again at the initials that formed the only signature of the cable. L.C. had to be the Black Widow. Lila Curran was the only one who could know she was here, because in all probability Lila was the only person who knew that Michael was here. And Beth hadn't hidden her intention to join Michael. She'd told Timmy flat out in the note she left him. A mistake perhaps. But not a mistake to reject any idea of hurrying back to England now. No matter how sorry she felt for Tim, Beth had switched her allegiances and now she knew where her duty lay. Lila had misjudged her. She must imagine that Beth was having a wild fling, intending to return to her husband someday. Well, she was wrong. It was Michael who—

A small black boy charged through the gate of the inn. His voice rang out in the still evening. Beth could not understand the words, but she recognized the desperation on the child's face and in his tone.

"Señor Curran, please! You *verdad* come quick!" The child hurled himself at Michael, tugging at his arm. "Quick, señor, you please come quick!"

"What is it, Obadiah? What's wrong?"

"Is Missy Doña, señor. She go off with them. Samsón, he try to stop her, but he *verdad* no can can. He go after her, señor, but he tell me get you. You come, señor. Missy Doña, she no think right these days. She *verdad* no understand—"

"All right, Obadiah, calm down. I'm coming."

Beth watched him leave with the boy. She hesitated a moment more. Then she made up her mind.

"Is all Assunta," Samsón muttered. "Is *verdad* Assunta what been doin' bad things to Missy Doña."

Samsón had waited for them on the edge of town. Michael and Obadiah had caught up with the old coachman in less than ten minutes. Michael was surprised to find him alone; if they needed muscle power it would have been logical for Samsón to bring a few of the younger men who worked at the bordello.

"Can't *verdad* trust none of 'em, señor. Assunta, she be strong magic lady. Be doin' whatever she likes with everyone in that house. 'Cept me and Obadiah." Samsón put his hand beneath his shirt and brought out a heavy gold cross. "Obadiah and me, we is *verdad* safe, señor. El Señor Jesus, he do protect us."

The boy pulled a similar cross from beneath his shirt and

turned huge, terrified black eyes to Michael. He nodded in agreement with everything Samsón said but added no word of his own. The child was frightened almost witless.

Michael still couldn't grasp the reason for the terror. "Where is Missy Doña now?"

Samsón pointed down a dirt track that wandered from the edge of San Juan into the forest. "At the farm over by that way. I know Assunta bring Missy Doña to that *verdad* bad farm. All her evil business Assunta do in that place."

"What evil business? What is Assunta doing?"

Samsón lifted his eyes to heaven and moaned. "Very bad black things."

Michael made an effort to hang on to his patience. "All right then, take me to this farm."

The road was dark, thickly overhung with trees that blocked out the moon. A few times the three men stumbled over large stones and deep ruts. "How much farther?" Michael asked after they'd been walking for a quarter of an hour.

"By that way another few steps, señor." Samsón pointed ahead of them and whispered the words close to Michael's ear.

The terror of the two blacks was contagious. Michael peered ahead and held up a hand to slow their pace. "Quiet. Try not to make any noise."

They saw the chickens before they found the house. The path bent to the right, curving around a stand of acacias. When they'd cleared the trees they were plunged into the midst of dozens of roosting hens. The birds squawked and squalled and flew a few feet into the air, flapping their wings at the intruders. Samsón moaned and Obadiah cried out.

"Quiet!" Michael commanded in a harsh whisper, beating off a hen that was thrusting its sharp beak at his hands. "Quiet, both of you. Stand still, don't move."

They waited. The chickens kept up their angry protests for a few seconds, then settled. "Now, come ahead." Michael led them forward, picking his way cautiously among the birds.

They'd only gone a few steps when Samsón tugged on the back of the Irishman's jacket. "Señor," he whispered, "look over there. *Madre de Jesus, verdad* protect us."

Michael looked and saw another man. The stranger was staring straight ahead, seemingly oblivious to their approach. He was as motionless as a statue.

"What in hell . . . ," Michael murmured.

"Is zombie," Samsón moaned: "Is *verdad* a zombie."

The man facing them was huge, about the same size as Michael. His head was shaved bald and his scalp gleamed in the moonlight. Michael could hear Obadiah's teeth chattering, and he could actually feel the boy's trembling.

"Is a zombie, señor," Samsón repeated, his words low and made toneless by absolute terror. "A dead man what *verdad* Assunta bring back to life. A zombie."

"Don't be a fool, he's real, not a ghost. Let's see if he means to fight." Michael started forward, then stopped.

A noise filled the night, the low throbbing beat of some kind of native drum. The sound and the rhythm were like nothing Michael had ever heard, they chilled his blood.

The zombie began to sway, his huge shoulders twitching in time to the drums. There was something hypnotic in his movements. Michael couldn't take his eyes from him. It was Samsón who broke the spell. "Missy Doña," he whispered. "The drums be *verdad* bad for Missy Doña."

Michael forced himself to take a few more steps, watching to see if Samsón's zombie meant to intercept them. He didn't. Whatever the creature was doing out here, it wasn't standing guard. They passed right beside him and he didn't seem to know they were there. The drums kept up their throbbing. Michael's skin was prickling; he felt the hairs standing up on the back of his neck.

"*Madre de Jesus,*" Obadiah kept muttering. "*Madre de*

Jesus." Both his small hands were wrapped around the gold cross that hung from his neck.

Michael thought of the old legend that said vampires could only be killed with a silver dagger. Right now he wouldn't mind a silver dagger, or at least a gold cross of his own. The drums were getting faster and louder, they were pounding inside his head.

Something dark loomed ahead of them. Michael squinted. They had arrived at a cabin of sorts. "Is that the farmhouse?"

"*Sí,*" Samsón murmured. "Is *verdad* de place where Assunta—" The old man broke off in a moan, too terrified to go on, yet driven forward by love and loyalty.

Michael realized that Nuria had to be in mortal danger to make Samsón and Obadiah overcome their fear and come to this place. He moved closer. The cabin had no proper windows, merely openings glazed with semitransparent paper. Behind them was a fearsome red glow.

Michael leaned forward, peering inside. He gasped. Whatever he'd expected, it hadn't been this. Nothing he was capable of imagining could match what he was looking at.

In one corner, on some sort of raised platform, were three very old men. Each held a skin drum between his knees and a large bleached bone that served as a mallet. In the middle of the room a fire burned in a pit dug into the dirt floor. In its red glare Michael saw the floor move.

It was impossible, but it was true. There were twenty or so people inside—men and women, arms wrapped around each other, all swaying to the drumbeat. And the floor they stood on writhed and heaved.

Jesus God almighty, a floor couldn't move. There had to be some explanation. He stared harder, willing himself to see whatever it was. Frogs! The floor was covered by frogs. There must be a thousand of them, all hopping and scurrying and looking for a way out. The people in the room were stamping on the slimy creatures, deliberately squashing the frogs.

"What you *verdad* see?" Samsón whispered. He was standing behind Michael, too terrified to look for himself. "You be seeing Missy Doña, señor? Be she inside in this bad place?"

"No, I don't see her. They're—"

Michael stopped speaking, unable to say what he saw. The people in the room were on their knees now, rubbing their arms and their faces with the blood of the squashed frogs. Plenty of the creatures were still alive, and the people lunged for them and tore off their heads with their teeth. Then they greedily sucked the frog blood into their mouths.

"Sweet Jesus," Michael murmured. He started to retch, stopped himself only by force of will.

"Missy Doña," Samsón moaned. "We *verdad* got to save Missy Doña."

Little Obadiah was a few feet away from the coachman and Michael, crouched down and hugging himself, rocking back and forth and weeping.

Samsón started whispering in Michael's ear because now the drums were so loud it was impossible to speak. Michael motioned him to silence with one hand and used the other to shade his eyes so he could see better. The people inside had drawn back to make room. Assunta appeared.

The big woman was naked except for ropes of beads and feathers. Her pendulous breasts hung almost to her waist, and there was a ring of blue paint surrounding each nipple. She stood in the middle of the room beside the fire. One man grabbed a writhing frog, ripped off its head with his teeth, and handed Assunta the body. She screamed and threw back her head and squeezed the frogs innards down her throat.

Michael's eyes searched the crowd. Maybe now that they'd changed positions he'd see Nuria. No, there was no one in the room who could be she, and no one he recognized among the women. Three of the men looked familiar. They worked in the bordello. So Samsón had been right about finding no allies there.

Suddenly everything stopped. The drums fell silent and no one inside moved.

The silence was a thousand times more terrible than the noise of the drums. Michael felt a new and more intense horror. He was conscious of Samsón standing at his shoulder, of Obadiah a little distance away, of the zombie somewhere out in the trees behind them.

"Ayeeyah!" The scream pierced the night. It echoed and reechoed.

Michael thought it had come from inside and he looked more closely, but Samsón was pounding on his shoulder in a wordless plea for attention. Michael turned around. The zombie was coming toward them, still shaking and shuddering, as if the rhythm of the drums was inside his soul. Every few seconds he stopped and uttered that ear-splitting scream. "Ayeeyah! Ayeeyah!"

Someone threw open the door and the light of the fire turned the narrow footpath into a red river. The zombie kept coming.

Michael and Obadiah and Samsón were in the shadows. No one inside could see them, but the zombie could. Michael braced himself for the attack that had to come, but the man walked by them as if he still didn't know they existed.

The zombie shrieked once more. "Ayeeyah!" Then the drums began again. They were faster this time, much more frenzied.

Assunta waited at the door to meet the zombie. She took his hand and led him to the middle of the room. The others were clapping and moaning, forming themselves into a circle around the pair. Then the circle broke and at last Michael saw Nuria.

She was lying on the floor at Assunta's feet, naked and apparently unconscious. Michael took a step toward the open door, not sure when the best moment would be. He clenched and unclenched his fists, raised himself on the balls of his feet, tried to shut his ears to the terrible music of the drums, tried to formulate a plan.

It was going to be difficult, maybe impossible. There were at least a dozen men in there. Only the zombie was as big as he was; still he couldn't fight them all. Speed was the thing. In like a flash of lightening, then out with Nuria in his arms. So fast they didn't know what had happened until it was too late. And please God he wouldn't lose his footing on the floor covered with slime and dead frogs.

Now? No, not yet. The moment of opportunity had gone by. The circle had formed again, the stamping and shaking dance was continuing.

Long seconds passed when he couldn't see Nuria, only the top of Assunta's head and the enormous shoulders of the zombie rising above the throng. Then the drumbeat changed a third time. Once more the pattern of the dance shifted and the circle was broken.

Michael took a step, then stopped again. A new element had been added to whatever diabolical ritual he was witnessing. Men and women began dropping to the floor. They seemed to be in some kind of trance. They knelt in one place, swaying their upper torsos in a circle and staring at the fire. It was as if they were drugged. Maybe the blood of the frogs . . .

Michael stopped analyzing and started to move, convinced this moment was his best chance. He could see Nuria, and there was a fairly clear path to where she lay. She was still unconscious, still lying on the floor in front of Assunta. But now the zombie was standing over her. He held a knife raised above his head, ready to plunge.

"No! What are you doing? Are you mad? Stop!"

It was Beth's voice that split the night in that cry of anguish and outrage, and pure English-accented fury.

Michael hesitated, almost frozen by astonishment. Most of the people inside acted as if they'd heard nothing. Some of them were drooling spittle from half-open mouths, others had fallen in a faint. But Assunta had heard. "Get dat woman!" she shouted at the zombie. "Go *verdad* get her like I say!"

The zombie dropped the knife and turned. His body moved like that of a lumbering giant—stiff, jerking, but coming inexorably forward to where Beth stood in the door.

Michael lunged for her, sweeping her out of the path of the oncoming man. "Go!" he shouted. "Run! Get away from here."

"Ayeeyah!" This time it was Assunta's voice uttering that eerie scream. "Ayeeyah! De man profane de service. Get him! Get him! Kill de Man Irish!"

A few of the bodies on the floor writhed as if they wanted to obey the command of the priestess, but it was too late. Whatever they'd drugged themselves with, they were too far gone to be pulled back by her will or their own.

The drummers picked up the tempo yet again. Assunta stood where she was, still screaming her rage and her commands. The zombie kept coming and he was between Michael and Nuria.

He lunged for the creature, hurling himself onward and delivering one stunning blow to the other man's chin. The zombie seemed to feel nothing. The two men stood only inches apart now, but the zombie didn't strike a blow. Instead he wrapped two enormous hands around Michael's throat and began to squeeze.

Out of the corner of his eye Michael saw Samsón and Obadiah dart past him. Once the boy slipped on the slimy floor, but the old man hauled him upright and they kept going. Assunta was still screaming. She'd picked up the knife the zombie had dropped and she slashed at Samsón, but she couldn't deflect him. The old coachman grabbed his mistress's shoulders and the child took her feet. Between them they began to drag her out of the room.

Michael couldn't help them. He was locked in a contest for his life. He couldn't breathe. There was a black veil descending over his eyes. He kept on struggling, called on every bit of his strength to break the grip of the zombie, but the hands on his neck continued to squeeze.

Seconds later, when his knees were starting to go and he knew it was over, he sensed a third presence. Whatever it was squirmed between his legs and the zombie's. Then something caused the zombie to shudder, to relax his grip for the merest instant. Michael knew he had only this moment to choose between life and death. He heaved his shoulders back, tearing one last time at the other man's arms. The grip broke and he was free.

"Michael! This way! Quick!"

His vision was still too hazy for him to find the door, but he could hear Beth's voice and feel her hand tugging him in the direction they must go. He followed her, running though he knew it was impossible for him to find the strength or the breath to run. Seconds later they were outside in the night and his eyes were focused again and the terrible burning pain in his chest was subsiding.

"Samsón!"

"I be here, señor. I *verdad* got Missy Doña."

"Good man. Are you hurt? Is Obadiah all right?"

"I be fine, señor. Only cut a little bit. Obadiah, he be fine too."

"Where's Missy Doña?"

"Here," Samsón repeated.

Curran could see them now. The three were sheltering among the chickens, beneath a tree some twenty yards from the house of horror. Michael glanced back at it. The drums were still beating and Assunta had come to the door. The zombie was with her; they were starting down the path.

"C'mon! We've got to get out of here." Michael looked at Beth. Her hair had come undone and hung free to her shoulders. Her dress was torn and filthy, but she seemed unharmed. How in God's name had she got here? What had she to do with these people? Not now. No time. "Can you manage without help?" he gasped out.

She nodded. "Yes. Yes, I can. Don't worry about me."

He wasted no more of his precious breath on words. He picked up Nuria's unconscious body, and the four of them began running along the dirt track that led to San Juan. In a few moments they realized they could walk, because the crashing sounds of the zombie following them got farther and farther away.

"He *verdad* no come into town, señor," Samsón assured Curran. "Zombies, they never come into the town."

"I hope to God he knows that." Michael was still finding it hard to breathe. "Doesn't matter, he can't move fast. Too clumsy. We can slow down."

Beth was trotting beside Obadiah, holding his hand. She looked at Michael and smiled. He grinned back. They went on.

They were halfway to town—Nuria still in Michael's arms, covered with his coat, beginning to moan as she regained consciousness—when he realized that in the instant when both women were in mortal danger, it was Beth he'd jumped to save.

Michael was reluctant to take Nuria to her own house, but Samsón insisted it would be best. "*Verdad* Assunta and her people no come back here, señor. They be too feared now we seen what they be *verdad* doing. Very safe on Calle Cruz now for Missy Doña."

Still Michael searched the little house before he let them go in, and locked and barred the door of the passage that led to the bordello. "Doña Nuria's ladies and their guests can look after themselves tonight."

"Is a *verdad* good idea, señor," Samsón agreed, grinning so his three gold teeth showed.

"I'm still not happy about leaving you." Michael glanced at Nuria. She lay on the sofa where he'd placed her when they arrived. Her eyes were open and she was looking at him. "Nuria, how are you? Can you hear me?"

"*Sí,*" she murmured. Then she closed her eyes and he realized she was sleeping. Whatever they'd given her was still having a powerful effect.

"Is going to be *verdad* fine now, señor," Samsón insisted. "I look after Missy Doña."

"Yes, I'm sure you will. You've been magnificent. I still wish there were some way to guard—"

Samsón's face split into a wider grin. "I get guards, señor. Is easy get guards for Missy Doña. Mens what *verdad* don't have Assunta messing with they's heads." He turned and shouted, "Obadiah! Where you *verdad* is, boy?"

The lad came running. He was holding something, shaking it free into the room. It was a large piece of native cloth, dark blue with white geometric patterns obviously he'd found it among Nuria's things.

Beth was standing alone in the shadows of a corner of the room. Obadiah held the cloth out to her. "Here, Missy Estranjera, you *verdad* take."

She stepped forward, understanding his gesture if not his words. She was only a little taller than the boy and he reached up and draped the fabric over her head and shoulders. Beth smiled and gracefully gathered the folds to her body. Her disheveled hair and her ripped and stained dress were effectively covered. "Thank you, Obadiah. That was very thoughtful. Michael, please tell him what I said."

When Michael translated, Obadiah's smile spread from ear to ear. Impulsively Beth leaned forward and kissed his cheek. He put up his hand and covered the spot, still smiling.

"Now you *verdad* stop bein' man lover and go get Missy Doña's friends from Calle Torina," Samsón told him. He turned to Curran. "Many mens in San Juan is good friends to Missy Doña, mens Missy Doña *verdad* helped before.

Assunta no be messing around in their heads. They come and guard us until everything very fine."

"Good, Samsón, that's good thinking."

Twenty minutes later the men were there—three burly youths, one black and two mestizos. "We can go now," Michael told Beth. "Sorry you had to wait so long."

"Not at all," she said, as formally as if they were at a dinner party. "It was sensible to wait until they arrived."

She preceded him out of the house, holding her improvised cape around her as if it were ermine.

It was a few minutes past eleven. The Puerto Ricans would be out in force, drinking endless cups of coffee and glasses of rum in the little cafés, doubtless talking about the *norteamericanos*. Michael led Beth to the inn through back alleys and side streets, by a route that avoided the Calle Fortaleza and its inevitable crowds. Neither of them spoke.

There was a rear entrance to the inn through the kitchen. Briggs had pointed it out, and on occasion Michael had found it useful. He planned to take Beth that way and avoid being seen in the lobby. It meant they had to cut across a narrow patch of weedy, abandoned garden. For a moment looming shadows made the evening's horror real again. He heard her indrawn breath and sensed that like him, she was remembering.

Michael took her hand, pulling her through the darkness into the bright moonlight. The night was fine and warm, the balmy air caressing. The white wall of the inn looked solid and safe and real. Michael approached it, then stopped. Beth waited, not prepared to speak until he did.

"In God's name," he whispered hoarsely, "tell me how you got there. I can't believe you're mixed up with those people. I won't believe it."

She went rigid, her eyes blazed, but her voice was cool.

"Is that what you think? That I was there before you? That I was involved with that—that abomination?"

"No. It's the only explanation, but I can't make myself accept it. Nothing would make me believe it."

A little of the tension went out of her. "It's much simpler than that. I was watching you from my window when Obadiah came. I followed you."

"Followed . . . Christ! What possessed you to do that? How could you take the risk? Beth, do you realize—"

"Do you realize that if I hadn't been there Nuria might be dead? And you as well. I provided the distraction you needed. Gave you those extra few seconds that made the difference."

Michael was staring at her as if he'd never seen her before, trying to take it all in. There were so many questions he didn't know which to ask first. "Why did you follow me? Have you ever—"

"Never. I've never followed you before in my whole life. I doubt I ever will again. But tonight . . . I can't explain it. Something told me I must do it, that if I didn't I'd regret it always. I had to, Michael. I simply had to."

He nodded, lay one hand on her cheek. "You were the bravest thing I've ever seen. Magnificent," he acknowledged. "Like an avenging angel."

She lowered her eyes. "I don't know what possessed me."

"Neither do I. One more thing, when that . . . creature had his hands at my throat, it was you who broke his grip, wasn't it?"

She nodded.

"Tell me how you did it."

Beth got very red. "I can't."

"You can. I want to know. Please." Laughter was brimming in him, a slightly hysterical urge to bellow. Michael knew it was a delayed reaction to the fear and the danger and he controlled it. "Tell me," he said again.

"I bit him."

"Where?"

She hesitated and looked away. "Between his legs," she whispered. "A very hard bite."

Michael let the laughter explode, and after a few seconds Beth was laughing too.

London, Midnight

The telephone rang in Norman's study. He picked it up instantly. "Yes."

"Mendoza?"

"Yes, sir. I was waiting for your call."

"Sorry to ring so late," Ransom said. "But you did want me to inform you as soon as my meeting with the chancellor was finished."

"Yes, of course I did. Good of you to take the trouble." Get on with it, he was thinking. Tell me, you damned fool, don't shilly shally, tell me.

"Look here, Norman . . . Are you still there?"

It was the first time Ransom had ever used his given name. It was not a good sign. Norman started to sweat, tension almost smothering him. "Yes, sir, I'm listening."

"Good, good. Can't get used to these damned instruments. Like to see a man's face when I'm talking to him."

"Of course, sir. Better that way, I agree. Still, the telephone's a great convenience. About the chancellor—"

"Yes. I was with him for over an hour. Left a few minutes ago. We had a very thorough chat, very thorough."

"I take it then that he understands the nature of the problem. That's it's only a temporary—"

"Won't do," Ransom interrupted.

"What won't do, sir?"

"Calling it a problem, saying it's temporary. The chancellor is quite clear about that. It's a crisis, Norman. And I must say, one of your own making. The decisions—"

"Sir, if Mendozas can have ninety days breathing time, there will be no crisis. I assure you." He knew he was wasting his breath. His body knew it. His stomach was churning and his mouth tasted of bile.

"Have to go the route we went before," Ransom said. "Same as we did with Barings. Can't ignore precedent, Norman. Once you start doing that no one knows what to expect. Then where will we be?"

"I take it then that the chancellor has refused any government assistance?" Get it out in the open and be done with it. There was no point to this stumbling around.

Ransom hesitated. "Yes," he said finally. "You have to recognize that though he's sympathetic, the chancellor really hasn't the means to help at his disposal. It would require a special act of Parliament. And that would mean a debate. That could get rather vicious, provoke exactly the kind of panic we're trying to avoid. Norman, are you still there?"

"Yes, I'm here. Is that it, then? The final word?"

"That's it. No government aid. It's up to the City to save itself. We're a free economy, Norman. That's our great strength. You know that as well as the chancellor and I do. In a free economy a man has to make his own way. For better or for worse."

"I see. Thank you, sir. Good night."

"Norman, hold on a moment."

"Yes, sir?"

"There'll be a syndicate, I imagine. A number of men who will put together the means to save Mendozas. That's what happened with Barings. I want you to know that I'm personally very sympathetic. I mean to call Johnathon at once. I shall tell him to put me down for a hundred thousand. Me personally, you understand. Nothing to do with the Bank of England."

"Thank you, sir, that's very generous."

"Don't mention it. Least I can do. Good night, Norman."

"Good night, sir."

Norman set down the receiver and stared at the telephone. He sat very still and tried to take it in, to find a way to turn this disaster to some advantage. The thing was spinning out of control, moving so fast he couldn't fit the pieces into a pattern. There were rogue elements in the mix, things only he knew about. Lila Curran and her son for one thing, Lord Sharrick for another.

"Sharrick," he said aloud. "Sharrick." The meeting the other day with the Irishman had gone more smoothly than he'd expected. Once Sharrick realized that Norman knew he was involved with the Fenians, Sharrick hadn't wasted time denying it.

"What do you want then?" Sharrick had asked.

"A loan."

His lordship had raised his eyebrows. "Blackmail is it?"

"Not at all. Nothing like that. I want the cash you cost me with your article in the *Times*. You planned that to come out the day of our new issue, didn't you?"

"You might say. Or you might believe it was simply a coincidence. Life's full of them, isn't it?"

"This wasn't a coincidence. Whatever you and Lila Curran think you're planning, whatever scheme you'd proposed to my son Timothy, I want you to know—" Norman had broken off, knowing he was letting his emotions talk rather than his brain. The important thing now was what he wanted, not what they dreamed they were going to get. "A non–interest-bearing loan. To be repaid in a single installment in three years time."

"Generous terms," Sharrick had said softly. "I rather doubt you'd offer them if the shoe were on the other foot, if the bank were the creditor."

"No, I wouldn't. But that's not the way things are at the moment."

"Very well. How much?"

"Half a million."

He'd worked the amount out beforehand, figured it was as much as he could expect to get in return for his discretion, and as much as Sharrick was likely to be able to find in cash as quickly as Norman wanted it. He'd been surprised by the speed with which the Irishman had agreed to his terms, but too pleased with himself to worry about the possibility that he could have got more. Then Hammersmith had overreacted and now the damned government was involved and half a million wasn't nearly enough to make a difference.

"Sharrick," Norman said again. Maybe the lord of Glencree still held the key to a solution. Or perhaps Lila Curran. God he hated that bloody woman. But there was something she wanted that he could give. So perhaps a trade might work. If it did, and if the Black Widow's resources were as vast as they were said to be, that could be the answer.

There had to be one, because what Ransom and the chancellor were suggesting was no solution at all. Norman knew quite well the details of the precedent Ransom was so fond of citing. He knew what had happened to Barings and the knowledge chilled his soul.

A few miles away in Bayswater, Johnathon Hammersmith was also the recipient of a late-night telephone call from his wife's godfather. He wasn't really surprised to learn that the chancellor had refused a government loan. He'd more or less been expecting it since the meeting between Ransom and Mendoza the night before. All that Jew business, the governor hadn't liked that. Hadn't liked Norman Mendoza either. Too pushy, too aggressive. Which was exactly what people always said about Jews. So maybe . . . Ah, the devil with all that. Religion and race didn't come into this. Or perhaps they did, his own at least. He was an Englishman and a Christian and he knew his duty.

Hammersmith opened a drawer of his desk and withdrew a notepad and began composing the cable he must send to Puerto Rico. His first obligation was to his client, and his client had a right to know the likely outcome of his demand for payment from Mendozas.

❧ 20 ❧

FRIDAY, JULY 16, 1898
London, Eleven-Thirty A.M.

Norman Mendoza stood in front of the Connaught Hotel, gathering his resources for what he had to do. Carlos Place was busy this morning. Hansoms and private carriages moved in both directions, many stopped in front of the hotel to discharge passengers or collect them. He took a final deep breath, then made his way through the throng and into the lobby.

"Yes, sir, may I help you?"

"I wish to see Mrs. Lila Curran." Norman produced his card. The clerk looked at it, then rang a bell. A young boy in hotel livery appeared, was instructed, and disappeared. Norman stepped to one side to wait.

He could have telephoned, but he'd decided it was better this way, more direct. She might refuse to see him, but he didn't think it likely. Lila Curran would derive too much pleasure from gloating to deprive herself of the opportunity.

In a few minutes the boy returned. "Madam says the gentleman's to go up."

• • •

"Well, Norman, it's been rather a long time."

"Yes, it has, Lila. I don't do much socializing since Penelope died."

"As far as my son and I are concerned, you didn't do much before. In fact, I don't recall Michael or I once being invited to your home when Penny was alive."

"That's true," he admitted. "We've never been fond of each other, Lila. There's not much point in pretending now, is there? May I sit down?"

She nodded and he lowered himself into a brocaded slipper chair. Lila settled on the sofa opposite. "I agree about not pretending," she said. "So I'm not going to play the hostess and offer you a drink. Why have you come?"

"To make a trade."

She smiled. "Yes, I thought that might be it. What did you have in mind?"

"I think you know, don't you?"

"Perhaps I do. Nonetheless, I'd like you to explain it to me, Norman. In the greatest possible detail."

Bloody bitch. She was enjoying this. But he'd known she would; in her shoes he'd have felt the same. Norman kept his face expressionless. He took out his watch, flipped open the cover, and studied it. "It's nearly noon."

"Is it? And what exactly has that to do with anything?"

"There's a meeting going on in the City at this moment. At the Bank of England to be precise. I'm not supposed to know about it, but I do . . . because one or two people involved are rather sympathetic." He glanced up at her. "To our plight, I mean. The circumstances the bank's in at the moment."

"I'm not sympathetic, Norman," she said softly.

"No, I realize that. But some are. So I know about the meeting and the probable outcome." She didn't say anything. He cleared his throat and continued. "Without a quite large influx of short term capital, Mendozas is going to have to stop. A group of City men are putting together a syndicate to produce that capital."

"How fortunate for you."

"No, not in the least." He glanced at a decanter on a nearby table, but she'd said she wouldn't offer him a drink, and he was damned if he'd ask for one. "I'm reasonably certain that if we solve our temporary problem by taking money from this cobbled-together syndicate, it will be the end of Mendozas."

Lila leaned forward, supporting her chin in her hand and studying him. "Will it, Norman? Mendozas as such? Or do you mean Mendozas of London?"

"It comes to the same thing."

"No, it doesn't. You and I know that the assets of Córdoba and London are held separately. No one outside the family knows how closely the two cooperate, or when they do and when they don't."

"That's true, but—"

"There are no buts," she interrupted. "It's true. Córdoba does not stand or fall with London. It never has."

"You presume you know everything there is to know about the operation, but you don't understand as much as you think you do. How could you? You're a woman, you've never been involved in the business decisions. Not even when you were with Juan Luis."

"Norman, let me save us both a great deal of time. First, I know as much as I need to know about this affair . . . and a great deal more than you think I know. Second, you mentioned a trade. I don't think you have anything I want."

"Yes, I do." He pitched his voice low. "You want Córdoba for your son Michael."

"That's true. But I'm going to get that with or without you."

"Believe me, you won't. Not unless—"

"Very well, Norman, let's leave that and go on. We're discussing a hypothetical trade. You are offering to give

Michael what is in any analysis his by right, and I am to give you . . . what?"

"Money."

"Ah, I see."

"A very great deal of money. Perhaps more than you have," Norman said frankly. "I'm not sure."

"How much did you have in mind?"

Ransom and Hammersmith kept talking about thirteen million, but that was absurd, real only if you viewed banking far more conservatively than he did. "Three, maybe four million," he said. "A loan for three years. And Michael withdraws his request to redeem the bond in his possession." He paused. "You do know about the bond, don't you?"

"Of course. I gave it to him."

"I know that. I mean you know he's requested payment."

Lila nodded. "I knew he expected to do so quite soon." She sat back, tapping her cheek with the folded fan that hung from her wrist. "So in effect we're discussing perhaps five million pounds. As you said, Norman, that's a very great deal of money."

"It is. But say three million in hard cash. Do you have it?"

"My, my, what an ungentlemanly question."

"There's no time for niceties, Lila. There's no deal until each party knows the other has something he wants. I have it in my power to put Michael into control in Córdoba. Can you produce three million sterling? Within five days at the most?"

She nodded. "Since you ask, yes, I probably can."

He let out a long breath. "I thought so."

"But I'm not going to, Norman."

"I think you may wish to reconsider that answer. If we go under, there'll be little worth having in Córdoba. Besides, you'll never get what you want without my help."

"Oh, yes I will."

"May I ask how?"

"Francisco has resigned. There's no one else to take over in Córdoba. Beatriz has decided that Michael should do so."

Blast her to hell! He hadn't thought she'd know about Francisco, at least not so soon. And bringing in Beatriz was something he'd not expected. He'd thought Beatriz would come to him for advice and assistance. "Ah, yes, Beatriz," he said, hoping none of his thoughts showed in his face. "She's here in England, isn't she? I believe she was at Westlake until a few days ago."

"She's in London now. At this hotel in fact."

That explained a lot. The two women must have remained friendly after Lila left Juan Luis. He'd never realized that. "I see," he said. "Well, whatever you and Beatriz may think, the directorship of the bank in Córdoba is not in her gift. In this family the men have always—"

"The men, at least those of this generation, have made an unholy mess," Lila interrupted. She stood up. "I think you'd better go, Norman."

"You're making a great mistake, you know."

"No, I don't think I am." She held the door open, waiting for him to leave. Norman hesitated, but there was nothing more he could do to pursuade her.

He played his last card. "If you refuse to help now, Michael will never take over Córdoba, Lila. I swear to you he won't."

"You're wrong, Norman. There's one last piece of information that I have and you do not. I'll give it to you. Free. Michael has Juan Luis's half of the medallion."

Rage was a sick thing in his belly; it made him tremble. Norman was glad it took his coachman over an hour to get through the melee of traffic between Mayfair and Knightsbridge; the delay gave him time to regain some control. God blast the woman to everlasting hell. No wonder they called her the Black Widow. Deadly—and enjoyed seeing her victims squirm. But the medallion, how in hell . . . Sweet Jesus, his head was spinning, his stomach churning. He had to think. He had to find a way out of this mess.

Norman touched his chest with the flat of one hand. His sliver of the medallion was home in his safe. He'd stopped wearing it years ago. But in a sense it was carved into his flesh. That was the point, wasn't it? The medallion had no legal force. Michael Curran might have the half of it that belonged in Córdoba, but what did it prove? That Juan Luis had meant his son to inherit after all? No, it couldn't be that. The man had written his wishes into his will in black and white. There was no doubt about them.

Still, there was a moral imperative in the possession of the medallion. It wasn't anything that would be understood outside the family, but they all knew it, and that was what mattered. "Superstitious claptrap," Norman muttered aloud. His voice sounded hollow in his ears. It wasn't true. The force of the medallion, the awe they felt for it—that was something so basic, so fundamental, he'd never be able to deny it. None of them would. Not Jamie or Henry or—"

"Here we be, sir."

They'd stopped, and the coachman had climbed down and opened the door for Norman before he realized they were on Basil Street. He yanked his mind into the present, grunted something, and got out of the carriage.

Tim's house looked quiet and peaceful. The front steps were carefully swept, flowers bloomed in the two urns that flanked the door, the brass knocker was polished. No passerby would know it had become a house of tragedy. Ah well, maybe there'd be some improvement today, some tiny element of hope. Something good had to happen soon; a man couldn't have luck so bad it would never change.

Harcourt let him in. "Doctor's upstairs, sir."

The butler looked morose, but then he had for days. Worried about his job no doubt. Norman walked past him and started up the stairs.

Miss Dancer met him at the door to Tim's room. Her

elephantine bulk blocked his way in. "If you wouldn't mind waiting out here a moment, sir. Doctor's with the young gentleman now." She closed the door in his face before he could reply.

Norman leaned his forehead against the ombré, striped wallpaper of the hall. Sweet Jesus, why did he care so much? After all, he and Tim had been at loggerheads for years, and the lad's duplicity was well proven. But it changed nothing. His gut ached with the need to hear that things were getting better, that Tim had a chance. My son, he told himself, my son—whatever else. Flesh of my flesh. A bond that no one and nothing could entirely sever. Like the moral suasion of the medallion, it was a reality that existed because of a long chain of events. If you denied such things, you wound up denying the meaning of your own existence.

The bedroom door opened. The doctor stepped into the hall. "Mr. Mendoza, I'm sorry . . ."

Norman stared at him. Knowing before he knew. The man's tone of voice said it all. "He's worse?" Norman demanded, the gruff question masking the deeper horror.

"Not exactly, not the way you mean. I'm sorry, I did everything I could. He's gone."

Hammersmith looked at the men seated with him at a table in a small anteroom of the Bank of England. "Gentlemen, it's getting toward lunch and we've been here nearly two hours. Perhaps it's time we took our collective temperature."

Never ask for a vote until you've counted heads and know the outcome, his father had told him, and Hammersmith had not forgotten the advice. He was fairly certain he'd got his sums right this morning. Most of the men present hated Mendozas, would have been pleased to see them disappear down a black hole. All the same, they had to help. The only other choice was panic and chaos.

He waited for some sign of agreement from the others, flicking his glance from one man to the next. By God, this was a gathering of power, the City in all its glory—and all its venality and venom as well. Some of the things said had been outrageous examples of spite and envy, but in the end they all knew they had their own hides to save, and that the price was saving Mendozas.

Hammersmith didn't think of the others as individuals; in his mind each man at the table was tagged with the name of the house he represented. He waited for agreement from the representative from the mighty Rothschilds, and in seconds had a barely perceptible nod. The man from Morgans raised a finger. Hambros actually smiled. Glyn, Mills coughed and nodded from behind a large white handkerchief. He looked at Barings. Barings shook his head.

Hammersmith was startled. He hadn't expected trouble from that quarter. If anyone should be sympathetic, surely it must be Barings. No, that's not what the gesture had meant. Barings was mumbling something about what a shame it all was. "I take it you're in support, however?" Hammersmith asked.

"Yes, of course. Nothing else we can do."

"I agree. And Coutts will pledge a like amount. So all together, we're committed for eight million." Hammersmith glanced at the papers in front of him. It was only a diversionary tactic. He'd been working with the figures for two days, and they were graven into his brain. He turned to Ransom. "That means we're still short five million, sir. If we're to put Mendozas on a solid footing, that is."

The governor of the Bank of England cleared his throat. "Yes, very good of all of you, very generous. In your own best interests, of course, but all the same . . ." Ransom took a sip from the glass of water sitting in front of him and went on. "Since the City is once again making this outstanding effort to save itself, the bank will guarantee the five million shortfall."

A collective sigh of relief echoed from the six men watching him.

"There are conditions, of course," Ransom added. "Have to be conditions if a public institution is involving itself so deeply."

"What conditions did you have in mind, sir?" The man from Hambros asked.

Ransom cleared his throat yet again. "The er . . . the present management at Mendozas. It's shown itself inept. I believe we must ask that his lordship and his two brothers relinquish their responsibility for the bank's affairs."

Five of the men nodded sagely. Hammersmith refrained from any reaction at all. Poor Norman, he was thinking, poor benighted sod.

"Are we suggesting then," Rothschild asked, "that Mendozas stop after all? I mean with all debts and obligations satisfied, of course."

It was Glyn, Mills who said quietly. "If Mendozas is going to cease to exist, who, may I ask, is going to repay this money?"

A small chuckle went round the table. The remark wasn't particularly funny, but they needed to laugh at something. "Well," Glyn, Mills pressed, "what is it we're suggesting?"

"A new company," Hammersmith said smoothly. "Something along the lines of the reorganization that Barings followed."

Barings smiled and nodded.

"Good suggestion," Ransom said, as if the idea were some original stroke of genius. "Up to them, of course, but we can support the notion if it's suggested. Meanwhile, there's one other thing. The Bank of England contribution to the fund must be secured by the personal holdings of all the principals."

"Secured?" Hammersmith asked. "Do you mean as pledged collateral, sir?"

"No. I'm sorry to sound so hard-hearted, but I'm afraid in this instance that's not sufficient. The bank must insist that the Mendozas liquidate their property at the earliest possible date. I'll tell them so myself."

San Juan, Dawn

Exhausted as he was, Michael didn't sleep well. His dreams were terrifying, and when the sun was climbing over the horizon he woke in a cold sweat.

He'd left the curtains open and the balcony door ajar, but the room seemed suffocating. Michael got out of bed and splashed water on his face, foregoing the bathroom down the hall and using the jug and basin Briggs always left in the room. Then he pulled on clean clothes and went out.

There was a *taverna* on Calle San Francisco that opened very early. He headed in that direction, longing for strong black coffee and a glass of rum. His neck was bruised and aching. He rubbed it, remembering. Jesus God almighty, what had the creature been? A dead man brought to life, according to Obadiah. That was insane, but what was the truth? And the frogs, why . . .

Michael shook his head, wanting to shake away the memory of the incredible scenes he'd witnessed. He thought of Beth and Nuria. He'd get his coffee and rum, then check on both women. He could stop by the Calle Cruz on his way back to the inn.

There was something he'd been trying to remember all night, while he slept his tortured sleep. It came to him now—the sound of Magdalena's voice echoed in his ears, crystal clear and limpid in the light of the new day. *Strength is holy, and the strength of a woman is the holiest thing of all.*

Beth. Great God, now that was strength. He'd always sensed it in her, been a little afraid of it, but . . .

"Señor Curran! Thank God you are here. I was going—"

"Good morning, Luz. You're up early."

The banker was coming out of the telegraph office, clutching an envelope. He looked terrible, worse than Michael felt. The Puerto Rican's skin and the whites of his eyes were sickly yellow. His forehead was beaded with sweat and he was shaking.

"What is it?" Michael asked. "What's the matter?"

"Señor," Luz murmured, then stopped, as if his mouth wouldn't form the words.

Michael took his arm. "Come with me. We'll go get some coffee and something to drink. Then you can tell me."

He had to half drag the banker across the road and through the alley that led to the *taverna* on San Francisco. Luz kept hanging back, trying to speak. "Not now," Michael told him repeatedly. "Some rum first, to put a little life in you. Then we'll talk."

There were a few workmen standing at the bar, and one toothless old woman sitting at a table in the rear. She was sleeping, her head propped against the wall, her mouth open. Michael pulled Luz to the back of the long narrow room, stopping only to tell the barman to bring two coffees and two double rums.

The cups and glasses were delivered quickly. Michael's reputation for wealth and power had been secure for some weeks. "Drink up," he ordered, doing the same. "Now, what's the matter? Something to do with that cable you're hanging on to, isn't it?"

Luz seemed to have forgotten the cable. He looked at it in mild surprise. "Yes, yes," he whispered. "The cable. It is for you."

He pushed it across the table. Michael smoothed out the wrinkles made by Luz's sweaty fingers, and saw that it was addressed to him. "When did this arrive?"

"Half an hour ago, señor. Maybe an hour. No more."

The envelope was sealed, but that proved nothing. Luz had to know what the message said, otherwise why would he be in this state? A smile began playing around Michael's lips. He could guess the contents. And if he was right, everything was perfect. "Tell me what it says."

"But, Don Michael, the cable is addressed to you. I only happened to be at the telegraph office when it came in. Because I was hoping for an advice from the bank in London. From Coutts. And then—"

"This is from Coutts, isn't it? Don't look so ridiculously sly. I know the telegraphist is in your pocket. In your position I'd have the same arrangement."

Luz nodded. His eyes were filled with tears. "Sí, the telegraphist told me. It is from Coutts. They say—" He swallowed the words, unable to continue.

"Let me help you," Michael said softly. "They say there's no money, right? They can't pay a million sterling into my account."

Luz nodded, his misery beyond words.

Michael allowed himself one whoop of pleasure. The old woman snored more loudly, protesting the noise. The barman glanced at them quickly, then looked away. "Everything exactly as planned," Michael said quietly, controlling his elation. "Right on schedule."

"But, señor, my bank." Luz's voice was a harsh whisper. He glanced around to make sure no one was close enough to overhear, then leaned forward. "There is no money to open with today. Everyone is very nervous because of the norteamericanos. They take out their savings and try to get away. If I had the advice from Coutts, the one I expected, I would go to the governor general and ask him—"

"Listen to me." Michael cut off the spate of words, pinned the banker with his direct stare, willed him to be calm and to pay attention. "Get hold of yourself. The million was based on a bond issued by Mendozas. It's supposed to be payable on demand. In ten days' time. If the money isn't coming, it's because Mendozas can't pay."

Luz stared at him, made silent by astonishment. He shook

his head over and over. "No," he croaked finally. "Mendozas, no, it cannot be."

"Yes, it can. It is." Michael ripped open the envelope and gazed quickly over the message. "Yes, it's exactly what I've said. Hammersmith, the man at Coutts, is very circumspect. That's his style. But that's what this means. Mendozas can't pay."

"But—"

"But nothing. It's exactly what I intended."

"You? But, señor, I trusted you. You told me—"

"I told you you'd do all right out of what I was proposing. You have. You've had the equivalent of fifteen thousand sterling out of it. Plus whatever you've been stashing away in banks in New York. Now's the time to go, Luz. Get a berth on the first boat available. Go to New York and live the way you've been planning to for years."

"How can I go? The bank . . . my customers . . . they will tear me apart."

"Not if they can't find you. Take what you need, and your money—" Michael stopped and peered at the other man. "You haven't used your own money to make good the shortfall at the bank, have you?"

Luz shook his head. "Not yet. Of course, if I were sure—"

"Fine. That's all right then. Go to ground, Luz. Hide until you can get off the island. I'll smooth your way as best I can."

"Señor, I do not understand. The bank, the planters . . ." He was weeping openly now, big tears dripping down his sallow, sunken cheeks.

"Get hold of yourself," Michael ordered. "Stop acting like a woman." *The strength of a woman is the holiest thing of all.* The words flashed into his head and Michael forced them away. Not now, there wasn't time now. "Listen to me. The planters are none the worse for any of this. They've had fifteen thousand pounds too. That's theirs to keep when I default on the purchase of the plantations. I wrote that clause into the contracts myself. Cost of doing business."

"You knew all along," Luz whispered. "You never intended—"

"Right. But it's unimportant." Michael pulled his watch from his pocket. "It's nearly seven. You've a little more than an hour. Go back to your place, get your money and anything else you absolutely need, then leave." He paused. "Have you someplace to go? Can you think of a place to hide until you can get a ship?"

"Of course," Luz said dully. "I was born and raised in Puerto Rico. Of course I can find a place to hide."

"Fine. Leave the bank locked up tight. Put all the keys in a sealed package marked with my name. On your way to wherever you're going—" Luz started to say something, but Michael held up his hand. "Don't tell me, I don't want to know. But on your way to wherever it is, drop the package of keys by the inn. Put them in the hands of my man Briggs. No, wait a moment." Michael hesitated, then made up his mind. "Ask for Beth—Doña Isabela—give the package to her. No one else, understand? See that you're there before eight. Then get the hell out of San Juan."

"The bank," Luz said again, hopelessly.

"The bank's mine now." Michael smiled. "I'll look after the bank."

There was only an hour before the bank was due to open its doors. Less now. His watch said five past seven. No time to go to the Calle Cruz; he'd have to leave Nuria to Samsón for the time being. Checking on Beth would have to wait too. But he was sure enough about her. *The strength of a woman, the holiest thing of all.*

Michael strode toward La Fortaleza. People were beginning to appear on the street, but he greeted no one, merely walked as fast as he could without obviously running.

There was a militiaman standing guard beside the door

leading to the governor general's private apartments. "I wish to see General Devega. Tell him it's Michael Curran, that it's a matter of utmost urgency."

The soldier straightened. "The general sees no one before nine. He will be in his office then."

"He'll see me. Give him my message."

"Nine o'clock, señor. In the office. The entrance is around the corner."

Jesus! He didn't have time to argue with the man. And knocking him out could involve consequences. The military were very protective of their privileges, here as elsewhere. Michael dipped his hand into his pocket and came out with a handful of pesetas. He had no idea how many. Enough apparently. The soldiers were as corrupt as their meager salaries insured they'd be.

The man didn't look at the money when he took it and shoved it inside his tunic. "Wait here. I will give the general your message. That's all I can do."

Michael nodded.

The wait was short, but the seconds seemed to take an eternity to pass. And all the while his head buzzed with the truths he was beginning to believe. It was working. It had worked. It was done. By God! he had his birthright in the palm of his hand.

"This way, señor. The general will see you."

Michael followed the soldier down a long corridor to a small sunny room overlooking the sea. Devega was breakfasting on churros and coffee. A cup had been placed for Michael, and the butler filled it as the Irishman sat down.

"So, Señor Curran, what is so urgent it could not wait another hour until I am in my office?"

Michael waited for the butler to leave the room before he spoke. "The Banco Mendoza can't open this morning. They've no money."

Devega stared at him. "That's impossible," he said after a few seconds.

"I assure you, it is true."

The general half rose. "Luz. He has to have embezzled the funds. I will send the soldiers—"

"Sit down, sir. Please, hear me out. Luz has done nothing. At least nothing illegal which involves you. It's Mendozas in London who have failed."

"Mendozas? How do you know this?"

"I have a cable right here." Curran waved the envelope, but didn't give it to the general to read. The message wasn't specifically what he was saying it was. Devega wouldn't understand the implications of what Hammersmith had written. "Besides, I am a member of the family."

"You are a Mendoza?"

"That's right. I was born in Córdoba. My father was Juan Luis Mendoza Calero. My legal name is Miguel Mendoza Curran."

"I knew your father, at least by reputation. But you never said—"

"Sorry. It suited me to keep the connection secret for a while."

Devega sat back in his seat, took a sip of his coffee, then spoke slowly and distinctly. "I begin to think there is a great deal about you and your plans which I do not know, Señor Curran—excuse me, Señor Mendoza. Perhaps you will have the courtesy to enlighten me."

"Curran will do for the time being. And I admit I haven't been entirely straightforward. But it doesn't matter now, does it? Your tenure here is almost over, wouldn't you say?"

"I take it you refer to the *norteamericanos*."

"Of course."

Devega nodded. "There is some truth to that. I mean that it is not an expectation without foundation."

"You don't plan to fight, do you? You've never planned to fight."

"Some battles are so unequal as to be absurd. Don't you agree?"

"Yes, I do. And a wise man knows which they are. So you will be going home to Spain in a short while. Perhaps we will meet there. I expect to be in Spain myself."

The general was unaware of where this conversation was leading, but he was prepared to be patient until he did. "Do you? In Córdoba perhaps?"

"That's right, in Córdoba. It's the bank in London that's in difficulty. The Banco Mendoza in Spain is as strong as always."

"I am glad to hear it," Devega said quietly. "A good bank, a reliable bank, can be a very useful asset to a man. Particularly when he returns home after a long absence."

"Yes, I agree. And I will be the *patrón* of the bank in Córdoba. It is my right as my father's son."

Devega nodded once more. "All of this is very interesting, señor. But meanwhile we are in Puerto Rico, and this island has only one private bank, and you are telling me it has no money, that it cannot open its doors this morning. So I must go at once and prepare my men to put down a riot."

"There need be no riot, General."

"Oh? I am glad to hear that. But how do you propose to prevent it?"

"I am going to take over the bank right now, supply it with funds from my private capital."

"I see. Very good. But where is this private capital of yours, Señor Curran? If it is in the bank which has no money . . ." He shrugged and let the words trail away.

"My capital is in London, General. What I need is cash— actual pesetas—here in Puerto Rico. Not a great deal, only enough to keep the bank solvent until more usual measures can be put into place."

"And how much do you estimate that to be, Señor Curran?"

"About two hundred thousand pesetas, somewhere around fifty thousand pounds sterling."

"I see. Well, señor, if I had such a sum at my command I would gladly lend it to you. But—"

"Thirty days," Michael said, biting out the words. "Interest of seven percent. The entire amount repaid into a private account in your name in the Banco Mendoza in Córdoba."

The governor's eyes narrowed.

"The *norteamericanos*," Michael said softly, "they will confiscate everything of value they find, will they not? Currency first of all."

"That is the usual way of invasions."

"Well then?"

Devega hesitated a moment more, then without a word he got up and left the room. Four minutes later he was back with a strongbox. "It's in here. This is the key. I'll send one of my men with you as a guard until you get it into the vault at the bank. And thank whatever God you believe in, Señor Curran, that the soldier will not know that this box contains the entire August payroll of himself and his brothers in the militia."

"I will not tell him, General. And by August it is unlikely to matter. Now, I presume there is something you would like me to sign?"

The governor produced paper and ink and a pen. Michael made two copies of the note, one for him and one for Devega, and they both signed each one. When it was done he stood up, smiling, nodding his thanks. In his head he was composing the cable he'd send to Norman Mendoza in London.

Beth was waiting for him in the courtyard of the inn. "I could understand very little of what Señor Luz said," she told him. "But I believe this is for you. That you had to have it before eight o'clock."

He took the package from her. It was wrapped in a soiled red bandana and it felt remarkably heavy. "Yes, right on both counts. Thank you. I'm sorry, there's no time to explain now. Are you all right? No aftereffects?"

"None I can't deal with."

She looked astounding—calm and poised and beautiful. Her hair was twisted into a chignon, her brow clear, her gown a tasteful blue linen that made her seem cool despite the mounting heat of the morning. "You're fantastic," Michael said and meant it. "There's never been your equal, Beth Turner, except perhaps for my mother."

"I think that may be the most meaningful compliment you've ever paid me, Michael."

He grinned. "A few days ago it might not have been; today it is. I have to go. Later," he promised. "Later we'll talk about everything." He leaned forward and kissed her. Her lips tasted soft and silky and wonderful. "Later," he said again. Then he ran to the street where the soldier with the strongbox was waiting.

The Banco Mendoza opened at five minutes past eight. The delay wasn't because Michael was late, only because it took him time to find the right key among the half-dozen Luz had left for him. The tellers were waiting on the fringe of a crowd. When he got the door open Michael motioned to the bank's staff.

"Señor Luz is not here," he said quietly. "I am in charge. You will go to your places and prepare to open for business." He turned to the rest of the waiting throng and raised his voice. "We will let you in, in ten minutes, as soon as the clerks are ready. Please excuse the delay and be patient with us. There's no need for any alarm; everything is entirely under control."

The crowd murmured unhappily among themselves, annoyed by the delay but ready to believe the *estranjero* because they needed to believe him. If he was lying, everything was lost and they would never again see the hard-earned pesetas they had deposited in this bank. Besides, everyone knew this Irishman was enormously wealthy. If he was in charge, then the bank must have funds.

Michael led the three clerks into the bank, closing the door firmly behind them. "Señor," one of them whispered as Michael started for Luz's office. "Señor Curran."

"*Sí, dígame.*"

The man glanced toward the street and the waiting customers. Instead of saying anything he pulled open the drawer beneath the counter holding the ledgers. It was empty. He looked at Michael in a wordless plea.

"*No passe nada,*" Michael said. "Nothing has happened. I'll bring you cash in a few minutes. Before we open the doors."

The clerk nodded, his eyes still wary; but like the crowd outside, he was prepared to believe because he wanted to.

Michael went into Luz's office and shot the bolt. There was another door leading to an alley in the rear. He hoped it too would be locked by a sliding bolt. It wasn't. He needed to find another one of those god-blasted keys. He fumbled with three of them before he came to the one that unlocked the door. Seven minutes had passed since he admitted the clerks.

The soldier was waiting, holding the strongbox in one hand, his musket in the other. Muskets for God's sake. The Spanish army was equipped as it had been in Napoleon's day. It was bad on the peninsula and worse in what remained of the colonies. No wonder Devega had no illusions of fighting the Americans. Curran reached for the metal box.

Michael watched the soldier leave, relocked the door to the alley, and opened the strongbox to reveal neat stacks of notes. He ruffled through one, estimating the amount because there wasn't time to count, then took three of the stacks to the change hall where the clerks were waiting. "This will get you started. If you need more I will give it to you. Don't hurry, take your time with each customer. Keep very careful records. Do you understand me?"

The three clerks nodded in unison. Satisfied, Michael unlocked the door of the bank. The crowd surged forward, each person anxious to be the first served, but there was nothing of panic in their movements or the sound of their voices. He was himself the best assurance of stability. Because he was here and the bank was open, it seemed less urgent to get one's money. Curran watched the transactions for a few moments, then returned to the office.

Luz's desk was in front of the picture of Maria Ortega. The old woman's eyes seemed to be boring into his back while he prepared his cable to London.

WITH PERMISSION OF GOVERNOR GENERAL OF THE ISLAND HAVE TAKEN OVER BANK HERE TO PREVENT A RUN AND CERTAIN FAILURE STOP MY PRIVATE CAPITAL GUARANTEES SOLVENCY STOP WILL RETURN LONDON AS SOON AS POSSIBLE TO MAKE ACQUISITION FORMAL STOP SIGNED MICHAEL MENDOZA CURRAN.

Michael read the message over and chuckled. That would give Norman Mendoza something to think about. Better still, the whole island would know the content of the cable as soon as the telegraphist did. Just as well.

He went to the door and satisfied himself that everything was proceeding nicely in the change hall, then slipped out the rear to send the wire.

Tillie arrived at the bank a little before noon. Michael was standing by the clerks' counter, pleased that the clients were orderly. And during the last half hour a few people had actually deposited money rather than withdrawn it. He'd stopped the rot, and two-thirds of Devega's cash remained untouched.

Tillie ran up to him, heedless of the crowd. "Miss Beth sent me, Mr. Curran. She said you'd probably be here. She says you're to go—"

"Come inside." Curran pulled the woman into the office.

Whatever Beth's message, he didn't want it babbled aloud in the change hall, even if it was unlikely that any of the customers understood English.

"Now," he said when he'd closed the door. "What's the trouble?"

"Can't rightly say, Mr. Curran. Only that a little black boy came looking for you at the inn a bit ago. Miss Beth talked to him. Leastwise she tried. Don't speak nothin' a body can understand, that child."

"Obadiah," Curran said. It had to have been him. There was no other little black boy likely to look for him at the Posada de San Juan Bautista. "Was the lad's name Obadiah?"

"I think that's what Miss Beth called him. Course she didn't rightly understand his words, but he was a pullin' and a tuggin' at her skirt and she went with him. I said she should wait for you, or at least take me and Tom, but she said she didn't need nobody but you." Tillie sniffed, her feelings obviously bruised.

Michael shoved the strongbox into the desk and locked it. He'd located the safe behind Maria Ortega's picture, but it worked by a combination, Luz hadn't remembered to tell him. The desk would have to do.

Michael showed Tillie the door to the alley. "All you have to do is follow your nose and you'll be on Calle Fortaleza. Go back to the inn. Stay with your brother until I return with Miss Beth."

"But I ain't told you where she went," the woman protested. "I ain't—"

"I know where she went."

Michael locked the door behind her, then went out through the change hall, making himself look unconcerned and walk sedately. Once on the street he lengthened his stride and headed for the Calle Cruz. He wanted to run, but he didn't dare. There were too many eyes watching his every move. Life in San Juan was poised to explode, and he'd become one of the elements keeping the town in balance. Thank God there wasn't far to go.

In minutes he was passing the bordello. Seconds later he'd turned into the alley and broken into a run.

Michael knocked, but nobody came. He turned the handle and the door swung open. Where the hell were the three guards they'd commandeered the night before? "Samsón!" he shouted. "Beth! Where is everybody?"

"Michael. Thank God! I came as soon as I could, but I was too late to stop her. She—" Beth broke off as she hurried across the hall to his side.

Michael put his hands on her shoulders. As disturbed as he was, he noticed they were bare above the scooped neck of her gown, and her skin felt like cream. "What's happened? Are you all right?"

"I'm fine. It's Nuria."

"What's happened?" he demanded again. "Where's Samsón."

"Come. I can't explain. You have to see for yourself."

She pulled him after her, and he realized that she was leading him to the patio between the house and the bordello. In seconds he heard the noise. It was an unholy screeching and cawing and squawking. It was almost as terrifying as the drums of last night.

"The birds," he muttered. "Those damnable birds of hers."

Beth didn't reply. They were in the patio now, and the air was thick with flying creatures. Half the cages that lined the walls stood open, their former occupants swooping and darting through the air of the walled space. The unbelievably brilliant colors of the macaws and parrots and canaries and finches and mynahs were swirling around him. For a moment they prevented him from seeing anything else. Then he spied Samsón.

The old man was kneeling on the ground. Obadiah was crouched nearby, and a little farther away were the three burly youths who'd been pressed into guard duty. They were huddled in a corner, hands covering their faces, obviously terrified by the insane behavior of the birds.

"Samsón, what is it? What's happened?" Michael went closer, beating off the winged creatures that settled on his head and his shoulders and screamed their displeasure in his ears.

The old man didn't look up. Nuria lay on the ground at his feet, her body wrapped in a long black robe of some sort. He spoke only to her. "Missy Doña," he kept repeating. "Missy Doña. I tell you is *verdad* no good you come out here. But you no be gonna listen to old Samsón. Old Samsón born in chains, what he *verdad* know?"

Michael squatted. Samsón was cradling the head of his mistress in his lap. Michael could see instantly that she was dead. Her skin was pulled mask-tight across her face, her eyes closed, her lips drained of color. "What happened?" he asked.

With one finger Samsón moved the black cloth and pointed to Nuria's neck. There was a gaping wound surrounded by dried and crusting blood. Michael gasped as understanding dawned. Nuria's shoulders were covered in claw marks; the tear in her flesh had been made by a beak. She had been pecked to death. "Oh, my God," he murmured, the words torn from a closed throat. "Oh, my God . . ."

Samsón was rocking back and forth, weeping openly now. "I tell her and tell her. You *verdad* no go out there, Missy Doña. They is *verdad* strange. Maybe that bad Assunta, she put a voodoo curse on your birds. Don't you go. That blue *papagayo* he be the worst. Bad luck *verdad* come to this place when you bringed home that blue *papagayo*."

Michael wrenched his gaze from Nuria and the evidence of the unthinkable, and looked up. There seemed to be still more birds in the patio. The roof was open to the sky, but none had flown away. Suddenly he spotted the hyacinth in the screaming melee. The parrot was going purposefully from cage to cage, hanging on to the bamboo sides with its clawed feet, then lifting the latch of each with its beak.

"Great God almighty," Michael said. "If I weren't seeing it I wouldn't believe it." He got to his feet, suddenly terrified for Beth. She'd moved back and was standing a few inches inside the door to the house. Not a single bird had crossed that barrier. Michael went to her, fighting off birds at every step.

"It's that blue parrot; he's found a way to open all the cages." He had to shout into her ear to be heard over the din.

"Yes," Beth shouted back. "I've been watching him. It's incredible. Nuria, is she—"

"Yes. The birds, or at least one of them, maybe the parrot—" Michael broke off, not wanting to expose her to the full horror.

Beth clutched at his arm. "Michael, look!"

He turned back to the patio. Every cage was open now, but the freed birds were no longer reeling drunkenly through the air. They were combining into some sort of purposeful configuration.

While they watched, the pattern of flight formed a V, led by the exquisite hyacinth parrot. As a single entity the pulsing mass moved toward the place where Samsón still knelt beside Nuria's body. Obadiah was there too, face pressed to his knees, hands protecting his head. The three guards still crouched in the corner.

For breathless seconds the birds seemed to hover in mid-air—then the hyacinth swooped down, came a few inches from Nuria's prostrate form, and rose again. As one, the other birds rose with him. The vivid colors were outlined against the blue sky. The hyacinth gave a single shrill cry, and the birds soared out of sight to freedom.

• • •

"He was saying good-bye to her," Beth said. "I know it sounds insane, but I'm sure that parrot was bidding Nuria farewell."

They were in the office of the bank. It was dusk and they were alone. "Everything that's happened since yesterday sounds insane," Michael agreed. "You'd only believe it if you lived through it. I must say, you look hardly the worse for wear."

Beth wrinkled her nose. "I can't say the same for you, Michael Curran. You haven't shaved. And you smell."

"Forgive me, it's been a very long day."

After the birds flew away they'd stayed with Obadiah and Nuria's corpse while Samsón went to make arrangements for the burial. "Aren't there any authorities we should notify?" Beth had asked.

"I can't think of any. This has always been a fairly simple and primitive society. Now, with everyone expecting the Americans to land any minute, what systems there were are breaking down fast. The governor and his troops are concerned with keeping order, preventing mass hysteria or a riot. They can't worry about one woman's death."

"Her death," Beth had repeated slowly. "Was it murder, Michael?"

"Murder by whom?" His voice had betrayed his weariness and his incredulity. "A bird? How is that possible?"

"No," she had said, answering her question, not his. "It wasn't murder. I think Nuria wanted to die."

"Perhaps. She had an extraordinary relationship with the parrot. It's too long a story to tell you now. I will someday. But I don't think the hyacinth would have done anything she didn't want it to do."

That was all they'd had time for because Samsón had returned, bringing a few old women. They would prepare the body for the funeral the next day. "I tell the priest man he give Missy Doña good Christian burial. He *verdad* say he do it."

Curran's opinion of the Jesuit went up considerably when he heard that. The priest could have denied Nuria Sanchez a Catholic funeral, and no one would have protested except himself and some former slaves.

So they'd left, he and Beth. Samsón and Obadiah and the others had their own kind of grieving to do. The two foreigners were out of place. "I have to go to the bank," Michael had explained. "But I'll take you to the inn first."

"No, please," Beth had protested. "Take me with you."

So he had. Now they were in Luz's office, the only occupants in the building. "Will you want to go to the funeral tomorrow?" he asked.

"Yes, I do want to go. Michael, listen—" Beth leaned forward to take his hand, then made a face and drew back. "I'm sorry, but you really do smell frightful."

Michael chuckled. "It's not surprising. I haven't bathed properly since yesterday morning, and a lot has happened since then. There's a bathroom upstairs in Luz's apartment. I'll go in a moment. First, are you sure you want to stay here with me?"

Michael had explained that he had to remain in the bank overnight. "I've a lot of cash on hand and the way things are, a wave of looting wouldn't surprise me. Can't get the safe open; I don't have the combination. I'll get someone to break in tomorrow, then fit a new lock. Meanwhile I'd better stand guard."

"Then I'll stay with you," Beth had said. "Don't say no. I really don't want to be alone."

She repeated the same thing now. "I'm much happier here with you than I would be at the inn. Even if you are filthy. Are we going to sleep down here or upstairs?"

"Here in the office, I'm afraid. At least I have to. It's really vital that I keep my eye on the cash. It wasn't easy to come by and it averted a crisis. There's no more to be had for a while."

She eyed the narrow couch, the hard tiled floor. "Hmm, very well. The life of a banker, always protecting his money. Are you sure that's the future you want?"

"Yes." The bantering tone was gone; he was dead serious. "I'm quite sure. Not here, of course. In Córdoba. It's what I was born to, Beth. It's my inheritance, my legacy."

She nodded. What about me, she wanted to ask, but she knew it was too soon. They were slowly and painfully rebuilding the intimacy they'd once had. She wasn't sure where the bridge would lead, but she wasn't ready to destroy it before she knew.

❧ 21 ❧

SUNDAY, JULY 18, 1898
London, Two P.M.

"... in sure and certain hope of the resurrection. Amen."
The vicar closed his prayer book.

The assembled mourners mumbled their amens, embarrassed and uncomfortable, as people always were at funerals, and intensely aware of the waiting gravediggers. In a few minutes they would heap black earth over the coffin of Timothy Mendoza.

It was a large crowd. There were a great many City types and a considerable number of dignitaries, including the lord mayor of London and a representative of the prime minister. The family had also gathered in force. A dozen or so were distant Mendoza cousins and aunts and uncles, who were still Jews. If they were slightly bewildered by this Christian burial that had so little connection to them and their ancient line, it did not show. Their behavior was entirely correct. The Anglicans of the family were in the ascendant for the moment, so be it.

Caroline had come down from Westlake. She stood beside Jamie and held tight to his arm. She seemed afraid he'd tumble into the grave if she let go. The way Jamie looked, that wasn't so far-fetched. Henry stood on the opposite side of the gaping wound in the earth, next to Sara, Charles's wife. Charles had arrived from Spain the day before. Now he took a few steps nearer the grave and stared down at the coffin, a look of profound horror on his face.

Norman was slightly apart from the cluster of relations, standing very still, very erect, beside the vicar. He avoided looking at the hole in the ground or at Charles. Norman seemed unable to acknowledge either his dead son or the one that was alive. He clutched his black top hat in his hand and his knuckles were white, as if the thing were heavy and he had to exert himself to hang on to it.

Lila and Beatriz stood together a few yards from the others. Both women wore black. Lila looked stunning despite the stark simplicity of her gown and veiled hat. Beatriz seemed more foreign than usual. Her mourning clothes were heavily embroidered with jet beads and festooned with lace, accentuating her Spanishness. Lila murmured something in her ear and they started to walk away.

Sharrick had placed himself at the rear of the crowd of relatives. Now he stepped into the women's path. "Lila, I have to speak with you. It's urgent. Will you wait for me a moment?"

They hadn't seen each other since that morning in Regent's Park. She looked at him for long seconds. He couldn't read anything in her eyes; they were obscured by her black veil. Then she nodded stiffly.

"Thank you. I'll come to your carriage as soon as I can." He turned back to the gravesite.

People were shaking hands. The northern races were absurd, only one physical gesture was allowed in public and it had to serve for any occasion. The Latins were more sensible; wailing and shouting got things into the open, cleared the air. He'd never manage that though, not in his blood. No longer in the blood of this lot either. The Mendozas had put down deep roots in English soil.

Sharrick moved toward Norman and the vicar, murmuring condolences to other members of the family as he passed.

Charles spotted him and started forward, then held himself back. Sharrick nodded in his direction but didn't go any closer. His eyes were still on Norman.

The vicar drifted off to say something to Westlake and his wife. Sharrick approached Norman. "My condolences, a terrible shame really." He didn't offer to shake the other man's hand.

"What the hell are you doing here?"

"I knew the lad," Sharrick said mildly, ignoring Norman's gruffness, the hatred in his eyes. "Look, sorry to bring it up at this moment, but there's not a lot of time. I must see you. No later than this evening. Will you be at home?"

At first he didn't think Norman was going to answer. The dark Mendoza stare went on for a long time. Finally Norman nodded. "Very well, this evening. I won't be at my place. At Gordon Square. Come at nine. I'll give you fifteen minutes."

Sharrick didn't react to the imperiousness. "Very well, nine at Gordon Square. Oh, one other thing, will Charles be there?"

Norman nodded.

"Good, that's fine then. Until nine." Sharrick made his way through the throng without speaking to anyone else.

Highgate Cemetery was in a quiet north London suburb. Beyond its walls ordinary people lived ordinary lives and usually ignored the presence of the dead. Today the houses across the road all had eager faces pressed to the windows, peering at the assembled carriages of the gentry and the black feathers and ribbons that decorated the horses' manes.

Sharrick spotted Lila Curran's hired vehicle parked a short distance from the rest. The curtains weren't drawn.

He could see the outline of her broad-brimmed hat behind the window.

He went to it, his limp barely perceptible today because the weather was fine and had been all weekend. She rolled down the window and leaned toward him, saying nothing.

"Good of you to wait," Sharrick said.

"What is it, Fergus?"

"A great deal has happened, is happening." He turned for a moment, looking over his shoulder at the mourners now streaming through the gate. "This sad business can't hold everything up. It's too late."

"I know that. Besides, I'm here because it's expected of me. I'm not pretending to be in deep mourning."

Sharrick peered past Lila to the other woman in the carriage. Beatriz Mendoza was leaning against the seat, watching him and her sister-in-law. He'd never met her and she didn't acknowledge his presence now. Like Lila, Beatriz wore a veil. He couldn't see her face but it didn't matter. He knew she had been party to the whole thing from the first. "We can't talk here," he said. The street was rapidly filling with people leaving the cemetery. "I'll come to the hotel in half an hour."

"No," Lila protested. Her voice was breathy, distraught. "I don't want—"

"Half an hour," Sharrick repeated. "Otherwise you could lose everything you've worked for."

Lila bit her lip, started to shake her head, then stopped. Her heart was beating like some idiotic schoolgirl's. "Half an hour then," she whispered. "At the Connaught."

"No, no, no," Lila said, her hands clenched into fists. "You can't."

"I can," Sharrick insisted. "Moreover, I must. Lila, in the name of God, don't you see what you're doing?"

"I see that you're undoing everything I've tried to achieve. Now, when victory is almost in my hands." She opened them, held them out to him palms upward. "I have them all right here, Fergus. Don't take them away. I beg you."

He wanted to go to her, take her in his arms, but Beatriz was in the room with them, sitting beside the window. She'd said nothing for nearly an hour, but Sharrick was very conscious of her presence. He stayed where he was, in the little chair across from the sofa. "Lila, what you don't seem to realize is that you've won. Michael is in complete control in Puerto Rico. Norman's known that since the cable reached him Friday afternoon."

"You're sure about that cable?" she asked hesitantly.

"Very sure. I told you, my source in Norman's house is impeccable. One of the servants. The man can read and write, thank God. He copied the entire text for me. You're looking at it."

Lila picked up the paper Sharrick had given her earlier and read it again. "Do you know anything about Michael returning to London?"

"No more than you do. You know I've no source of intelligence on the island."

She nodded, then pressed her hands to her temples as if she were in pain.

Beatriz got up and poured a small glass of brandy from the bottle on the sideboard. "Here, *mi niña,* drink this, you'll feel better. May I give you another, your lordship?"

"Thank you, that's most kind." Sharrick held out his empty snifter and she filled it half-full, then took one for herself.

"Elizabeth, the wife of Timothy," Beatriz said as she returned to her chair by the window. "She was—how do you put it in English?—conspicuous by her absence."

"Yes," Sharrick agreed. "That's how we put it."

Lila was sipping her brandy; she didn't say anything. Sharrick turned to her again. "My dear, it has to be the way I've outlined it. For your son's sake as well as for—" He stopped speaking.

"For what? What were you going to say, Fergus? For mine?"

"Yes, that's what I had in mind."

"You're wrong. Oh, if only you weren't such a strong-minded bull, Fergus. If only I could convince you of what the Mendozas owe me." She looked guiltily at Beatriz as soon as she uttered the words.

Beatriz shrugged. "Me, I don't think I owe you anything, Lila darling. And you certainly had payment from Juan Luis before you left." She sat back against the brocaded cushions of the chair. "How many millions was it, *mi niña*? I've never known exactly."

"The equivalent of two million sterling in cash. And I've invested it quite well." It wasn't necessary to be sparing with the facts, not any longer. "Plus the million pound bond."

"And Michael," Beatriz added. "Juan Luis let you take your son, don't forget that. And the medallion of course. That's the thing that has always amazed me the most. You left with Michael and with the medallion."

"He had no choice." Lila spat out the words. "If Juan Luis could have done anything else, I'd still be locked in that room. Probably chained to the bed like a dog." Her voice was rising with every word. "Chained, do you understand?" She put her hands to her neck. "With a collar around my throat, like an animal." She began to shake and she covered her face with her hands.

This time Sharrick went to her, no longer caring what Beatriz thought. He sat beside her, took her in his arms. "Lila, if you keep the memory alive, allow it to torment you, then Juan Luis has won after all. Don't you see that? Sweet God, lass, you've got to see it."

"How did you do it?" The words exploded from Beatriz; unable to suppress them any longer. "You said you'd tell me when it was over. When we'd won. Well, we have, and I still don't know."

Sharrick didn't share the Spanish woman's curiosity. His

concern was with Lila's future, not her past. But maybe this
was a way out. Maybe if she could be made to tell the whole
tale for once it would finally be finished for her. "Doña
Beatriz has a point," he said, his face against her hair. "Tell
us what happened. Tell us how you got away."

A few seconds passed, then Lila pulled out of his arms
and went to the desk in the corner of the room. "I always
keep this with me. Wherever I am, always. This letter came
from Puerto Rico, and . . . God, how can I explain? The whole
thing is so strange, so—" Again she stopped speaking, but
she handed Sharrick the envelope.

He saw that it was addressed to her in Córdoba. It wasn't
sealed. Sharrick withdrew the pages. There were many of
them, each covered with large, childish writing. The paper
was beginning to yellow at the edges. "Do you mean me to
read this?"

"Yes. I think—no, don't." She snatched it back. "I'll tell
you. I can quote it word for word. Word for word," she
repeated softly. She sat down again, the letter still clutched
in her fingers, a white square against the black silk of her
gown.

Beatriz leaned forward, peering at the envelope. "I remember that. The day it came I was in the Patio del Recibo.
That's our entrance court," she said quickly to Sharrick. "I
was there and so was Michael. It was a coincidence. Nothing
but that. I—"

"It wasn't a coincidence," Lila interrupted. "Nothing that
happened was an accident. It was all planned."

"By whom?"

"I don't know. It doesn't matter. I only know that everything was planned. Michael, he—"

"'Don't tell Papa, Tía Beatriz,' that's what he said," the
other woman interrupted. "'Don't tell Papa. Mama won't
have her letter if you do.'"

"He was right. Juan Luis never would have given it to
me." Lila turned to her sister-in-law. "Those days, the things

he was doing to me, what did you think? For God's sake, why didn't you do something?"

"I couldn't, you know that. Juan Luis controlled everything, every centimo we lived on. And he was mad. My brother was insane with jealousy, not in his right mind. Francisco said . . ." She shrugged hopelessly.

Lila leaned back, weariness and memory etching deep lines in her face. "I know. Forget I asked, Beatriz. I've never blamed you. There was nothing you could do."

"One thing only. I let Michael into the patio below your room. So he could climb up to the balcony and get in."

Lila nodded. "That's another thing I hate Juan Luis for. That my son saw me like that. A prisoner . . ."

"The letter," Sharrick prompted gently, afraid that he'd made things worse by encouraging her to remember all this. "What did the letter say?"

Lila spoke softly, as if in a dream. "The letter told the story of what happened. How Moses the Apostate made all the Mendozas of Córdoba Muslims."

"In the twelfth century!" Beatriz burst out. "That happened seven hundred years ago. But you say Juan Luis cared so much he—"

"Be quiet." Lila sounded as if she were in a trance. "Be quiet and I'll tell you. It wasn't Moses, it was his grandson, Ishmael ibn Mohammad."

"There was a ruler of the house named Ishmael once. I remember being told about him. He disappeared and—"

Lila cut her off. "He was murdered—" she paused, "by his own flesh and blood."

"No, that's not what happened." Beatriz pressed her hands to her forehead and tried to remember the story. It was but one of many Mendoza legends she had heard. "It was something to do with the *Reconquista,* the time when the Christian Spaniards from the north took back Córdoba. There was a battle. That's how this Ishmael died."

"There was a battle," Lila agreed. "But it wasn't the way

you heard it. Ishmael signed his death warrant years earlier, when he decided that the family must have a Jewish heir. The Christians hated the Moors, but for a time they were tolerant of the Jews. So Ishmael wanted to change back. But it wasn't easy. There was a fanatic Muslim sect in control of Córdoba then."

"Yes, so you told me. The Shi'a. Because of them Moses became a Muslim, so the Mendozas wouldn't have to leave Córdoba."

"Yes. But fifty years later Ishmael decided it was time to undo what Moses had done."

Sharrick got the brandy bottle and refilled all their glasses. "Tell us, Lila. What did this Ishmael do? You said he signed his own death warrant."

"He did. He wanted a Jewish son, so he kidnapped Miriam bat Yakov, a beautiful young girl who lived in Toledo. And on the journey back to Córdoba he raped her. That way her father wouldn't try to get her back. She wasn't a virgin anymore so she was worthless. Ishmael paid her family a bride price and he married her."

"She was a Jew, this Miriam?" Sharrick asked.

"Yes, of course, that's why her son would be one. And in the Palacio Mendoza she continued to live like a Jew, at least in the secret apartments where Ishmael hid her. She had her own slaves, her own food—everything. All the same, at first she hated Ishmael. Eventually she loved him."

"She could forgive him for kidnapping her and raping her?" Beatriz murmured.

"She had good reason. Ishmael was very clever." Lila paused, looked once at Fergus, then continued. "He was a magnificent lover. Miriam became drugged with him. Besotted. Besides, she gave birth to a son that first year. They named him Daniel. Miriam loved her son. Do you know how hard that is? To love the son and hate the father?"

Lila paused, but neither Sharrick nor Beatriz replied. "I can tell you that it is a torment," Lila whispered. "A torment.

So because of Daniel, Miriam let herself love Ishmael. Then he betrayed her again."

The room was warm and very still. Sharrick and Beatriz listened, not interrupting now, completely captivated by Lila's story.

"When Daniel was a year old Miriam was expecting another child. Ishmael had always slept beside her in the secret apartment. Then one night he said he would not return for some time. He told her he was going to marry again, take a second wife the way the Muslims do. Miriam went mad with grief. She got a knife and—"

"*Ay mi Dio!*" Beatriz whispered. "She murdered him."

"No. She cut herself. Her face and her breasts and her legs. And she slashed open her belly so the child she was expecting would die too."

Sharrick had withdrawn to the shadows of the room, listening to the story, watching the two women. Despite the warmth, Beatriz had forgotten to fan herself. Her eyes were huge with astonishment as she leaned forward, hanging on Lila's words.

"The child did die, but Miriam didn't. She was horribly disfigured though, covered with scars. One eye wouldn't open, and one side of her face wouldn't move. She couldn't walk without dragging one leg. She was repulsive; no one could look at her. Ishmael left her entirely alone after that. And when Daniel was seven years old Ishmael sent him to Barcelona where there were Mendoza cousins who were still Jews because the Moors had never conquered that far north.

"Twelve years later everything Ishmael had been afraid of was on the verge of happening. The Christians were about to reclaim Córdoba. So he brought Daniel back from Barcelona. The boy thought of himself as a Jew, but he didn't reject his Muslim father. And naturally he wanted to see his mother. But he couldn't; Miriam had managed to hang herself three years before.

For eight months father and son were always in each

other's company. Ishmael wondered if Daniel nursed re-
sentments because of Miriam, but the boy never mentioned
her name. Instead he learned everything his father could tell
him about the family's business, their investments, who were
their enemies and who their friends. Oh, Daniel was very
clever.

"When he wasn't with his father, Daniel walked around
the city, getting to know it. Those were terrible times. Córdoba was under seige. People were starving. Daniel found
out about a plot to smuggle two Christian spies inside the
walls. The plotters only wanted to lift the seige so the people
could live. Daniel had reasons of his own.

"He was the one who opened one of the gates and let
the spies in. Two nights later the Christians attacked, and
thanks to Daniel Mendoza they knew everything about the
city's defenses, they almost won. Ishmael didn't know what
his son had done, but he knew it was only a matter of time
before the walls of Córdoba would fall.

"He'd already made his plans. Months before he'd sent
three of his brothers and their families to Cairo to find a
home. The only Muslim Mendozas left in Córdoba were
Ishmael, his two Arab wives, and their seven children, five
boys and two girls. Ishamel told them to get ready. They
would take slaves and horses and as much gold as they
could carry, and flee to Egypt and safety.

"By this time Daniel was completely in his father's confidence. He helped Ishmael plan the route he would follow
between Córdoba and Cairo. A few days later word came
that more Christian troops were arriving and Ishmael and
his family started on their journey.

"The next morning Daniel sent word to the Christian
lines, and after dark he met again with the soldier he'd
helped to smuggle inside the walls. 'My father left last night
with his wives and children. He is going to Cairo,' he told
him.

"At first the soldier didn't understand. 'Why do you tell me?'

"Daniel told him about Ishmael's gold and about the women and the children. 'They have many jewels. And two of the children are girls, young and virginal. They would bring an excellent price in the slave market.'

"'You speak of your father, your sisters,' the Christian said.

"'My half-sisters. Yes, I do. I also have here a map of their route.'

"The soldier shook his head, 'I don't understand your kind, I never will. You mean me to follow and kill them all, don't you?'

"Daniel said that was exactly what he wanted. 'Except the women. You may kill them or have them or sell them, as you wish. But if you bring me the heads of my father and my half-brothers, I will pay you well. And you may keep whatever you take from them.'

"The Christian refused to shake Daniel's hand, but the bargain was made.

"Ten days later the two met again. Córdoba belonged to the Christians by then. The soldier went to the Palacio Mendoza with two of his men. They carried a wicker basket. There was a stench so horrible Daniel had to cover his nose with a linen handkerchief. 'Show me,' he demanded.

"The men lifted the lid of the basket and four terrible souvenirs tumbled to the ground at Daniel's feet. Ishmael's eyes were open and his mouth drawn back in a horrible grimace. His three sons had similar expressions of terror frozen on their dead faces. The necks were evidence of the butchering, jagged things of hacked bone and bloody rotting flesh. Daniel simply looked and nodded. Then he handed over a sack of ducats that stood as tall as the soldier's knee.

"That night Daniel didn't sleep. He wandered through the palace. Finally he went to the apartments where his mother had lived, to the room where they'd told him she'd died. 'It is done,' he said. '*Aleha ha-shalom*, Miriam. Rest in peace.'"

Lila stopped speaking. The silence in the room was total, even the noise of the street beyond the windows seemed to have disappeared.

"It's a terrible story," Sharrick said finally. "Incredible."

"But it explains nothing." Frustration made Beatriz's voice shrill. "Because you knew all this Juan Luis let you go and—"

"No," Lila interrupted. "It was because he was, as you said, mad. And evil. And because I knew where the bodies were buried."

"The bodies?" Beatriz leaned forward. "Lila, are you telling me that you knew where Ishmael—" She broke off, shuddering.

"That and something else. On the last page of the letter"— Lila caressed the envelope with one finger—"she told me that it was Juan Luis who had arranged his own father's death."

Beatriz gasped. "No, he could not! My father died when his horse threw him—"

Lila turned to her, at last telling the secret she had kept so long. "How? Why? Rafael was an excellent horseman, you know that is true. But when your brother was a child of nine, the streak of evil was already there in him. The bad seed that sometimes flowers among the Mendozas was planted in Juan Luis. He was angry because his father had denied him something he wanted. I don't know what, some childish thing. So Juan Luis hid in the bushes along his father's route with a slingshot, and when Rafael came close his son jumped into the road and shot a rock into the face of the horse. Naturally the creature reared up, then bolted. As luck would have it—Juan Luis's luck, not his father's—Rafael was thrown and broke his neck and died."

For some seconds Beatriz said nothing. "My mother told me she removed the half medallion from my father's neck with her own hands, before they prepared the body for burial. She herself gave it to Juan Luis."

"Don't you see?" Lila demanded. "She didn't know. Only the woman who wrote me the letter knew. She told me and I told Juan Luis. 'You murdered your own father,' I told him. 'Do you think if that becomes known you will be forgiven? Do you think your enormous wealth can buy you the respect of your peers when they find out about your patricide?'"

Lila's voice was soft and almost musical; she crooned the words. They were a love song of sorts, the melody which had brought her freedom. "At first Juan Luis pretended he didn't care and told me I could prove nothing. But I had proof, I told him so. 'There is an old arch in the wine cellar. It's been walled up for years, but behind the wall there is proof.'

"I kept tormenting Juan Luis with that. He didn't know how I knew any of it, but he couldn't stop himself from listening. All that night he kept coming back to me, asking more questions. Finally he unlocked my door and we went down to the wine cellar together. We found the arch, and Juan Luis took a sledge hammer and knocked down the old wall. All by himself. He was too frightened of what he would find to let any servant do it."

Lila paused again, her face composed and still now, remembering.

"What was there?" Beatriz whispered, demanding to know it all.

"The heads of Ishmael and his sons. In a wicker basket. The way the mercenary had brought them to Daniel. They were skeletons, of course, but still you could see how horribly they died . . ."

"And the story about my poor father, could you prove as well that Juan Luis murdered him?" Beatriz was rocking back and forth, comforting herself with rhythmic movement like a child.

Lila shook her head. "No, in reality I could not, but Juan Luis didn't know that. I had given him proof that the first story was true, so he assumed I had some way of exposing his own crime as well."

"Whoever sent you this letter," Beatriz exploded. "She must be a witch."

"That's what Juan Luis said. Only he didn't know about the letter. I'd managed to hide it. He thought I was the witch. 'You're a witch! A witch! I cannot have you in my house.'" Lila laughed softly. "His brain was so addled he was as terrified and superstitious as an old woman. He was terrified that all Spain would know he had murdered his own father, and they would believe it because it had happened before. Because they would know about the heads in the basket in the wine cellar of the Palacio Mendoza."

Sharrick spoke for the first time in many minutes. "He had an option, didn't he? Right then your husband could have chosen to kill you and leave you with the corpses and wall up the wine cellar again."

"Yes," Lila admitted. "That was the risk I took. But these days it's a little more difficult to make someone disappear and be asked no questions. Even in Spain. Even for a Mendoza. I had decided to take the chance because it was the only one I had."

"So he let you go and gave you the money, and Michael, and the medallion." Beatriz was fanning herself again, breaking the spell of her sister-in-law's words.

"That's right."

"But that wasn't enough revenge for you?"

"It might have been," Lila admitted. "If he hadn't put it in his will that Michael should never have Córdoba. That was the final injury. I could never forgive him for that."

"You're right," Sharrick said. "You shouldn't have forgiven him. You didn't. You've had your revenge."

"Yes." Lila turned to him, eyes blazing as they had been before. "But now you want to take it all away."

"No. I'm going to make it sweeter."

"What do you mean?"

Sharrick crossed to her, took both her hands in his. "I'm going to give you the ultimate pleasure of keeping them alive. Lila, isn't your frustration now caused by the fact that Juan Luis is dead? What do you think will happen to Jamie and the others if you strip them as thoroughly as you mean to do?"

"I don't know. I don't care."

"Yes, you do. At the funeral today, you saw the way they looked. Jamie particularly. They'll die, Lila. Sooner rather than later. The Mendozas have become hothouse plants. They can't survive without the insulation of their wealth. If you allow me to do what I want, they'll be around for a good many years yet. They'll have the things that money buys, but not the power. The power will all still be there, but beyond their reach. Tantalizingly close, but denied them. Forever."

He stopped speaking and watched her. He could see her waiver, struggle against giving in, then waiver again. "And there's Michael," Sharrick added softly. "If you do it my way, your son will be much safer in Córdoba."

He saw the glimmer of change, of agreement in her eyes. Finally Lila nodded.

The lovely house in Gordon Square was full of people, all speaking softly, sitting in various rooms and helping themselves to nuts and fruits and glasses of wine. Lila had told Sharrick what to expect. "It's the Jewish way. Even the ones who think of themselves as Christians still do it. When there's a death the family all mourn in one house. Everyone comes to see them there."

Lord Westlake's butler took Sharrick's card, glanced at it, and placed it on the foyer table along with dozens of others. "The immediate family are in the small sitting room, milord. The others are in the drawing room and the library and the morning room."

"Thank you. I'll pay my respects to his lordship first, if I may."

The butler nodded and led the way. "Sharrick of Glencree," he announced as he opened the door.

What they called the small sitting room was really quite large, and beautifully decorated in tones of pink and red. Norman was sitting beside Charles, on a small red velvet sofa. He looked at Sharrick with pure malevolence. Charles started to rise. His father put out his hand in a quick gesture and the young man sat down again. Sharrick looked for Jamie, spotted him sitting in a corner, his wife on the hassock beside him, holding his hand. God, the man looked terrible.

Sharrick went to him. "My condolences," he murmured.

Jamie looked at him vaguely. He didn't seem to remember who Sharrick was, certainly not the article in the *Times*. "Thank you, good of you to come. Have some sherry. Or whiskey if you prefer." Jamie tried to stand up but he couldn't muster the strength. "My dear . . ."

"Of course." Caroline patted his hand. "I'll see to it." She got up and led Sharrick to a table where a footman was standing. "What can we offer you?"

"Sherry, thank you. A Mendoza fino if you have it."

"I'm sure we do." She smiled, but she looked as if she'd been weeping. Not for Tim most likely. It was her husband and her own future the woman was crying over, not her nephew. Still, Sharrick felt sorry for her.

She took the sherry from the footman and handed it to him. Sharrick murmured his thanks, conscious of Norman's eyes on his back.

Caroline drifted off in the direction of her husband. Sharrick stood where he was. A few more people came into the room, but over the hum of chatter he didn't catch the butler's announcement of their names. The newcomers surrounded

Jamie, then moved to Norman. The paterfamilias before the blood father. It wasn't surprising.

He sipped his wine and waited. Somewhere a clock struck nine. Norman detached himself from a cluster of people and came toward him. "Nine o'clock, that's what I said. Come with me."

"I think perhaps Charles should be with us."

"I'll decide that after I hear what you have to say."

They left the sitting room and walked down a long corridor that led to the back of the house. The sumptuous carpet muffled their footfalls, the buzz of talk faded as they penetrated deeper into the private wing.

"In here, it's Jamie's study. We won't be disturbed." Norman opened the door but didn't wait for Sharrick to go ahead of him. It was Sharrick who closed the door.

"Well, what do you want?"

"To give you a hand, get you out of the mess you're in."

Norman laughed mirthlessly. "I'd say you'd already meddled quite enough in my affairs."

"Perhaps. But it's not over yet."

"What's not over? The failure of the Paraguayan issue started the rot and you're responsible for that. Now Tim . . . I don't think things would have turned out like this if Tim hadn't been involved in your plots and schemes."

"I hope that's not true," Sharrick said softly. "I don't want any blood on my hands."

"No blood? Look, you bastard, I've just said—"

"You're talking about money. It's not the same. Though I admit plenty of blood is spilled over it."

Norman dismissed the comment with a gesture. "I don't want to stand here and chat with you. What have you come for? Tell me and get it over with."

"I have told you. I'm prepared to see you out of your present difficulties. At least the worst of them."

"Meaning?"

"Meaning I'll arrange security for the five million the Bank of England's putting up."

Norman stared at him. "What did you say?"

"What you heard. I'll back the Bank of England's loan. There'll be no need for you and your brothers to sell your private holdings. No need to change your personal lives at all."

"I don't understand. The other day I had to squeeze five hundred thousand out of you. Now you're saying—"

"I'm saying that things are not the same today as they were the other day," Sharrick said softly. "But if we're going to continue this conversation, I must insist that your son Charles join us."

Norman stared at him for a few seconds. "Wait here," he said finally. "I'll get him."

Once he was alone Sharrick took the chair Norman hadn't offered him. This too was a lovely room, mostly dark woods and green leather, the only other color was provided by the matched bindings of the many books. Westlake had exquisite taste, you had to give him that. There were a series of paintings of horses on the wall behind the desk. Stubbs, no doubt about it. And he'd noticed a Rubens in the sitting room. Empty out this house and you'd go a long way to raising the capital the Bank of England demanded. But you'd kill the former owners.

Norman returned with Charles. He was carrying a bottle and three glasses. "Here," he said ungraciously, handing Sharrick a schooner of sherry. "Now you've got Charles and you've got a drink. So perhaps you'll tell me what's going on."

"With pleasure, but first—cheers." Sharrick toasted the other two men. They merely nodded in reply. Charles was pale, his forehead beaded with sweat. Sharrick decided it was time to put the young man out of his misery. He turned to Norman. "I've already had one private meeting with your son. Have you told your father about our little chat, Charles?"

Charles shook his head.

Norman swiveled to look at his son, then turned back to the Irishman. "More treachery, Sharrick?"

"No. More contingency plans to save your house."

"My affairs are none of your da—" Norman broke off, remembering that an offer of five million pounds was on the table. "What did you two talk about?" His voice was lower, more controlled.

"The future of Mendozas. I told Charles the house was going to topple, that the only possibility of survival would be to form a new limited company. I also said that he should prepare himself to be at the head of it."

Norman turned to his son. "Why didn't you report all this to me?"

"There wasn't time, Father. His lordship and I met right before you sent me to Córdoba. Besides, I didn't believe it would happen as he described."

"That's true," Sharrick said mildly. "He didn't. But he did indicate that he'd be willing to take over when the time came. It's come."

"For the sake of the house, Father." Charles spoke quietly, his confidence seeming to grow with every second. "I wasn't interested in pushing you or my uncles out. But if what his lordship said was true, then I'd no choice but to save Mendozas—whatever that required."

Norman stared at Charles for some seconds. Finally he nodded. He turned to Sharrick, hesitated, then made up his mind. "You seem to know a great deal. I presume it includes Ransom's terms?"

"Yes. That you and your brothers resign. But that doesn't include Charles. If you form a limited company, he can be put in charge; he's not a senior partner so he's untainted by the present mess. Besides, there's no one else. It will take time to restore the City's confidence in Mendozas, but it can be done. Barings has done it."

"Yes, I know that. We all do. We don't need you to tell

us any of this. The papers of the new company are being drawn right now. Charles is named as director."

"Good, good. But the capital to start operations . . ." Sharrick let the words trail away.

"We have capital. It's not really as black as Hammersmith and Ransom have insisted it is." Norman leaned forward, almost his old self again. "Listen to me, Sharrick. If you're really interested in making this big a loan, if you're able to make it, we can stop the whole thing before it goes any further. I don't need those fools, Ransom and the rest. I can—"

"No," Sharrick said simply. "No, that's not what I have in mind."

"Why not? It's because of her, isn't it? Lila Curran's got her fingers in this. You're in league with her."

"You might call it that. I plan to marry her." He turned from Norman to Charles. "I'm about to trust you with something that you can, if you wish, use against my wishes. I promise that if you do, I will bury you so thoroughly and so deeply that Mendozas will never crawl out of the hole. Never. Do you understand me?"

Charles nodded. "I'm sure I do."

"Now look here—" Norman tried to interject.

"Be quiet. You're no longer in charge. Your son is." Sharrick took some papers from his pocket and handed them to the younger man. "Take your time. I want to be sure you're clear about the terms."

Charles looked at Sharrick, then unfolded the documents. He read silently for a few minutes; finally he looked up. His father was staring at him, but Charles concentrated all his attention on Lord Sharrick of Glencree. "I have power of attorney on this account?"

"That's correct."

"What account?" Norman demanded. "What the hell are you two—"

"This is notice of a deposit account with the Bank of

Ireland, Father. They're holding five million sterling for his lordship. I've power of attorney."

"I made the arrangements last month," Sharrick said. "It took some doing, investments that had to be changed, that sort of thing, but I managed to get all the documents to Dublin." A vision of young Donald O'Leary flashed into his mind. Too bad he'd tried and failed with the boy who had unwittingly helped him make all this possible.

"Everything's in order as of yesterday," he continued after only a second's pause. "Five million in cash. There's also a note signed by me which says part of the funds—as much as two million in any calendar year—may be used in support of the activities of Mendozas Limited. With that and with what the syndicate's loaned you, you can tell Mr. Ransom that the Bank of England funds are not required. So there's no need to have a fire sale. Everything can go on as it has."

"In our personal lives," Norman said softly, repeating the phrase Sharrick had used earlier.

"Exactly. It won't bring your son back, but it will lift a lot of the gloom from this house I think."

Norman nodded. He was beaten and he knew it. The fight had gone out of him. At least for the time being. "Yes, it will. The others, Henry and Jamie, they only want a quiet life. They were in the bank because it was expected of them. Me, I—" He stopped speaking.

Sharrick nodded. He knew that Norman was going to say he loved the business of business. Lila's revenge was more complete than she knew. "One other thing," he said. "This matter of the Russians withdrawing their deposits with the house here and in Spain..." Sharrick's voice trailed away. Both Mendoza men looked at him expectantly.

It was Norman who spoke first. "That was a lie, wasn't it? A false trail?"

Sharrick nodded.

"I thought so from the first," Norman murmured. "But I couldn't afford to..." He let the words die and shrugged.

It was too late now—from his point of view, too late for everything.

"Sharrick," Charles said. "I've one more question."

The father's strength seemed to be flowing into the son. Charles seemed to be coming to terms with his own guilts and opportunities. His voice was firmer, the look in his eyes more direct. "Do you expect to own any part of Mendozas because of this?"

"No. I'll expect to be paid interest on my money, but that's all. Oh, there's one other—"

"Córdoba," Charles supplied.

"That's correct. Córdoba. Your cousin Michael gets what's rightfully his or I cancel everything."

Charles smiled. "That's already taken care of. As my father explained, the papers for the reorganization are already being drawn up. I cabled Michael in Puerto Rico yesterday afternoon."

Norman gasped. "You didn't! You had no right."

"I'm sorry, Father. I not only had the right, I had the responsibility. Francisco doesn't want to stay, and besides, he's incompetent. I have his signed resignation, exactly as you instructed. And choosing a replacement for him is now my obligation."

Charles turned to Sharrick again. "I'm going to propose we also adjust the legal structure of the Banco Mendoza in Spain. That way there will be no difficulties made about Juan Luis's will."

Sharrick smiled and nodded. He wondered if Charles remembered who had first suggested that to him. It didn't matter. The young man was growing in stature by the minute. He'd fit the Mendoza cloak soon enough. That's what would enable him to live with whatever responsibility he bore for Tim's death, that was the Mendoza legacy. Lila's story was one more example. Spill any blood you must as long as it protects the house. Yes, he decided, Charles would do fine.

✣ 22 ✣

TUESDAY, JULY 20, 1898
San Juan, Three P.M.

Michael stood on the balcony outside his room and watched the *Arabella* steam out of the harbor. He knew Luz was aboard; the man had managed to get a message to him this morning. He was glad of it. He'd never had any quarrel with the banker. "Good luck to you," he murmured aloud. "I hope New York lives up to your expectations."

He went inside, leaving the balcony door open in hope of a breeze. The afternoon was stifling, airless. He'd not minded the heat of the morning in the bank; he'd been too busy and too full of his own thoughts and plans to notice it. Now he was conscious of the sweat pouring down his chest and his back.

Michael stripped off his sodden shirt and flung it into a corner. He poured water from the jug into the basin and splashed it over his face and shoulders, then slipped the leather thong of the medallion over his head and grasped the half-moon of gold in his hand. He stretched out on the bed and studied it.

If I forget thee, O Jerusalem, may my right hand forget her cunning. That was the whole motto, but it had been engraved on the full circle. He'd always wondered which of the words were written on his half, but he couldn't read Hebrew so he didn't know.

Would he have to learn Hebrew to be a Jew? He didn't know that either. He did know about being circumcized, though, and had been worrying about that for weeks. Michael laughed aloud. A small enough price to pay—a bit of his prick in return for a kingdom. Not even a vital bit. He'd checked with a doctor in Dublin and been told it wouldn't affect his performance. So Beth...

Sweet God, what was he going to do about Beth? She was sleeping in her room down the hall now, exhausted by the tumultuous events of the past four days. First that terrible night of voodoo and the zombie, or whatever he'd been. Then Nuria's horrific death and her small, strange funeral.

The mourners had comprised Beth and Michael and the whores and Samsón and Obadiah, and some black people and Indians he didn't know. They had gathered in one corner of the darkened church while the Jesuit performed his rites and rituals with an elegance and calm that comforted even the nonbelievers. But afterward, when they followed the coffin up the aisle, Michael had noticed Devega standing in the shadows in the rear. He'd liked that, the governor general arriving silently to pay his last respects. Nuria would have liked it too.

Then, when he thought things were settling down, the world beyond the island reminded him of all that remained to be settled. The message came in the form of two cables received within thirty-six hours of each other.

The first arrived on Saturday afternoon and it was in code. Michael had stared at it, totally frustrated. Luz had known the code, but Michael's ostracization from the family insured that he did not.

"The safe," Beth had suggested. "Señor Luz must have kept a codebook in the safe."

"By God, you're right girl! My brain's turning to cotton wool these days, but not yours."

Michael had forced the safe open. "I can have a new one installed," he'd said, breathing hard as he applied all his weight to the crowbar he'd wedged into the door. "Better than—There, that's got it. Damned thing shouldn't have sprung so easily. A new one's a good idea."

There wasn't much inside—Luz had apparently taken anything of monetary value—but they'd found the code-book. He and Beth had sat side by side at the desk, laboriously translating each word. Michael's heart was pounding with excitement by the time they were halfway through.

NEW LIMITED COMPANY BEING FORMED HERE STOP MYSELF AS HEAD STOP APPRECIATE YOUR PROMPT ACTION PUERTO RICO STOP SUGGEST YOU LOCATE NEW MANAGER FOR BRANCH OR CLOSE SAME DEPENDING LOCAL CONDITIONS STOP IMPORTANT WE . . .

"They're offering me Córdoba," Michael had said, reading over the partially decoded message. "They have to be."

Beth had been very pale, her voice subdued. "Yes, I imagine you're right."

"What is it? What's wrong? Córdoba's what I've wanted all along. It's what I've been working to get."

"I know."

"But you're miserable about it, why?"

"Not about Córdoba." She'd looked again at the cable. They hadn't yet decoded the signature.

Michael's glance had followed hers. "It's Tim, isn't it? You think this is going to turn out to be from him."

"I'm not sure. There's something I haven't told you."

"What? For the love of heaven, Beth, there's no time for more secrets and intrigues. Not now, not between us."

"I know. I'm ashamed of myself for not telling you sooner.

I was going to, but you weren't speaking to me when it
came, then everything—"

"When what came?"

"This cable. It arrived last Thursday." She'd taken the
thing from her pocket and handed it to him. "I'm sure it's
from your mother. She's the only L.C. I can think of. Besides,
she's the only one who could have figured out where to find
me."

Michael read the message about Tim's accident and the
suggestion that Beth return. "Did you consider going?"

"No, not for a moment. I'm sorry Timmy's been hurt,
but I never intended to go back to him. I'm sure your mother
thinks I will, that you're just a passing fancy. But she's
wrong."

He'd put his hand over hers. "I know that. Let's finish
decoding this cable, shall we? Then at least we'll know who
sent it."

It took twenty minutes more to get to the end of the
message.

. . . MEET LONDON SOON AS POSSIBLE AND DISCUSS
DISPOSITION OF CORDOBA STOP PRESUME YOU ARE
WILLING TO ASSUME RESPONSIBILITY THERE STOP
PLEASE ADVISE IN CODE STOP SIGNED CHARLES MEN-
DOZA.

"Charles," Beth had said. "Then Timmy must be—"

"Not necessarily. Charles is the elder brother. It's logical
that—"

She'd shaken her head. "No, if you know Timmy it's not
logical. He can run rings around Charles, always. And Norman prefers him. Timmy and his father don't always like
each other, but underneath they're two of a kind. Poor
Timmy," she murmured. "Poor Timmy."

Then, late Sunday night, the mystery was solved. Another
cable, this one for Beth and written in plain English.

REGRET INFORM YOU TIMOTHY DIED FRIDAY STOP
BURIED SUNDAY AFTERNOON STOP.

There was no signature.

"My mother again?" Michael had looked puzzled.

Beth shook her head. "Somehow I don't think your
mother would rush to inform me I was a widow. She doesn't
approve of me. And now there's one less obstacle to—"
She'd blushed and stopped speaking.

Michael wanted to finish the sentence for her. One less
obstacle to our being together. He didn't dare. Because the
biggest obstacle of all remained, and thinking about it was
tearing him apart. Instead he had said, "Sorry about Tim."

"So am I. Truly sorry. He wasn't a bad man, not really.
It was Norman who made him the way he was, made him
think he must always fight to be first. But I won't pretend
to be a grieving widow. We were never truly married. Not
the way I think marriage should be," she added softly.

"What do you think it should be?" Michael was half-
afraid of her answer but unable to stop himself from asking
the question.

"A partnership, two people sharing their lives and their
goals. Children." She'd paused. "Timmy never wanted children. He always made sure I wouldn't have any."

"Why not?" Michael had been startled. "That's not normal. Besides, if he meant to take over Mendozas he'd have
needed an heir."

"Yes, I know. I said that to him a few times. 'I don't want
to share you,' that's what he kept saying. 'I don't want you
fat and ugly.'" She'd looked hard at him. "Michael, do you
think a pregnant lady is ugly?"

"No, not at all. If it's your child she's expecting, then . . ."

Beth had waited for him to finish what he was saying, to
open the floodgates to the future they must speak of soon.
He'd said nothing more and all Monday the topic had been
between them, a tinderbox waiting for a spark.

Yet they were happy together. For the first time in weeks it was the way it used to be. Michael sure of himself, overjoyed with the success of everything he'd planned, Beth sharing his mood, laughing with him. Monday had been a good day, despite the shadows that lingered in the backs of both their minds.

Now, lying on the bed, the medallion still in his hand, Michael groaned. He had to face facts soon. What he needed to do was clear enough. Put the bank here in competent hands and get on the next ship for London. The second problem wasn't one he could solve. He simply had to wait. According to Briggs there wasn't another ship expected in port for at least five days. Maybe not then if the Americans came first. But the bank was different. Michael had made up his mind about the bank.

His watch was on the table beside the bed. He glanced at it, nearly four. Late enough.

Michael pushed open the door with the crude painting of the rooster. The Taverna El Gallo was deserted except for Rosa's son Pedro behind the bar, and one man at the far end. The customer was drinking purposefully, as if he planned to get quite drunk in the shortest possible time.

"*Beunas tardes, Pedro. ¿Dónde está su padre?*"

"*Buenas tardes*, Señor Curran. He is not here." The lad kept polishing a glass with a filthy towel. "Nobody is here. Everyone is hiding, waiting for the Americans."

"They'll come," Michael assured him. "But don't worry, it won't be a war, it will be a rout. Where can I find your father?"

"You have been to the house?"

"Not yet. Is he there?"

Pedro shrugged. "Maybe. You will have to go and look, señor. I am alone here and I cannot leave. Across the street, then through the alley on your left. Number Ten Calle Jesus."

The end of siesta always brought numbers of people into

the streets. They were there today, huddled in small groups, and talking about *la guerra*. Some war, Michael thought, muskets against Gatling guns.

Number Ten Calle Jesus was a small cottage. It was freshly whitewashed and the front walk was swept clean.

A woman answered Michael's knock. "*Sí*, señor?"

"*Buenas tardes.* I wish to see Señor Rosa. His son thought he might be here."

She was small and dark, with the shadow of a mustache on her long upper lip, and one eye that didn't focus correctly. She shook her head. "He is not here."

Michael was suddenly curious about Rosa's personal life. "*¿Usted es la mujer de Señor Rosa?*"

"*¡Yo! ¡Qué va! señor.* The *peninsulares* come here and do many things, but they do not marry Puerto Rican women." She smiled, showing three or four missing teeth. "I am not the sort of woman a man takes for a mistress, eh? No, I am the housekeeper."

"Can you tell me where I can find Señor Rosa? It's very important."

"I am sorry, señor. I do not know."

Michael turned away. "Señor," the woman called after him, "I can tell you that he goes often to look at the sea from El Morro. I think Señor Rosa looks and thinks he can see all the way to Madrid."

Michael found Rosa sitting on the rocks that tumbled down to the sea from the high walls of the fortress of El Morro. He was not alone; Beth was with him. She sat with her knees drawn up to her chin and her arms wrapped around them. The white lace of her petticoats showed below the hem of her mint-green frock.

Michael watched the pair a moment, then climbed down to where they were. "Afternoon. I didn't realize you two were so friendly."

"Hello, Michael." Beth looked up at him, her eyes made greener by the color of her dress. She wasn't wearing a hat and her parasol lay forgotten by her side. Her hair was coiled atop her head, and in the sunlight it was like spun gold. "How did you find us?"

"With some difficulty. *Buenas tardes,* Rosa."

"*Muy buenas,* señor." He switched to English. "I have stolen your charming companion for a while. Will you forgive me?"

"Beth usually does as she likes. May I join you?"

"Do please sit down," Beth said with mock formality. "Choose any rock you like. Charming, aren't they? The latest thing in decorating."

Michael found a place to perch and looked out to the sea. It was very quiet. They were too high to hear the noise of the waves crashing against the cliff below. "If we stay here long enough we're bound to see the stars and stripes looming on the horizon," he said.

"I expect you are right," Rosa agreed. "It will be interesting, this invasion."

"There won't be any fighting worthy of the name," Michael said.

"No, I don't think so. They are too unequally matched. Besides, I hear that His Excellency the bishop is having urgent consultations with the leaders, assuring them that Holy Church does not require them to fight for her honor."

"Are they listening?" Michael asked.

"Of course. It is what they wish to hear. People always listen to advice which confirms their natural tendencies. What about you, señor. Will you wait until the Americans come, or leave before they arrive?"

"When they get here is up to them, but I'm planning to be aboard the first ship available." He heard Beth's sharply indrawn breath. "If I can make the arrangements I wish to make," he added.

"What arrangements?" Rosa asked. "I'm told that in Lares there are sixteen plantation owners who cannot decide whether they want to kill you or light candles in church in praise of your name."

"They're considerably richer than they were before I came."

"*Sí*, but not as rich as they expected to be."

"But they still own their land. They were paid for doing nothing, only for existing. They've nothing to complain about."

"A rather Talmudic argument. You don't know what that means, do you?"

Michael shook his head.

"Never mind," Rosa said. "Perhaps you will someday. The point is, men do not like to be duped."

Michael shrugged. "True, but sometimes that's how things happen." He looked directly at Beth for the first time since he'd arrived. "What about women, do they object to being duped?"

"Women are accustomed to it," she said quietly. "At least they're accustomed to the fact that men often think they're duping them. Sometimes it's not as it seems."

"I'm sure you're right. What happened to the nap you told me you were so desperate to have?"

"I decided to visit Señor Rosa instead. There were questions I wished to ask him."

"I see. And has he answered them?"

Beth looked at Rosa. "Yes. Very well. Things are much clearer now."

Michael sensed the current of understanding between Beth and the old man, and for no logical reason resented it. "Fine, I'm delighted to hear it. Meanwhile, I have business to discuss with Señor Rosa. Will you excuse us, my dear?"

His tone and the peremptory way he was dismissing her brought two spots of color to Beth's cheeks. She rose quickly, with her customary grace. "No, don't get up, either of you. There's no need. Thank you for speaking with me, Señor Rosa. Now I think I shall take a stroll along the shore."

She scooped up her parasol and started down the cliff, holding her skirts in one hand, springing from boulder to boulder with astonishing agility.

Michael jumped to his feet. "Beth, wait! Don't do that, it's dangerous."

She acted as if she hadn't heard him. He started to go after her.

"I would not do that if I were you, señor," Rosa said softly.

"Why the hell not? She'll kill herself."

"I do not think so, señor. Look."

Beth had reached the base of the cliff. The tide was on the way out and there was a strip of wet sand between the rocks and the sea. She'd tucked up her skirts and was carrying her shoes in one hand, walking along the temporary beach. "She is a woman well able to take care of herself," Rosa said. "A remarkable woman."

Michael watched her a moment, then sat down. "Remarkable," he agreed. "And as stubborn as a mule."

"Women are not stubborn," Rosa said. "They're tenacious. It's in their blood. We like to think they are gentle and need our protection, but they are made for endurance. Women are prepared to withstand, Señor Curran. Some of them are very strong." He nodded in Beth's direction. "Like her."

"You seem to have thought a lot about Doña Isabela."

"Doña Elizabeth. I prefer the English name. Much prettier. And yes, I have thought about her. In some ways she reminds me of your mother."

"I know."

"A man is very fortunate if such a woman loves him."

The words were spoken so softly Michael wasn't sure he'd heard. He couldn't believe that Rosa would have the cheek to make such a remark. "What?"

"Nothing, señor. I was just dreaming aloud. Now, what did you wish to see me about?"

Michael made himself concentrate on the business at hand. "I wish to offer you employment."

"What kind of employment?"

"I want to make you manager of the Banco Mendoza in San Juan."

"Ah, I see."

"I doubt it. You imagine I'm looking for a scapegoat, someone I can leave holding the bag, as the Americans say. It's not like that. The bank is solvent. It will get stronger. My cousin Charles Mendoza and I, we're going to be in charge in London and Córdoba. There's a new day dawning, Rosa. New opportunities. We don't intend to miss them."

"For the Mendozas there are always opportunities. I have not had the good fortune to be born a Mendoza, Señor Curran."

"We look after those who work for us. Always have. The people who make our wine in Jerez, the Ruez family, they've been associated with us since the fifteen hundreds."

"I know nothing about banking."

"You are an educated man. Oh, I know you try to hide it, particularly here on this island, but it's obvious. At least to me. You will learn whatever you have to know very quickly. I can start training you tomorrow. Anyway, I plan to keep you on a short rein. You may as well know now, that all major decisions will be made by me from Córdoba. We'll arrange a private cable link through New York as soon as the Americans get here."

"Yes, we return to the Americans. What will they think of your Spanish bank, Señor Curran?"

"I'm gambling that they'll think nothing at all. There's no reason for them to upset those institutions on the island which work—God knows there are damned few of them. I plan to lay over a few days in New York on my way to London. I'll deal with the Americans."

Rosa didn't say anything for long seconds. Finally he shrugged. "Why not? Very well, I accept."

"Good. I hoped you would."

"You thought I would," Rosa corrected. "And you were right. Why should I refuse? What do I have here that is more interesting? Being a banker can be no more boring than being the keeper of a bar."

Michael heard the bitterness in his voice. "There is one thing that's worrying me a bit. Do you plan to go home to Spain sometime soon?"

"If I could do that I would have done it years ago."

"I don't understand. Look, if there's something hanging over your head, back in Madrid I mean, maybe you should tell me about it. I don't care about your past, not any man's. But I don't want any nasty surprises later."

"No, there is nothing hanging over my head, not the way you mean. It is simply that I can see very little point in being a rabbi in Spain, Señor Curran. Even now."

Michael stared at him. "You're a rabbi?"

"Yes. I was sent to France to study when I was very young. My family believed that by the time I returned everything would be different in Madrid. They were wrong. Oh, we are not persecuted, not like in the old days. There are even some appropriate things one can do." He looked sideways at Michael. "Appropriate for a rabbi, I mean. Such as helping a woman who is fleeing a lunatic. A woman with a young boy."

"I don't remember you. When we were crossing Spain on the way to Ireland, my mother was terrified that my father would change his mind and come after us. It was a terrible journey. There were people who helped, but I don't remember you at all."

"I was in the background, señor. You can ask Doña Lila if you wish. As a rabbi one has connections, one can make certain arrangements to smooth the way. But for our people there can be no public religious life. That remains illegal in Spain. It is very difficult. It killed my wife. So I came here."

"But why here? What could you have expected to find

in Puerto Rico, for God's sake—Excuse me, I'm not accustomed to thinking of you as a man of the cloth."

"It's all right, Señor Curran, I am very accustomed to not being one. As to why Puerto Rico . . ." He shrugged. "I don't know. The opportunity presented itself and I took it, and here I am."

Michael stood up. "It's none of my business anyway. Tomorrow morning then. Nine o'clock at the bank?"

"Nine o'clock. I will be there, señor."

"Please, call me Michael."

The other man smiled. "Yes, I would prefer that. Now, I think perhaps the señorita will require some assistance to climb back up this cliff. There's no other way into town. I can leave her to you, Michael?"

"Oh yes, you can leave her to me."

She'd left her parasol wedged between some rocks. Michael picked it up and walked to where she stood at the far end of the strip of tideland. "You forgot this."

"I didn't forget it. I left it behind."

He pulled back his arm and hurled the parasol into the sea. "You don't need it now anyway. Sun's going down. Besides, I'll buy you a new one in New York. Something much nicer."

Beth didn't answer immediately.

"I'm asking you to go to New York with me," he said. "Will you?"

"As what?"

"I don't understand."

"Yes, you do. Are you inviting me to go to New York as your mistress or your wife?"

"My wife," he said instantly. "I suppose we'll have to wait a bit, since Tim's just died. But I want to marry you."

"What about Córdoba?" She was staring out to sea; she hadn't looked at him once since he joined her.

"What about it?" Michael asked.

"I realize that I'm not acceptable to your family there. That's always been the problem, hasn't it?"

"Yes," he admitted. "But I've decided they can take me or leave me. And my wife. Besides, you're less unacceptable as a widow than you would be as a divorcée. That wouldn't have changed my mind, but there's no denying it's easier the way it's worked out."

She turned to him at last. A breeze was building over the sea, ruffling the waves and tossing the few curls that had escaped her upswept hair. "You'll want children, won't you? Sons."

"Of course."

"They have to be Jews, don't they? Isn't that part of your arrangement?"

"How do you know that?"

"I don't know it. I guessed. I've been around the Mendozas for some time now, Michael. I know how the wheels always turn within the wheels."

"Yes," he admitted. "I have promised to bring the family back to the practice of Judaism. I don't know how I'm going to do it. But I've promised, so I'll try. Will you object to that, raising our children as Jews?"

Beth had one hand in the pocket of her skirt. Her fingers clutched the piece of paper Señor Rosa had given her before Michael joined them. On it was written the name of a rabbi in New York, a man Rosa promised would continue her instructions in Judaism and oversee her conversion. She wouldn't tell Michael about that yet, she decided. She smiled. "No, I won't object to making the children Jewish."

"What are you grinning at?" he asked, taking a step nearer and putting his hands lightly on her shoulders.

"Nothing. I'll tell you someday soon, but not now. There is something important, though, we have to talk about. When we go I want to take Obadiah with us. Samsón too if he wants to come. And Tillie and Briggs, of course."

"Take whom you like. Overseeing the household has to

be your responsibility, I've other things to worry about." His eyes darkened the way they did when he was very intense. "Listen, I'm going to say this only once, but I mean every word. You and me, what we did to Tim. I want to tell you that if you cheat on me, I'll kill you."

Her chin came up. "And what about you, Michael Curran? Is it sauce for the goose and not the gander? You thought very little about seducing a married woman. Do you plan to do it again?"

He shook his head. "No. I'll be faithful to you until the day I die. I swear it. But I meant what I said. I love you. If you betray me I'll kill you."

Beth leaned her head against his chest. "I will never betray you," she promised. "As God is my witness. Never. I will teach you things about fidelity that you didn't know existed, Michael Mendoza Curran. Things I'm only now discovering myself."

Ireland, Five-Thirty P.M.

Sundown was still hours away, but the Wicklow hills were dark purple in the angled light of late afternoon. O'Leary felt dwarfed by the hills and a little drunk with the fresh air. He'd been born in Dublin's crowded streets, spent his entire sixteen years in the city's alleys. The open country did not feel natural.

He climbed to the top of the path he was following, then stopped and stared at the long narrow valley below. The estate of Glencree was spread in front of him. He could see the great mansion built of gray granite; its many slate-covered roofs and countless chimneys formed a maze of angles and planes. Surrounding the big house were the out-buildings, a veritable forest of barns and cottages. It was beyond him to imagine the use of so many different buildings. Well, he'd find out soon enough. Maybe.

O'Leary was torn between wanting to rush forward, and being afraid. He compromised by sitting down on an out-cropping of rock, slipping the pack from his back, and untying his boot. There was a pebble in his shoe that had been annoying him since he left the City. At first it had been easy to ignore; he was too busy looking over his shoulder and trying to control his beating heart to worry about such a small annoyance.

He cast one more look back the way he'd come, but he no longer expected to see anyone following him. He'd left the Fenians behind, at least for the moment. Would that moment last? He couldn't know the future. No man could. He'd been thinking it through for days. Ever since Paddy Shea reported it wasn't the council that had in-structed him to go to Glencree, and that they didn't want him to do it.

He shook the gravel out of his boot, then put it back on, still staring at the scene spread below him and the hills all around. "Ach, and isn't this what we're fighting for?" The sound of his own voice intruding on the silence startled him. O'Leary twisted quickly to check behind him, then laughed aloud when he realized his mistake. "Yes, it is," he said. Then again, louder this time. "Yes, it is what we're fighting for. Ireland free and beautiful. And every man able to do what he likes."

He remained what he'd been from the time he could understand the words, an Irishman and a patriot—in one sense a Fenian. "On the day they rise to throw the British out," he whispered, "sure and I'll rise with 'em. God as my judge, I will. But meantime I got me life to live."

O'Leary stood up and adjusted his pack. Somewhere a bird sang and he paused to listen to it, then started down the path to the estate. Perhaps he was too late, perhaps the agent would tell him the job he'd been offered was gone. No matter if he did. There were other places, other jobs. In any case, he'd be free. "Free," he said. "Young and Irish and free. Sure and a man can't ask for more blessings than that."

London, Ten-Thirty P.M.

At Victoria Station there was a sizable crowd waiting to board the boat train. "I was a child, the first time I heard it mentioned," Lila said. "I thought the train must somehow turn into a boat and sail off across the sea. It sounded miraculous. It never occurred to me it was something as simple as putting the railway coaches on the ferry."

Beatriz laughed. She was flushed and happy, her face animated with pleasure, her plump body swathed in purple silk and black braid. Lila thought her sister-in-law looked like a Christmas parcel done up by someone with ten thumbs, but Christmas parcels were a joy, however they were wrapped. "Will Francisco be glad to see you home?" she asked.

"Probably. For five minutes. It doesn't matter; I shall tell him about the arrangements for our future, that he's rid of me as well as the bank, and—"

Sharrick joined them, interrupting the conversation. "Here they are. Everything's in order." He gave Beatriz a fistful of tickets. "Your berth is in coach twenty-two. I've spoken to the porter. You'll be well looked after. These blue ones are for the wagon-lit to Seville. You have to take a third train between there and Córdoba."

"Thank you, Lord Sharrick. You are most kind."

"I thought you'd agreed to call me by my given name," he said with a twinkle.

"So I did. Thank you, Fergus." She turned to Lila. "A man can be very useful, can't he? The right man, of course. Not one that only knows bim-bam. Lord Sharrick, I don't think he's a bim-bam."

Lila's smile froze; she glanced at Sharrick. He looked

puzzled, but not shocked. Obviously he hadn't guessed the meaning of the words. "Yes," she said quickly. "I'm sure you're right. Now, it's time we got you settled."

They escorted Beatriz along the platform, checked that her luggage had been loaded, and saw her ensconced in the small comfortable compartment where she'd be until she changed trains in Paris. A porter arrived who said he'd make up madam's bed whenever madam wished, and that breakfast would be served at seven.

"You're sure you'll be all right?" Lila asked anxiously. "Perhaps I should have accompanied you as far as—"

"I will be fine," Beatriz insisted. "I enjoy traveling. I have told you. From now on I will travel and travel, until I'm so exhausted I want to stay at home. Then I will buy a little house in Córdoba and watch over your Michael and the *niños* he will have. By then, many *niños*."

"I'm sure." Lila pressed her cheek to her sister-in-law's. "No more bim-bam," she whispered in the other woman's ear.

"But for you, lots of good bim-bam I think." Beatriz rolled her eyes toward Sharrick, waiting in the narrow passage beyond the compartment. "Very good bim-bam."

"You're impossible. *Adiós, Beatriz. Hasta la próxima.*"

"What was she talking about back there on the platform?" Sharrick asked as he and Lila made their way through the enormous glass-roofed terminal.

"Nothing. A private joke between ladies, that's all."

"Bim-bam. It sounds rather descriptive. I think I can guess what it means."

"You can't. Don't you dare try."

He chuckled. "Very well, I won't." Sharrick took her arm and drew it through his. "Do you know what I wish?"

"What?"

"That you and I were setting out on a journey together. An adventure. Have you ever been to India?"

"Never."

"The maharaja of Jaipur's a friend of mine. He wants me to come tiger hunting. I've been dreaming of taking you. It's incredible, Lila. You travel about on an enormous elephant. You can't imagine how big until you see one face-to-face. Anyway, the natives put this thing on the beast's back. Call it a howdah. It's a kind of throne, fantastically decorated. Then your—"

"Fergus, stop chattering, listen to me."

They were outside now, nearing Sharrick's waiting carriage. "I am listening. I always do."

"It's about Michael. And that woman, Timothy's wife, though I suppose now I must say his widow."

"Hmm . . . yes, you must. Listen, it's a lovely evening. Would you care to walk a bit?"

"Yes, I'd like that."

He signaled the coachman. The man approached and they exchanged a few words, then Sharrick took Lila's arm again and led her down Victoria Street toward the houses of Parliament.

"About Beth," Lila said. "I sent her a cable last week, informing her of Tim's accident."

"Oh, what made you do that?"

"Don't play the innocent with me, Fergus. I told her he was very ill, possibly fatally ill. I hoped she'd come back to look after her interests, if nothing else. She had to expect Tim to leave a considerable fortune. Thanks to you, he probably has."

"And what was the result of your bit of meddling?"

"I don't know. Even if she set out for London as soon as she knew, she wouldn't be here yet. That's why I'm asking you about it. Have you heard anything?"

"Not about the young woman, no. But I know Tim's estate won't go to her. He'd already changed his will, accused her of desertion. Didn't leave her a penny."

"Damn!" The expletive burst out. Lila was quick to apologize. "Sorry. But you know the Moore Street brat isn't buried very far below the veneer of the proper lady."

"I like the Moore Street brat, as you call her. She has courage, she's intrepid. Look, about India, I——"

"Fergus I can't think about going anywhere until I know that Michael isn't doing anything foolish, throwing away everything I've worked for."

They'd arrived at Westminster Bridge. Sharrick led her a few steps forward and they leaned on the railing, the breath-taking buildings behind them, the Thames an inky black ribbon below. "Michael worked for it too," Sharrick said, choosing his words carefully. "You have to stop thinking of this coup as something you manufactured and handed to your son. He was in on the planning from the first, and apparently he executed his part in things brilliantly."

"Yes, I know that, but——"

"There are no buts. He's a grown man, Lila. His own man. Would you want him any different?"

She shook her head, her gaze fixed on the tower of Big Ben.

"I didn't think so. And if you recognize all that, you must recognize that he will choose his own wife, that it's no affair of yours."

"It is! He has an obligation, he's made a promise."

"And he's an honorable man who will determine how best to keep his promise." Sharrick thought of the cable he'd sent informing Beth Mendoza that she was a widow. "Leave him to do as he sees fit, Lila. Leave the pair of them to work out their own destiny. You've your own to be concerned about."

Lila turned, leaning back against the railing of the bridge. He could see the rise and fall of her breasts beneath the black bodice of her gown. "What is my destiny, Fergus?"

"I'm not a seer. Destiny's perhaps too grand a word. Maybe we should call it future, the immediate future. I believe that's the term."

"And?"

"And I see travel in my crystal ball." He lay one finger along her cheek, the caress so light it almost didn't happen, a touch that contained only the whisper of a promise. "First Glencree. We're Irish you and I, we need to smell the turf and look up at an Irish sky. At least long enough to make us clean again."

"You said first. Then what?"

"India, as I said. Unless you'd prefer something else. Africa perhaps. Or China if you fancy it. China's a wonderful place. We could go to Hong Kong first, then arrange a journey into the interior. Shanghai, Canton, Peking, it's quite marvelous, I promise—"

Lila breathed a deep sigh. "Oh, Fergus."

"What does that mean. It worries me a bit, that tone of voice."

"It means that I can't imagine living in such a fashion, not having an overriding goal, a passion so strong it—"

"I'm offering you passion, lass. Never doubt that. A great passion."

Her eyes found his, she looked at him as if she wanted to see into his soul. "You're offering to replace hate with love," she said softly. "I know. I do understand. Believe me, I do."

"And?"

She hesitated. "I'm not sure. I've hated for such a long time, I don't know if I can make the change. But I'd like to try, Fergus. If you will be very patient, perhaps I'll succeed."

His carriage had followed them. It was parked a discreet distance away, under a gas lamp on the Embankment. Sharrick took her arm again and drew her toward it. "I can be very patient, Lila. I promise you I can. Now I'll take you home."

Lila held back, caused him to stop walking. "I've a wild idea."

"Tell me. I adore wild ideas."

She nodded toward the waiting carriage. "If we left right now, this minute. Could we really go home? I mean could we be in Liverpool in time for tomorrow's Dublin ferry?"

Sharrick tipped back his head and roared with laughter. "You're a wonder, lass. A miracle among women. No wonder I love you. We can and we will!"

He broke into a run and Lila ran beside him.

ও Afterword ৫৩

On July 25, 1898, troops from the U.S.S. *Gloucester* raised the American flag at Guánica on Puerto Rico's southern shore. Hours later thirty-five hundred fighting men from the battleship *Massachusetts* occupied Ponce. San Juan surrendered within two days. The island had been taken virtually without a shot.

The victors proclaimed that they had not come to "make war upon the people of a country that for centuries has been oppressed," but "to bring protection, and the blessings of enlightened civilization."

Whether those promises were fulfilled is best left to the judgment of Puerto Ricans, but the liberal elite rejoiced at the coming of the Americans, and for the most part life on the island was unchanged. A movement to sue for statehood began immediately, though not everyone supported it. At this writing the issue remains unresolved, but Puerto Ricans were granted U.S. citizenship in 1917.

The Irish Republican Brotherhood, the Fenians, took part in the famous Easter Rebellion of 1916. With the political separatists, Sinn Féin, they were active in the bloody insurrection known as the "troubles," which lasted from 1918 to the signing of the compromise treaty of 1922, which created the divided Ireland of today.

And the Mendozas? What happened to them after 1898 remains to be told in *The Firebirds*.

If you enjoyed **THE FLAMES OF VENGEANCE** you won't want to miss **THE FIREBIRDS**, Beverly Byrne's final book in this enthralling trilogy about the Mendoza family.

For the third novel, the setting moves to England and the United States in the recent past. All the mysteries of the Mendozas are intricately resolved in a stunning conclusion. **THE FIREBIRDS** will be a May 1992 FANFARE book, on sale in April.

· The following excerpt begins the book.

Prologue

England: 1939

At a few minutes past two P.M. on the seventh of April, a single ray of sunlight glimmered on the sodden earth of a rainswept garden in Sussex. Lady Swanning tipped her extremely pretty young face upward and felt the welcome warmth. At that moment she heard the first cuckoo of spring.

The bird's distinctive call echoed in the stillness of the garden. It was Good Friday, and most of the staff of the great house had been released from their duties for the afternoon. Lady Swanning and the bird had the far-flung lawns and the beds of tender spring flowers entirely to themselves.

She thought about the cuckoo. Somewhere it would find the nest of another bird and deposit one of its eggs. When the hatchlings emerged, the cuckoo baby would destroy the rightful children, either by pecking them to death or pushing them to the ground. The conscripted foster parents, unaware of how they'd been duped, would nurture the changeling. Lady Swanning believed the cuckoo was a marvelously clever creature.

The sunlight faded and another bank of clouds rolled across the Sussex downs. Lady Swanning glanced at her elegant gold watch. Two-thirty, almost time. Casting a last look at the garden, she began walking toward the great stone house built centuries before.

How sad that she must leave all this. She had loved her life since marriage, adored the excitement of race meetings and dinner parties and balls, thrived on being the feted and admired young wife of Emery Preston-Wilde, the thirteenth Viscount Swanning.

Regret did not alter her decision.

As she had anticipated, the servants had left for church and the house was hushed and still. Lady Swanning and her husband were also expected to attend the service. Emery was to read one of the lessons, as his forebears had done for generations. This year would be different, for reasons which only Lady Swanning understood.

In the gun room she quickly found what she wanted, a Mauser that Emery had appropriated from a German officer in the Great War. Like all her husband's guns, the pistol was oiled and ready. To become a lethal weapon it had only to be loaded with the cartridges kept in a locked drawer in the sixteenth-century Jacobean cabinet. The night before, while Emery slept, she'd taken the key. It had been quite simple.

Loaded now, the small snub-nosed pistol fit easily into the pocket of her tweed jacket. Lady Swanning returned to the long corridor, her footsteps making no sound on the Oriental carpet. Moments later she stood before the study door and looked again at her watch. It was two forty-five.

"I'll be in my study," her husband had said at lunch. "Meet me there and we'll go on to church. Say, quarter to three?" He'd looked up from his poached salmon. "Do try for once to be on time, my dear."

She was exactly on time. Lady Swanning smiled, then went in. Emery stood with his back to her, staring out the tall French doors that led to a walled rose garden. He was a big man. His form blotted out much of the gray light.

"Damned rain's starting again," he said without looking around.

"Yes." She took the pistol from her pocket and thumbed off the safety catch. It made only the tiniest sound.

"Well, nothing for it, we have to go."

"No," she said quietly. "I don't think so. Not today."

"Don't be silly. There's no way we can—" He turned, an expression of annoyance on his face. Then he saw the gun. "What are you doing with that?"

She didn't answer. It seemed to her unnecessary since her intention must be obvious.

The cook, the parlor maid, the chauffeur, and her ladyship's social secretary were the skeleton staff in the house that afternoon. At five minutes to three the cook and the maid heard two explosive noises and ran to the study. They found Lord Swanning lying facedown in a pool of blood. Their first impression was that he'd fallen and injured himself. The cook struggled to roll the viscount over. That's when she saw his staring eyes and the gaping, bloody wound in his chest and began to scream.

The chauffeur and the secretary arrived within moments, summoned by the screams, though both subsequently denied hearing the shots.

Lady Swanning was nowhere to be found. The police looked long and hard—until a few months later when war broke out and diverted them—but she seemed to have vanished from the earth.

Fielding, Massachusetts: 1955–63

Most folks in the small town of Fielding felt sorry for little Lili Cramer, who lived in the big house on Woods Road and had only one parent.

It was the child's mother, Irene Petworth Cramer, who

made the townspeople uneasy and stirred their sympathy for Lili. Irene was one of their own, born and raised in Fielding, but they'd always had doubts about her. She had left home years before, and they would have forgotten her entirely if she hadn't come back in '51 as a widow with a baby daughter. Since then the vaguely negative reactions had grown more pronounced.

For one thing, Irene never permitted Lili to call her Mom or Mommy. The little girl always had to say "Mother." For another, according to Rose Carmichael, who cleaned for the Cramers, the child was made to be unnaturally careful with her toys. " 'It was expensive, Lili,' that's what Irene always says," Rose reported.

Each time Rose left the house on Woods Road she went to the grocery store on Fielding's main street to gossip. "I don't know what's going to become of Lili," she said on one of these visits. "It's not right, the way she's being brought up."

The other women nodded their heads and made disapproving noises. "Call her Irene Petworth or Irene Cramer," one of them said. "Marriage didn't change her a bit. And now she's giving herself airs because she's living in the big house."

"Nothing new in that," another added. "Irene always gave herself airs. Grew up an iceberg and she still is. And she's freezing that poor little girl to death."

What they didn't know was that the child had found something to love. Long before she understood what made the house she lived in unique and beautiful, Lili fastened all her affection and trust on it. In her mind it became a substitute for the father she'd never known.

"He died when you were born," Irene explained each time Lili asked. "Then we came home."

By the time she was five and the women in the grocery store were talking about her, Lili had drawn two conclusions from Irene's terse explanation. Her father's death was somehow connected with her birth, her fault in some way, and home was where people didn't die and you were safe. "You used to live here when you were a little girl, right?" she pressed her mother.

"Yes, I lived in Fielding. All the Petworths did."

Lili understood that Irene had been named Petworth before she married the man who died. What she never realized was that in those days the Petworths hadn't lived in the house on Woods Road.

She found out about that the following year, when she turned six and started first grade in the Abraham Lincoln School. As well as getting used to hearing Miss White call her Liliane—no one else ever used her full formal name— Lili had to accept certain other realities of growing up.

Irene was unaware of what was happening until a rainy November afternoon when she decided to pick up her daughter after school. Lili was trembling and trying not to cry as she ran from the playground. The accusing words burst out as soon as she clambered into the old Chevrolet. "Is it true our house isn't really ours?"

"Lili, what nonsense, of course it's ours."

"Miss White says it's somebody else's. Their name is Kent."

Irene stiffened and didn't respond.

The little girl's story tumbled out in a rush. "Miss White read us the sign in the hall across from the principal's office. It says a man named Samuel Kent gave the money to build the school and named it after Abraham Lincoln."

Irene nodded agreement. "I know that, Lili. I went to the same school when I was a little girl. I told you so."

By now Lili was sobbing inconsolably. "Yes, but Miss White said Mr. Kent built our house too. And everybody who lived there was always named Kent. She says it's the Kent house."

Irene took a deep breath. "Stop crying, Lili. The Kents

used to own our house and it was called the Kent place. But it's not theirs now, it's ours."

Despite that simple explanation, the pain of the teacher's revelations did not go away. Lili felt threatened in her very soul. All the emotion Irene never allowed her to display was vested in the big shingled house with its slate roof, oak floors, and screened porch hung with wisteria vines. Even though she didn't have a father, she was safe because of the square rooms, the two big fireplaces, and the dining room full of sparkling colored glass. Now Miss White had made Lili's haven feel less safe, less inviolable. Now she must cling to the house with all her strength, or the Kents would come back and take it away.

There were a great many Kents in Fielding. By the time she was seven, Lili could read the signs that said KENT'S PHARMACY and KENT INSURANCE COMPANY. It helped that neither of those places was as big as Petworth's Department Store. "There are lots of people named Petworth in Fielding, aren't there?" she anxiously asked her mother.

"Yes," Irene agreed, her attention on something she was sewing. "Why?"

"I was wondering if there were more Petworths or more Kents."

"The things you think of, Lili. I haven't the faintest idea. You have a great many Petworth cousins, in any case."

Christmas was the only time Lili ever saw these distant relatives. Each year on the holiday Irene took her to a house across town where lots of Petworths lived. They gave one another presents and ate a lot and seemed quite friendly, but none of them ever came to the house on Woods Road. Lili was nine and in the fourth grade before she learned anything of their past.

The teacher was a local-history enthusiast. She explained about fourteen settlers arriving from England in 1650 and choosing the site fourteen miles southwest of Boston and naming it Fielding.

"A man named Josiah Kent came to Fielding in 1652 and dammed a section of Willock's stream to make a millpond. Josiah built a mill and there have been Kents here ever since." The teacher's eyes lighted on Lili. "Of course the Petworths are our other 'first family.' Lili, your ancestors were mostly farmers until Tom Petworth became a miller and took over the Kent mill. That was in 1756."

Lili listened intently. Here was another instance of Petworths replacing Kents, the way she and her mother had done on Woods Road. That was some comfort, but she longed to learn more about her house. Who had built it? When? She asked her mother, but Irene said she didn't remember any of the details, and she got that look on her face that meant it was better to drop the subject. Lili knew the look well and she usually backed off when it appeared, but she always went on thinking about whatever it was that had roused her curiosity. And sooner or later she'd ask again.

Lili's questions about her dead father, for instance, always made Irene's eyes go blank and her mouth tighten. But when Lili was twelve she decided to bring up the subject once more.

Irene was working on a set of needlepoint covers for the dining room chairs. The pattern was of pink roses on an ecru background. It was slow, infinitely painstaking work, but when Irene stitched she was placid and composed. "I'm restoring the covers that used to be on the chairs long ago," she explained. They were upholstered in dull brown velvet now, and Irene said she wouldn't change them until she had embroidered seats and backs for all eight. Lili sometimes thought that might take a lifetime.

On the afternoon that Lili posed her question her mother's blond head was bent over the frame that held the fabric, and she didn't look up when Lili asked, "Can't you tell me anything about my father? I know he died when I was born, but what else?"

Irene went on stitching. "He was English. I lived in England until you were born and he died and I brought you home."

"Then I'm half English?"

"Yes, that's right."

"Why did he die?"

"Nobody knows why people die, Lili." Irene always insisted on correct speech. "What you want to ask is how did he die. An automobile accident."

Lili's hazel eyes took on the color of her surroundings or what she was wearing. When she was concentrating hard, as she was now, they seemed to become darker, more greenish-blue. "Was I in the car?"

"Not exactly. You hadn't been born. I was expecting."

Here was new information, more clarity. Lili plunged ahead, eager to take advantage of Irene's unusual willingness to supply a few details. "What was his first name?"

"Whose?"

"My father's, of course."

"Don't take that tone with me, please," Irene said softly. She never shouted, even when she was annoyed. "His name was Harry Cramer."

"Do I look like him? Are there any pictures?"

"No, you don't look particularly like Harry Cramer."

"Who, then?" Lili demanded. "I don't look like you."

"I think you do, a little. Anyway, there are hundreds of ancestors you could look like, generations of marrying and intermarrying. That's particularly true in a town like Fielding."

"But—"

"If you don't mind," Irene interrupted, "I don't find this a pleasant topic of conversation. I really don't care to discuss it further."

End of inquiry. And confirmation of what Lili had begun to suspect. Her mother wasn't sorry when her husband died. Probably if he hadn't, they'd have divorced. Lili wondered if English people did that. That same afternoon she took her bike and went to the public library. Lili had devoured books since she'd discovered how many questions they could answer.

The library didn't disappoint her; there was plenty of information about England. "Try this, Lili," Miss Demel, the librarian, urged. "You like Dickens." The book she offered was *A Child's History of England*.

Lili shook her head. Her hair was the color of dark mahogany, absolutely straight, very thick, and always shining clean. She wore it short, with bangs, and it bobbed when she moved her head. Irene always said, "You're not pretty, Lili, but your hair is very nice." Lili often despaired of her small, turned-up nose, what she thought of as her funny-colored eyes, and the little crease in her chin, but she'd learned to like her hair.

Now she pushed the heavy bangs aside in an unconscious gesture and refused the book Miss Demel was suggesting. "I like Dickens's stories, but I want to know about England now."

"Oh?" Miss Demel sounded surprised. "Why England?"

"Because my father was English."

"Oh, yes," the librarian agreed. "I knew that, but I forgot." Of course she knew. In Fielding, people always knew all about their neighbors. What mattered to Lili was that Miss Demel didn't try to stifle her curiosity. "Let's see what we can find," the librarian said.

At the end of her investigation Lili decided that most things in England today were a lot like they were in America, not strange and old-fashioned like they were in *Oliver Twist* or *Great Expectations*. So Irene must have been going to divorce Harry Cramer, that's why she never talked about him. Especially since then he'd died and it was sad and tragic, and probably she felt awful about what she'd planned.

Lili had not thought much about the picture hanging over the fireplace in the front parlor until she read about it in a book, *Fielding in the Nineteenth Century*, published by the Historical Society in 1921. She and her mother seldom used that room. They preferred the sitting room because it had thickly upholstered sofas and chairs. The parlor wasn't comfortable. It had stiff Victorian furniture with carved wooden frames and unyielding cushions covered in dusky red velvet. But according to the book, the picture was important.

Lili went back to the library. "Constable, John, 1776–1837," she read in a reference work on famous artists. "With Turner, J.M.W., England's most famous landscapist." She wanted more information, but she didn't know where to look. Miss Demel was home with the flu and the temporary librarian wasn't anyone Lili knew. She decided to wait.

That night Lili couldn't fall asleep. When she heard the clock in the hall chime one A.M. she got up and went downstairs to the front parlor.

Lili stood in the dark for a moment or two, loving the house, feeling somehow that it was loving her back. Finally she switched on a tiny lamp on one of the marble-topped tables and immediately pulled the cord that closed the heavy velvet drapes, so if her mother happened to be awake she wouldn't chance to see a reflection on the driveway. Then she turned and looked at the painting.

Lili knew nothing about art; why this picture was supposed to be so special was a mystery. It was a painting of a field with a haystack and some big trees and a few people. It didn't excite her because of its beauty, but its associations. The Constable had been given to Sam and Amanda Kent, the first occupants of the house, Lili had learned from the Historical Society book. It had hung right over the fireplace since they moved in. It belonged to the house—and to her.

Lili started to switch off the light. The small bulb highlighted a section of one wall while leaving the rest in darkness. That made her really notice the wallpaper for the first time in years. The design was wreaths of tiny dark rosebuds on a beige background. One of the marvels of the house was that the paper in the front parlor was the original; unchanged in nearly a century. "Because the room's used to seldom" was Irene's explanation. True, but Lili realized it must also be true that the paper had faded.

She turned to the painting once more. It had been hanging there almost since the paper was put up. So behind it the wallpaper would be absolutely fresh and new.... Lili couldn't resist; she had to look.

She pulled one of the red velvet chairs close to the fireplace and climbed up on it, then moved the painting a bit, but it didn't reveal what she wanted to see. The light was behind her, shielded by her body. She bit her lip and hesitated. What if there was an accident? What if she damaged the precious Constable in some way? But she wouldn't; she'd be very careful.

The painting was heavier than she expected. Lili braced herself for a real effort and lifted it off its hook. Then she lowered the painting, propped it against the back of the chair, and climbed down. She stepped back a few paces, looked up at the portion of wall she'd revealed, and caught her breath.

The newly exposed rectangle of wallpaper was a revelation. The rosebuds were vivid red, their twined stems a vibrant green. The background color was rich yellow-white cream, not the insipid beige she'd looked at all her life. Sam and Amanda had chosen a bright, gay paper. Their front parlor had been planned for parties and good times and happy people.

"I'll find some way to have it made new again," she whispered. "When I'm rich and famous I'll have parties here too, and the paper will be like it was in Sam and Amanda's day." It was a promise to their ghosts.

Lili looked down at the Constable. The picture wasn't much different now than it was at eye level, and still didn't seem particularly special. Beyond the closed door she heard the clock strike two. She'd better hurry back to bed.

Lili climbed on the chair, gripped the gilt frame of the painting, and glanced down to see the exact position of the hanging wire. What she saw was a little wad of paper shoved between the frame and the canvas backing of the painting. Without a moment's hesitation she reached down and gently worked the screw of paper loose.

When she'd rehung the painting and climbed down from the chair, she carried her find nearer to the lamplight. Very carefully she undid the numerous folds, and found that she was holding a small envelope. She could feel that there was something inside, and see that there was nothing written on the front. She turned the envelope over. It was sealed, and there were a few words in faded ink below the flap. The creases made the writing difficult to decipher, but not impossible. "Córdoba, Spain. The house of . . ." It was M something, but she couldn't read the last bit. The ink was smudged, as if it hadn't been quite dry before the envelope was folded over and over.

Lili resisted the urge to rip it open. If she was going to do it without tearing through the writing, she needed a tool. Her nail file should be perfect. It never occurred to her that perhaps she was disturbing her beloved ghosts, that perhaps Sam and Amanda would disapprove.

FANFARE

Sandra Brown

_____ 28951-9 TEXAS! LUCKY .... $4.50/5.50 in Canada
_____ 28990-X TEXAS! CHASE .... $4.99/5.99 in Canada

Amanda Quick

_____ 28932-2 SCANDAL .... $4.95/5.95 in Canada
_____ 28354-5 SEDUCTION .... $4.99/5.99 in Canada
_____ 28594-7 SURRENDER .... $4.50/5.50 in Canada

Nora Roberts

_____ 27283-7 BRAZEN VIRTUE .... $4.50/5.50 in Canada
_____ 29078-9 GENUINE LIES .... $4.99/5.99 in Canada
_____ 26461-3 HOT ICE .... $4.99/5.99 in Canada
_____ 28578-5 PUBLIC SECRETS .... $4.95/5.95 in Canada
_____ 26574-1 SACRED SINS .... $4.99/5.99 in Canada
_____ 27859-2 SWEET REVENGE .... $4.99/5.99 in Canada

Iris Johansen

_____ 28855-5 THE WIND DANCER .... $4.95/5.95 in Canada
_____ 29032-0 STORM WINDS .... $4.99/5.99 in Canada
_____ 29244-7 REAP THE WIND .... $4.99/5.99 in Canada

FANFARE

FANFARE

Rosanne Bittner

_____28599-8 EMBERS OF THE HEART . $4.50/5.50 in Canada
_____29033-9 IN THE SHADOW OF THE MOUNTAINS
$5.50/6.99 in Canada
_____28319-7 MONTANA WOMAN .... $4.50/5.50 in Canada

Dianne Edouard and Sandra Ware

_____28929-2 MORTAL SINS .... $4.99/5.99 in Canada

Tami Hoag

_____29053-3 MAGIC .... $3.99/4.99 in Canada

Kay Hooper

_____29256-0 THE MATCHMAKER, ... $4.50/5.50 in Canada
_____28953-5 STAR-CROSSED LOVERS .. $4.50/5.50 in Canada

Virginia Lynn

_____29257-9 CUTTER'S WOMAN, ... $4.50/4.50 in Canada
_____28622-6 RIVER'S DREAM, ... $3.95/4.95 in Canada

Beverly Byrne

_____28815-6 A LASTING FIRE .... $4.99/ 5.99 in Canada
_____28468-1 THE MORGAN WOMEN .. $4.95/ 5.95 in Canada

Patricia Potter

_____29069-X RAINBOW .... $4.99/ 5.99 in Canada

Deborah Smith

_____28759-1 THE BELOVED WOMAN .. $4.50/ 5.50 in Canada
_____29092-4 FOLLOW THE SUN .... $4.99/ 5.99 in Canada
_____29107-6 MIRACLE .... $4.50/ 5.50 in Canada